RICHE

Katherine Hastings

RICHES TO RUINVILLE

For information contact:
katherine@katherinehastings.com

eBook ISBN: 978-1-949913-44-6
Paperback ISBN: 978-1-949913-45-3

First Edition:
Editing: Tami Stark

www.katherinehastings.com

CHAPTER ONE
Diane

Maurice topped off my glass of champagne while I settled into the leather chair in the private shopping area. I took a sip, and the bubbles tickled my lips.

"Can I get you anything else before we get started, Mrs. Whitlock?" he asked, then stepped aside.

"No, thank you, darling. I'm ready when you are."

I must be the only socialite in New York City who hated shopping. Abhorred it, actually. So, discovering the option to have a privately curated collection brought directly to me was a game changer. For the last twenty years, I'd embraced this luxury, settling into the private room season after season, eagerly taking or passing on the exclusive items presented to me. Within an hour, I was fully stocked for the season, bypassing the need to step foot in a store again.

With a soft smile, he tipped his head then snapped his fingers. The first salesperson stepped out from the curtains holding a beautiful Gucci gown.

"This is the newest addition from Gucci, and I think it suits your style very well, Mrs. Whitlock," Maurice said as the salesperson turned the dress over to show me the elegant back.

"I love it. Keep," I answered, already planning on which fundraiser to wear it to.

The salesperson smiled and hurried off, and another stepped forward with a pair of Manolo Blahniks on a silver tray.

1

"Perfect. Take," I answered.

When a salesperson emerged with a gorgeous blouse, Maurice leaned down and said, "I picked this one because it matches your blue eyes perfectly. And with that new light brown shorter-hair style you're sporting these days, which I love by the way, I think it's absolutely perfect for you."

I brushed a hand through my shoulder length hair and smiled as I looked up at Maurice. "Thank you. I thought I'd change it up a bit."

"Well, it's working. Really chic and sleek," he said.

I smiled wider. Now at sixty-two years old and losing the battle against my greys, I'd switched to lightening my naturally dark brown hair. The new softer shade with highlights made it easier to hide a stray gray when it popped up now and again between my twice-monthly styling appointments. "You know, this is your third time working with me, and I have to say, no one has ever done such a great job of understanding what I like. You know me too well. I don't even know why I bother coming in anymore. I should just have you send over your choices and fill my closets."

"Why thank you, Mrs. Whitlock. That's a wonderful compliment." He beamed a proud smile back at me.

I took a sip of my champagne then smiled back at him. "Please, like I told you last time, call me Diane."

"Of course, Mrs. Whitlock." He closed his eyes for a beat. "I mean... Diane."

"See? That wasn't so hard, was it?"

His bashful smile preceded the flush in his cheeks. "No. Not so bad at all."

"You've done such an excellent job already, I insist you pour yourself a glass of that champagne, sit in this chair and join me." I patted the seat my husband, Rick, usually sat in.

His eyes flipped open wide. "Mrs. Whitlock, I'm not allowed to do that."

I arched an eyebrow. "Diane. Call me Diane. And I'm the customer, and the customer is always right. My husband usually comes to keep me company, but he's been unusually busy lately, so he couldn't make it. I feel strange sitting in this chair all alone like some weird, wicked evil queen on a throne. I want someone to sit beside me and make it feel less formal."

Rick usually joined me for shopping, as the only "friends" I had in New York were vapid housewives and rich socialites who ran in our circle. I had no interest in spending any more time with them than was absolutely necessary. I saw those wicked women enough at all the functions I had to attend regularly. Fundraisers, brunches, lunches, galas, and every other event where we had to make an appearance.. As Rick Whitlock's wife, my life represented a constant battle to fit among snobby, rude, and materialistic people. But, after forty years married to him and navigating the affluent circles of his 'silver spoon' upbringing, I'd mastered the art of blending in. Part of that was a killer wardrobe, even if it meant sitting in a private room at a fancy department store all alone. And lately, Rick was so busy I barely saw him, so having a friend join me, even a paid one, sounded lovely.

"You won't get in trouble," I said to Maurice. "In fact, you tell your boss that if you don't join me for a glass of champagne while I shop, I'm leaving immediately and taking my business, and my obscene spending account, elsewhere."

He glanced over at a salesperson off to the side, and after a quick exchange of expressive looks, she shrugged and gestured for him to sit.

I patted the empty chair beside me. "I don't bite. Come. Sit, sit."

He took a few tentative steps toward me, then slowly sat down. "I hope I don't get in trouble."

I leaned over. "If you do, I will buy this store with cash on the spot, then fire your boss and promote you to manager."

He pursed his lips together and stifled a smile then nodded his head. "Okay. Let's do this."

I grinned wide as I handed him the bottle of champagne, and a moment later, a salesperson hurried over with an empty glass and filled it.

"Cheers, Maurice. Thanks for not making me shop and drink alone."

"My pleasure, Mrs... Diane," he said as he clinked his glass to mine.

Now feeling less like an evil queen ordering around my minions, I nodded to the salesperson to start again. Maurice and I spent the next hour laughing and talking as we went through all the exclusive clothing and shoes he'd curated for me, and I said yes to almost everything he suggested.

When we reached the end, with the bottle of champagne gone and the bubbles still tingling on my tongue, I let out a happy sigh. "Now *that* was fun. I insist you join me like this every season when I come in."

"Girl, you have yourself a deal!" With a flick of his wrist, he lifted his hand, and I gave him a high five.

"See! A little champagne and some laughs, and you're loose as a goose!"

"Just promise you'll have my back if my boss is pissed." He arched an eyebrow.

"I promise." I stuck out my hand and he shook it.

"So, I think that's everything?" I asked as I glanced at the enormous collection on the keep side, and the few paltry items on the pass side. "I think we have every event on my calendar covered plus all my day to days."

"That's everything," he said, but then his eyes lit up with a mischievous sparkle.

"What? What is it?"

He pursed his lips, then leaned in close. "I really shouldn't. I'm not supposed to show it to anyone, but I think for you, I can make an exception."

"What is it?" I leaned closer.

His face bloomed with excitement. "The new Hermes is in. And it. Is. Stunning. It's not available yet, but what the hell. Do you want to see it?"

"Yes!" I clapped my hands. "Oh, yes!"

Maurice jumped up and hurried out the door. I twirled my empty champagne glass between my fingertips, and a few moments later, he popped back in with a bright pink purse clutched tight to his chest.

"Here she is. Isn't she *stunning?*"

When he released his grip on the purse and held it out in front of him, I smiled.

"It's beautiful," I answered, though in my head, I knew I didn't want it since hot pink wasn't my esthetic. I preferred more muted colors and understated style. That purse, in fact, looked exactly the opposite of my style. It looked exactly like something that the queen of all the New York socialite snobs would love.

My eyes narrowed just thinking about her.

CeCe VanTramp.

My nemesis. My frenemy. The bane of my existence.

CeCe made all the vapid, self-centered, snobby socialites I ran with look like playful schoolyard children based on how horribly elite and awful she was. I'd met Rick my junior year of college when I was twenty-one and he was twenty-five, and CeCe, who was six years older than me, was already married to Rick's business partner, Arthur. From the moment we'd been introduced, she insisted on making my life a living hell. After a few years of putting up with her passive aggressive remarks about my modest clothes, plain hair, and everything else about my person she deemed beneath her, I reached the end of my rope and started to fight back. Ever since I stopped letting her use me as her emotional punching bag, I'd made it my mission to repay her years of condescending remarks by making her life a living hell.

For decades, we'd been in a constant, quiet war. Anything she wanted, I tried to get my hands on first. She did the same to me. Even though I hated the socialites we ran with, she and I engaged in a silent battles behind toothy grins over who led them. It was nothing but snarls behind smiles between me and CeCe as we jockeyed for position as the most prestigious woman in the city. From clothes to purses to jets to vacations, everything we did seemed to be just to one up the other. As I envisioned the look on her overtightened face seeing me strolling into the luncheon on Saturday with this coveted purse dangling from my arm, my heart palpated with excitement.

My eyebrow inched up. "Has anyone else gotten this bag yet? Is it really the first one in the states?"

Maurice shook his head. "Nope. Just came in this morning. No one has it. I'm not sure who the order came in for, but I just knew you had to see it."

Knowing full well how much CeCe would seethe over seeing me with the new Hermes she would die for, a smirk lifted one corner of my lips. "Can you sell it to me?"

He froze. "Oh, I'm sorry but I think it's already claimed."

I held my smile until he kept speaking.

"You know, hold on. Let me check."

"Please do," I answered as I crossed my legs the other way. "I would *really* love that purse. So, can you see if you can make it happen for me?"

"Of course. Let me see what I can do." Maurice hurried off, then a few minutes later, he returned wearing a frown. "Unfortunately, this purse is already spoken for. CeCe VanTramp asked for first dibs on it, and she's stopping in this afternoon to see it."

I almost snarled just hearing her name.

CeCe. Of course it would be her. Why was I not surprised?

My smirk grew. "Maurice, darling. What would happen if, say, you didn't realize this purse was going to CeCe

VanTramp?" I said her last name the way I always did, like *van tramp* even though she seethed with anger and always corrected me since it was pronounced *von tromp*. I'd just shrug and pretend I couldn't get the simple name straight. "Let's say you didn't get the memo, and I offered your store an exorbitant amount of money to let me walk out of here with it right now."

His eyes bulged. "That would be very bad. CeCe would be livid."

My eyebrow inched up higher. "Yes, I suppose she would, wouldn't she?"

It didn't take him long to catch the meaning of my intent, and his own smile grew sinister. "Oh, Diane! You are bad!"

With a flick of my wrist, I huffed out a sigh. "What? You can't tell me you like working with her. She's unbearable."

He pulled his fingers across his lips like a zipper. "I can't speak ill of a client."

I leaned forward. "You don't have to. I can see it in your eyes. I've known CeCe for forty years, and I've never met anyone who *actually* likes her. She's filthy rich and well-connected, so everyone pretends to adore her. But I know the truth, and I also know how she treats sales staff, so I can only imagine how she's treated you."

His face twitched with what I imagined was some horrifying memory of being belittled by that monstrous woman... likely the same way she'd belittled me when I'd come from modest means and married into one of New York's most prestigious families. One that rivaled her own legacy of old money.

Unwilling to let this perfect opportunity to torture her pass, I looked Maurice in the eyes and said, "So, tell me. What will it take for that bag to leave with me today?"

Maurice shifted nervously on his feet then finally said, "Okay, fine. I'll do it. I'll ring it up and have it delivered with your other stuff. But seriously, if I get fired, you are going to have to buy this place and rehire me."

I hopped up from my chair and clapped my hands. "Done and done! You are an angel, Maurice! And no need to have it delivered. I'm carrying that baby out of here today. Send the rest of my stuff to the penthouse."

"Anything for you, Diane." He walked over and we air-kissed cheeks.

I took the new bag and tucked it under my arm then pulled out my black card from my other purse and handed it to him. "Please, put a few things for yourself on there. You've been wonderful, Maurice."

His grin grew. "Thank you, Diane. I really appreciate it. I'll start looking at the fall collections and picking out things I think you'll like. We'll meet again in September."

"Perfect. I'll meet you up at the register in a few minutes."

He disappeared with my credit card, and I gathered up my purse and raincoat then headed out into the busy store. I found Maurice at the desk, but instead of waiting with a receipt for me like he normally did, he met me with a concerned expression.

"Everything okay?" I asked.

"This is so embarrassing, and I'm so sorry to do this, but your credit card isn't working."

"Oh," I answered, furrowing my brow. "That's strange. Maybe there's a problem at the bank. Oh, I hope our card didn't get stolen again. Those damn scammers. Such a pain in the ass. Okay, here, use this one."

I handed him a different card and waited while he swiped it. A few moments later, his face dropped again.

"I'm so sorry, Diane. This one is declined too."

"What?" I leaned over the counter to look at the computer screen flashing the word *declined*. "That's impossible."

Maurice looked up. "Do you have another card?"

"Of course," I answered, still stunned that two of my cards had been compromised.

Maurice took the third card and swiped it, and when his concerned eyes met mine, I breathed out, "Again? Another one is declined?"

"I'm so sorry, Diane. I'm sure there is some logical explanation."

"There must be. Hold on. Let me call my husband."

He nodded and stepped aside to push around some paperwork while I pulled out my phone and dialed Rick. But instead of ringing, I got an instant message telling me the number had been disconnected.

Disconnected? Why the hell would his phone be disconnected? A strange sense of doom pierced my gut as I started worrying for his safety, and my heart plummeted to my feet.

What in the hell is going on?

"Maurice, I'm so sorry, but something is wrong. Can you just hold this stuff for me? I'll stop in later today or this week when we get things sorted out."

"Of course, Diane. I'll have everything waiting for you. Good luck. I hope it's nothing serious."

"Me too," I answered, then handed him the bag I unfortunately couldn't steal from CeCe. After giving it one last look and feeling sad she may get to it first, I quickly hurried out of the store to find Rick and figure out what the hell was going on.

I walked briskly along the busy street the five blocks to the penthouse downtown where Rick and I had lived for the past twenty years. When I arrived at the door, Harold, our door man, wasn't waiting in his usual spot. Instead, a man in a dark black suit stepped forward and blocked the door.

"Mrs. Whitlock?" he said, his stern, muscular jaw clenching as his piercing eyes met mine.

"Yes. That's me. Who are you?"

"I'm Agent Mercier with the FBI." He flashed me his badge, and my stomach dropped like I'd been on a rollercoaster.

"FBI? What's wrong? Is Rick okay? What's happened? Where is he?"

My hands flew to my mouth as I prepared for him to tell me my husband was dead or kidnapped and held for ransom somewhere. My mind reeled with all the possibilities of terrible things that could have happened that would send the FBI to my door.

"Why don't *you* tell me where he is, Mrs. Whitlock," he said, and the way he glared at me had me shrink back a step. "That would make things go a lot smoother for you."

My heart took off at a gallop. "What are you talking about? Where is he? Is he hurt? Did something happen?"

"You really don't know where he is?" Agent Mercier's stare bore deeper into me.

"No. Please, tell me what the hell is going on! My cards aren't working, Rick's phone is disconnected, and I have to find him. Please, let me through. I need to find Rick."

Instead of moving aside, he further blocked the doorway. The simple step further into my path made me stiffen, a slither of fear crawling up my spine. I glanced around looking for a familiar face to give me comfort, a neighbor to run to for help, but instead, an empty lobby met my eyes.

"I'm afraid I can't do that, Mrs. Whitlock. It seems your husband and his business partner, Mr. VanTramp, have been embezzling tens of millions of dollars for years, and they have fled the country. Your assets have been frozen, and you're under investigation as well."

The world shifted on its axis as I stood staring up into the face of the man looking at me like I was America's Most Wanted.

"What... what are you talking about? What? That can't be right. There's a mistake. This must be some kind of mistake."

"There's no mistake," he answered abruptly. "And now we're gonna need you to come with us for questioning." He gestured to the black SUV parked on the street.

"What?" I stepped back. "I don't know anything about this, and I'm not going anywhere with some strange man. For all I know this is some expansive kidnapping plan, and to hell if I'm dumb enough to get in the car with a stranger just because you flashed me a badge... which could be fake! Now, let me through!"

I tried to push past him, but he grabbed my arm. I shrieked and pulled it loose, then scurried back out onto the street.

"You can't go into your home. It's currently being searched by agents. You'll be allowed in briefly when we are done to get your basic necessities, but it's a large place. This could take a while."

I pulled out my phone and tried calling Rick, but once again, a message told me the number was disconnected.

"Where is my husband? What have you done with him!" I demanded.

"That's our question to you. Where did he go? Where are they hiding?"

Still unable to process the wild accusations, I shook my head. "No. This is ridiculous. You aren't the FBI. I'm calling the police," I said as I dialed 911.

"I can show you the warrant, though I suspect you still won't believe me. So go ahead and call the cops," he answered. "Then they can come here and explain that we're the FBI, your husband is a suspect on the run, and we can figure out if you're involved. I'll wait."

With my mind spinning out of control, I asked the operator to send a police officer to assist me, then I waited safely on the busy street until the police arrived. A few minutes later, a squad car pulled up. I raced up to the uniformed officer, pointing at the man in the suit. Then I explained he was impersonating an FBI agent and trying to kidnap me, and he may already have my husband.

"Stay here, ma'am. I'll handle this." The officer stepped around me, hand hovering over his gun, and headed toward Agent Mercier. After they spoke for a while, he talked to a few other men in dark suits who came down carrying boxes of what looked like contents of Rick's desk. While I waited breathlessly for him to pull out his cuffs and arrest the nefarious criminals intent on kidnapping me and holding me for ransom... the ones who may already have Rick for all I knew... the police officer strolled back over to me.

"I made some calls and verified the badges. These men are FBI. You're going to need to go with them for questioning, Mrs. Whitlock."

"What?" I struggled to inhale my next breath. "This... this is real? This is really happening?"

"I'm afraid so," he said. "They are searching for your husband and his partner, but it does seem that they fled the country last night."

"What? Rick is gone? He's... what? This can't... I... this... this can't be happening. This isn't happening." As the world seemed to tip again, my entire existence suddenly tumbling around in question, I stumbled and collapsed into a heap on the street.

"Mrs. Whitlock!" the officer shouted, and I saw his concerned face appear in front of mine just before I passed out.

CHAPTER TWO
CeCe

"Not that one! Leave that!" I barked at Julian, my assistant, when I saw him grabbing last year's Dior from the closet. "I meant the new Gucci!"

"Sorry, CeCe!" he shouted back, then tossed the dress on the ground.

I gasped when I saw it lying in a crumpled, pathetic heap. "Well, don't just toss it on the floor! It still has feelings even if I can't take it with me!"

He spun around on his Prada loafer and picked it back up. "Sorry! You're right. It's not the dress's fault this is happening to it."

When he took it back into my giant walk-in closet, my throat constricted knowing it may be the last time I saw that dress, or most of the other clothing, shoes, and purses that the despicable government claimed were no longer mine. Anger seethed through my body as I stared at the collection I'd so carefully cultivated over the years. Memories of the events I'd worn them to... the envy they'd been of everyone who'd seen them. Once upon a time, they were the bells of the ball, like me. And now... their fate, as much as mine, hung in the air. My poor babies. The innocent bystanders in the shitstorm my crappy husband had left me standing in.

"Maybe I should burn them all. It may be better to put them down than let them fall into the wrong hands. What if these grubby, greedy government people take them from me and they end up on..." I paused and gulped... "Ebay."

Julian spun around, and his hands flew to cover the perfectly trimmed and shaped stubble on his face. "Don't say that!"

"Well, it could happen. Who knows what the government does with couture! Oh, my poor sweet babies." I hurried to the closet and opened my arms, pulling a clump of gowns into my embrace and hugging them against me. "Mommy loves you. She'll always love you. This is barbaric," I whispered, hugging a Dior gown to my chest. "This dress was on the Cannes red carpet!"

"And now," Julian said solemnly, "it'll be on some girl named Brittany's Poshmark for five hundred dollars." His mouth drooped in a frown, pain twisting his face into a puckered mess. "Or worse. At Goodwill."

I let the internal scream I'd been holding for too long bubble out of my mouth.

I gasped, shaking my head wildly. "No. No they can't. They wouldn't. These beauties can never find themselves dangling on the sales rack with some common rabble from... Kohl's!"

Julian swallowed and nodded, lifting his chin higher. "No. You're right. They would never let them fall into those grubby little thrifter hands. These are pieces of art. They'll be treated with the dignity they deserve."

I mustered all of my strength as I stared at the clothing that had once been my armor in the war zone of the Upper East side. They had done me proud, and I would miss them far more than that deadbeat husband who'd run out on me.

"Okay. We have to focus. We don't have time for hysterics. What about this one?" Julian pulled a Gucci and held it up.

"Yes. That one. We can't let them get that one."

As we'd been doing for the past half hour, he carefully folded it into one of the black garbage bags we were using to confiscate my favorite couture and jewelry. We couldn't take it all as I'd been told repeatedly by the stiffs in the suits planted at my front door, but they'd allowed me to come in and take a "few non-valuable things that fit into an overnight bag". Once I left this penthouse, they couldn't tell me when I'd be allowed to return.

If I was allowed to return to it as that cranky woman in the cheap suit had said with a smirk. When she'd said the words, they'd crippled me to my core.

"This is the last thing that can fit in this bag, CeCe. We have to leave the rest behind."

I whimpered looking back at all the beauties I would have to say goodbye to... maybe forever.

"Finish up!" A deep voice from one of the agents called through the closed door.

We both jumped, then shot each other a panicked look.

Julian's brown eyes widened. "I'm going to lower it down. We need to hurry!"

His quick steps moved him across my large bedroom to the balcony where we had been lowering down the bags of clothes, shoes, purses, and jewelry I intended to sneak out. The agents didn't know it, but the Maloneys, my downstairs neighbors, were in Tuscany for the month. They had given me a key to their place when I'd told them I needed extra kitchen space for my caterers to use during the party I was supposed to host tomorrow... the one that had been canceled since my husband was on the lam and I was now a suspect in some heinous financial crimes. It had been Julian's brilliant idea to smuggle out what we could and protect it from the government, then after the FBI left, we could sneak back up to the Maloney's suite and grab the bags off their balcony.

I'd seen this happen to Margaret and John Long after he'd evaded taxes for years. They'd lost everything and ended up God knows where without a penny to their names. To hell if I was going to let them take my favorite, precious belongings. Though I still clung to hope this was all some terrible mistake soon to be remedied, I knew deep down how much the government must be drooling over getting its hands on our wealth. With money like ours, they could make a sizeable dent in the deficit once they snatched it from us. For a moment, I started to wonder if they made this all up just to take our money, but then I remembered my husband had disappeared after wiping out every remaining dollar from our bank accounts.

Not exactly making him look innocent.

"Careful!" I whispered as I stood at Julian's side watching my bag of coveted belongings creeping toward the pile below.

We held our breaths until the bag touched down, then when he released the rope made of sheets and it fluttered down and out of sight, with a big simultaneous breath, we turned toward each other and fell into a hug.

"We did it," I whispered into his shoulder... the one I'd collapsed on when I'd gotten the news last week about my husband's extracurricular criminal activity. The shoulder I'd sobbed into when I got out of the FBI questioning room having learned so much about my husband that I never wanted to know. The shoulder that had supported me when I'd been told everything I owned was in limbo. The houses... jets... bank accounts. Everything.

The shoulder I'd clung to that was the only thing keeping me from sinking into a boneless heap on the floor, unable to move even an inch as I watched my perfect life smoldering in a pit of never-ending flames. Even knowing I couldn't pay him a penny of his salary, Julian had stayed loyally by my side. Of all the people that I'd called friends who had already turned their back on me since news of the scandal broke, Julian was the only one who remained steadfast and true.

My one and only friend.

"We did it," he whispered back. "Those bastards are never getting their hands on that Gucci."

I pulled back from our embrace and looked into the face of the man who had been at my side for twenty years.

I'd found him when he was only twenty years old and new to the city having moved from some Midwestern suburbs to pursue a career in high fashion. I'd needed a new personal assistant, and he'd been introduced to me by my trusted hairstylist. They'd met at a club a few months before, and he'd known Julian was looking for work after having no success breaking into the tough world of fashion.

Since Julian had no real resume, I'd taken a big risk in hiring him, but he'd shown a natural talent for fashion and was highly organized. So, after a trial run where he'd proved invaluable helping me prepare for events and keeping my social calendar running smoothly, I'd taken him on full time. He'd been so grateful for the job that allowed him to work with fashion and high society helping me with my shopping and household, he'd worked for pennies on the dollar when he'd started. But soon, he'd proved to be my most beloved friend, and now I never left the house without him. We'd traveled the world together, attended the most prestigious events, and for all intents and purposes had been glued at the hip for twenty years and counting. Now he was all I had left in this cruel and vindictive world I was getting tossed out into, and I was eternally grateful he hadn't abandoned me in my time of need like everyone else I knew.

"That's it! Times up!" an agent said as he pounded on the door.

"Quick! Get the dummy bags!" Julian squealed as he broke our embrace and sprinted across the room to get the bags we'd filled with toiletries, pajamas, and a few pieces of couture we hoped they'd let us leave with.

When the door opened and the FBI agent who resembled Frankenstein stepped in, Julian and I stood side by side clutching our Louis Vuitton bags.

"I'm ready." I lifted my chin high as I looked him in the eye.

He glanced at our bags. "We said no valuables can leave. And I don't need to be a fashionista to know that suitcase is valuable."

I looked down at my bag. "I don't have any suitcases that aren't valuable. I'm CeCe VanTramp. Where do you think I shop for my luggage? Walmart?"

He grumbled then strode over and pointed at them. "Open them up. We need to check them for jewelry or any valuables you may be trying to smuggle out."

"The audacity," I breathed. "Treating me like some kind of criminal."

Julian started to glance over his shoulder at the balcony behind us, but I bumped him with my shoe to stop him from giving us away.

"Well, considering you're in this situation because of the allegations against your husband, and the strong possibility you're involved, can you blame me?" the agent said as he started going through my bag.

Julian lifted a finger, and his voice rose with it. "I'll have you know, *sir,* that CeCe was completely unaware that her husband was a Shady McShaderson. We are *victims* here and would appreciate being treated as such, thank you very much."

"Exactly," I said. "If I were part of the crime, don't you think I would be sitting on some beach somewhere sipping margaritas with my husband? But no. I'm left behind here to deal with our lives in shambles, penniless and alone while he's off God knows where doing God knows what with the money he stole. Money he stole from *me!* He took *my* inheritance as well!"

The rage bubbled inside me again. It wasn't even that he'd stolen money and done some underhanded things that got me so wild with anger. It was the fact that he'd hidden it from me, hadn't trusted me with the information, and then had just left me behind like yesterday's garbage. As if the forty-seven years I had spent with him, more than half of my life, meant nothing. At sixty-seven, those years as his wife had defined my life. I had *thought* I was his most trusted confidant. We weren't a passionate marriage filled with romance and mushy love, but we had been partners.

Or at least I'd thought we were until he'd up and left me broke and alone.

I'd been more shocked he'd left me behind in this mess than that he'd run off with tens of millions of dollars. Not even a word. Not a warning. Not a call. Just... gone. If he'd have just come and told me what was going on, I could have helped him fix the trouble he'd gotten himself into. I could have prevented this from happening. Or, at the very least, I could have grabbed Julian and jumped on the jet with them as they made their big getaway.

Instead, I was here. Left behind with nothing.

The agent peeked up at us, grunted, and kept rifling through my bag. When he got done with mine, he checked Julian's. Julian huffed and crossed his arms, tapping his little black Prada shoe on my mahogany floors while he waited for the inspection to be complete.

"Looks good," the agent said. "Now, zip them up and let's go. You won't be allowed back in here again until the investigations are over, so make sure you have what you need."

"And we *will* be allowed back in here though, right?" Julian asked.

The agent shrugged. "We won't know until after the investigation. But if your debt is more than your assets, then everything you own, including this place and all of your things, can be confiscated toward restitution. So, just take what you need, and they'll sort out the rest after they complete the investigation."

"What I *need* is everything in that closet!" I spit out, my temper flaring as I glanced back at my closet one last time. "That's *my stuff* and I think *you* are the criminals here for stealing it from me!"

"Just doing my job," he said flatly. "Now, let's go."

With one last glance at my decadent boudoir, I fought back the tears threatening to spill out. But I refused to let them see me fall apart. They wouldn't break me. I was leaving here with my dignity at the very least.

"No!" Julian screamed, then bolted across my room and tossed himself on the bed. His arms spread wide as he clung to my eiderdown comforter. "Please don't do this to us! Please! We have nothing left! Please, sir!"

Julian sobbed as he continued clinging to my bed.

The agent marched over and planted his hands on his hips. "We can do this the easy way, or the hard way."

"Julian," I soothed, my voice cracking a bit before I cleared my throat and took a breath. "We have to go. Don't give him the satisfaction of seeing you fall apart."

"I won't go. I'm staying here. We belong here." He sniffled into the world's softest comforter... the one I'd paid a fortune for and would miss dearly.

"Sir, you need to get up," the agent said sternly.

"No," Julian snapped back. "I'm not going."

"Sir," he said. "This is your last warning."

"Julian," I said softly as I sat down beside him. "We can't stay here. We don't even know if we live here anymore. This may not be my bed anymore. I don't even know if I have a husband anymore." As I started saying the truth aloud, the lump in my throat grew bigger. Even if by some miracle we did get to return here, we'd surely have to sell it and downsize to survive. Arthur had cleaned out every one of our accounts, and unless he planned on coming back for me to whisk me away to the new life he'd started, everything I knew would never be the same. "We have to go, Julian. And I have no idea where we're going." As I finished the sentence, my fight to put on a tough façade collapsed, and so did I.

I wailed as I flopped forward onto the bed beside Julian. His sobs intensified, and together we lay on my cloud soft comforter sobbing away our woes.

So much for leaving with my dignity intact.

"Oh, for Christ's sake," the FBI agent grumbled. "Would you two get up?"

"No," we answered in unison.

"So, you're not rich anymore. Well, guess what? Neither am I. Neither are most of the people in this country. About time you learned what the rest of us have to go through. Now quit crying and get up."

"He hates rich people." Julian sniffled. "That's why you're being so mean to us. You hate the rich, Mr. Jerky Agent Man. That's prejudice."

"Julian isn't even rich," I said into the white blanket. "I barely pay him anything. He just gets a free ride in the life of luxury as his salary."

"Got," Julian corrected. "I *got* a free ride. And now... it's over. I didn't even save a dollar from my salary. I didn't think I needed to. I spent it all, and now I'm as broke as you."

He wailed again, and it set me off as well.

"Okay. That's it. We're going," the agent said, and I felt his hand wrap around my arm. He hoisted Julian and I to our feet, then pointed us toward the door. "Pitty party is over. Now get your bags and let's go."

How had this happened to me? Just last week I'd been planning trips around the world, parties with societies' most elite, and spending money like it would never run out. Then I'd come home to find FBI agents tearing through my things as they told me my husband and his business partner had stolen tens of millions of dollars, cleaned out our accounts, and were gone. There was no word in the English language to encompass how shocked I'd felt... how angry I'd been that I'd been so clueless to it all happening right under my nose. I couldn't help but wonder if Diane, Rick's intolerable wife, had been in on it too. Even though I doubted it with how uppity and holier than though she usually was, part of me hoped she had. Then she'd be in the slammer, and I could go there and tell her how orange washed out her skin tone and made her look sickly.

Ugh. *Diane*.

If there was one silver lining in this whole messed up disaster that was now my life, it was that at least now that our husbands were no longer business partners, I'd never have to be near her again. Never have to fake a smile and kiss her cheek when I saw her at a social function. Never have to bite my tongue until it bled when she'd show up with something she *knew* I'd want and then I could never have because of how tacky it would be if we both owned it. She did it on purpose. She'd never admit it, but I always knew. It was the look in her eyes when she'd ask me if I liked her dress, or purse, or shoes.

Spite. Pure spite.

Jailtime is what she deserved after all the hell she'd put me through. Even if she turned out to be innocent and I couldn't go laugh at her in a cell, with the government having frozen her assets as well, it seemed she was just as broke as me. So, at least there was that. I would crawl straight out of my skin if Diane could peer down from her penthouse while I scrambled for a place to lay my head.

"Time to go." The agent leveled us with a stern stare. "And I *will* drag you out of here if I have to, so I recommend no more outbursts."

Julian whimpered. "But I have nowhere to go. I can't do this."

With more tears pouring down my cheeks, I lifted my chin and wiped them away. "We *can* do this," I whispered.

"We can't," he answered with how I really felt.

"Well, we have to anyway." I took his hand, and after giving one last glance to the bedroom I may never see again, we marched through my penthouse like we were marching down death row.

After an elevator ride brought us down to the ground floor, they escorted us out onto the streets. The ape of an FBI agent gave us a quick nod of his head, then he disappeared inside and left us standing on the street corner.

Several long minutes passed while Julian and I stood in stunned silence. Finally, he softly asked, "What do we do now? The guy we talked to yesterday said there may be some government housing we can stay in during the investigation. Should we find out more about that?"

My eyes bugged. "Government housing? Like a homeless shelter? Never! I'd rather sleep on the streets than be caught in one of those!"

"Then is there anyone to call that we can stay with? *Anyone?*"

Is there anyone to call?

Knowing the answer to that question made me feel even smaller. My parents had died years ago when I was in my fifties, and I'd never had children. I had no siblings, no husband, no living relatives, and it turned out after this scandal hit and everyone showed their true colors, I had no friends either.

"No, Julian. There is no one to call. We've tried everyone we could think of, and with the scandal, none of our 'friends' want anything to do with us. And even if there was someone to call, I don't even have a phone anymore anyways. Those bastards took both our phones as evidence, and it turns out I have no money to buy a new one or get one of us a phone plan."

"Those bitches." His tears turned to rage as he spun to look at me. "I can't *believe* that none of those hussies would take us in! After all the years spending holidays on yachts, having brunches, dancing at fundraisers, and now they are treating us like lepers! Like lepers covered in crap!"

"I'm just so sorry my crap ended up on you too. If you want to leave me and try to get a job with one of them, I won't blame you," I said, though deep down, I definitely didn't mean it. If he left me for one of those treacherous women who'd slammed their doors in my face, I'd skin him alive too.

"I wouldn't leave you like this," he said. "And even if I wanted to, your stank is all over me as well. I'm as untouchable as you are, CeCe. No. I'm not going anywhere. We're stanky together."

I reached out and took his hand in mine. "I'm lucky to have you, Julian. And don't worry. Once I find that no-good husband of mine and all my money he ran off with, after I divorce him or perhaps kill him with my bare hands, I'm going to treat you to the most extravagant vacation you've ever dreamed of. Nothing but first class all the way for your loyalty to me during this impossible time."

His face lit up but then quickly dropped and he softly whispered, "But what if we don't find him? What if he's really gone forever? What happens to us then?"

My stomach clenched at the thought. Was it possible my money really *was* gone? For good? I swallowed down the bile in my throat at the horrifying future that I could barely comprehend.

Me.

CeCe VanTramp.

Poor.

Destitute.

Destroyed.

My life of luxury ripped away leaving me in the gutter with nothing but the clothes on my back and loyal Julian at my side.

Preposterous!

Seeing the worry in his eyes that mirrored my own crippling concerns, and refusing to let this be our life, I let my seething anger over our situation wash away the worry. I dug deep down into my resolve, refusing to accept our fate.

"Well, if that happens, and we can't find him or my money, I may not be as young and beautiful as I once was, and men my age are looking for twenty-something bimbos, but I think I can still snag some old millionaire to pull us out of this mess. If Arthur really did leave me and doesn't come back, we just have to find one, get him to marry me, then wait him out until he dies, and we'll be back in business again."

Julian smiled, and it was the first time in a while I'd seen those flashy teeth I'd paid to have whitened last month. "You mean it, CeCe? You really think you can find a new rich husband we can marry?"

I lifted my chin. "I'm CeCe VanTramp. If I say I'm going to find us a rich, old husband to lift us back out of the gutter, then that's exactly what I'm going to do. We just need to find somewhere safe to land for now, and I'll get us back into the penthouse again soon, with or without Arthur. You just wait, Julian. We're getting out of this mess."

Tears welled in his eyes, but this time not from sadness. "Oh, CeCe. I know you still have it in you. You can woo the pants off some old geezer. Or diapers. Maybe you'll be wooing the diapers off him."

He pulled a face, and I mimicked it. "Ugh. Gross."

"I'm not changing his diapers." Julian lifted a finger. "Seriously. That's not happening."

"Of course not, darling." I touched his cheek. "I would never ask you to do something so horrific. He'll be rich. We'll have people for that."

He blew out a breath. "Okay, good. Then let's do this thing. We need to find somewhere to stay, and then Operation Diaper Daddy is going into action."

"That's a horrible name," I responded, my face puckering at the thought of how far I'd fallen. Once the most esteemed woman in high society, my fall from grace had taken me so low I was planning on groveling at the feet of some shriveled up prune to beg to be his wife.

"I'll try to think of something else, but for now, it's Operation Diaper Daddy."

I cringed again. "Ugh. Fine. If that's what it takes to save us, then that's what we'll do. We're going to be okay, Julian. We have a plan. And since you've been so loyal to me all these years, I promise I won't let you down. We're getting back to where we belong. Together." I smiled back at him, and even though I felt completely lost in the moment, that little glimmer of hope that we could crawl our way back out of the gutter again fluttered inside of me.

His eyes swelled with hope. "I trust you, CeCe. I know you'll get us out of this."

"I will." With a deep breath, I straightened my shoulders. Even though deep down I would miss Arthur, and I had no idea if he would show up again to save us or if I'd have to trudge forward to find a new husband to take care of us, I knew Julian and I could sort things out like we always did.

Together.

He paused then sucked the air through his teeth. "Well, maybe don't go hunting for a new husband just yet. You've got mascara running down your face like Tammy Faye Bakker."

I gasped and covered my face. "Julian! How could you let me stand on the streets looking like this! What if a reporter sees me! I'll never catch a new husband if I end up in the society pages looking like a pathetic mess!"

He gasped. "You're right. Quick, CeCe, let's get you off the streets stat. We can't be spotted like this."

Though I had no idea where we were going, I took his hand, and together we hurried away from the penthouse I no longer called home.

CHAPTER THREE
Diane

I pushed open the door to the building where our lawyer's office was, then stepped inside. I'd met Arnie many times at social functions, but I hadn't been to his office before because Rick always handled the financial and legal stuff for us... a fact I once appreciated, and now resented. Maybe, just maybe, if I'd been an active participant in our finances and billing, I would have seen what was going on right under my nose. But instead, I had been clueless to the money schemes that had left me broke and alone with a criminal for a husband who'd run off to God knows where.

The rage I had felt over the past month since I'd found out rose inside me again. But, like I did every time I felt it boil through my blood, I took a deep breath and let it out slowly.

There's nothing you can do about it, Diane. All you can do is move forward.

But how? Even though I kept telling myself I would be okay, I still hadn't figured out the how. After the investigation proved they'd swindled money from just about every one of our friends, our entire social circle had turned their backs on me. I was lucky I had one friend who'd felt bad enough for me that she'd let me stay in her apartment while she and her husband were on a cruise. But they would be home in three days, and then I'd be back out on the street again. My only hope was that this meeting with our lawyer today would tell me that the investigation was over, and they would unfreeze our assets so I could get back into our penthouse and get started on the new, uncertain life awaiting me.

With hope guiding me to his office, I rode the elevator to the fifteenth floor then got out. That hope that had me walking a little lighter extinguished immediately when I saw my arch nemesis sitting in a chair outside his office.

CeCe.

I growled her name in my head. This was probably all her fault. Her husband's fault at least. He always seemed shady to me, and no doubt he'd led my husband astray and caused me to end up in this crappy position.

Those piercing blue eyes widened when she saw me. "Diane? What are you doing here?"

She elbowed her "assistant," Julian, if you could even call him that since he never lifted a finger to work. It seemed his only job was spending his life glued to her side like a flamboyant one-man entourage. He turned and looked at me, and that pretentious lift of his nose preceded the half smile he gave me.

I stiffened as I slowed my steps moving toward them. "Hello, CeCe," I answered in the formal tone I always took with her— a tone almost as formal as the gown she wore. An odd choice of clothing for a trip to the lawyer's office, but nothing surprised me with CeCe anymore. "I got a message to meet Arnie here today. What are you doing here?"

"I got a message too." She rose, then swept a hand through her dyed blonde hair, and I noticed it wasn't as shiny and perfectly coifed as usual. It seemed her fall from grace had lost her that daily hairdresser she'd spent a fortune on.

The thought of her reaction when she'd found out she was penniless and had to do her own hair made me quirk a smile. It almost softened the blow of being penniless myself.

Almost.

"Hello, Diane," Julian said in his usual haughty tone as he stood.

"Hello, Julian," I answered back, my tone matching his.

"I didn't realize you'd be here as well," CeCe said.

"Nor I you." I avoided the empty seat beside her and sat down in the chair across from them.

After a few moments of uncomfortable silence, she finally said, "Well, I hope at least he has some good news for us today. I'm ready to get back home."

"Yes, me as well," I answered, then went silent again.

Normally, when CeCe and I had seen each other over the decades and our husband's partnership had forced us into the same rooms, we'd always grinned and kissed each other's cheeks, our fake smiles and greetings a necessity in the world we lived in. But now as we both sat broke and abandoned outside our lawyer's office, it didn't seem important to force myself to make small talk with her anymore. The one benefit of this disaster we both found ourselves in.

"He's ready for you," a woman said then opened the door and waved us to come in.

With a quick smile and a thank you, I hurried in first with CeCe and Julian rushing in behind me.

"Welcome." Arnie gestured to the two seats in front of his desk.

I settled into the seat on the right. "Hello, Arnie."

"Pleasure to see you again." CeCe stood beside the other chair, then gestured to Julian. "Do you have a third chair?"

I looked to see her minion standing beside her, his arms crossed tightly against his chest.

"Of course, of course," Arnie said, then asked his assistant to grab an extra chair.

A few moments later, she arrived with the third chair and scooted it into place. Julian and CeCe sat, then we all looked toward Arnie.

"Well? Any news?" I asked, crossing my legs as I settled in.

"Yes," CeCe said. "Please tell us this is all settled now, and we can at least get back into our penthouses. It's been a month. This is ridiculous."

"Your husbands have both been clients of mine for decades, and I've come to know you both as friends over the years. Because of that, I've worked very hard to try to right this sinking ship." He paused and arched an eyebrow. "And at no cost to you since I know that you have no money or assets right now, and the regular monthly retainer ran out twenty hours ago."

"We appreciate it so much," I said quickly.

"Yes, yes," CeCe said. "We appreciate it. But why are you looking like that? What's going on?"

Arnie ran a hand through his grey hair, then leaned forward and pressed his hands together in a steeple. "Well, there is good news, and there is bad news," he started.

My heart stalled out as I saw the concerned look tighten his aging face when he said, "bad news."

"What's the good news?" CeCe asked.

"Well, they have decided not to press charges against you two. They found no evidence to tie you to the crimes, so you are both free and clear of any wrongdoing in the mess your husbands made."

"Oh, thank God," I breathed. I had hoped the investigators would figure out that I was innocent of any crimes, but I'd seen enough movies to know that innocence wasn't always a safe bet. "So, no charges? We're safe?"

"You're safe." Arnie smiled.

"Well, of course we are." CeCe rolled her eyes. "We didn't do anything wrong. Well, at least *I* didn't. I don't know about her."

"I didn't either," I snipped back.

CeCe shrugged. "Well, you never know. I mean, with your husband getting them into this mess, who knew if you were involved."

"*My* husband?" I sat up straight. "I think it's pretty safe to say if anyone concocted this illegal plan, it was *your* husband! He was always up to no good! This amount of treachery has *van tramp* written all over it," I said, pronouncing her name wrong as always.

She spun and narrowed her eyes at me. "*Von Tromp!* How hard is that to remember? It's pronounced *Von Tromp! Von Tromp Von Tromp Von Tromp!*"

I shrugged. "My mistake."

"Whatever. Well, it's ridiculous you'd think *my* husband was the mastermind here. I know it was your husband who did it. My husband is probably just an innocent bystander in his underhanded business dealings."

I opened my mouth to argue back, but Arnie raised his hands. "Ladies, ladies, ladies," he said, and we both glared at each other then looked back at him. "This is not the time to fight. And I have to tell you, from what the investigation has turned up, *both* of your husbands were complicit in the criminal dealings."

"Well, her husband probably started it," CeCe snipped.

"He did not!" I started back, but Arnie raised his hands again.

"Okay, okay. I can see tensions are high right now," he said. "But this isn't the time to fall apart. Both of your husbands were, without a doubt, stealing tens of millions of dollars. They have enough evidence to prove that fact ten times over. So, let's not worry about who started it. But, that brings me to the bad news."

"How bad is bad?" I asked, noticing the lines on his forehead deepening as he stared between us.

"Well, things are worse than we thought."

"Worse? How could things be worse?" CeCe spit out. "Our husbands emptied our bank accounts and fled the country! How can it be worse than that?"

"Because they stole tens of millions of dollars from dozens of victims, and also got into so much trouble with the IRS, the government has agreed to let you walk away without any legal repercussions. However, in exchange, they will confiscate what is left of your assets. Everything. Those will be used to pay back the victims for the money they lost in the scam investments your husbands created. Hopefully, any attempt at restitution will protect you from the normal flurry of civil litigation in cases like this."

"What?" I breathed out. "Nothing? We'll get nothing back?"

"Preposterous!" CeCe snapped. "Those thieves can't take *our* things! And what about the things I bought with *my* money from *my* inheritance? Those things are mine! They can't take them too!"

He shook his head. "Over the forty years you two were together, you comingled your money so much that anything you purchased with him after the marriage is a joint asset, therefore it's susceptible to being taken as restitution. You had a prenup to ensure you both walked away with what you walked in with, but that doesn't protect you in this situation. He cleaned out the bank accounts, and now all that is left is your joint assets to try to repay his victims. The government has every right to them. And the things they are taking aren't actually *your* things. At least most of them, anyway. This investigation turned up a lot of information, including information that over a decade ago, your husbands made some bad investments, and as a result, they were going to lose everything. You all would have been bankrupt."

"What?" CeCe sat up. "When?"

"I know when," I said softly, remembering how a decade ago, Rick had been so stressed for a month he'd lost fifteen pounds. He'd canceled some of our trips and started cutting back on spending, and any time I'd ask him what was wrong, he'd just storm away instead of talking to me. The man I'd married had become unrecognizable as he'd stayed up all night every night locked in his office like a crazy recluse. But then, one day he'd stepped out all smiles and soon after, he'd started buying even more expensive things than normal, like our new penthouse we still lived in. "Yeah. It was ten, no, eleven years ago. Rick was so stressed out for a month, then one day, he was fine again."

CeCe grew quiet. "I think I know when too. Arthur was acting strange for a while and sold some of his favorite cars, a few of our houses. Then soon after, he bought us a jet and even more houses than he'd sold."

"Well, what happened was," Arnie started, "Your husbands lost everything. But instead of filing bankruptcy, they came up with a plot to get investors to give them money for a business idea that didn't exist. They were smooth-talking salesmen with great reputations and rich connections, so they got millions of dollars invested into a pyramid scheme. That money was used to bail them out of financial ruin. Then, to pay back those people, they did the same thing to the next investors, using the money from the new people to pay off the old ones. And again, and again for a decade, increasing what they took each time. But, it finally caught up with them when an investor caught on and wanted his money back, and since they hadn't stolen from their next victims yet, they couldn't. That's when the whole thing came crumbling down."

"I can't believe this," I said in disbelief. "They were stealing money for a decade?"

"Yes. And this is where the bad news comes in," Arnie said softly. "Because they cleared out the bank accounts, and technically most of your remaining assets were bought and paid for with stolen money, everything you own will be sold off to pay back the people who were victims and pay the government in back taxes. I did everything I could, but the government is seizing every asset you own."

"Everything?" I breathed.

He nodded his head. "Everything."

"Wha... what?" CeCe choked out. "You can't be serious! You're not serious!"

"I'm afraid I am, Mrs. VanTramp. There will be nothing left for you two. Technically, you lost everything a decade ago, but it's just catching up with you now."

A guttural wail erupted from CeCe, followed by a shrill cry from Julian. I was too stunned to make a sound or even exhale the breath trapped in my chest.

"As of today, your penthouses, vacation homes, clothes, shoes, cars, jets... everything... belongs to the United States Government."

"Noooooooo!" CeCe screamed as she fell forward into a dramatic heap, her head collapsing onto her folded arms while she sobbed into his mahogany desk.

"They can't take it all! They can't!" Julian cried. "We didn't do anything wrong!"

"I understand that," Arnie said, "But that doesn't mean the government cares. The assets that you have are going to be used to repay the debt, and even with that, it's not going to cover everything, so just be grateful I was able to fight to get you freed from any additional monies owed. You can try to fight it, but I don't recommend it."

CeCe sat up. "What? Fight it? How?"

"Well, you could roll the dice and say no to the deal they are offering. But that opens you both up to a lengthy investigation and countless legal battles with every victim your husbands stole from. They will be coming for their money back, and with your husbands gone and you two in control of the remaining assets, it's going to fall on you to fight for them."

"Then we fight!" CeCe lifted a fist in the air, and Julian mirrored it.

"Why don't you recommend it?" I asked, remembering those words.

"Honestly? Because you'll lose," he stated simply. "It's a fact that the money was stolen. It's a fact that your assets were purchased with the victim's money. No jury is going to side with you. They are going to tell you that you lost your money a decade ago and you're lucky you got ten extra years of living the high life, and now it's time to give back the investors' money. And you're going to spend a fortune in lawyer fees fighting them all, plus likely end up owing even more than you have and having to pay restitution for the rest of your lives... *after* they take everything."

My heart stalled out again.

"Just be grateful you're getting out without jail time or owing more money than you have."

"Grateful?" CeCe sat up, and her eyes narrowed, her smudged makeup making her look more unraveled than before. "You want us to be *grateful* you did such a shoddy job that you literally lost us *everything!* What kind of crap lawyer are you?"

"I'm so sorry, Mrs. VanTramp. I assure you that I have put in ample time and effort to help you ladies out. At no cost to you, mind you." He lifted his eyebrows.

"Where are we going to go? What are we going to do?" she cried, then collapsed forward onto her folded arms again.

Finally, the words that had been trapped in my throat formed. "So, we literally have nothing? No place to live, no money, no clothes. Nothing?"

"I'm so sorry, Mrs. Whitlock, but that is correct. It seems your husbands have been at this for many years, and the sheer amount of money stolen is astounding. And with them cleaning out the bank accounts before they fled, all that's left goes straight to the victims."

"So... we're homeless?" I said, still struggling to believe this new reality... the one that was far worse than what I'd ever imagined. In my mind, I'd be able to sell the penthouse and lots of my belongings and get enough money to start over. It seemed, however, that the government had other plans for me.

"There are some programs to help out people in your situation. Perhaps some temporary government housing and employment assistance programs. I can get you the information if you'd like it."

"Oh, God. I'm going to throw up." Julian covered his mouth, his pallor taking on a tinge of green and gray.

"We're ruined!" CeCe sobbed into her arms. "How is this happening to me? I'm CeCe VanTramp! I can't be broke! Please, Arnie. There must be something you can do!" CeCe looked up, and the black tears from her mascara streaked down her face. "Screw it. I want to fight! Let's fight!"

"Yes! We're fighting!" Julian uncovered his mouth and the color flooded back into his face. "How do we start?"

"I'm so sorry, Mrs. VanTramp. There's nothing more I can do. My retainer alone is fifty thousand dollars, which you don't have, and I wouldn't feel right taking your money because I truly don't believe there is any way to win. If you want to seek another legal opinion, of course, you're welcome to, but I can tell you you're just going to waste your time and money... money you don't have. I've exhausted all our options, and this is it for you. Just be grateful you won't be in a criminal trial or facing potential jail time."

"No!" she screamed again, then tumbled over onto Julian's shoulder. "It's our money. They can't take it!"

He pressed a hand to her head and together they embraced as they sobbed.

"Well, if he's really gone and our money is gone too, then I need you to help me divorce that bastard." CeCe released her grip on Julian and looked up, eyes red, now narrowing in anger. "I need to be single so I can get us out of this mess."

Arnie sucked the side of his cheek. "Divorcing a man you can't find is going to be tricky. It can be done, but I'm not a divorce lawyer. I don't know how to advise you in this situation. I'm sorry Mrs. VanTramp, but you'll need to find a lawyer appropriate for this situation, and unfortunately, you have no money to pay for one at this time so it could be tricky navigating your way to a divorce for a while."

"Ugh!" She threw her hands up. "This is a nightmare! Now I have nothing *and* I'm still tied to that scoundrel! When I find him, I'm going to wring his neck with my bare hands before I demand a divorce!"

I gave a little snort. "The entire FBI is looking for them CeCe, and they can't find them. Unless they decide to show up again, I don't see us being able to sleuth them out from whatever corner of the world they're hiding in or pay some PI the five pennies we have left between us to hunt them down. We just have to accept this is our new reality. They stole everything and left us with nothing. They're gone, and we're still here cleaning up their mess. I'm not wasting another minute trying to find Rick. I just want to move on with my life and start over, even if I'm doing it with nothing."

CeCe's angry eyes met mine. "Oh, I'll find Arthur. I *refuse* to be married to that man one more minute than I have to. I *can't* be if I have to start over again. I don't know how, but I'll find my way to get a divorce whether I can find him or not."

I was about to argue back at her, but Arnie lifted a hand to stop me.

"Well, actually, Mrs. Whitlock," he said. "It seems you do have one asset left."

I sat up straight. "I do? What is it?"

"I was contacted a few days ago by an attorney trying to find you. It seems that when your aunt passed away, you were her last remaining family, and she left everything to you. She left you her house, all her worldly belongings, and a small inheritance of five thousand dollars. Since this happened after the crimes were committed, I was able to negotiate for you to keep that inheritance. The property and the money are yours, and you can claim them anytime you want."

It wasn't the shock of finding out I had a home and five thousand dollars that kept me from inhaling another breath. The thing that kept me frozen and wide-eyed was finding out my aunt, my last remaining family, had passed away, and I didn't even know it.

Memories of summers at her place flooded into my mind like movie trailers in fast forward. Every summer from the time my mom passed away when I was nine until I graduated from high school at eighteen, my father had sent me to stay with my mother's sister, Aunt Addie, so I could get a little time with a female influence, and someone who had once been my mother's very best friend. He'd thought spending time with her would help me cope with my own loss, and he'd been right. Every year I'd counted the days until I could get to Aunt Addie's, then I'd spend the summer running around barefoot drinking iced tea and helping her bake her famous cookies. My whole body warmed with the memories the two of us had created, and then a cold wave of regret washed over me when I realized how long it had been since I'd even picked up the phone to call her.

Five years? Ten years? My heart constricted when I remembered the event that had been the last time I'd seen or spoken to her.

My father's funeral almost twenty years ago.

Twenty years. That was how long I'd gone without even picking up the phone to check in on her and say hello. And now she was gone, and deep regret washed over me that I hadn't said goodbye or even let her know how much those summers had meant to me. I'd been so consumed with my life in the city and trying to prove that I belonged in my world that I'd completely forgotten about who I'd been. I'd completely forgotten about her. And now... she was gone.

"She's... she's gone? Aunt Addie is gone?" I whispered.

Arnie's face froze. "Oh, I'm so sorry. I didn't realize you didn't know."

A tear slipped past my quick-blinking lids and slid down my cheek. "No. I didn't know. When?"

"Two weeks ago," he answered. "I'm so sorry for your loss, Mrs. Whitlock. I had no idea this would be news to you, or I would have informed you much more gently."

It shouldn't have surprised me that no one would reach out to me to let me know of Aunt Addie's passing. I hadn't been there since I was eighteen years old, and with my phone being confiscated by the government, it wasn't like anyone would have known how to get ahold of me. But still, the guilt and sadness that she'd been gone two weeks already and I hadn't known sank deep into a part of my soul I'd forgotten existed. It was the part that always came to life when I was with her, running wild and free through the gardens, and swinging on the old tire swing out in her front yard. I'd loved her dearly when I was younger, and once again I cursed myself for letting so much time pass without getting in touch.

"Wait," CeCe said as she pointed a finger at me. "So, *she* has a house and money? Then what do I get? That's not fair that she gets something and I don't!"

"Yeah!" Julian said. "We should get something too. It's only fair."

"Excuse me?" I said, spinning to look at them. "My aunt just died. That's why I have something. It's not exactly something I planned on or am celebrating here."

CeCe waved her hand in the air. "Yes, yes. I'm sorry about your loss. Okay? Whatever. It's just not fair that both our husbands did the exact same thing, and *she* is going to have a place to live! Where the hell are Julian and I supposed to go?"

"I don't have an answer for you," Arnie said. "But I'm sure you'll land on your feet. You must have some friends or family to help you out."

CeCe and Julian went quiet, and I knew why. Everyone had turned their back on me without a second thought. Considering I'd always been nice to everyone, and CeCe had been a holy terror, I only imagined her nose must be bruised from all the doors slamming in her face.

"We have nowhere," CeCe whispered. "Please, Arnie. You must be able to negotiate them leaving me at least one house. What about the beach cottage? That one is small."

He lifted an eyebrow. "The twelve-bedroom house on Martha's Vineyard?"

She nodded. "Yes. The summer cottage. Can I at least keep that one?"

If I didn't know better, I'd have sworn I saw a smile start on his lips before he tightened them. "That house is worth millions, Mrs. VanTramp. Unfortunately, they aren't going to let you keep it."

"Ugh!" she screamed, then tossed her hands in the air. "Then we're fighting this! We'll figure out a way! It's our money, and they can't take it!"

"But it's not," I said, turning to face her. "It's not our money. It's the victims' money. And Arnie is right. No one is going to side with us. We're broke, CeCe. And apparently we have been for a decade. I'm not fighting this. I'm taking the deal, Arnie."

"Well, that's easy for *you* to say since you aren't completely broke! At least *you* have somewhere to live!"

"I'm sorry, CeCe. But it's the right thing to do to pay the victims back. I'm not fighting to steal their money again. I just won't."

She glared at me, crossed her arms and looked away.

"I'm sorry I don't have better news for you, ladies." Arnie sat back and then pushed a stack of papers toward me. "Now, this is all stuff you and I can go over to officially transfer things into your name. But after this, I hate to inform you that I won't be able to work pro bono anymore. I hope you can understand."

"Of course," I answered. "We just thank you for helping us through this trying time. Your loyalty is appreciated."

He smiled at me then looked to CeCe. She just rolled her eyes. "Yes, fine. Thank you. Whatever. Come on, Julian. We're leaving. It seems we need to find someplace to live now that we're *homeless!*" She directed that last word she hissed out at Arnie.

A whimper escaped Julian's lips, then he slowly stood. "But the Maloney's come back in two days. We've been sleeping at their place, and they don't know it. They are not going to let us stay when they find out we're there. Where are we going to live?"

"I wish I had an answer for you," Arnie said. "The best advice I can give is to reach out to get some government-assisted living for the time being. But I'm sure you two will land on your feet."

"At this rate, maybe I should land on my head. Off the top of the Empire State building. Just put myself out of my misery," CeCe grumbled as she grabbed Julian's hand and yanked him toward the door.

"Goodbye, CeCe," I said to her, spinning in my chair and giving her a small wave. "It's been nice knowing you," I lied.

She glared at me then stormed out with a whimpering Julian in tow. I watched her go, and for a moment, I felt sorry for her. Then I remembered all the horrible things she'd said to me over the years, and I narrowed my eyes and thought "good riddance" as I watched her walk out of my life for the very last time.

"This shouldn't take long," Arnie said, as he started flipping through the paperwork.

Together we went through it all, and as I signed all the forms and read the documents, I couldn't stop fighting the tears threatening to spill. My aunt had been the one who got me so interested in giving back, and before I met Rick, I had a whole life planned of things like joining Greenpeace, building homes for the needy, and working as a nurse who could travel to impoverished countries and heal the sick. Then Rick entered the picture, and soon I became swept away in his world, forgetting completely about my own goals... the ones I knew Aunt Addie would have been so proud of. She hadn't appeared to judge me when she saw me at my father's funeral, but I'd been so embarrassed when she'd asked what I'd been doing, and I had nothing to answer other than shopping, playing tennis, and hobnobbing with New York's elite. And now she was gone, and I was left with nothing but regret.

"That ought to do it," Arnie said. "Here are the keys for you, and I'll get that paperwork filed."

"Thank you so much for your help, Arnie."

"You're welcome, Mrs. Whitlock. I'm just so sorry this happened to you."

"Yeah. Me too," I answered as I stood. "But I'll find my way through."

"I have no doubt you will." He rose and shook my hand, then with one last wave, I walked out of his office.

When I got to the hallway leading to the elevator, I stumbled to a halt when I saw CeCe and Julian standing in front of the elevator doors. They both looked at me, then their gazes dropped down to their feet.

"Um, Diane?" CeCe said softly, in a tone I'd never heard in her voice before. A tone that resembled... humbleness?

"Yes?" I arched an eyebrow.

"Julian and I were leaving when we realized that we literally have nowhere to go. Then we were thinking a bit about you and your house and wondering... Um... do you think that Julian and I could uh, maybe we could..." She paused, slamming her eyes shut as she inhaled a deep breath then blurted, "stay with you for a little while?"

"What?" I choked out on a laugh. "Are you serious?"

Her eyes snapped open. "Of course, I'm serious! And there is no need to laugh at me about it! Do you think I *like* having to ask for your help? No! I'm mortified! But that should tell you just how desperate we are!"

I couldn't help but start a nervous, awkward laugh. "You... you want to live... with me?"

"Don't laugh!" She stomped her foot. "This is so embarrassing!"

"Please, Diane. We have no one. We have nothing. We are literally homeless. Just for a little while," Julian begged. "I promise we'll stay out of your hair. Just let us stay with you at your aunt's house for a tiny bit while we enact our new plan. Operation Diaper Daddy."

"Julian!" CeCe spat. "We're not calling it that! And don't tell Diane about that!"

"Operation Diaper Daddy?" I asked, arching an eyebrow.

CeCe waved a hand. "Just never mind that part. All you need to do is give us a place to stay for a tiny little bit while we figure out our next plan. Please, Diane. I..." She paused, then slowly lowered herself to her knees, grabbing Julian's hand and pulling him down with her. When she looked up at me with desperation filling her eyes, she finished with, "I'm begging you. Please don't leave us behind."

Even though I wanted to throw a party just to celebrate getting rid of that awful woman, and seeing her on her knees begging for my help should have been the highlight of my existence, my heart constricted at the desperation I saw in her. From the sag in her shoulders to the defeat welling inside her eyes, I understood her emotions. I knew she had nowhere else to go. I could almost hear my Aunt Addie whispering in my ear that it was the right thing to do to take care of your neighbors whether you liked them or not.

From the smallest spider she'd carry outside instead of squishing it, to the endless fundraisers it seemed we'd constantly baked cookies for those summers I was there, my Aunt Addie made it her life's purpose to help any and all in need. And even though I wanted nothing more than to tell that wretched creature and her minion "Hell no" then laugh at them as they shook a can for change on the street corner, I felt like the best way I could honor my Aunt Addie was to follow in her footsteps.

"Please?" Julian stuck out his lower lip, pressing his hands tight together.

With a heavy sigh, I slumped my shoulders. "Even though I know I'm going to deeply regret this.... Okay. Fine. You can come stay with me."

They launched up off the ground and collided into a hug as they started jumping around in circles.

"We're saved! We're saved!" Julian blubbered out between tears.

"We're not homeless!" CeCe exclaimed, and they continued jumping around.

"Just until you're back on your feet," I added, and they finally broke up the celebration.

"Of course," CeCe answered. "We'll get out of your hair as fast as we can. We promise."

"Well, I was just going to go book myself a ticket to get to my aunt's, and I suppose you don't have any money to buy your own tickets?"

They shook their heads.

"We are quite literally penniless," CeCe said.

I knew how she felt. Well, other than the five thousand dollars I now had. "Okay. I'll pay for your tickets too. But then you're on your own. I don't have much, and I can't afford to support all three of us. Deal?"

"Deal!" they answered quickly.

"Wait a minute. Tickets?" Julian asked. "Where is your aunt's house? Is it not in New York?"

I shook my head. "No. It's in Louisiana."

Their eyes nearly bulged out of their heads.

"Louisiana!?" CeCe shrieked. "You can't be serious!"

"Did you not want to come then?" I arched an eyebrow and tugged my lips into a smile. "Because you are welcome to stay behind. Arnie said there may be some government housing for you. Perhaps you could look into that?"

"Never!" CeCe stiffened. "I'm *not* living in a glorified homeless shelter! I'm CeCe VanTramp and I will *never* allow myself to fall that far."

I tipped my head, fighting the smile on my lips. "You sure? Because you didn't seem very excited about Louisiana. You really want to come stay with me?"

They exchanged a worried look, then with a quiet cry, they nodded their heads.

"No. Louisiana is great. Perfect," CeCe said. "After you."

With a big smile, I pushed the button on the elevator, then we all got in and started our descent to the new life awaiting us below.

CHAPTER FOUR
CeCe

When I stepped off the bus and out into the hot, humid southern summer air, I caught a whiff of my own body odor, and my nose crinkled in response. "Ugh. The heat just made everything worse. I smell, Julian. I smell like... bus people!"

He stepped down behind me, his face scrunching to match mine. "To be more specific, we smell like sadness, failure and B.O. all mixed into one horrifying aroma of despair."

"Well, after twenty-four hours on a bus, I *feel* like sadness, failure and despair, so I guess it's only fitting."

"If it makes you feel any better, we all smell." His face soured more as he sniffed his Gucci shirt.

"It doesn't. I'm never going to get this smell out of my hair. It's permeated too deep. I'm going to smell like a bus person until my dying breath."

"Oh, quit your griping," Diane said when she came down the stairs. "Just remember that if you wouldn't have insisted on lugging all those boxes with you, we could have flown. But you refused to ship them, and we couldn't afford to check them all. So, it was this, or you could have stayed behind in New York. Just be glad I brought you down here with me."

She was right, of course. My boxes of pilfered couture, the ones I'd refused to let out of my sight, had caused us to be unable to afford even embarrassing coach plane tickets. But those boxes were all I had left in this world, and to hell

55

if I was going to let them out of my sight... even if it meant spending a full twenty-four hours living in a never-ending nightmare surrounded by men who spit chew into a can and women who seemed to all have forgotten about a little thing called deodorant.

Disgusting.

Regular humans were disgusting.

And now without my millions of dollars that kept me elevated above the rabble, I had no choice but to be surrounded by them.

"Yes, yes. I know. It's all my fault we had to take the bus," I admitted. "But *you* have a house and an inheritance. All I have are these boxes we smuggled out with my most cherished possessions. What if I shipped them and they got lost? It's not like I could claim insurance on them since, technically, I'm not supposed to have them. Then I would have nothing, Diane! Nothing!"

"Okay, okay." She lifted her hands. "I get it. These are your babies. And I paid the extra money out of the small amount of inheritance I got to get them on the bus with us, so just be grateful and quit complaining about how we got here."

Just be grateful. Those words were like fingernails on a chalkboard every time she said them... which had been a lot since I'd waved goodbye to the last of my dignity two days ago by getting on my knees and begging her for help.

After Julian and I had stormed out of Arnie's office, we'd realized quickly we had nowhere to storm to. With no one to help us, we were, quite literally, homeless. It had been Julian's idea to ask Diane for help, and as much as saying the words to her had felt worse than vomiting hot lava, I'd been overwhelmingly relieved when she'd agreed to let us stay with her. But ever since that moment, any time I complained about our situation, she just kept reminding me to "be grateful." That "things could be worse." She was right, of course, but it still didn't make me want to bop her in the nose any less.

Frowning when I caught another whiff of myself, I sighed. "Fine. Thank you. I appreciate it. Now, can we get out of this bus station to somewhere with a hot shower so I can try to wash away the smell of ruin?"

Julian nodded. "And a bath. I really think this is gonna require a full soak to get it out of my pores."

"My aunt's house has a bathtub," Diane answered, then paused. "Or, I guess I should say it used to. I have no idea if she remodeled or anything. It's been over forty years since I've been here."

A mosquito buzzed around Julian's head, and he slapped his neck when it landed. "Eew! It's starting already! Bugs!"

Diane slung her bag over her shoulder. "We're in Louisianna, Julian. You'd best get used to bugs."

"Oh, man. How is this happening?" he whispered.

How is this happening was right, yet after two days of processing the horrifying information Arnie had dumped on us, I was finally starting to grasp my new reality. My sad, scary, and embarrassing reality. The reality that I was... poor.

I shuddered at the thought for the hundredth time, wondering when that realization would stop making my whole-body shiver.

Probably never.

"Who gets our bags?" Julian pointed to the boxes the bus driver was unloading. "Do we have a driver or something to grab them?"

Diane chuckled. "We do, Julian."

"What?" he and I gasped.

"We're supposed to get our own bags?" I asked, appalled.

Diane rolled her eyes then planted a hand on her hip. "Yes, CeCe. I know you've never lived without millions of dollars, but for the rest of the world, we haul our own bags."

Diane hadn't grown up rich like I had, so this was easier on her than it was on me. At least she had some semblance of what to expect out here in the cold, harsh reality of the real world. My entire life I'd been pampered and spoiled, and the thought of carrying my own bags sent another one of those now-too-familiar shudders through me.

"Fine. We'll get our own bags," I said, accepting another one of the horrors of brokedom. I waved a hand at Julian. "Be a doll and get our bags and boxes."

Julian furrowed his brow. "Me? You want *me* to get all the luggage?"

"Well, you are technically her assistant, aren't you?" Diane arched an eyebrow. "Or are we finally done with the ruse that you've lifted a finger to work in the last twenty years with her?"

"I had responsibilities." He pointed up his chin. "Lots of responsibilities. But none of them were handling luggage."

"And those responsibilities were what exactly?" Diane asked, knowing full well that Julian had no real job with me and was just a friend I took everywhere... something she'd continued needling us about at every opportunity this entire trip together.

"They weren't bags," he answered, then turned up his nose. "And there is no way I can carry all of those."

Diane chuckled. "We all carry our own bags and boxes. I'll call a cab, and we'll get going."

Diane pulled out the prepaid flip phone she'd bought since the government had taken her phone too and she couldn't afford a new plan. "Well, crap." She closed it up. "That's right. This prehistoric thing doesn't have internet. How in the hell do you find a cab company or Uber without Google?"

We all stood silently staring at each other.

"Don't look at me." Julian shrugged. "We've had a driver ever since I've been with CeCe. I wouldn't even know how to Uber *with* a smart phone."

Diane scrunched up her face., then after taking a good look around, she marched over to the ticket counter inside the small, rundown bus station. A few minutes later, she came back smiling. "They had the number to a cab company! It will be here in five minutes. We need to get our bags to the curb over there."

When she pointed, I looked between the curb and my piles of boxes and luggage now all unloaded from the bus.

"Can the nice lady at the counter also help us move all this stuff?" Julian asked, batting his eyelashes with a smile.

"No," Diane answered abruptly. "We all carry our own stuff. I suggest you two get moving."

With a groan, Julian and I sauntered over to our luggage, then one at a time, we took turns schlepping it the few hundred feet to the curb where Diane stood with her one large rolling suitcase. One stood guard over our precious belongings while the other moved the rest to the cab stop.

"You're not going to help?" I asked Diane, puffing as I dropped off another bag.

"I wish I could, but I'm watching for the cab." She flashed an overly sweet smile.

Withholding my glare, I spun on my heel and click-clacked on my heels back across the pavement to tag out Julian as he dragged off the next load. Finally, with both of us panting and sweating in the hot, Southern summer heat, we finished our last load.

"That's everything," Julian said exasperated. "And look! I have a blister!"

"Oh, honey!" I grabbed his hand and looked at it. "You poor thing."

He nodded, sticking out his lip in a big pout. "It hurts. Everything hurts and I'm dying." With an exaggerated sigh, he slumped down onto my Hermes suitcase, using it like a chair. I gave him a warning stare for sitting on my precious belongings, and he quickly hopped off. "Sorry."

"Oh! There it is!" Diane waved at the ancient-looking yellow cab heading our way. When it pulled up, she greeted the driver, and he got out. I cringed at the small dirt stains on his ripped-up jeans and the unprofessional t-shirt stretching over his pot belly. The cab drivers I'd seen in New York always at least looked more... hygienic.

He took one look at our large pile of luggage, then in his deep, thick accent that made my eardrums scream in horror, he pointed at our pile of luggage. "That's ain't gonna fit in the trunk."

"What? What are we supposed to do then?" I asked, panicked he was going to tell me to leave it.

"I can put it up on the roof. I got me some tie down straps I 'spose we can use."

"Put my things on the *roof?*" I gasped. "No! Never! They can't be out alone in the elements!"

He spit on the ground then sucked his teeth. "Only other option is to leave 'em behind or call another cab to take the bags separate."

I started to agree with the second statement, but Diane turned and faced me with a stern stare. "I'm not paying for *two* cabs. If you want a second cab, you can pay for it yourself."

"But I have no money!" I stomped my foot.

She shrugged. "Well, then your crap rides on the roof or you can leave it here. Or if you want, put it in the back seat and you and Julian can take the roof. Your choice."

Julian and I shared a worried look, then finally, I gave a slight nod. "Fine. Put it on the roof."

With that smug smile I knew too well, Diane gave the driver the go ahead. He pulled some strange orange straps out of his trunk, then we all took turns putting the luggage on the roof, and when it was done, he secured the straps through the open windows and ratcheted it down.

"Careful!" I said as he cranked one more time.

"Well, we don't want 'em to fall off, now do we?" he answered, and I shook my head.

"No. No we don't."

"There. That'll do it," he said, then walked over to the driver side of the car and got in.

Diane jumped in the front, and Julian and I went to the back. We shared a look at the worn velour fabric, and with matching cringes, we climbed inside.

"I'm Dwayne," the driver said as he started up the car. "What's the address?"

Diane rattled it off, and he turned to her and smiled. "Oh, sweet Aunt Addie's place, huh? Oh, how we all do miss her."

Diane spun to face him. "You knew my aunt? Wait. How did you know she was my aunt?"

He grinned, and when I saw it in the rearview mirror, it showcased a smile that could have used about a gallon of bleach and whiteners. "Of course I did. Everyone knew Aunt Addie. And everyone calls her Aunt Addie on account of how she takes care of us. Is she your real aunt?"

Diane nodded as he pulled out.

"Lucky girl to have had her as a real aunt. That must have been a hell of a treat. All us in town just had her as our honorary aunt. Always there when we need her. Sure gonna miss that gal. Didn't see you at the funeral though, did I?"

Diane didn't answer, and instead grew quiet as we rode along.

"What brings you to her house?" Dwayne asked, ignoring her non-response.

"Uh, I inherited it. We'll be staying there for a while."

"Get outta town!" He slapped the steering wheel. "Well, that's great news! Hopefully we'll be seeing you 'round town then."

"Yes, I'm sure you will," Diane said softly, then went quiet again while he drove on. Eventually, we reached a sign that said *Ruinville: Population 276.*

My eyes went big. "Wait. Is this town actually called *Ruinville?* That wasn't just the way we were referring to it since we're, you know, ruined?"

Diane chuckled. "Yes. It's actually called Ruinville."

"Ruinville? Seriously?" Julian clutched his chest. "I thought you were just joking too. Like it was Poorville or Loserville or some other word to encompass what we are now ville."

"Nope. The town really is called Ruinville."

"Well, isn't that ironic," I said with an eyeroll.

"We're literally ruined in Ruinville." Julian sighed.

"From riches to Ruinville. Fitting." I joined him in the heavy sigh. "If I die down here from malaria, or more likely shame, go ahead and etch that on my tombstone. 'She went from riches to Ruinville and she died of shame. RIP.'"

Diane chuckled. "I'll see it done."

"And did that sign say the population is two hundred seventy-six people? That's the entire population?" Julian said. "You've got to be kidding."

The driver grinned his horrifying smile. "Well, with you guys moving in, guess that takes us to two hundred seventy-nine! Really getting booming it seems!"

I withheld my groan as he turned down a street that took us into an almost quaint-looking little town. There were houses lining the streets with white picket fences and flowers blooming everywhere. As we drove the few blocks past them, we arrived in a small town square with a white gazebo and more flowers smattered around the green grass filling the area.

"That's the Ruinville town square," Dwayne said as we drove by. "We have all our festivals and fundraisers here."

"It's kind of pretty," Julian said. "You know, in a sort of dumpy, vegetation covered way."

"I remember this," Diane said softly as we drove by the admittedly pretty little space. "And look! The old ice cream parlor is still there! And the candy shop! Oh! It's the same! It's exactly the same!"

"Nothin' in Ruinville ever changes," Dwayne said as he turned a corner and took us away from the little street lined with small businesses. "When is the last time you were here?"

Diane's smile faltered. "Uh, it's been forty years."

"Gosh darn that's a long time!" he said, then he pressed on the gas to speed us up as we drove out of town.

"Why are we leaving? Isn't her house in Ruinville?" Julian pointed out the window. Then he shrunk down and whispered into my ear, "Oh, God. We're being kidnapped aren't we. Sold off to cannibals."

Dwayne kept on driving. "Aunt Addie didn't live in town. She liked her peace and quiet. Her place is just ten minutes out of town."

"Thank God," Julian whispered. "I thought we were goners."

As we kept driving, the scenery started to change again, and now instead of quaint little white houses, we sporadically saw rickety old shacks that all looked like they could blow over in a bad wind.

"It is cannibals," Julian whispered when we passed a homestead with at least a dozen junked up, rusted old cars scattered around the front yard, and a man wearing no shirt and overalls staring at us as we passed by. "My God. It's cannibals. Or *Deliverance.* We're in *Deliverance* aren't we. I think I just heard the banjos."

"Can we go back to the town and stay there?" I asked. "Maybe she kept an apartment in town or something?"

"Don't let ol' Whacky Wade scare you off." He waved out the window at the man in the overalls. "He's perfectly harmless. And he rarely wanders over to Aunt Addie's house."

I gripped Julian's hand as I watched the scary man disappear behind us.

Rarely? So that meant there was a chance we'd wake up and Whacky Wade would be standing in our yard? I started to question if we'd be better off on the streets of New York.

"Almost there," Dwayne said as he turned onto another road. "Just another half mile to go, then you'll be at Aunt Addie's house."

Diane remained quiet as we drove deeper into the vegetation, and shortly after the turn, I realized we were following some sort of body of water. With trees and shrubs growing in it, I realized what it was from photos.

I gulped. "Is her house... *in* the bayou?"

"Oh, yeah," Dwayne said. "Real nice place she's got out here. And you're right up next to the water. Super peaceful. Aunt Addie sure did love it out here."

Diane still rode in silence, and I couldn't figure out why she wasn't talking more. Usually, she was chatty with everyone from doormen to diplomats, but for some reason on this ride, it seemed like one of the cannibals Julian and I feared had already pulled out her tongue.

"Here we are." The cab turned down a driveway lined by tall trees with dangling branches that looked almost like moss or something. We drove between them, twisting and turning down the long driveway until we came through the trees to an opening with a big lawn butted up against the water, and a decrepit, white two-story house in the center of the yard.

"What... what happened to it?" Diane breathed out, clasping a hand over her mouth. "It's so rundown. It used to be beautiful."

Dwayne shrugged. "It ain't bad. Could use some paint I 'spose, and maybe new shutters. You know Aunt Addie. She never liked to spend a penny on herself. Always thinking' 'bout everyone else first, and I guess she just let the place get away from her." He frowned. "Guess we should have popped out here more often to help her out. Didn't realize she needed the extra help these last years. Dang. Now I feel bad. Don't know why she didn't just ask. I'd a been over lickity split with the boys and some cans of paint and extra boards. But then it wouldn't be Aunt Addie if she ever asked for a dang thing for herself."

The cab pulled to a stop, and we slowly stepped out. Diane's face was as white as a ghost as she took slow steps toward the house.

"It used to be so pretty," she said quietly.

"When were you last here?" Julian asked. "The fifteen hundreds? Because that's how long it's likely been since this place looked shiny and new." Diane glanced over her shoulder and pinned him with a glare. He shrunk back behind me then whispered, "Damn. Diane is a little mean these days, don't you think? Isn't she supposed to be the nice one?"

She was supposed to be "the nice one." It was part of why I hated her so much. Ever since she'd arrived in our world with her bright shiny skin and her bright shiny smile, everyone had fawned over Rick's "sweet, new girl." I'd been pushed aside as they all swooned over her like she was Cinder-freaking-ella. Then year after year, everyone always went on and on about beautiful Diane and her kindness and generosity.

Blech.

Annoying.

Yet, Julian had been right. She wasn't herself right now.

Dwayne's cell phone rang as he was unstrapping our bags from the roof. "Yello? You what? Oh dang, Miss Ellie. I'll be right there."

He hung up the phone and set our luggage down. "Normally I'd help you load this in the house, but that was Miss Ellie. She swerved to miss a gator and plum ran her car right off the road. I gotta go get her quick. You all okay?"

"Yes, we'll be fine," Diane said softly. "Thank you for the ride."

"Any family of Aunt Addie's is family to us too. You just holler if you need anything."

"We will, Dwayne. Thanks."

With a quick final wave, he jumped in the car and pulled out, leaving the three of us standing in front of the looming disaster of a home.

"So... we're actually staying here? In this dump?" Julian asked.

Diane spun and faced him, planting her hands on her hips. "You don't have to stay here, Julian. You can go back at any time. This was my Aunt Addie's home and it's my home now too. Now either quit your bitching and come in or start hiking back to New York!"

We both recoiled at the unusual sharpness of her words, then she stormed up the steps and onto the porch.

"Damn. The heat must be getting to Suzy Sunshine," Julian whispered, then we followed along behind her.

The rickety porch floor creaked beneath our feet, and the screen door, barely held on by rusted old hinges, let out a loud, cringe-inducing *eeeek* as we pushed it open. Diane stepped in first, and Julian and I squished together tight as we followed her inside. Slowly, we all moved into the first room, a sitting room filled with old antique furniture and décor that belonged in some seventies museum filled with oranges and browns making me want to poke my own eyes out.

Diane said nothing as she kept moving forward, and her slow steps took us to a doorway that led into the kitchen. When we turned the corner to step inside, Diane gasped and froze as stiff as a board.

"Don't. Move," she breathed out.

Julian and I both peeked over her shoulders, then when my eyes clapped onto the alligator on the kitchen floor, I tipped my head, wondering why in the hell she would have had such an odd and cumbersome decoration just taking up space on the ugly vinyl floor. But when its eyes blinked, my mouth opened, and a scream ripped straight out of my lungs.

Julian's scream dwarfed mine as we flew backward. It hissed and snapped its head in our direction.

"I said not to move!" Diane scolded, stepping back with us. "Just stay calm."

"I watched somewhere if an alligator chases you, you're supposed to zig zag," Julian whispered.

"Let's just step back slowly," Diane said quietly.

We all took one step back together, but Julian bumped into a wall and let out a bloodcurdling scream. The alligator jumped from the sudden noise, then snapped towards us with another hiss.

"Run!" Diane shouted, spinning around and pushing into us as we started stumbling backward away from the irritated creature.

"Zig zag!" Julian shouted as he took off. "Zig zag!"

His youth and fitness sent him flying out leaps and bounds ahead of us as Diane and I huffed along after him. We sprinted out the front door, tumbled down the steps and continued chasing Julian through the yard as he ran erratically back and forth yelling, "Zig! Zag! Zig! Zag!"

Finally, when we had enough distance from the house and there was no alligator hot on our tail, we stumbled to a stop, pressing our hands to our knees as we puffed.

"What in the holy hell was that?" I breathed out. "Is that normal? That can't be normal!"

"I have no idea," Diane answered breathlessly. "She didn't used to have an alligator."

"You didn't zig zag!" Julian said as he trotted back. "They always say to zig zag! It could have gotten you!"

"It's not chasing us." Diane stood up, and we looked at the porch door. Slowly it creaked open, and the five-foot alligator slid through it, down the steps, and sauntered back into the water while we watched in stunned silence.

"I can't believe we were that close to an alligator," Julian said. "The closest I've ever been to one before this was when I bought those red alligator boots during Fashion Week."

"We can't stay here," I blurted. "We absolutely, positively cannot stay here. The house is falling apart, and it's infested with alligators. What are we going to do?"

Tears started pouring down my face, and I collapsed to my knees. The reality of my new life struck me like a lightning bolt as I stared at the house I couldn't imagine setting foot in again.

"I can't do this. I can't do this. I can't do this," I repeated as I struggled to catch my breath.

After heaving a heavy sigh, Diane placed a hand on my shoulder. "We can do this. We have no choice. Let's just try to make the best of it."

Make the best of it. How in the hell was I supposed to make the best out of being abandoned by my husband, shunned by my society, completely penniless and now forced to live in an alligator-infested shack in the bayou surrounded by overall-wearing cannibals with names like Whacky Wade?

But Diane reached down and extended her hand. When I looked in her eyes, I saw the same pain in them that mirrored mine. But unlike me, she was standing tall. I didn't know how she had so much strength when I felt so weak and defeated, but I reached out and took her hand and let her pull me up to my feet.

"We can do this," she said as we stood staring at the house.

"What if there's another alligator in there?" Julian asked. "We can't go back inside."

"We can and we will. Let's find something to defend ourselves with and start going through the house together."

After sharing a look, we all lifted our chins then started toward the house side by side. On our way, we grabbed anything resembling a weapon we could find in case we stumbled onto any other predators inside. With our shovel, hoe and metal fence post clutched tight in our hands, we tip-toed back inside our new home.

CHAPTER FIVE
Diane

Wave after wave of nostalgia hit me as we moved room to room through my Aunt Addie's house, each looking closely for critters with every door we slowly pushed open. Everything was exactly the same as the last time I'd been here when I was just seventeen years old. My last summer before I left for college, and after that, I never returned, though I always meant to.

Though everything was the same, it was also so different. When I was young, the house had been warm and clean, filled with laughter and joy. Now it felt dark and sad. Although there was dust on the ledges and picture frames throughout the house, it wasn't necessarily dirty. There wasn't garbage and junk piled up, or old food rotting in the kitchen. It wasn't that it was falling apart, but more that nothing had been updated or maintained since my last visit here. The walls had cracks and paint chips missing, the lights didn't all work, and the carpets and rugs were all at least forty years old and worn down to bare threads. I hated thinking that Aunt Addie had spent her last years in a rundown house that I'd never returned to.

We pushed open the door to the second-floor bathroom, and like most doors we opened, Julian screamed in anticipation of some animal launching itself at us.

"Would you stop screaming!" I batted a hand at him. "You scare me more than whatever could be waiting behind these doors. I'm going to need a hearing aid by the time we finish clearing the house."

"Sorry, it's just so scary! I think I have PTSD from seeing that alligator. I really thought it was stuffed, but then it moved." He shuddered. "It was straight out of a horror movie. Now every corner we turn, I think something is waiting."

"I agree with Diane. My ears are ringing. Just stop screaming out loud. Scream on the inside. Like me." CeCe straightened taller. "I've basically been screaming since the moment we set foot in this house, but no one is going deaf from it."

"Bathroom is clear. Nothing nefarious awaiting us that required your blood-curdling scream." I glanced back at Julian and scolded him with a stare. After taking one last peek around the room Aunt Addie had taught me to apply mascara in, we backed out and moved toward the last doorway down the hall... the one that had been my summer room all those years of my childhood.

"I feel like we're Navy SEALs or something," Julian whispered as we got closer. "You know? Like clearing a building filled with terrorists or something."

I looked over my shoulder and snorted out a laugh. "You? A Navy SEAL? I think even CeCe would have a better chance at that."

"Hey, I'm very fit," he snapped back. "I work out at least two hours a day. How else do you think I have this physique? Although, since we lost our home, and our gym pass, I've only been able to do sit-ups and push-ups. I think I'm starting to lose my tone already."

"Well, if you're so strong, maybe you should be going first so you can fight off the woodland creatures awaiting us behind this last door."

"Nope. No way. It's your house, your battle. We're just here as backup."

I chuckled at him as I kept moving. Despite often finding him annoying and uppity at the parties we'd attended, I had to admit, since embarking on this adventure together, he had made me laugh more times than I could count.

Though, it was mostly at his expense.

I put my hand on the doorknob I'd turned so many times, and readying my shovel, I pushed it open. When nothing jumped out the door at me, I stepped inside.

My heart constricted in my chest when I saw every single poster I'd put on the walls were still there. The same bedspread we'd picked out at the thrift store together still spread across the twin bed she'd tucked me into each night. On the bedside, the photo of the two of us holding up her famous cookies at the summer bake sale for the church.

My room. It was still... my room. She hadn't changed a thing. Like it was a tomb enclosed since the last time I'd left. Like all this time she had expected me to come back, and she'd left it untouched. And yet... I hadn't. I hadn't come back. I'd gone to college, got busy interning over the summer, then I'd met Rick and jetted off to my new life... a life without her.

A gut-wrenching sob shook my shoulders as my hands flew to my face. I stood in my old room sobbing at the guilt I felt for abandoning her and the regrets I had for not being there for her even in the end. While I'd been living in the lap of luxury, I hadn't even thought to send money so she could enjoy some of the creature comforts I'd taken for granted. I could have easily sent money to fix everything for her and should have. How selfish. After everything she'd done for me, while I was flying around on private jets and buying ten-thousand-dollar purses just to piss off CeCe, she couldn't even afford to upgrade her carpeting or have a fresh coat of paint on the walls. I'd left her here. All alone.

"What's happening? Are you okay?" CeCe asked.

"I'm a horrible person!" I cried, stumbling forward toward my old bed. A plume of dust floated up around me when I sat down on the mattress that likely hadn't been used since the last time I'd sat on it.

"Uh... What's happening here?" Julian asked.

I looked up to see him and CeCe staring at me with confused expressions.

More tears dripped down my cheeks. "My aunt. She gave me so much when I was young. After my mother died, each summer I came here to stay with her. She did everything she could to be the female role model for me. She taught me everything a mother would have taught a daughter, and each night she'd sit here in this rocking chair and tuck me in, telling me stories about my mother so it would keep her memory alive."

I looked at the picture of the two of us on the nightstand again, and for a moment, I could still hear her voice softly soothing me to sleep.

"She was so wonderful to me, and look at this place? It hasn't been updated in decades! I met Rick then just left her to her fate all alone. How easy it would have been for me to pick up the phone to call her, to take the jet down to see her, to send money to make sure she never wanted for a thing. But I didn't. I was... I was too ashamed. I couldn't face her, so I just let her disappear from my life," I admitted to them as well as myself.

"What are you talking about? Why were you ashamed?" CeCe came over and started to sit beside me, but when more dust floated up, she hopped up then just patted me on the shoulder in what I appreciated as an awkward attempt at comforting me.

"My aunt gave everything to everyone else. She never kept a thing for herself. She was the one who had inspired me to go to college and do something where I could spend my life helping people. But then I met Rick, and I got swept up in his world, and slowly but surely, I forgot about myself... my goals. My desire to help others."

"You donated to charity fundraisers all the time. Hell, you outbid me at the auctions more times than I can count." Her eyes narrowed for a moment.

"Sure, I wrote checks to the fundraisers getting all the publicity, but I didn't actually *do* anything to help. And I ignored all the causes that I felt passionate about because Rick wanted to make sure our donations were flashy and appreciated by the public, you know, so we looked good."

"Well, isn't that why people do charity stuff?" Julian tipped his head.

"Well, yes, but also for tax write offs," CeCe added.

"Not *good* people," I answered quickly. "Good people do it to help others, not for recognition. I'm a terrible person for abandoning her and for forgetting who I am, and my goals of a life devoted to helping others. That's why I'm here, broke in the bayou. It's penance. My punishment. I've been smited."

"Smited in Ruinville," Julian said on a sigh. "That's what we all are. Broke in the bayou. Destitute in Dixie. All trapped here in this hellhole together."

"Well, I deserve it. That's for sure. I turned into a terrible person when I got rich."

CeCe tutted and waved a hand at me. "Nonsense. I think your money did plenty of good. We helped fund schools, supported medical research, and lots of other changes that yes, maybe we didn't get in and get our hands dirty, but our money still helped. You have nothing to feel ashamed about," CeCe said, and it felt unnatural to have her being kind to me.

I looked up at her and paused, waiting for her to finish with some backhanded compliment like she normally did, but instead, she just gave me a sympathetic look.

"Thanks, CeCe. I wish I believed that, but deep down, I know that I did a terrible thing abandoning her. When she came to my father's funeral, I saw the disappointment in her eyes when I told her about my life. She would never say it outwardly, she was far too kind, but deep down, she was disappointed that I was just writing checks and hiding out in my penthouse far away from the problems of the world. I think that I never called her again because I was too ashamed of who I'd become. But that feeling is nothing compared to what I'm feeling right now seeing how she lived and knowing she died alone."

My shoulders slumped under the weight of my admission. It hadn't even occurred to me that the reason I'd avoided Aunt Addie all these years was my own selfish need not to see the look in her eyes when she asked how I'd been helping people... and my answer was so far from the one I thought I'd be giving her.

I just got back from a missionary trip in Serbia feeding orphans.

I became a nurse and joined Doctors Without Borders. I've helped treat so many unfortunate people.

I helped build houses for Habitat for Humanity. We just finished moving a new family into their home.

Those were the words she'd expected to hear from me when I'd run up and hugged her at my father's funeral. Instead, I'd told her that I had been busy planning parties and traveling. Then, after seeing the look in her eyes, I'd quickly blurted. "I do give a lot of money to charities though. A lot."

"That's nice, dear," she'd answered with a soft smile.

I'd shrunk beneath it, knowing in that moment that I'd come nowhere close to living up to her expectations... or mine. But instead of using that moment to propel myself back to the person I'd set out to be, I'd just hugged her goodbye and hid from her, returning to my old life as Rick's socialite wife writing checks for charities and trying to torture CeCe.

"Can I... do anything?" CeCe asked, and again the unnatural kindness in her voice sounded foreign to me.

I looked up, shaking my head. "No. I don't think so but thank you for asking. What's done is done. All we can do now is move forward, and I can try to be a better person this time around. Try like hell to be the person we both thought I'd be."

"I still think you weren't as bad as you think. In fact, I would say you were an annoying do-gooder if that makes you feel any better."

A small smile started on my lips. There was the CeCe I knew. "I suppose compared to you, I was Mother freaking Theresa."

We exchanged a look, and behind her glare, I saw the playfulness in her eyes... a softness I hadn't seen before.

"Ah! A car! I hear a car pulling in! It's the cannibals!" Julian rushed to the window and peered out the sheer drapes.

"What? Who's here?" I asked, hopping off the bed and hurrying to his side.

The three of us peered out the window together, and I saw an old brown cop car pull up and park in the gravel drive.

"Cops?" CeCe asked. "I thought that we were cleared of all that criminal nonsense!"

"Cannibal cops!" Julian gasped. "I swear I've seen this movie. He's going to use his power to trick us into getting in the back seat of that car and then..." He slid a finger across his throat. "We're sandwiches, bitches."

"He's not a cannibal." I chuckled as I squinted at the familiar, though aged, face of the man stepping out of the car. "I think that's Deputy Boshaw. I remember him from when I was a teenager. He was just a new, young cop then."

"And you're sure he's not a cannibal?" CeCe asked. "Julian might be onto something here. Maybe we should grab our weapons again." She gestured to our shovel, hoe, and fence post propped against the wall.

"He's not a cannibal. He was kind of a hard ass, but he didn't give off the eating humans vibe when I had to ride home in his cop car," I answered, then started toward the hallway to go out and meet him.

"You got arrested here?" Julian gasped as he hurried behind me.

"No. Just silly kid stuff," I responded, and the memories of that night wrapped around me like a warm hug.

The last time I'd seen Deputy Boshaw, I was riding home in the back of his car after I'd gotten in trouble "borrowing" a rowboat with my summer love, Johnny. My stomach erupted in a whirlwind of butterflies when I thought back to that particular summer day where I'd given up my virginity to him in that "borrowed" rowboat that got us into so much trouble.

On my last weekend before heading back to college, and after spending those past few summers together madly in love, it was going to be our last night together. We'd ridden our bikes down to the water, and while giggling wildly, we'd hopped into Old Man Ewan's rowboat and paddled out away from shore. I'd lost myself in him that day drifting around the lake, the romance of young love and new experiences making that one of the most magical days of my life.

It turned out we hadn't been as stealth as we'd thought, and Old Man Ewan had seen us sneak off with his rowboat and called the cops on us. Deputy Boshaw was standing on the pier with a scowl waiting for us to come back in. Even though I was terrified to get in the back of the cop car while he drove us home, I couldn't stop grinning. Johnny was beside me in the back seat, those beautiful dimples of his deepening as he'd smiled at me. We'd even snuck another kiss while Deputy Boshaw was giving us an upbraiding about bad choices turning us into lifelong criminals and that he should be taking us to jail to teach us a lesson. Instead, the sheriff, who was friends with Johnny's dad, had told him just to scare us then drive us home. I'd kissed Johnny goodbye that night, not knowing it would be the last time I saw him.

My heart constricted thinking about that one other piece of my past I'd walked away from and never looked back.

Johnny Alden.

My first love. The man I'd swore I was going to spend the rest of my life with. And then college happened, I got busy with a summer internship, then I met Rick and well... that had been the end of my youthful romance that still made my heart flutter thinking back on it all these years later.

"Afternoon," Deputy Boshaw said as he approached the house.

"Deputy Boshaw? Is that you?" I asked as I stepped out onto the front porch.

He sauntered up the walkway overgrown with weeds. "It's *Sheriff* Boshaw now."

As I came down the steps, he lifted his head, finally showing me his face hidden beneath his tan hat. Though his eyes were the same, he'd aged forty years, and I don't know why it shocked me so much to see the difference. I wasn't a seventeen-year-old girl anymore, so I didn't know why I expected to see the young version of him. Instead, grey hair and weathered skin met my eyes as I stopped at the bottom of the stairs and faced him.

"*Sheriff* Boshaw. It's great to see you again. I'm not sure if you remember me but I'm—"

"I know who you are," he responded, the words sharp with his Southern drawl. He clamped the piece of straw tighter between his teeth. "I remember you. Got in some trouble back in the day if I recall."

CeCe and Julian stepped out the front door but kept their distance behind me up on the porch.

I chuckled. "Yeah. I guess I made a few bad decisions as a kid. I think that was the last time I saw you was the time Johnny and I borrowed that rowboat."

"*Stole* the rowboat. And that wasn't the first time you two had gotten on the wrong side of the law." He leveled me with a stare.

"Oh, come on." I chuckled again, suppressing the laughter reliving those memories induced. "It was just kids' stuff. Toilet papering houses. Egging a couple bullies on bikes. Maybe taking a piece of candy from the store once on a dare. It's not like Johnny and I were *that* bad."

"You two were lucky I didn't put you in the slammer that day I caught you stealing that boat. Although, knowing what I know now, I should have. Could have scared you straight and kept you from becoming a lifelong criminal."

"What?" I stepped back, furrowing my brow. "What are you talking about? Me? A criminal?"

He rocked back on his heels, his thumbs settling into his holster. "Just because we're down here in the South doesn't mean I don't hear things. When Aunt Addie died and her lawyer was looking for you, I helped track you down. Found out you were caught up in some embezzlement scheme where you'd stolen millions of dollars from people. Nasty business. Not surprising though. Once a thief always a thief, I 'spose."

"I didn't do anything wrong!" I defended. "We were victims!"

He smirked. "Likely story. Not the first time I've heard a criminal cry out their innocence. Just wanted to stop by and let you know there's a new sheriff in town, and unlike the sheriff who was in charge the day who wrote off what all you hoodlums did as "innocent kid stuff", I don't play things so nice 'round here. They may not have been able to put you away for your crimes in New York, but I'm not gonna look the other way this time. You even think about stealing anything from the nice people of Ruinville, and I'll be ready with my handcuffs and a nice cold cell for you."

"Deputy Boshaw, I would never! I can't even believe that you—"

"Sheriff Boshaw," he corrected. His firm glare fixated on my shocked eyes. "I know you inherited this place, though I doubt your Aunt Addie would have brought you back to town if she'd known what kind of riff raff you'd be when you got here. But what's done is done. You're here, and I just wanted to stop by and let you know that I ran into Dwayne on the road, and he told me you're back in town, so I wanted to welcome you back to Ruinville... and let you know that I'm watching you." He looked up at CeCe and Julian and pointed toward his eyes and then them. "*All* of you."

"Sheriff Boshaw. There is a serious misunderstanding here. We aren't criminals. I swear. We had no idea what was going on, and we're victims here."

"Yeah. Victims," Julian added, but he went quiet when Sheriff Boshaw impaled him with a warning glare.

"Just keep your noses out of trouble, ya hear? I'm watching you."

He spun on his brown boot and sauntered back to his car, giving us one last gesture where he pointed to his eyes then us before he climbed in and drove off.

"Friendly town," CeCe said as she came down the steps beside me.

"I can't believe he thinks *we're* the criminals! We're broke! How in the hell could *we* have stolen the money and then ended up down here without a damn penny!"

"At least he wasn't a cannibal," Julian said. "I know I'm tasty, but I really don't want to pass through that crabby old man's digestive system."

"Eew." I puckered my face. "That's a horrible picture in my head."

"I'm traumatized by the thought," CeCe agreed.

Julian huffed. "I'm just saying, I don't want to be anyone's dinner. So, let's get to work figuring out how in the hell we're getting out of Brokeville."

"Ruinville," I corrected.

"Same difference." Julian shrugged.

Though CeCe and Julian seemed to have some plan to get back to the penthouse they wouldn't stop crying about, I didn't have any plans right now. I was still too shell shocked by such a dramatic turn of events in my life to even begin to figure out my next steps. At the moment, all I could think about was the next five minutes of my life, and I hoped that eventually when my brain finally processed the horrifying turn my life had taken, that a path forward would suddenly become clear.

Standing on the porch of Aunt Addie's house, I glanced up at two unlikely companions fate had thrust upon me. It appeared, for the foreseeable future, this bewildering new life had chosen us for each other.

CHAPTER SIX
CeCe

Diane stood staring at us on the porch before marching inside. "Well, we have a lot of work to do to get this house cleaned up. I think we should start unpacking and then get cleaning."

"Ourselves?" I recoiled, then hurried after her. "You mean you want *us* to clean this place up?"

"Yep. You gotta earn your keep. Everyone puts in equal effort."

I pressed a hand to my chest, still struggling to process her horrifying idea that I *clean*. "But... but I already smell like bus people! And now you want us to, what? Scrub the toilet? Mop the floor? Dust the cobwebs?"

"Yep, yep, and yep." She spun around and grinned. "I expect us all to do every single one of those things. It's up to you if you want to wash the bus people smell off first or wait until after we've all put in a little cleaning time before we shower."

Julian and I stared at her dumbfounded as she stared back at us, then we slumped our shoulders and followed her back into the house. When we got into the living room, we all looked around at the rundown surroundings.

The sheer amount of things that needed to be done before this place would be hospitable in my eyes overwhelmed me. My whole life I'd lived in the lap of luxury, and now I was surrounded by orange shag carpet, dusty old furniture, and not a single extravagant item in sight. "I don't even know where, or how, to start."

After a long moment, Diane took a deep breath. "Well, we have to start somewhere. Maybe we should just get our bedrooms cleaned up and the laundry started so we have somewhere to sleep tonight."

"Good plan," I said. "I'm so tired I just want to nap, but there is nowhere I feel is clean enough for me to ever lay this body down."

"Who's sleeping where?" Julian asked.

"I'll take my old room, and you two can share my Aunt Addie's room."

"You want us to *share* a room?" I gasped.

She shrugged. "Aunt Addie never married or had kids. The boy she loved died in the military when she was twenty, and she vowed she'd never love again. She chose to give her love to the town and her people and bought this smaller house for herself. It's a two-bedroom house, and now it's *my* two-bedroom house, so I'm taking my old bedroom. I'm certainly not building a third bedroom for you guys, so, you can share the other room, or one of you can take the couch."

Julian and I looked at the rundown brown and orange couch and then looked at each other, eyes wide with horror.

"Honestly, I think I'd be too scared to sleep out here in the bayou by myself. We'll share a room," I said.

"Thank God," Julian breathed. "I'm not sleeping on that hideous old couch *or* on the ground floor where the alligator could just saunter in and devour me while I sleep. I don't want to be eaten by cannibals *or* alligators. At least alligators can't climb stairs." He tipped his head. "Right? They can't climb stairs, can they? Like, their legs are so short there is no way. Or... is there? Crap. We're fixing the front door first, then we'll do the bedrooms."

"Actually, that's a good idea. I have no idea why that alligator came in here, but we certainly don't want it back, and the door doesn't lock. Does anyone know how to fix it?"

We looked at each other, each awaiting someone to pipe in they knew how to fix a door. When no one answered, I pressed a hand to my head. "None of us have the faintest idea how to repair a door. How shocking."

"Julian? You don't know how to fix a door?" Diane asked him.

He popped a hip and lifted his eyebrows. "What? Because I'm the *boy* I should suddenly just know how to build a damn house, Diane? I grew up playing with Barbies, not helping my Dad with household repairs. It's not like carpentry is actually in our DNA. My penis doesn't know how to swing a hammer."

"I know that," she snapped back, but the way her face fell, I didn't think she did.

"So, what do we do?" I asked, turning to look at the door barely hanging on by its hinges. "We have to fix it."

"Yeah. Otherwise cannibals and alligators are going to saunter right in here and swallow us whole."

"I'll try," Diane said decidedly. "It's been over forty years since I've picked up a tool, but when I was a kid being raised by a single dad, he showed me a few things."

"Thank God," Julian breathed. "Because if we can't get that door fixed, I'm sleeping on the roof. I *know* alligators can't get to the roof."

"But then we'll be on full display for the vultures likely circling knowing that we're weak, wounded creatures who won't survive out here."

Diane ignored my comment. "I'll go find the toolbox and see what I can do. In the meantime, you two get started on the bedrooms. Since I'm fixing this, Julian why don't you work on my bedroom while CeCe cleans the one you two will be sharing."

His face soured. "By myself? You want me to go in there by myself?"

"We already checked it for alligators. It's safe. You'll be fine. Since we need somewhere to sleep tonight, bring down the sheets right away and we'll get them washed," she said, then she marched off into the kitchen.

Julian and I shared a pained look, then knowing we had no other options left and a maid wasn't going to suddenly appear, we slowly trudged up the stairs, giving each other one last pathetic look before parting and disappearing into separate rooms.

As I stepped into Aunt Addie's room, I felt a little relief that it was fairly clean. Since she'd been sleeping in it just a few weeks earlier, the dust was minimal, and the sheets didn't send up a plume of it when I walked over and touched the bed. I heard Julian wail from the other room, and I could only imagine what horrors awaited him inside something that hadn't been used in over forty years.

Pulling out the gumption I would need to partake in my first cleaning expedition, I gathered up the sheets and blanket and carried them down to the laundry room. The white machines sat pressed against the wall as I stood there staring at them, completely perplexed on the next step.

"Uh, Diane?" I called.

"What?" she called back.

"How does this thing work?"

"What thing?"

I pointed at the machines I'd never touched in my life. "The washing machine."

I heard her groan, then her little footsteps marched my way. "Seriously? You've *never* done laundry?" she said as she came into the little utility room.

"Why would I have ever done laundry? I've always had people for that."

She rolled her eyes. "Good lord. How are you ever going to survive without your money?"

My heart clenched at those words. I wouldn't. Bottom line was I wouldn't, and wouldn't want to, survive without my money. This whole life of dirt and toil wasn't something I was interested in experiencing. In fact, if Julian and I didn't have a solid plan of getting ourselves back to the penthouse, I may as well just go jump in the water outside and offer myself up as dinner to that damn alligator. But as I stood staring at the washing machine wondering how I'd ever gotten here, I just kept reminding myself this was only temporary. I was CeCe VanTramp, and I would reclaim my place on the throne. And when I did, I would punish every last one of those disloyal bitches who'd turned their backs on me.

"Go ahead. Put it in." Diane gestured to the washing machine.

"Wait! Do mine too!" Julian burst into the laundry room with an armful of Diane's old sheets.

"They won't all fit," Diane said. "You'll need to do two loads. But I'll show you both how to do it with this load, then you can do it yourself next time."

We watched in awe as she pushed the buttons and spun the dial, pouring some liquid soap in before closing the lid and telling it to start.

"Wow. You're like, really good at this being poor stuff," Julian said.

"You didn't grow up with CeCe's fortune. Why don't you know how to do any of this stuff?" she asked him.

He huffed. "I had a stay-at-home mom, and she handled all the cleaning and cooking stuff. My Dad worked and I just went to school and dreamed of the day I could get out of that small town and find my way to the big city. I always knew I was destined for great things, so I never bothered to learn this, you know, piddly stuff. I mean, I had my friend help me do some laundry at the laundry mat when I moved to the city before I met CeCe, but that was like, forever ago. I have no idea how this thing works anymore."

Diane chuckled. "Every person on the planet should know how to do laundry. And now you both will too. So, when this machine beeps that it's done, we'll put it in the dryer together, and then you'll both know how to do a full load."

"Then we just keep doing this every time we need clean stuff?" I asked.

"Yep. Every time."

"Wow. People must do a lot of laundry in their lives," I answered, feeling a little silly I didn't really pay much attention to how much laundry my staff must have been doing all these years.

"Lots and lots of laundry." Diane clucked the side of her cheek. "And everyone hates it."

"Being poor is sad," Julian said. "You just spend your life doing stuff you hate every day. How awful."

Diane chuckled again. "It's not that awful. You'll adjust."

But I wouldn't. I knew I wouldn't. Someone like me just wasn't born to be poor. I was cut from a different mold. Generations of my family had been rich. It went back so far I wasn't even sure where we originally got our money from. But now I was the first one in my lineage to lose it all. How horrified my ancestors must be staring down at me watching me do .... laundry.

Julian's stomach rumbled, and he pressed a hand to it. "Sorry. I'm starving."

Diane tipped her head. "Actually, I am too. Maybe we should go and get some food first, then we can come home and finish cleaning the bedrooms."

"Oh, a proper meal sounds amazing," I agreed.

"Is there an organic tapas restaurant around here?" Julian asked. "That sounds incredible right now."

Diane snorted. "Um, no. Maybe some other restaurant or two has popped up in the last four decades, but the only one I know is Mawmaw's if it's still there. There is definitely not an organic tapas restaurant in Ruinville."

"Mawmaw's?" I asked. "What the hell is Mawmaw's?"

"It's a bar and diner just a few miles from here. Mawmaw means grandmother, and the woman who owned it was like a grandmother to everyone. It was a very popular restaurant. Everyone in town gathered there regularly. Well, at least they used to."

"And it's not organic?" Julian asked. "CeCe and I only like to eat organic."

Diane smirked. "Nope. Not organic. And I'm not paying for you two to eat like queens. I've got a little money left from my inheritance, but I'm not spending it frivolously. We'll go to Mawmaw's and get some cheap food, then we need to figure out how to get some more money flowing. Let's all head up and take turns getting showered and cleaned up, then we'll head out in an hour."

"An hour?" I gasped. "It takes me that long just to do my makeup!"

"An hour," Diane said sharply. "If you're not ready in an hour, I'm leaving without you."

I whined, then stomped my foot. "Fine! But I shower first!"

I took off running up the stairs with Julian hot on my heels. I got to the bathroom and slammed the door shut, then grinned as I locked it. "Ha! I go first!"

Feeling happy I would have the most time available to get ready, I turned and looked at the old baby blue bath tub with a faded cream shower curtain, and my smile turned into a frown. "Eeew."

Despite fearing the old, ugly shower might leave me feeling dirtier than before I stepped into it, I recognized this as my new reality, and I would need to adjust to these modest accommodations. But not for long, because I had a plan, and I was coming back.

***

"Time's up!" Diane called from downstairs. "Anyone not down here in one minute is getting left behind. I'm starving!"

I squealed as I hurried to put on my lipstick, then dropped it in my purse and rushed down the stairs.

"I'm ready! I'm ready! My hair isn't even close to set properly, and I look atrocious, but I'm starving too. I'm not getting left behind here to starve to death!"

As I marched off the last step, Diane's wide eyes met mine. "Whoa. What the hell are you wearing?"

I glanced down at my couture Valencia gown. "What? I'm dressed for dinner."

Her eyebrows shot to her hairline. "It's just that you look like you're heading to the opera, and I hate to break it to you, but Mawmaw's isn't exactly upscale Michelin Star dining. You may want to change into something a little... well, a little less."

I placed a hand on my hip. "Less what? Fabulous? That's impossible because I only pilfered my nicest wardrobe. Other than the skirt and blouse I was wearing for travel and one other pantsuit that needs a dry cleaning, I didn't take anything with me that wasn't the cream of my couture."

"So... you have nothing to wear but evening gowns, a pant suit or that *one* blouse and skirt you wore today?"

I lifted my chin. "Yes. And that outfit smells like bus. I'm not putting it back on until it's been properly sanitized."

She stifled a smile. "Oh. I see. Well, I guess you're ready then. Unless... do you want to borrow something of mine? Or maybe Aunt Addie has something in her closet? You were about the same size."

I snorted. "I don't do hammy downs. This dress will be fine for dining this evening. I used to snap necks wearing it around New York, everyone spinning so fast to appreciate me."

I waved a hand over the black beaded gown, smiling inside as I remembered how enamored everyone was of me the time I wore it to the opera.

Diane lifted her hands. "Be my guest. You just may... stand out a little."

"Good. I like standing out." I stepped past her and checked myself in the dusty little mirror by the door. My hair wasn't anywhere near what I had been accustomed to all these years, but it was as good as I could get it without my hairdresser and less than an hour to prepare for our evening out. My makeup I was getting better at, though I still missed Maggie, who'd been applying it every morning on me for years.

"Wow! You look amazing!" Julian rushed down the stairs and gave me the gesture to do a little turn.

Smiling, I twirled around, ending with a flourish.

"Gorgeous. Absolutely gorgeous!" He clapped.

"You look dapper too." I pointed at his brightly colored Gucci shirt and accenting bright blue pants.

He took a bow. "Thank you, milady. I'm so glad you let me shove some of my faves in your stash when we stole it."

I reached forward and touched his cheek. "Of course, Julian. Anything for you."

Diane cleared her throat. "Well, now that you two are ready for the Met Gala, let's go to Mawmaw's."

I scrunched my nose at her plain outfit of khaki pants and cream-colored shirt. "We're ready. Are you sure *you* are?"

She looked down at her outfit. "For Mawmaw's? Oh yeah. I'm ready."

Julian furrowed his brow. "Wait. How do we get there? Do we need to call that Dwayne guy again?"

Diane shook her head. "No. Part of my inheritance was Ol' Blue. My Aunt Addie's old truck." She held up the keys in her hands.

"Wait. That monstrous blue thing in the yard I saw? That truck? It still runs?"

Diane frowned. "I guess I'm not sure. I just assumed since it was part of the inheritance."

"Do you even *drive?*" Julian asked, eyes wide. "Like, do you have a license to operate that monstrosity?"

Diane frowned deeper. "Uh. Well, I used to know how to drive, and I do have a license. I actually learned how to drive right here on these roads in Ol' Blue. It was a new truck back then, and it's been awhile since I drove, but I think I remember how."

I probed her with a stare. "And that was how many years ago since you've driven?"

Her face fell. "At least thirty years, I guess. Forty since I drove Ol' Blue, which is a stick shift."

"Oh God, we're going to die. Just call that Dwayne character," Julian said.

Diane looked at the keys in her hand then shook her head. "No. We can't afford to be taking cabs everywhere out here. We need to start taking care of ourselves, and that means driving ourselves. We'll be fine. I'll figure it out."

Julian and I looked at each other with matching worried eyes. Diane lifted her chin then walked past us out the front door... the one now hanging properly from the hinges.

"Hey! You did it! You fixed the door!" Julian clapped.

Diane turned back and smiled. "It's gonna hold for the night, but I'm going to need to work on it some more for tomorrow."

We walked out behind her, and she turned around and took a piece of rope she'd nailed to the wall beside it and tied it around the handle. "I didn't know how to fix the lock, so this will have to do for tonight. Should at least keep the alligator out."

"Clever girl." I smiled, appreciating her inventiveness. All those years of seeing her trouncing around the balls and galas, and it turned out she had a little handy side hidden beneath the couture.

"Thanks." She smiled back. "My daddy would be proud right now. I remembered how to use a few basic tools."

"I'm great with tools, just not the kind you find in a toolbox." Julian grinned a mischievous grin, and Diane and I chuckled at him.

"Okay. Let's go," Diane said, then carefully made her way down the creaky stairs. "Careful on that one. It really seems like it's gonna break."

Julian held my hand, and we made it safely to the walkway, then he escorted me by the arm across the yard, which I struggled to cross in my heels. When we reached the big blue truck with the faded and chipped paint, Diane hopped in the driver's seat. Julian and I went around to the passenger side, and after he opened the door for me, I stared straight across the seat at Diane.

"Wait. There isn't a back seat. Are we all supposed to ride up front together?"

"Yep. It's a bench seat. Just hop in and slide into the middle."

"Oh, good lord," I breathed out, then tried to lift my leg to get it into the truck.

"You need help?" Julian asked.

"My dress. It's too tight to lift my leg this high. Crap."

Diane looked at me and grinned. "You sure you don't want to go back and grab something out of Aunt Addie's closet?"

I scowled. "I'll get in."

"Here. Just lean forward on the seat and I'll push your hiney," Julian said.

I tried once more to get my heel up into the floor of the truck, but it just slipped back down. "Damn it! Aren't there steps or something? Why is this truck so tall?"

"It's really not hard to get into if you're not wearing a snug couture gown." Diane shrugged. "Now hurry up. I'm hungry!"

I tried one last time and failed, then slumped forward onto the seat. "Fine. Do it. Push me in."

"Hold on, CeCe! I've got this!"

I felt Julian's hands cup my ass, and I groaned as I relished in my own humiliation while he grunted and shoved as I wiggled my body like a dying fish trying to flop back into the sea. Finally, I slithered up onto the seat and tipped sideways, crawling back up into a seated position.

"This truck is stupid. Ruinville is stupid. Louisiana is stupid. I hate this!" I pouted as I crossed my arms.

Diane just chuckled and continued staring at me with that "I told you so" look I wanted to smack right off her face.

"I'm in!" Julian announced triumphantly as he hopped spryly into the seat beside me. With a loud creak and a heavy grunt, he closed his door.

"Everyone in?" Diane asked.

"We're in."

"CeCe, I need to use that shifter your knees are touching. Just angle your body toward Julian so I don't hit you when I shift."

"Oh, for Pete's sake," I grumbled, then scooched my body to aim toward Julian.

With a deep breath, Diane turned the key, and the big blue truck rumbled to life.

"Hey! It started!" she cheered. "That's one big hurdle we're over!"

"Now the next hurdle is to have you not kill us while trying to remember how to drive," I said, looking over at her.

"Did you want to drive?" she asked, meeting my accusatory stare.

I shrunk a little. "Definitely not."

"Julian? Would you like to drive?"

He shook his head. "No way. I wouldn't know the first thing about piloting this behemoth. CeCe and I get our licenses renewed anytime they come up just so we have them, but it's been actual decades since either one of us has driven."

"Then unless you two can suddenly produce a boat load of money to pay for cabs, you're gonna need to shut the hell up and stop making me more nervous."

I pursed my lips tight, and Julian did the same.

"Okay, here we go." Diane pushed on the pedals as she started the truck forward. It chugged and jerked causing Julian and I to scream as we lurched our way forward.

"Stop screaming!" Diane shouted back as she pressed on the pedals some more. "You're freaking me out!"

"You're freaking *me* out! Why is it doing this?" I said, the jolting movement of the truck making my words sharp and stuttered.

"Hold on, I'm in the wrong gear!" She did some weird movements with her feet and after a loud grinding noise when she moved the shifter, suddenly we started forward more smoothly. "Ha! I'm doing it! I'm driving again!" Diane proclaimed proudly as she started us slowly down the driveway.

"We're not dead!" Julian cheered, then whispered. "Yet."

"I can't believe I remembered! It's been so long! Oh man, does this bring back memories." Diane smiled as we continued down the drive toward the road. "I used to love when Aunt Addie would let me drive this truck to town. I can't believe it's still running after all these years."

"Just try to keep it in once piece," I said as she carefully pulled out onto the road. "I really don't want this to be the way that I go. I need to get back to my wealth and status before I die, because to hell if I'm going out like this. Just drive careful."

"I'm being careful." Diane continued a slow crawl down the road.

"You're doing great, Diane," Julian chimed in. "It's like we're in the Indy 500... just in slow motion."

She laughed as she maintained our turtle speed down the road. "I'll learn to go faster in a minute. For now, let's just stay at this pace."

"As long as we make it back to Shitville in one piece, I'm fine with this pace," Julian said.

"Ruinville," Diane corrected.

"Same difference," Julian said.

Same difference was right. Shitville. Ruinville. It was all the same to me. All I knew is I wanted it to be AQuickStopOnMyWayBackToThePenthouseville.

And it would be. I had a plan, and to hell if this was going to be my life.

Diane shifted into second gear, and as we sped up a few miles per hour, we all cheered.

CHAPTER SEVEN
Diane

The truck tires ground on the gravel as I pulled into a parking spot in front of Mawmaw's, then we jerked to a stop when I hit the brakes too hard. As the truck settled to a halt, I looked up at the familiar neon lights glowing from the windows of the wooden building set back just off the along the tree line. The log cabin-like restaurant looked exactly the same as it had forty years ago. Little waves of nostalgia washed over me remembering how many times I'd been here with Aunt Addie.

"Holy shit. We made it! We're alive!" Julian continued holding the handle on the roof tight. "I mean, you're parked all weird at an angle, but I guess, who cares?"

"Not me." I wiggled the stubborn key to turn the engine off, letting out a big sigh of relief that I'd managed to get us there safely. "I parked this big beast good enough. I'm calling this a win."

CeCe appeared downright elated as she looked around us. "I can't believe you actually did it! You drove! Look at us out here just learning how to get by on our own!"

She was right. This was a big deal in the steps we'd need to take toward complete self-sufficiency. No limo drivers were going to be shuttling us around anymore. Now we had Ol' Blue, and me as the driver. And I'd done it. I'd driven. A stick shift, no less. Pride flooded through me as the engine sputtered off.

BANG!

"Gun!" Julian shrieked before beginning an ear-shattering scream that CeCe and I joined as well, though we didn't quite hit the same octave as him. The loud blast sent the three of diving down into the center of the truck, folding on top of each other into a terrified pile.

After a few long moments of screaming in sync, we finally ran out of air. Panting and puffing, we remained locked in a huddle as we froze, listening closely for another shot.

"Is it cannibals?" Julian whispered. "Please don't let it be the cannibals."

"I'm too beautiful to die in this hideous truck," CeCe sobbed.

"Was that really a gunshot?" I whispered, still frozen in place on top of CeCe.

"It had to have been," Julian whispered. "The cannibals are hunting us. Is anyone hit?"

I shook my head and felt CeCe do the same.

I tried not to lift my head but looked for my purse with the one flip phone the three of us shared. I saw it on the floor by CeCe's feet. "We need to call 911. My phone. It's in my purse. Can you reach it?"

CeCe turned her head then stretched out her arm, stopping just inches from it. "I can't reach!"

"Reach, CeCe! Reach!" Julian encouraged her on.

CeCe tried one more time then retracted back into our tight ball of terror. "I can't! I'm gonna get shot sticking my head out there like that! You get it!"

"No!" Julian snapped back in a whisper. "I'm not going to be the sacrificial lamb! If I lift my head up, a sniper could get me!"

My heart rattled against my ribcage as the fear continued coursing through my body, but with every moment that ticked by, my common sense started to trickle back in.

"Are we *sure* that was a gunshot?" I asked. "Why would someone be shooting at us?"

"What else could it be?" CeCe whispered back. "It sure as hell sounded like a gunshot."

A knock on the window caused the three of us to start screaming again, our little huddle of helplessness tightening as we all clamped onto each other.

"Hello?" a man's voice asked.

"It's them! The cannibals!" Julian cried out. "We're sandwiches!"

"Y'all alright in there?" the voice asked. "Do ya need help 'er somethin'?"

Slowly, I turned my head, looking up over my shoulder, and saw the man's face pressed up against the driver's side window.

"Don't hurt us!" I called back to him, then remembered my self-defense training and making sure to humanize myself to make them less likely to kill me. "My name is Diane. This is CeCe. This is Julian. We're people! We're people! Please, don't hurt us!"

"I want to live!" CeCe cried.

"Hurt you? What the? Why would I hurt you? I saw Ol' Blue pull in, and since we lost Aunt Addie so I know it ain't her in there, I was just wondering who the heck was driving him, and why the heck they were screaming like a banshee."

"You... you knew my Aunt Addie?" I asked, my heart rate starting to lower.

"'Course I did. We were good friends. Just wondering who the heck you are driving Ol' Blue. She loved this truck, even though the damn thing backfired every time she turned it off. Sounds like it still does."

Backfired.

After my adrenalin started to simmer down and my good sense began to seep back into my body, I finally started to think rationally.

"The truck... it backfired? That was the sound?" I asked.

"Yep. Been doing it for years," the man answered. "Aunt Addie never liked spending her money to fix things that weren't broke, and since it still ran fine, she just joked it was her way of announcing her arrival, and she never fixed the damn thing."

"Backfired? What the hell does that even mean?" CeCe asked.

As the fear drained from my body, I suddenly felt like an idiot the way I'd reacted to the sound. A backfire. Of course, that's what it was. "Sometimes vehicles backfire, and it sounds like a gunshot."

"So... not a gunshot?" Julian peered up at me but stayed low.

I calmed down a little more. "Not a gunshot," I said with confidence. "The truck backfired."

"Not cannibals?" CeCe asked.

I rose back to sitting, straightening my hair as I sat upright. "Not a gunshot. Not cannibals. The truck backfired." I turned to see the man with the long white beard grinning at me from the window.

"Y'all thought you were getting shot at?" He chuckled.

"I'm embarrassed to admit it, but yes. It's my first time driving this truck in decades. We didn't know it backfired, and we thought someone shot at us."

His cheeks swelled with his smile as he laughed. "Can't imagine who'd be taking cracks at you at Mawmaw's, but that at least explains why y'all were screaming like a bunch of banshees. Y'all okay now then?"

"Yes, we're fine," I answered, gesturing for CeCe and Julian to get up. They slowly did. "Thank you for checking on us. I'm Diane, Aunt Addie's niece."

His eyes lit up. "Diane? Little Diane? Well, I'll be. I ain't see you since you was a teenager! Probably don't remember me, but I'm Hollis."

Though he was much older now, I started having flashes of his face from my youth.

"I do kinda." I tipped my head as I studied him. "You didn't used to have a beard, right?"

He stroked a hand down the long, gray strands. "Nah. I just grew this out ten years ago or so. Been a long time since I've seen you running around here."

That pang of guilt struck hard again. "Yes, it has been awhile since I've visited Ruinville. But I'm living here now. In Aunt Addie's house, actually."

"Well, welcome back," he answered with a smile. "Wish I could stay and chat, but I gotta get going home. My program starts in twenty minutes, and I don't have those fancy TiVo's or whatever the hell they're called. Don't wanna miss it. I'm sure I'll be seeing you around."

"It was great to see you again, Hollis."

"You too, Diane. And I'm really sorry about your aunt. She was a good woman."

"Yes, she was," I answered with a soft smile.

With the tip of his head, he sauntered off to a little red truck then hopped in and pulled out.

"Well, that was terrifying," CeCe said. "I really thought we were under attack."

"Me too," I agreed. "It seriously sounded like a gunshot."

"I don't think we should eat here." Julian pointed up at the rustic restaurant. "Not only does it look horrifying with those tacky, glowing signs, but clearly, it's dangerous here. I think we should go somewhere else."

I rolled my eyes. "The gunshot wasn't real, so it's not dangerous. We just established that. And not to mention, we have no search capabilities or maps on the stupid flip phone, so I wouldn't have the faintest idea where to go or how to get there. Mawmaw's is the only restaurant I remember. And we're here, miraculously, so I don't want to go driving around in this truck all night looking for something fancier. It's Mawmaw's, and you're broke so I'm paying, and that means I pick."

He went quiet, biting his lip as he swallowed a sigh. "Fine. But I don't like it already."

"No one said you have to," I answered as I opened the truck door, the creaking hinges making me cringe with their loud *squeak*.

The three of us walked up the three steps to the covered porch with a few chairs scattered around it, then we pushed open the door and headed inside. The moment we entered, the eyes of the dozen or so diners all lifted from their tables and snapped onto us. Those same eyes went big as they watched us walk into the quaint little restaurant. I was half expecting to hear the music screech to a stop, and after glancing back over my shoulder at CeCe and Julian in their glamorous outfits appearing ready for a fine dining experience in New York, I knew why.

We didn't fit into Ruinville at all, and as we stood looking like three-headed monsters to the shocked locals, I began to wonder if I'd ever be able to fit back into this life here again.

CHAPTER EIGHT
Diane

"Why are they staring like that?" Julian whispered. "This is like that scary horror movie where all the townsfolk are like brainwashed or something."

"They are staring because we don't exactly fit in," I answered in a hushed tone. "Just don't stare back."

CeCe dropped her gaze to her Jimmy Choos. "I'm not making eye contact. I don't want to get shanked or whatever."

I glanced around at the diners, and even though deep down I knew the people in this town were known for their kindness and generosity, after having been away so many years, I felt like an outsider. Though I hated to admit how uncomfortable I felt in a place I used to love so much, I pushed down the feelings, took a deep breath and walked straight to the booth Aunt Addie and I always sat at. "They aren't going to stab you. You just look a little out of place in that outfit. You look more ready for an Oscar party than a diner in Louisiana."

She sat quickly, sliding across the smooth wood to smoosh up tight to Julian. "Well, we don't have anything designed in whatever the hell that plaid pattern is everyone seems to be wearing. How is that my fault?"

"Those are flannel shirts," I answered, noting most of the men, and some of the women wore them in different colors. I didn't exactly fit in wearing my khaki pants and cream shirt, but I didn't stick out like a sore thumb either.

"Welcome to Mawmaw's!" a woman's voice said in her thick Southern drawl. "I've got some menus here for ya."

I looked up to see the older woman, likely in her eighties, grinning down at us holding the laminated menus in her hands. Her round cheeks swelled with her smile, and in her blue old-fashioned waitress dress with the white frilly apron hugging her curvy frame and her grey hair tied up in a messy bun, she looked like she'd stepped straight out of a nineteen fifties diner.

"Thank you," I said as I took a menu.

Julian and CeCe looked at the oversized plastic menus with disdain, but when I gave them a warning with a flash of my eyes, they each took one with a smile.

"Special tonight is a Fried Catfish Po'boy and soup tonight is Shrimp Bisque plus we got our famous Gumbo our cook, Gumbo Gus, makes every day. His secret recipe. I'm the owner and even I don't know it! Can I start y'all off with something to drink?"

The owner? I tipped my head as those words sunk in. Mawmaw was a wonderful woman who'd opened the diner years before I'd ever set foot in Ruinville. When I'd come here with Aunt Addie, she always took such good care of us and even let me bus tables one summer when I wanted to save up some money to buy a new bike. The diner was named Mawmaw's because she was like a grandmother to everyone in town, and everyone called her Mawmaw. If this woman was the owner, then that meant Mawmaw was likely gone along with my Aunt Addie. It shouldn't surprise me. She'd been older than Aunt Addie by at least twenty years, but once again the length of my absence shocked me.

On one hand, it felt like nothing had changed in Ruinville, and yet on the other, so much had since I'd last set foot in this town decades ago. My heart constricted at the thought of such a kind, wonderful woman I'd never see again either. Before I could ask if Mawmaw was truly gone, CeCe lifted her finger.

"There's a bar here, right?" CeCe craned her neck to look around.

The server pointed toward the small bar where two men sat belly up against it. "Yes ma'am. We've got a full bar. Can I get you something from it?"

"Martini. Straight up. Extra dry. Two olives," CeCe answered.

"Make that two," Julian said, then he paused. "And you have top shelf vodka right? None of that cheap crap."

She recoiled a little at the sharpness of his tone, and I scolded him once again with a flash of my eyes.

"Whatever you have back there is just fine," I said, my eyes locked with Julian's. "And I'll just have a glass of white wine please."

Her soft smile warmed me right to my insides just like I used to feel when Mawmaw would smile down at me. "Coming right up, Cher."

As she walked away, Julian leaned in and snorted. "Cher? Does she really think you're Cher? I mean, come on now."

I rolled my eyes. "Cher is a term of endearment in Louisiana. Like dear or hon."

"Oh, I was gonna say." He looked down at his menu. "Ugh. What is this crap? Is anything on here not fried?"

"I can't eat fried food." CeCe turned up her nose. "It will go straight to my hips, and I can't afford a tailor anymore to alter what's left of my wardrobe. Is there a salad section or something?"

They pressed their heads together as they studied the menu, and I couldn't help but chuckle at the sight of two of New York's most discerning diners who rarely ate anywhere without a reputation for excellence studying a menu with things like fried alligator and frog legs.

Nostalgia washed over me as I looked at the menu, and I remembered sitting in this very booth with Aunt Addie picking out all the things we wanted to share. We always got a few appetizers and a couple entrees then took turns passing them around so we could get a few bites of everything.

"Here you go," the server said as she came back holding the tray of drinks. "I hope I made your martinis right. It's been a long while since anyone ordered somethin' so fancy here. Plus, my bartender moved away last month, and I'm still looking to fill the position, so it's just me serving and making the drinks."

Before they could say something snobby and terrible, I smiled and answered, "I'm sure you did a wonderful job. Thank you."

She smiled back, the rosy hue in her cheeks deepening in response to my words. As she set our drinks in front of us, she asked, "Have you had a chance to look at the menu? Ready to order?"

"I have a few questions," CeCe said, her eyebrows lifting as she lowered the menu.

I groaned outwardly, worried about what was going to come out of her mouth.

"Is the lettuce here organic? Do you know where it's sourced from? Is it handpicked?"

The server's eyes widened. "Uh, I don't actually know. Would you like me to find out?"

"Yes, please," CeCe answered as Julian nodded along.

"You don't have to do that," I interjected, but she just smiled.

"No trouble. I'll go ask Gumbo Gus, the cook. He does all the ordering."

As she hurried back to the kitchen, I leaned forward. "Would you two behave?"

"What?" CeCe shot back. "I can't afford to be putting crap inside my body just because we're poor. I need to stay fit and in shape so I can catch a new husband."

"Amen to that." Julian nodded. "We can't afford to pack on the pounds."

The server came hustling back. "Sorry. He doesn't know either. He just said its regular lettuce."

CeCe and Julian both twisted their lips into matching frowns.

"What about the fried chicken? Is it possible to get it grilled with no breading? And in olive oil. Just a dash. Extra virgin. Not butter."

"Uh..." the server glanced back at the kitchen. "I'll see if that's a possibility."

She spun on her little flat blue shoe and rushed off again.

"Seriously?" I asked. "You can't find anything on the menu to just order as is? It's like five pages long!"

"I don't even know what half of these words mean," she argued back. "I just want something organic, gluten free, and not doused in some artery clogging oil."

The waitress came rushing back, her breathing quickened with all the running she'd been doing. "He said it's prebreaded, so he can't grill it. I'm sorry."

CeCe grumbled. "For your house salad, what are your gluten free dressings? And any low-calorie options that are also gluten free? And is there anything like grilled salmon or something back there that the chef could toss on a salad?"

"Oh! A grilled salmon salad sounds good," Julian agreed. "With like a lemon basil dressing like we had that one time at... where was that again?"

CeCe's eyes lit up. "Oh yes! I can't remember the name either, but that sounds perfect. Can you ask the chef if he can do a grilled salmon salad with a lemon basil dressing? Just hold the croutons. I don't need the carbs."

The server stared down at them blinking. "I... I don't think we have that. We definitely don't have salmon."

"Can you just ask if he can do something similar? Find out what kind of fish is back there, fresh caught, of course, and we can go from there."

"I'm so sorry," I said quickly. "You don't have to do this. They don't need dinner. They can starve." I turned my sympathetic stare from the server and narrowed my eyes at CeCe and Julian.

"I'll just go check," the server said. "We'll see what he can think up."

As she hurried away once again, I leaned forward on the table, my fingers threading together as I steepled my hands.

"I swear to God if you don't just pick something on the menu and order it, I'm not paying for your dinners, and you can starve for real."

"I'm not asking for the world." CeCe tossed up her hands. "What's so hard about a salmon salad?"

"Um, the fact there is no salmon on the menu for starters."

"Well, any kind of fresh, good fish would work I suppose," Julian said.

Just before I started tearing into them for the ridiculous requests, the door to the kitchen swung open and our server walked out with the hulking form of a man behind her. She started towards us, her little steps two for every one of his ground-covering slow strides. His eyes, bright white against the contrast of his dark skin, scanned the room, and I wanted to sink straight into the wood bench I sat on when the weight of his intense gaze landed square on us, and his chiseled jaw ticked and tightened when his lips pulled into a frown.

"Holy hell," Julian whispered. "Look at the size of his arms. I work out every day and my arms look the size of the vein running up his."

"I brought Gumbo Gus to answer your questions directly and save me some steps." Our server arrived to us smiling, waving her face as she puffed. "I'm not as fit as I used to be, and I'm down a server too, so this will make it easier instead of me running back and forth. I'll leave you to ask Gumbo Gus all your questions while I go help this other table. I'll be back to take your order when y'all are ready."

She smiled wide then buzzed off to another table, and the three of us sat dwarfed beneath the man standing at least six foot six with bulging muscles popping out the sleeves of his white t-shirt. He wiped his hands on the apron tied around his waist then crossed his arms tight over the expansive chest filling up every inch of his t-shirt.

"You got a problem with my menu?" he said, his voice so deep it may have been bottomless.

"No. Of course not," I answered quickly. "Everything looks wonderful."

CeCe and Julian sat wide-eyed staring up at him blinking fast.

"Then what you got all these questions for?" he asked.

I pointed at them. "They have weird diet requirements, but it's fine. We're fine. We'll just pick something off the menu as is. Right guys?"

They started nodding slowly, their eyes still glued to the man making them crane their necks to meet his gaze.

His jaw tightened again as he passed a slow gaze across us. "Good."

Without another word, he turned around and those large strides took him back to the kitchen where he disappeared behind the swinging door again. We all let out an echoing sigh.

"Holy crap. I thought he was gonna skewer us up and serve us for dinner," Julian said.

"You deserved it," I answered. "All those crazy questions. You're lucky you didn't get us tossed out."

"We just don't know what to order!" CeCe said too loudly.

"Try the catfish," a man sitting at the bar said.

We turned to look and saw the back of a man wearing a red flannel with the sleeves ripped off hunched over a bottle of beer.

"What? Are you talking to us?" Julian pointed at his chest.

The man spun around on his bar stool. When he looked at us, a smile played on his face the moment he locked eyes with CeCe. He let out a long, slow whistle and pulled off his camouflage baseball cap, running a hand through his salt and pepper shaggy hair before putting the cap back on. "Well, hot damn. No wonder you were asking for all that fancy schmancy crap. Didn't realize the Queen of Sheba was sittin' behind me."

CeCe acted offended for only a moment, but when she saw the size of the appreciative smile he gave her, she pursed her lips and shrugged. I could see how much she enjoyed being admired, even if it was from a scruffy faced man she'd normally go screaming from if she saw him on a city street.

"Get the catfish if you're looking for fresh. I'd know how fresh it is. I catch 'em for Mawmaw's. Tonight's was just swimming this morning, and I dropped it off an hour ago. You'll love it."

"He said you'll love his meat," Julian whispered under his breath and chuckled. CeCe elbowed him in the ribs.

"Catfish. That sounds disgusting." CeCe turned her nose up.

"Don't knock it 'til you try it, Pretty Girl. You never know what you're gonna love until you give it a spin."

I stifled a smile catching the look in his eyes that said he was talking about a lot more than catfish. CeCe huffed and looked away.

Undeterred by her obvious rebuff, he kept on. "Everyone 'round here calls me Bayou Bill. I run the swamp boat tours."

"Nice to meet you, Bayou Bill," I said with a little wave. "I'm Diane, and this is CeCe and Julian. Thanks for the suggestion."

"I'm here anytime you need me. For anything at all." He tipped his hat at us, then gave a wink to CeCe before spinning back to the bar. If I didn't know better, I'd think she blushed.

"CeCe has a boyfriend," Julian whispered.

"Stop." She waved a hand at him. "He's not even clean enough to be a pool boy."

Julian shrugged. "I dunno. If you shaved Crocodile Dundee up, gave him a haircut and put him in a Gucci suit, he may shape up all right. In fact, with that bone structure and those eyes, better than alright. At least good enough to scratch a few itches if you know what I mean."

"Stop." She swatted him again. "Don't be crude. I'd never consort with someone like that."

She shuddered, and I rolled my eyes. "Would you two stop arguing and just pick something off the damn menu?"

They matched my eye rolls and pushed their heads back together to look at the menu. Our server came toward our table, but this time instead of a big smile, she walked towards us staring at me looking stunned.

"Diane? Did you say Diane? Is that really you?"

"What?" I asked, looking up at her stunned expression.

She looked at my face for a long moment, then pressed her hands to her mouth. "It *is* you! Oh heavens! It's been so many years! I thought I heard the distinctive sound of 'Ol Blue backfiring in the parking lot, but then realized my dear Addie was gone so I must have been hearing things. But it was 'Ol Blue wasn't it, because you're Diane. Her niece. And you've finally come back."

"Yes, I'm Diane," I answered slowly, the tears welling in her eyes causing me to stumble over the simple words. "Do I know you?"

She nodded, a tear slipping down her cheek. "Oh, she'd be so happy you were here again. She always dreamed you'd come back."

A twist of guilt tore up my gut hearing those words. She'd really dreamed I'd come back? My God how had I been so selfish... so disconnected from my old life that while she pined for my return, I barely thought on her.

"It's me. May. Well, now that my mother passed on and left me the diner, everyone calls me Mawmaw or Mawmaw May. Do you remember me?"

I gasped and pressed a hand to my chest. Though her face had changed with age and the extra weight, I finally recognized those familiar eyes.

May.

My Aunt Addie's very best friend.

"May!" I jumped up from the booth and tossed my arms around her neck. "It's been so long I didn't recognize you!"

She enveloped me in her warm hug, and I choked back the tears as we stood clinging to each other in the diner. Memories of countless hours spent with her and my Aunt

Addie crashed back into me like a tidal wave. Baking cookies. Swinging on the porch swing squished between them on starry summer nights. May teaching me how to knit. Their laughter. Oh, their laughter. The two of them would laugh so hard when they were together they'd often run out of air. My mind reeled with the wonderful memories that induced joy mixed with a potent blend of pain that Aunt Addie was gone.

"I hoped to see you at the funeral, but I'm so glad you finally made it, Diane. I can't tell you how wonderful it is to see you again."

"I can't believe it's you." I squeezed her tighter. "And you're Mawmaw now?"

She gave me one last squeeze then stepped back and slid her hands onto my shoulders, leaning back far enough to take a good look at me. "I am. My ma passed fifteen years back. I've been called Mawmaw May ever since. Kinda like your Aunt Addie was Aunt Addie to everyone, not just you. I'm the town grandmother, and she was the town aunt." She sighed. "Sure do miss her."

"I'm so sorry for the loss of your mother and Aunt Addie. I know how close you two were."

She pressed her lips together and nodded. "Best of friends. Born just nine days apart right here in Ruinville. From cradle to grave we always said. I'm just sad she was the first to go. Sure isn't the same around here without her."

"She was a special woman. I'm so sorry I wasn't around much these last years."

Mawmaw May tipped her head and reached out, touching my cheek. "She knew you were out living your best life. That's all that mattered to her... that you were happy."

Happy.

Was I? Had I been? Or had I just been going through the motions all these years, parading around with my money and a husband it turned out I didn't really know at all. Her simple words twisted inside my mind.

"How long are you staying here? I'm assuming you inherited her place? I know that was always the plan and she secretly hoped you'd come back and keep it, but do you have any plans with it?"

"I'm not sure how long we're staying," I answered honestly. "Life has kind of taken a bit of a turn as of late. It's why I missed the funeral."

Before I could fill her in on what was going on, a man at a nearby table waved at her.

"Dang. I'd better go help him out. I'll be right back to take your order, and then we can set aside some time to catch up. I can't wait to hear what you've been up to all these years."

"I'd like that," I answered.

She squeezed my hand then turned around and hurried off to her table. I watched her go, seeing more clearly now the woman I'd adored so much inside the aged body of the woman in the little blue dress.

"Wow," I breathed as I slid back into my seat. "That's incredible. I used to love May. And now she's Mawmaw May. Amazing."

"Since you have a personal in, do you think that means you can get her to find us some salmon for a salmon salad?" CeCe asked.

I glared. "No. When she comes back, you'd better be ready to order. And it had better be something on this damn menu." I tapped it with my finger and they both scowled.

A minute later, Mawmaw May returned grinning at me just like she used to. "Okay. You ready to order?"

"We are," I said, then spit out my order. CeCe and Julian did the same, each getting a salad with no extra requests.

"Wonderful. I'll get this put in for you straight away. And while you're here, if you need anything at all, you just give a holler. That house has a lot of silly quirks I'm happy to help you sort out. I'm always here if you need me. For anything."

"Thanks, Mawmaw May." I smiled.

Julian lifted his eyebrow. "Actually, if you're offering to help us, can you get rid of the gator that we found in the kitchen? I'm still scared to go home and find that thing waiting for me under the covers." He paused, then spoke louder. "Or maybe that's a request I should be asking you, Crocodile Dundee."

The man at the bar spun around and smiled. "Bayou Bill, and the answer to your question is hell no. You're talking about Aunt Addie's beloved gator, Peggy. She'd crawl right back out of her grave and kill me if I ever laid a hand on that creature."

"Wait." I lifted a hand. "That's a *pet* alligator?"

Mawmaw May chuckled. "Oh, you know your Aunt Addie. Always a tender heart. She found that little baby gator with an injured leg and knew it wouldn't survive. So, she brought it home, raised it up until it was healed and healthy, then she let her go. Named it Peggy on account of her little injured peg leg. But danged if that little alligator with a limp didn't come back all the time sitting on the step begging for chicken." She chuckled again. "Just toss her some scraps now and again and she'll slide back off into the bayou."

"Will it... bite?"

"They all bite," Bayou Bill answered. "She's still a wild animal so don't forget that part, but yeah. Mawmaw May is right. Just toss her some food and stay out of her way and she won't bother you none."

"Great. It's a freaking pet." CeCe palmed her head. "And just when I thought this hellscape couldn't get any worse, I find out we have a pet freaking alligator."

"I'm never going back to that place again. Never." Julian crossed his arms and shook his head.

Even though I was horrified my new home came with a predatory house guest, I couldn't help but smile realizing nursing a baby alligator to health is *exactly* what Aunt Addie would have done. I didn't want to have it in the kitchen again, but I certainly could try to pick up where she left off and take care of it for her. It was the least I could do after I abandoned her all those years. I couldn't take care of her, but I could take care of her house, her gardens, and even her pet alligator.

With a renewed sense of purpose to try to make Aunt Addie proud even though she wouldn't be here to see it, I sat quietly through dinner. The nostalgic foods all tickled my heartstrings, and with every familiar bite of the recipes we used to share, I swear I could almost hear her voice and her laughter again. I didn't even get annoyed with CeCe and Julian squabbling over how many calories were in the creamy dressing.

This food. These people. This place.

Aunt Addie was everywhere, and I hadn't noticed how much I'd missed her.

"Your first meal is on me, Cher," Mawmaw May said when I asked for the check.

"Oh, you can't do that. Please let me pay. I insist," I argued.

"No, no. It's my pleasure to give you and your friends a good welcome meal."

"Please. We can't take advantage," I said, but Julian flashed his wide eyes at me.

"We don't have much money left, Diana. Take the free meal!" he whispered in a sharp tone.

I was about to start arguing since I normally would have spent enough on a meal I could have fed everyone in this place, but then I remembered how little funds we had left ... and no other source of income to replenish our dwindling reserves.

"Well, I appreciate it so much, Mawmaw May. Thank you. We'll be coming in to visit you a lot. Well, as often as we can afford to dine out."

She paused and looked at the three of us. "Is everything alright, Diane? Are you short on money? Aunt Addie always made it sound like you were as rich as an oil sheik."

"I was," I answered, "but we hit a bit of an issue. But please, nothing to worry yourself over. I'll figure it out."

Julian lifted a finger. "Just for the sake of asking. How exactly do people get more money in this part of the world? Is GoFundMe a thing down here? Do you think we could start one?"

I grumbled. "We're not starting a GoFundMe, Julian. No one is going to give a bunch of broke millionaires money."

"I don't know what that whole GoFundMe is, but I'm hiring if you're interested in work," Mawmaw May said with a smile.

CeCe and Julian gasped in unison.

"A... a job?" CeCe sputtered out. "At... at a diner?"

"Thank you for the offer," I quickly said before CeCe said something horribly offensive. "We'll think about it."

"You just let me know, Cher. In the meantime, when I need a little extra spending money, I have a rummage sale. Maybe you could find some things lying around and we'll let the town know."

"Oh! That's a great idea. I'm sure we could find some stuff to sell," I said, then my gaze passed over CeCe's Louis Vuitton bag wondering how much we could get for it. The look didn't go unnoticed, and she grabbed it and clutched it tight to her chest scolding me with a warning stare.

Mawmaw May didn't notice the small interaction and kept on. "Should get a good turnout if I tell Chatty Cathy. Her real name is Cathy, but the chatty part is because she spends all day running around spreading gossip... both good and bad. No one here has had to put up a flyer or advertisement in years. We just tell Chatty Cathy. If you decide to have a rummage sale, you just give me a call and tell me when. I'll let her know and the whole dang town will find out about it."

"That sounds great. I'll let you know. Thanks so much for all your help. It's really wonderful to see you again." I stood up and hugged her, closing my eyes as familiar memories flooded through me once again.

After we broke apart our embrace, CeCe and Julian stood up and followed me out to Ol' Blue. When we got the truck, I turned around and said, "She's onto something with the garage sale idea. We need some fast cash, and you've got a lot of stuff worth some serious money."

I looked at her bag again.

CeCe's eyes narrowed. "You'll sell my stuff over my dead body!"

I leveled her with a stare. "You're going to be one well-dressed corpse when you starve to death, because if you don't start contributing soon, we'll be too broke to buy food."

Her lip quivered as she glanced down at her purse. "Ugh. Fine. But not this purse. This is my baby."

"I'm sure even a few of your dresses will keep us well fed for months."

We both looked at Julian. He shrugged. "I didn't get as much out as CeCe. Unless you want me walking around naked, I don't have much to part with. Although." He pressed a finger to his chin. "If I'm walking around naked a lot, maybe I could start an account on that site where people pay to see you doing stuff. You know... OnlyFans. Maybe that can be how I contribute."

"You're not selling your body online like a prostitute. We'll figure something else out," I said as I jumped in the truck. "Let's go home and look. But we're doing this. We're all sacrificing some of our things to pay for food and living expenses while we figure things out."

They both grumbled then agreed.

Once they were in, I fired up the engine, and this time, with a little experience under my belt, I wasn't so scared driving Ol' Blue home.

CHAPTER NINE
CeCe

Gripping the wheel tight, Diane bit her lip while she guided the giant truck into the gas station parking lot. Our truck dwarfed all the small cars as she navigated the blue beast around, and a little squeal escaped my lips when she wound between them toward the pumps.

"Careful!" I whispered, then held my breath as we got closer and closer.

"Shh! I need to concentrate!" she snapped back.

We all ceased breathing as she inched her way to the pump, the truck jerking while she tried to slow it down without stopping, and finally, with a lurch, we slammed to a stop.

"I did it," Diane breathed. "Phew. It's been decades since I've had to fill up a car at a gas station, and I've never had to maneuver something this big into such a small space."

"Well done." Julian leaned around me and gave her a nod of approval. "I couldn't have done it."

"Me neither," I agreed. "I'm never driving this thing."

I hated to admit that we were dependent on Diane for yet another thing. Not only was her minuscule inheritance of money and home the only thing keeping us alive, but now she was the only one who could drive us around in the giant hunk of hideous blue metal.

"Second day driving this thing and I'm getting good at this." She grinned and turned the key.

The loud bang echoed again, a sound we'd heard twice last night—once at Mawmaw's and again when we got home. Yet somehow, we'd all managed to forget it. Our three screams shook the cab of the truck.

I pressed a hand to my chest and puffed out a breath. "Ugh! Why does it *do* that? That is just horrible! I forgot to brace myself!"

"I'm getting PTSD I think," Julian said between sharp breaths.

Diane grimaced. "I forgot about that damn backfire too. Wow. Really wakes you up in the morning!"

"I'll stick to coffee for my morning jolt," I said. "Can we get this thing fixed so it doesn't do that?"

Julian leaned around me and looked at Diane. "Agreed. Getting scared to death every time we turn off the truck isn't good for our heart health."

Diane opened the door and it creaked loudly. "Sorry, guys. Truck repairs are very expensive, and we can't waste the money. Aunt Addie lived with it, and so will we. We're just going to have to get used to it."

She slammed the door, but then a moment later, pulled it back open again with the horrible *creak*. "Damn. The tank is on the other side."

"The what is on the what?" I said, confused.

She jumped in the driver's seat and leaned forward, pressing her head on the steering wheel. "The gas tank… where I put the gas… is on the other side. I have to drive around and line this behemoth up again."

"Oh no. We barely made it the first time!" Julian whined.

I saw a large, camouflage-covered man walk in front of the truck toward the gas station. "Should we ask that guy to do it for us? He looks like he could handle a truck like this."

Diane breathed out then sat back, gripping the wheel with both hands. "No. I need to learn how to do this myself. We can't depend on anyone but ourselves ever again."

With another deep breath, she fired up the engine and shifted the stick between my legs. Julian reached over and squeezed my hand tight as we started creeping forward. Inch by inch, Diane guided the truck past the pumps, and then began the painstaking process of reversing and going forward over and over until we were finally lined up with the other side of the pump. When she made it back into a straight line and got us lined up like a plane coming in for landing, Julian squeezed my hand harder as we jerked and lurched toward the pump, then finally arrived safely.

"I did it!" she proclaimed, then shut off the truck.

The loud *bang* caused us all to jump and let out a small scream, but this time we were more prepared.

"I hate that!" I closed my eyes and tightened my fists, wondering for the millionth time how this was my life now.

"Just wait here, and I'll fill up, then we'll head off to Walmart." Diane jumped out of the truck and started filling it up with gas.

Walmart.

Just hearing that word come out of her mouth sent the bile churning in my stomach, inching up toward my throat.

The whole point of this outing was a shopping trip to... Walmart. We needed supplies for our rummage sale, and apparently, they also sold food there. After last night's discussion at Mawmaw's, Diane had jumped into action toward this plan to sell off my beloved pieces of couture like prostitutes to the highest bidder.

The bile churned again.

As much as I hated the idea of parting with even one more piece of couture after the government whisked most of it away, she was right. Up to this point, I had contributed nothing. My only value now was selling the clothing, shoes, jewelry and purses I pilfered to get some money to survive. Realizing how far I'd fallen nearly crushed me, but I resolved to get the name and number of every buyer. After I figured out how to divorce my current, lying, useless, missing criminal of a husband and snagged a new, rich husband, I would hunt down every single item, buy it back, and bring it home where it belonged. That knowledge was the only thing keeping me from screaming at the top of my lungs over the thought of losing my little beloveds.

Diane finished pumping and came back, the creaking door causing me to cringe as she climbed back up into the truck. Pride radiated off her face.

"Okay! I did it! We're over another hurdle."

"Well, we didn't crash or blow up, so I guess that's a success," Julian said.

"I'm getting good at this." Diane grinned and fired up the old truck.

We pulled out and cruised down the rustic roads the fifteen miles to the Walmart just in the next town, or the "big city" as Mawmaw May had referred to it. As we reached a little town filled with half a dozen chain stores, a grocery store, and an oil change garage, Julian puckered his face.

"What the hell? I thought we were going to the city. This is the 'city' they were talking about? I mean, I know Brokeville is a small town, but no one should ever call this little hole in the wall a 'city.'"

"Ruinville," Diane corrected. "Not Brokeville."

Julian shrugged. "Same difference."

Diane chuckled. "Well, compared to Ruinville, this is a city."

I lifted my chin. "To call this dump a city is an insult to New York City. *That* is a city."

"Amen." Julian nodded.

Diane rolled her eyes as she pulled into the Walmart parking lot. "You're welcome to return to fabulous New York City anytime you want." She looked over and smirked. "Oh, yeah. You can't. You're broke and have nowhere to live. I suggest you quit your bitching and get your heads in the game. We've got a list of things to get and not a lot of money to spend."

Julian and I sighed in unison while she gripped the wheel tight and pulled into a parking spot in the middle of nowhere.

"Why are we parking so far from the entrance?" I asked.

"Because I'm too scared to try to squeeze in between parked cars. We'll park way out here alone and then walk the rest of the way."

I was about to argue that I wanted to be dropped off at the door like I'd been accustomed all my life, but seeing the anxiety twisting up her face, I shut my mouth and let her concentrate on maneuvering the hulking machine I would never be able to, nor want to, drive.

"There. That will work," she said as she took up two spots.

"People with expensive cars like to take up two spots so no one dings them," Julian noted. "But I don't think we need to worry about getting dings in this thing. It already looks like someone took a sledgehammer to it."

"I'm not moving again. This is fine." Diane turned off the engine.

Bang!

We all screamed, and I clutched my chest. "Dammit! I am never going to get used to that!"

"I hate this truck!" Julian stomped his feet on the dirty floorboards.

Diane took a breath and sighed. "We'll get used to it. We'll get used to all of this. All we can do is make the best of what we've been given. Now, who has the list?"

I reached into my purse and pulled out the list we'd made of supplies we needed for the garage sale. Paper tags, pens, and stickers at the top.

"Here." I handed it to her. "But I still think we need some mannequins and lighted jewelry displays if my stuff is going to look its best."

Diane snorted. "We have a hundred dollar budget today... and that *includes* food. Paper tags, pens, and stickers are all we need to price your items. That should be like five or ten dollars, I think. Then since none of us know how to cook, let's just go to the grocery section together and pick out what we need as we go. But we keep it cheap. Only the bare essentials."

Grumbling, I climbed out of the truck behind Julian, and the three stood staring across the sprawling black asphalt that ended at the monstrosity of a store.

Tears erupted from my eyes as I wailed, my shoulders shaking with my grief. "I can't! I won't! I'm not going to Walmart! I'm CeCe VanTramp for cripes sakes!"

"It's okay, CeCe. It's okay." Julian soothed me with a hand on my shoulder.

"Oh, for the love," Diane sighed. "Would you pull it together? We're just going shopping at Walmart."

"Exactly!" I cried. "That's the point! He took *everything* from me! My money, my parent's money, our money, his money. And now, my dignity. That lying, stealing, treacherous bastard left me with nothing, and now I'm here at... at Walmart. And I can't even afford to buy anything." I sobbed louder.

Julian sniffled and threw his arms around my neck. "How did this happen to us?"

We clung to each other in the Walmart parking lot, and tears flowed freely down my cheeks. Finally, I felt Diane's hand on my back.

"Hey. It's okay, CeCe. I know you lost everything, and it's a big shock. Remember, I lost everything too. But we're alive. We're okay. And we're going to rebuild our lives."

I glanced over my shoulder to look at her, and even though it didn't feel like it since she seemed to be handling everything in stride, I remembered that she had lost everything too. Her husband. Her money. Her home.

Everything.

"How do you do it?" I sniffled, letting go of Julian to turn and face her. "How are you so strong? I can't do this, Diane, and you make it look so easy."

She snorted. "Easy? Oh, no. This is a nightmare, CeCe. I think I'm still in shock that it's all gone. My home. My things. My husband. I may never see him again." Her eyes narrowed for a moment. "Not that I'd want to after what he did, other than to hand him divorce papers of course, but still. He was my husband for forty years, and now he's just gone. Grieving all of these losses feels like mourning a death. Facing any one of them would be harrowing, but together, they're utterly crushing."

Her chin dimpled, and I reached out and took her hand. I shouldn't feel joy in seeing her start to break, but at least it made me feel like I wasn't such a wimp compared to perfect, unbreakable Diane. She hurt inside too.

She squeezed my hand back, then after a big swallow, she lifted her chin. "But I'm accepting what happened to us and trying to move forward as best I can. That's all we can do. One foot in front of the other. Right now, that means we're going shopping at Walmart, and we're not going to die when we do. Okay?"

My shoulders slumped. "I may die of shame when someone sees me in there."

"You won't even know anyone in there," she said. "These people are strangers. Who cares who sees you shopping at Walmart?"

I sniffled and wiped the tears from beneath my eyes. "I guess that's true."

She smiled. "See? Who cares? Everyone shopping at Walmart is fine shopping at Walmart. They won't be judging you. The majority of the world doesn't have personal shoppers and an account at all the finest stores in the world. The majority of the population does their shopping right here. At Walmart." She paused and pointed to the blue and white sign looming in the distance. "Now, let's stop feeling sorry for ourselves and go get some food so we don't starve, and some stuff so we can sell your clothes, also, so we don't starve."

With a deep sigh, I nodded my head. Knowing I'd likely streaked my makeup, and not wanting my face recognized, I slid on my oversized, black Cartier sunglasses. "Okay, fine. Let's just get this over with."

Side by side, we started our walk across the seemingly endless asphalt. When we reached the electronic doors, Julian reached over and slid his hand onto mine, squeezing tight.

"I'm scared," he whispered.

"Me too." I squeezed his hand back.

"It's Walmart, you guys, not Alcatraz. Let's just go in and get this over with."

Diane marched through the dreaded doorway first, and after taking one simultaneous sigh, Julian and I hurried after her. Even in sunglasses, the horrible lighting assaulted my eyes, and I cringed against it. A man in a blue vest wearing a goofy grin waved at us as Diane grabbed a cart.

"Welcome to Walmart!" he said.

"Welcome to hell is more like it," I muttered under my breath while we followed Diane into the vast expanse of my own personal hell.

"Thank you," Diane responded to him as she pushed past with our cart.

"Wow. It's huge in here!" Julian said as he slowed his steps, his head swiveling around in all directions.

"It is," I agreed breathlessly, overwhelmed by never-ending aisles in all directions. "How do we even know where to start?"

Diane pointed toward the ceiling. "I was only in a Walmart a few times many, many years ago, but I think those signs above our heads should tell us what's in each aisle," she said as she started walking us past the clothing section.

Julian paused and tipped his head. "Is it just me, or is that shirt actually kinda cute?"

I looked toward the shirt he pointed at and pursed my lips, shutting them tight before the embarrassing truth popped out. It *was* kinda cute.

"Oh! Check out these sunglasses!" He took off at a brisk walk and hurried to the sunglasses, popping them on his face before turning to look at us. "Cute, right? Do they fit my face shape?"

As I walked toward him, a pink sweater caught my eye, and I paused to touch it and take a closer look. The minute I thought about trying it on, I dropped the soft sleeve like it had scalded my hand and stepped back with a gasp. "Oh my God. Julian, take those off! We're in *Walmart!* We don't shop at Walmart! My God, have we fallen so far that we're starting to think Walmart fashion looks good?"

Diane shrugged. "I actually see a lot of cute things in here. Who knew Walmart actually had some fashion sense? And yes, Julian, those look fabulous on you." She stepped forward and pulled the sunglasses off his face and put them back. "However, we have zero dollars in the budget for clothes or fashion. So, let's just hurry away past this section to get the tags and pens first."

Julian frowned. "I liked those." He frowned deeper. "Oh my God. Am I really pouting that I can't buy a pair of sunglasses from Walmart? My God, CeCe. You're right. We've fallen too far."

"Come. Let's just forget that happened." I opened my hand, and he rushed forward and took it, then we hurried after Diane farther into the belly of the beast. I couldn't resist taking a little peek back over my shoulder at the sweater I really wanted to take home, and I noticed Julian looking back with longing in his eyes as well. When we caught each other in the embarrassing act, we quickly looked forward and caught back up with Diane.

After getting lost in the maze of endless items several times, our cart now had clothing tags, stickers, and markers for pricing my items during the rummage sale.

"Okay, that part is over." Diane turned the cart and aimed it toward the grocery section. "Now we need to figure out what kind of food we need in the house."

"I'm really missing my organic smoothies in the morning," Julian said. "Do they have an organic fruit section here? And preferably with some passion fruit and kale. Then I like..."

Diane raised a hand. "I'm gonna stop you right there. We have nowhere near the budget for fancy organic fruits and whatever other crazy request I know you both are about to make."

Her gaze flicked over to me, and I pretended to look shocked even though I had been about to open my mouth and start rattling off the ingredients for the smoothie I wanted.

"We keep it simple. Cheap. I'm talking mac-n-cheese, frozen pizzas, that kind of thing. That's all we can fit on our budget."

Julian and I both gasped in unison.

I opened my mouth to argue, but Diane stopped me with a hand. "I already know what you're going to say. 'But the carbs!' 'I only eat organic!' 'Food in a *box?* Ugh! Never!'" she said, mimicking both my voice and what I was going to say a little too perfectly.

My face dropped.

"Simple. Cheap. That's the goal, and that means I'm in charge of picking out foods, okay? I don't want to spend this trip fighting with you like a couple of toddlers throwing a tantrum they can't get their sugary cereal, but in your case, it will be over Wagyu beef. My money. My choice of groceries." She looked between us.

Julian crossed his arms, and I shrugged. "Fine," we answered in unison.

With one last warning stare, Diane spun round and pushed our cart off into the grocery section. Julian and I shared an annoyed look, and he pulled a face, mimicking Diane while using his hand like a talking head.

I chuckled.

"I know you're making fun of me back there," Diane said without turning around. "Careful or I'll only buy you the highest fat, highest carb, highest sugar foods in here."

Our eyes bulged as Julian snapped his mouth shut, then we rushed off after her.

It felt like hours passing as we went up and down every single aisle. Having never shopped at this store, or in a grocery store in decades, Diane took her time checking prices and trying to meal plan for all of us.

"Ugh. I'm going to be over budget. Groceries are way more expensive than I expected. Unless I want to make us live on nothing but pasta or mac-n-cheese, I'm going to need at least a hundred and fifty. Wow. Grocery prices have really gone up since I was shopping last."

"Thank you for not making us live on mac-n-cheese," I said. "I need to keep my figure so I can snag another husband."

Diane turned around. "How do you intend to do that? I mean, find another husband while you're still technically married to another man. We haven't really discussed this stuff yet, but can we get divorced without them present? I wanted to hire a lawyer to figure this out, but I can't afford one."

"We looked into it a little while we were in New York," I said. "Basically, if we can't find them to serve them papers, we have to put out a notice in a newspaper or something."

"What?" Diane's eyes bulged. "Are you serious? In public?"

I cringed. "Yes. In public. I'm not sure how it all works, but my plan is to find another rich man and when he wants to marry me, which of course, he will, I'll have him pay for my lawyer to figure out the whole divorcing my jackass, absentee husband. So, I'm just not going to worry about it. I'll let my next husband handle things."

Diane stood silently for a few long moments. "Wow. I really don't want to have to put a divorce notice in a public paper. How embarrassing."

"Just stay married until you find your next rich husband. I'm sure with some money to grease some wheels, he can help you avoid the public humiliation. Lord knows we've endured enough of that with this whole nightmare."

Diane's eyes flickered for a moment with anger. "No. No way. I'm not going to live my life just waiting to find a new man to depend on. Not after what happened. And why would you want to go right back down the same road that lead us here? Don't you want to learn to stand on your own two feet with no one to support you?"

"No!" I answered quickly and with certainty. "I want a new husband as fast as humanly possible!"

"We need a sugar daddy," Julian agreed. "It's our master plan."

"You really don't want to remarry?" I asked, shocked to hear she wasn't on the same path back to redemption as me.

Diane shook her head quickly. "No. Not even a little. I used to be so independent and self-reliant, and I have no desire to ever let some man control my life again. I'm in charge of me now, and what happened to me will never happen again."

"Wow," I breathed. "So, this is like gonna be it for you?" I looked around at the discount products surrounding us. "You're just gonna give up on being rich again and become a regular Walmart shopper?"

She paused then answered, "If that's what it means to be independent, then yes. I'll be here shopping the sales."

I blinked as I looked at her, stunned to hear she may actually just accept this fate instead of warring against it like I intended to do. It hadn't even occurred to me not to run out and remarry for money, and I assumed it would be her plan too.

"Well, I guess if this is enough for you."

"Maybe it is." She shrugged.

"It's not enough for me." Julian snorted. "No offense, Diane, if this is like your thing now, but no. Hell no. We're gonna be rich again. Right, CeCe?"

"Right. Definitely right." I nodded quickly then turned back to Diane. "And really, Diane? You're trying to tell me that after living the life we've lived, you're going to be content bargain shopping in Louisiana for things like..." I paused and looked at the shelf beside us, reaching out and grabbing a yellow bag. "Pork rinds?"

"That won't be all my life is about," she argued back. "I'll find something to fulfill me."

"Well, these certainly aren't going to do it. I mean, unless it turns out you love whatever the hell pork rinds are."

"They sound disgusting," Julian agreed.

"Look at me. I'm future Diane and I'm having the best day ever because pork rinds are on sale!" I started mimicking her and doing a happy dance as I pretended to clutch the strange bag of snacks to my chest like I was embracing a long-lost lover.

"The only thing I love better than pork rinds is a pretty girl who loves pork rinds too," a deep male voice said from behind me.

I spun around, and my eyes popped wide when I saw Bayou Bill strolling down the aisle toward us. His alligator boots clicked on the tile floor with each slow, deliberate, and dare I admit, sexy step that brought him closer.

When I locked eyes with his pretty blue ones, my heart fluttered inside my chest the same way it had last night when he'd looked right at me. I cursed it now like I'd cursed it then for responding to such a crude, inappropriate man... no matter how good he looked in those tight jeans.

"These aren't mine," I spit out, then dropped them on the floor.

Bill slowly reached down and picked them up, his soulful eyes locking with mine as he rose to standing. My heart did that infuriating flip-flop thingy again.

"You dropped these, Pretty Girl," he said as he held them out for me.

"I said those aren't mine. I don't even know what pork rinds are. They sound revolting."

"Fried pig skin." He held the bag out.

I gasped and pressed a hand to my chest, and I heard Julian gag behind me. "Disgusting! Who would ever eat that?"

Bill crooked that sly, sexy grin and tipped his head. "Like I said last night, don't knock 'em 'til you try 'em. You may love pork rinds if you just take a little chance on 'em."

"I will never, *ever* love a pork rind. Nor will such a horrific, disgusting thing ever make its way into my mouth."

Julian snorted behind me, and the realization of what he was implying made my cheeks burn from the flush of heat racing to them.

Bill smirked again, his chiseled, scruffy jaw ticking while he hid his smile as his gaze remained locked with mine. "Well, if you ever change your mind, I've always got a bag of pork rinds at my house. You're welcome anytime you want to sample 'em. Enjoy the rest of your day. I hope to see you around, Pretty Girl."

With a tip of his head, he bid us goodbye and held onto the bag of pork rinds as he walked away. I didn't want to turn and look, but damned if my disobedient eyes didn't lock on to that ripe looking behind filling out his ripped, faded jeans.

"He may be disgusting, but he's kind of hot," Julian said. "God. Or is it like the lighting in Walmart that's doing this? Suddenly the clothes look good, the sunglasses looked good, and even Bayou Bill looks good. Or maybe like some happy gas they feed through the vents to make Walmart shoppers not feel so pathetic? Could it be that? Because I don't want to admit it, but I kinda want to climb that jungle man like a tree."

Though he kept talking, I couldn't. My mouth went dry as images of *me* climbing Bayou Bill like a tree invaded my mind. Long, passionate kisses. His muscular arms lifting me off the ground. Those electric eyes locked with mine as we lost ourselves to primal passion. It had been decades since my husband and I had shared any real passion. More like obligatory birthday sex, and considering all men my age in the city lusted after twenty-year-old models, one hadn't looked at me the way Bill just had in years.

And it felt... good.

Dirty. Naughty. Disgusting... but good.

I kept watching him walk away, my heart stalling in my chest as he paused and looked over his shoulder, catching me ogling him like he had ogled those pork rinds. A quick wink let me know he could see my appreciation for his fine assets, and I gasped and spun away, fanning my heated cheeks.

"You okay, CeCe?" Diane asked, smirking. "Did you find something else at Walmart you want to take home?"

"Stop!" I wafted my hand at her. "Disgusting. Never. No way. He's gross. And even if he wasn't, he's got to be at least fifteen years younger than me."

"So." Diane shrugged. "Men have been dating women decades younger for eternity. Women our age are practically relics for the museum back in New York because men our age won't touch us. Do you really thing you're going to be able to find some rich, handsome husband now when he's likely off seducing some twenty-year-old blonde with a brain the size of a pea?"

She wasn't wrong. I knew I wouldn't be able to snag a Grade A husband this time around, but a good solid B with a big bank account should still be well within my reach. Balding and a pot belly would likely be on the menu, but once we were married, and I had access to the bank account, I wouldn't have to endure him touching me again.

Not the way I envisioned Bill touching me.

My face flushed again.

"I know I'm not going to snag New York's most eligible bachelor anymore, but I've still got enough in the looks department to grab myself an older, rich man."

"The older the better," Julian added. "You know, so he dies sooner, and we get his money."

Diane rolled her eyes. "If that's really what you want in life, then I hope you find yourself a decrepit old man soon. Me? I'm doing things differently this time. I'm going to find my own way without depending on a man to save me."

"You do you, and I'll do me." I lifted my chin up high, annoyed by her holier-than-thou attitude once again.

"Let's just get the rest of the stuff on this list and get out of here," Julian said. "Because I'm seeing a button-down shirt across the way over there, and it's looking really good. I think the Walmart happy gas is getting to my head. We need to go before those funny looking plaid flannels start calling to me."

"I think we have everything we need for a week of meals," Diane said. "All we need is a whole chicken to feed Peggy."

"That gator is going to be eating better than us," I said, looking down into the cart filled with things I was terrified to try.

"Better than her eating us." Diane lifted a brow.

"Valid," Julian agreed. "Let's go get that chicken and get the hell out of here."

The three of us found the frozen whole chickens, tossed one in the cart then made our way to the checkout line. After fumbling our way through self-checkout, we pushed the cart the lengthy distance back to the truck parked off on its own.

With a triumphant grin, Diane tossed the groceries in the back.

"We did it! We got gas, we got groceries, and we're still alive!"

Though I faked a smile to share her enthusiasm, instead of feeling triumphant, I just felt like I'd been through a war zone.

And I'd left my pride somewhere in aisle six.

CHAPTER TEN
Diane

I hurried across the yard toward the tables scattered around with CeCe's couture beautifully displayed on them. When I reached them, CeCe and Julian were arguing over the price of her sparkly Louboutins.

"Four hundred dollars? No way! These were sixteen-hundred new, and I've worn them once. Let's do a thousand," CeCe said.

"Yeah, good point," Julian agreed. "We don't want to give the goods away. We need this money. Now that Diane has informed us we need to pay for health insurance, chip in for groceries, and God knows what other expenses we're facing in this hell hole. We don't have a dollar for it, so I agree. A thousand it is."

I cringed as I approached them holding the pitcher of lemonade. "Um, how much are you listing stuff for?"

"Pennies it seems." CeCe spun to face me and rolled her eyes. "Practically giving it all away."

I sucked the air through my teeth regretting not being here for the pricing of her couture. Instead, I'd run to town to get mix to make lemonade so we had something to serve people on the hot, humid day. "These people don't have money like the people in New York had. I thought I told you to get out some of your less expensive stuff."

"This *is* my less expensive stuff!" she snapped back. "What, did you think I had a secret Walmart collection hidden in my closet? No! These are my things. My beloved, important, beautiful things I can barely stand to part with. And I picked the least expensive stuff like you suggested."

"I guess I wasn't thinking this through." I paused, a bit of panic palpating my heart as I looked at her collection of couture that no one in Ruinville would have ever heard of, and definitely couldn't afford. "Even a hundred dollars is going to seem like a lot for a pair of shoes."

Her eyes bulged along with Julian's. "A hundred dollars? For Louboutins? Preposterous! If I'm forced to sell my babies, I'm not going to let them feel shame for bringing in next to nothing. I'm not selling them for a penny less than I've got them listed for."

She wasn't wrong that her stuff was worth far more than it would sell for here in Ruinville, but I knew if prices were too high, we likely wouldn't sell a damn thing. And having just been in town and hearing how many people were coming to check out our rummage sale, I knew I had to try to get CeCe to lower her prices.

"Let me just put this pitcher down and get the cups set up, then let's take a look at pricing together."

She crossed her arms and lifted her chin, looking away. "They are priced as low as I will go. Period."

I arched an eyebrow. "If nothing sells, we're back to square one and you have no income to contribute to our funds. And if you think I'm going to keep footing the bill for your groceries and living expenses, not to mention that's on top of things like home repairs, property tax, insurance and all the other expenses coming our way. My five-thousand dollars isn't going to last us long at all. We need you to sell some stuff to help us stay afloat while we get things figured out. People are coming here expecting to buy things. You need to lower your prices to make some sales. Today."

She continued stubbornly looking away. "I won't. This is what they're worth."

Anxiety twisted up a knot inside my stomach that we wouldn't make a penny during our sale, and with no other sources of income in sight, we needed the money. Why hadn't I realized how out of touch CeCe was with reality that she would expect an average person to buy a thousand-dollar pair of shoes at a rummage sale? Instead of getting into a war with CeCe I knew I would never win, I set down the lemonade on the little wicker table. I hurried inside to find some reasonable items the people of Ruinville may want if CeCe's couture pricing sent them screaming away.

Each item of my aunt's I picked up and considered selling filled my soul with sadness. Everything had a memory attached to it, and I hated the idea of parting with a single thing that she'd used during her lifetime here. But knowing she'd be okay with some of the less sentimental things going to make sure I had food in my belly, I started tossing trinkets and knickknacks into a cardboard box. After twenty minutes of scurrying around every room in the house, I came out with the final box.

"Is this for the garbage man?" Julian asked as he looked at the weird contents of my boxes.

"No, it's for the rummage sale. Thought I'd contribute some of Aunt Addie's stuff I don't need."

He snorted as he pulled a brown and orange crotchet potholder with a chicken embroidered in the middle out of the box. "Who in the hell is going to want this when they can have a Gucci gown?"

"I have no idea," I admitted, and the anxiety over the minutes ticking down to our rummage sale deepened. In less than fifteen minutes, our yard would be filled with all the locals in Ruinville, and I was terrified to meet them. It'd been years since I'd been in a small town, but I knew all too well about the gossip mill that would be churning about us... and likely already was.

Ignoring the nagging guilt in my stomach for selling some of Aunt Addie's things, I grabbed the tags and stickers and went to work putting the modest prices on each of them. From twenty-five cents to five dollars, I priced as fast as I could and displayed them on the extra table.

A plume of dust coming up the driveway announced the first shoppers were coming, and the three of us scurried into our positions. A black pickup truck led a caravan of cars, and I could barely believe my eyes when dozens of people poured out of their vehicles.

"Holy crap. That's a lot of hillbillies," Julian whispered as they started coming our way.

A tall young, redhead wearing a crimson dress and matching lipstick led the way with four little belles hurrying behind her in their flouncy dresses. When she arrived at us and flashed her toothy grin, I smiled back.

"Hi, y'all. I'm Ruby and we are the Magnolia Maidens," she said, and all the girls gestured to the matching magnolia flowers pinned in their hair. "We just wanted to come and welcome you to Ruinville. We Magnolia Maidens are here to help you in any way you need, and you'll see us around town organizing all the fundraisers and social gatherings. If there's anything you need, you just give us a holler."

Her smile grew, and the four clones behind her grinned as well.

"Wow. Thank you for the warm welcome," I said. "We appreciate it, and I'll be sure to let you know if we need anything."

"You do that now, ya hear?" She winked, and the girls fell into line as she started moving through the couture clothes.

They squealed with excitement at first, but the moment her painted red nails touched a price tag, she dropped it like it had been dipped in molten lava. The girls all pressed together in a huddle as they flipped tag after tag, then judgmental eyes moved our way.

"I told you that you priced too high," I whispered to CeCe.

She scoffed. "Whatever. Those 'hillbelles' wouldn't know fashion if it smacked them in their overpainted, trashy faces."

"Wow. They are really giving us the mean mug," Julian said. "They are meaner looking than the New York City socialites when you accidentally wore the same dress as Franny McMahon to that cancer fundraiser."

"Southern girls are as sweet as they come but they can turn on a dime and be meaner than a venomous snake," I whispered back. "Just try not to piss them off. We don't need the local popular girl group badmouthing us all over town."

We didn't have time to pay any more attention to the Magnolia Maidens because it seemed the entire population of Ruinville was clamoring to come and meet us. One by one they introduced themselves, and I struggled to remember anyone's names. But then a woman in a pink plaid dress two sizes too tight came up to our table. She smiled, and it showcased the pink lipstick stuck to her teeth.

"Afternoon, y'all. I'm Mayor Marjorie." She stretched out her hand, and I rose to shake it. CeCe and Julian remained seated and gave her a small, unimpressed wave.

"Thanks so much for stopping by Mayor Marjorie."

She waved her hand. "Wouldn't dream of missing it. Mawmaw May had such fine things to say about you, I wanted to come by and introduce myself. She says she's sorry she can't make it, by the way. Short staffed and all, so she couldn't leave."

"Of course," I said. "I completely understand."

Mayor Marjorie glanced at my lemonade pitcher and furrowed her brow. "Did you leave the sweet tea inside?"

"Sweet tea?" I asked, freezing as I remembered in that moment that everyone in the south drank sweet tea and not lemonade. "I'm sorry. I don't have any. Just the lemonade."

Her eyes flashed wide for a moment, then she cleared her throat. "Oh, if you don't have any, I suppose it's not the end of the world. Just a little hot out here is all. I guess I'll be fine."

As she waved her gloved hand at her face, I looked back at the house. "I, uh. Let me go see if I can find the tea. I'm sure Aunt Addie had some."

She grinned as she stopped fanning her face and pointed at the house. "Actually, allow me. I've made tea in Aunt Addie's house dozens of times. I know exactly where it is. And if you don't mind, while I'm in there, I'm just gonna grab back the blender she borrowed from me a few months ago. Never got around to picking it up before she, you know." She frowned.

"Oh. Yes, of course. I'll just go unlock the front door for you and we can find it."

A hush fell over the crowd of people perusing the tables around us, and Mayor Marjorie gave them all a look then giggled.

"Oh, dear. You're in Ruinville. We don't lock our doors around here. We're a neighborly kind, and we don't have any criminals hidden among us." She paused then made a face and leaned down. "Well, unless the rumors about you three are true, and in that case, I do hope that you don't go causing no trouble in my town, you hear?"

My teeth clenched. "We aren't criminals. We're victims, and we won't be causing any trouble here. Just follow me into the house, and I'll get that blender for you, and we can make some tea."

"Perfect, dear," she said as she rose back upright.

I started to get up out of my seat, but Julian caught my arm. "We're door lockers, understand? I've seen Whacky Wade, and after looking at all these weirdos out here, we are absolutely, positively locking the damn doors."

"I'm getting a deadbolt next time we go to Walmart," CeCe whispered. "I swear that woman over there is a witch. And I'm pretty sure she just hexed me when I told her I wouldn't lower the price on my Chanel sweater to five dollars. She mumbled a bunch of weird Cajun mumbo jumbo at me."

I looked over at the woman with the long, gnarled grey hair and the black, draped fabric that fashioned a sort of disheveled dress. CeCe wasn't wrong when she said she looked like a witch. The woman suddenly spun to look at me, and I nearly tumbled backward over Julian's chair with the fright her intense look impaled me with.

"Holy crap," I spit out as the woman glared then pointed her fingers at me before mumbling something and turning away again.

"See! She just hexed you too! Damn it! We're all hexed." CeCe slumped forward. "I hate this place."

"Don't mind her," Mayor Marjorie said as she came over and took my elbow. "That's just Zadia. She thinks she's a Voodoo witch, but she's harmless. She's hexed us all and no one has croaked yet. Now, let's go make that tea."

I went inside with Mayor Marjorie, and after a little digging, we found the sweet tea. She showed me how Aunt Addie used to make it, and the memories of helping her in the kitchen during my childhood came flooding back. When we finished, I helped her carry it outside, meeting even more people along the way. Many were asking about certain items they were hoping to find at the sale today, so after dropping off the tea and parting with Mayor Marjorie, I met some of them back in the house and found the items they were looking for.

One wanted the lamp from the living room, and she paid me almost forty dollars for it. Seemed she's always coveted it when she visited. Another had always loved a red sweater Aunt Addie wore often, and though it pained me to part with it, I took her ten dollars and found it in the closet. When we cleared out of the house, I had almost two hundred dollars of extra money I desperately needed.

"I best get going, dear," Mayor Marjorie said after she left the little huddle of ladies who'd been gossiping in the yard... likely gossiping about us, I noted.

"Thanks so much for stopping by," I said to her. "I look forward to seeing you again."

"And which charity were you raising money for today? I forgot to ask."

"Oh." I paused and bit my lip. "Um, actually we need to keep the proceeds of the sale today."

Her eyes flashed wide then she furrowed her brow. "Oh. Well, you see, in Ruinville, we are always trying to raise money for charity. Your aunt used to throw rummage sales to help fundraise. I guess I just thought you were doing the same."

"We're the charity," CeCe said as she stepped up behind me. "Our piece of crap husbands emptied our bank accounts and fled the country, leaving us penniless. Every dollar we make today goes to making sure we don't starve to death. So just keep that judgey look off your face. We're the poor, starving people this time."

"Seriously," Julian said. "Someone just get Sarah McLaughlan to play that song and put us on a commercial. We're that damn needy right now."

"I see." Mayor Marjorie gave us each a look. "Well, I guess I understand, but just so you know, we do expect you to help with charities and fundraisers if you're going to be part of the community here. We take care of our own, and the loss of your aunt was a big one. She worked tirelessly to help out in any way she could."

"I understand," I answered quickly. "And once we're on our feet, we'll be sure to help out where we can."

"I hope so," she said. "We wouldn't want to let your aunt down, now would we?"

I felt like I shrunk a foot with the weight of her stare, but I just shook my head and answered, "No. We wouldn't. It was nice to meet you."

She smiled at us then spun on her pink shoe and started back toward her car.

"Bitch," Julian whispered under his breath. "We're literally starving and poor and she's gonna go judging us for trying not to starve to death?"

"Well, at least she bought some stuff," I said. "And with the sales from outside, I'm up at least five hundred dollars. How are you guys doing."

They both looked down at the green grass.

"Uh, we, uh... we haven't sold anything," CeCe admitted.

I growled under my breath. "I knew you were pricing things too high!"

She tossed up her arms. "Well, how in the hell was I supposed to know that these hicks wouldn't appreciate fine couture! They aren't my target audience."

I pressed a hand to my forehead. "You're right. I'm sorry. A rummage sale was the wrong place to try to do this. I just... we need money, you guys. We have to find somewhere to sell your stuff."

"We'll make the most money if we can list them on the internet," Julian said. "People who know fashion will pay good dough for this stuff."

"You're right," CeCe agreed. "But we don't have a computer or anything."

I sighed, then lifted my head. "I heard someone today talking about using the internet at the library. Maybe Julian could spearhead going to the library and finding out how to sell our stuff online. There must be a dealer or something who could handle doing pictures and stuff."

"Me?" Julian pressed a hand to his chest, his voice jumping five octaves. "You want me to go sit in the stinky public library chairs and work on the communal computer? No. Hell no."

CeCe and I both turned to face him, our eyebrows raising to match.

I narrowed my eyes. "I'm supplying a house and money to live. CeCe is going to donate her beloved clothes to help us survive. And..." I pressed a finger to my chin. "What exactly are you contributing here?"

He shrank a little. "Uh, I'm here for entertainment. I make you laugh. I'm nice to look at. I'm... I'm Julian!"

I shook my head. "Not anymore. From now on, if you want to stay, you pull your weight. And right now, figuring out how to sell couture for top dollar is your new job. Even if it means going to the library."

CeCe nodded. "Julian, darling. I've been supporting you for years and have never asked you to do a damn thing. You didn't have to. We were crazy rich. But now I'm broke as a joke, and the free ride is over. You're going to the library, hon."

He tossed up his hands, then with an overly dramatic sigh, he agreed. "Fine. I'll do it. But I don't like it."

"No one said you have to like it, you just have to do it." I smiled.

CeCe looked over her shoulder, and it wasn't the first time I'd seen her eyes scanning our surroundings as if she was searching for something. Finally, I realized *exactly who* she was looking for.

"Looking for someone?" I asked, grinning.

"What? No." She quickly looked back to me.

"Someone named Bayou Bill, perhaps?" I grinned wider.

Her eyes widened then narrowed. "Ew! No! Of course not. Why would I be looking for him?"

Julian's face lit up. "Oh! You *are* looking for him, you little minx! You little southern slummin' harlot!"

"I am not!" She swatted him on the arm, but that familiar red rushed back to her cheeks. "Gross. I hate him."

"Just because you hate someone doesn't mean you don't want to," Julian paused then started shimmying his hips as he said, "Bow chicka wow wow!"

"No! Stop! Gross!" CeCe swatted him again, but I noticed the girlish smile she couldn't keep off her lips.

She and Julian started batting their hands at each other, but then Julian stopped abruptly. "Speaking of bow chicka wow wow... who is this handsome hunk heading our way?"

I turned to look where his gaze had landed, and the moment I clapped eyes on him, the breath whooshed out of my lungs. Though forty years had a way of transforming people beyond recognition, his was a face I could never forget.

He stopped when he saw me. "Diane?"

My heart skipped a beat at the sound of my name spoken by a voice I hadn't heard in decades. I remained frozen, my breath caught in my throat as he came closer. He stopped in front of me, and I stared, stunned, into the warm, expressive brown eyes that I'd gotten so lost in many nights under the Louisiana stars. My long-lost love that had captured my heart during those sun-drenched summers in the bayou.

"J-Johnny?" I stammered, my voice barely above a whisper.

He smiled, a smile that held the same easy charm that had captivated me all those years ago. In that moment, the years melted away, and it was as though time had folded in on itself. Of course, ever since I'd returned to Ruinville, I'd been wondering if Johnny still lived here, and every time I went anywhere in Ruinville, I was always secretly looking for him, though not daring to ask anyone to satisfy my curiosity. He'd always planned on making a life right here in town, following in the footsteps of generations of family fireman. And it seemed he hadn't left, because the beautiful boy I'd shared my first kiss with... along with so many other firsts... was standing before me in the body of a handsome, silver-haired man.

"I heard you were back," he said in a voice much deeper than I remembered.

"Uh, yeah. Hi. How... how are you?"

I stood awkwardly, unsure if I should hug him or not. He slid his hands into his jeans pockets and dipped his chin toward the ground. "Good. Pretty good. Been a long time," he said, and as his eyes lifted up to meet mine again, my heart pounded with the same intensity as it had the first time he'd leaned toward me to steal a first kiss.

"Yeah. Really long time. I... gosh. How many years?"

"Forty-four," he answered quickly as if he'd been keeping track since the day I'd kissed him goodbye then never returned.

My heart clenched over my betrayal. Was he angry? Hurt? Or had he forgotten my promise to return the summer after I started college so we could start a life together. Get married. Settle into the quiet life I'd dreamed about but then started to regret when I'd gotten to college and seen what the world had to offer. Suddenly, I hadn't felt ready to settle down and I'd wanted to travel, help people all around the world and explore life before returning back to him... before returning to Ruinville.

But I never did.

That summer, when I'd landed a nursing intern job, I'd swore I'd return to him. We'd clung to phone calls, my promises to visit dangling like fragile threads. But as my passion for nursing and helping others had engulfed me, those calls had dwindled, stretched thin by the demands of my new life. I'd never made it back to Ruinville that year, despite all my plans.

And then I'd met Rick.

Standing before Johnny now, the past cascaded over me, reigniting feelings I thought I'd left behind. Back then, on my wedding day, seeing Aunt Addie had briefly stirred old memories of Ruinville. Of a simpler time including our summers and the love we'd shared. Yet, I'd never wavered, convinced that my future lay beyond this small town's borders, chasing ambitions too vast for its small confines. Ironically, despite the world at my feet, I'd achieved none of those dreams. I'd transformed into a socialite, unrecognizable even to myself—a far cry from the person Johnny once knew.

Unsure whether to apologize or not, and now feeling the prying eyes of CeCe and Julian boring through me, I just smiled and said, "It's been a long time. You look great. I didn't know if you'd still be here."

"Yeah, thought about venturing off a couple times, youthful ideas and whatnot, but never made it past the county line long," he answered. "My dad got sick the summer I turned nineteen, so I stayed back to take care of my mom and little sister and step up into the family business early. Ended up staying forever."

"Wow. That was so thoughtful of you to take care of them, Johnny."

"You gotta take care of family above all else," he answered. "And it ended up turning out fine for me. I love firefighting, and just like my father before me, I'm the Fire Chief now. And by the way, no one has called me Johnny since I was a teen. Just go by John now."

"Oh," I said, embarrassed to be referring to him by a name he hadn't used in decades. "Sorry about that."

"No. No worries. Just didn't want to start getting teased by the guys if anyone hears me called Johnny." He chuckled.

I smiled softly. "Fair enough... John." The word stuck on my tongue, but it did suit the strong, distinguished man standing before me better than his childhood nickname. I flicked a gaze to his hand and noted the absence of a band circling his most important finger. "Glad you got the life you wanted."

"Yeah. Me too. And I heard you're back here now? For good?"

"God, I hope not," Julian whooshed out.

John arched an eyebrow and looked over my shoulder at him.

"Uh, sorry. John, this is CeCe and Julian. They are my..." I paused, wondering what words to say to encapsulate the relationship we had. Enemies? Frenemies? Arch nemeses and her sidekick? Roommates? Partners in poverty? Finally, I settled on, "They are staying with me for a while."

"Nice to meet you." John tipped his baseball hat with the Ruinville Fire Department emblem on it.

Julian giggled and gave a little wave. "You too, Mr. Fireman."

CeCe straightened her shoulders. "Nice to meet you, John. I look forward to hearing more about you." Her gaze slid over to me, and it narrowed in a knowing stare.

Someone down by the tables started waving a floral blanket at me. "Hi! How much for this? I can't find the tag!"

"Uh, sorry, John. I have to go help her out."

"No problem. Just thought I'd drop in to tell you I'm real sorry about your aunt. I know how much she loved you and every time I saw her, she always reminisced about the summers you used to spend with her. So, yeah. Just wanted to come and say how sorry I am. Aunt Addie was a hell of a woman."

"Yes. She was." I smiled. "And thank you. I appreciate you coming by."

He gave a slight nod of his head. "Yep. No problem. I'm sure I'll see you around."

"Yeah. Definitely. For sure," I answered awkwardly. "It was good to see you again."

Once again, I stood in front of him unsure if I should reach forward and pull him into the embrace I so desperately wanted to feel, but instead I just stuck out my hand. He looked at it for a moment, then crooked a smile and reached out his hand. The moment I felt his skin on mine, every nerve in my body seemed to crackle back to life. Like they'd been dead since the last time he touched me, and now just one brush of our skin was breathing them all back to life.

"See you around, Diane," he said, then let go of my hand.

I struggled to exhale my next breath as I watched him walk away.

"Damn, girl. You better spill the beans on that one. And if you even try to say nothing happened between you, I'm gonna call you the biggest liar I've ever seen, because..." Julian paused to wave his hand at his face. "You two are like *fire!*"

"You definitely slid down his fire pole," CeCe teased. "And by the way you looked at him, looks like you want to go for another ride."

"It was a long time ago," I said quickly, and the pain and guilt of abandoning him like I'd abandoned Aunt Addie sunk into the pit of my stomach. "I need to go help this woman."

Before they could ask another question, I hurried off to help the woman still waving the blanket at me. I glanced across the driveway and watched John climb up into his big, black truck, and our eyes connected once again. He gave me a little smile, then I stood silently watching him as he drove out of my driveway, and I wasn't sure whether I was excited or terrified about his reappearance in my life.

CHAPTER ELEVEN
CeCe

I puckered my nose against the stench as I struggled to dislodge the trash bag from the waste bin. "It's too full! I can't get it out!"

"Maybe you should have thought of that before you refused to take it out and let it get too full," Diane said as she scrubbed a dish at the sink.

"I told you. I don't do garbage!"

She glanced over her shoulder and smirked. "And now you do. No one is too good for the chore list. And as you're learning tonight, if you drag your feet with chores, they only get harder."

After three days of refusing to do such a disgusting task, and the garbage can starting to overflow with stinky refuse, I finally realized Diane wasn't going to cave and let me off the hook of her horrible chore list. I glanced up at the big chalkboard on the wall with the list of chores doled out between the three of us. This week, I was in charge of garbage, sweeping the floors, and cleaning the bathrooms. Julian was on dusting duty, laundry duty, and lawn mowing. Diane assigned herself dishes, cooking, and grocery shopping... the same tasks she'd assigned herself every one of the three weeks since we'd arrived in Ruinville and she came up with that cursed chore chart.

"I just love that every week you take the same three tasks, and Julian and I get stuck with the crap jobs."

She paused and turned around, her yellow gloves full of white suds. "Can you drive the truck to go to the grocery store?"

I shook my head.

Her eyebrow inched up. "Can you cook?"

I shook my head again.

"Can you do the dishes without gagging and vomiting, as we learned the first time you tried?"

I shook my head a third time.

"Then these are my jobs since you two invalids can't manage them. That leaves the rest of the jobs for you two to split. This week, you're on garbage duty. Get over it."

"Fine! I'll do it. But I don't like it."

"No one said you have to."

With a tug and a growl, I finally dislodged the bag. Carefully, I slid it out and tied the top shut.

Julian walked into the kitchen, and Diane paused her scrubbing and quirked an eyebrow. "What in the hell are you wearing?"

I looked up to see him in one of Aunt Addie's white, frilly aprons, a bandana on his head and clutching a feather duster in his hand.

He glanced down at his outfit. "I think I kinda look like a sexy French maid in this. It makes doing this horrible chore of cleaning a little more tolerable if I role play."

"You look more like Orphan Annie than a French maid," I said.

He narrowed his eyes at me and cocked a hip. "Well, alright then, Oscar."

I looked at the garbage in my hand and caught his joke. I narrowed my eyes to match his. "Whatever, Annie."

"Whatever, Oscar."

Diane chuckled. "Will you two quit your bickering and finish up chores? I'll be done with dishes in a few, and then we can pick a movie to watch tonight."

"Oh! I saw that Aunt Addie had Casablanca. I would love to see that again," Julian said.

My eyes lit up. "Yes! Great movie! A classic."

"Casablanca it is." Diane grinned.

We all hurried off to finish our chores, and when we were done, we met in the living room. I tipped my head. "Did something change in here?"

Julian grinned. "I did a little redecorating while I dusted. Moved things around a little too. What do you think?"

I wasn't even sure what was different since the cluttered room was so full of knickknacks and furniture, but somehow, it did look better.

"I mean, it's not like the *Queer Eye* crew got their hands on this wreck, but better right? Kind of like..." He paused and looked around. "Garbage chic."

"It looks great, Julian. You did a nice job." Diane sat on the sofa and patted the spot beside her. "Come. Sit. You worked hard. Time to relax a little."

Julian popped the movie in then pulled off his apron and climbed in on her left. I settled in on her right, and the three of us shared the Afghan blanket as we settled in for our nightly movie time. Aunt Addie had hundreds of movies in a cabinet beneath the TV, and since we had no money to go out, it had become our nightly tradition to pick one and watch it together.

I picked up the movie case Julian had set on the coffee table and sighed as I looked at the picture. "Wasn't she beautiful? Look at her perfect skin."

"She was something," Diane agreed.

"And so was he." Julian waggled his eyebrows then grabbed the remote.

"Speaking of perfect skin, we need to go to the library tomorrow to use the computer and find out who does Botox around here. I'm really starting to wrinkle. Can you give us a ride, Diane?"

"Botox?" She laughed. "We can't afford Botox! We can barely afford the boxed hair dye we all splurged on!"

I looked at her with her smooth, silky skin and narrowed my eyes. "You've already got a Botox guy, don't you? That's why you don't want me to get it done so you can look like that, and I can turn into a wrinkled old prune!"

She scoffed. "I do *not* have a Botox guy! This is just my skin!"

I rolled my eyes. "Yeah, right. No one in their sixties has skin as smooth as that without a lot of cosmetic help."

"I eat well, I moisturize, and I stay out of the sun. Plus, good genes. Aunt Addie and my grandma on her side had pretty smooth skin too."

With a snort, I shook my head. "Good genes? Please. Everyone says that even though I know the guy that stretched their face within an inch of its life. So, tell me. Who's doing your skin? Let me in on the secret."

She laughed. "I'm serious! I'm not getting work done. This is just me."

"You're telling me that's natural?" I pointed at her face.

She nodded, and I could see the honesty in her eyes.

"Ugh. Now I hate you more," I grumbled.

"You don't need Botox. You're just fine the way you are, and we can't afford it."

I spun and furrowed my brow. "Um, I have sold over three thousand dollars worth of couture online already. I may have agreed to use that crappy box dye and let Julian cut my hair, but there is no replacement for Botox. That's my money, and I'm spending it on Botox."

Her eyebrow rose. "It's *our* money since I've spent a ton of *my* money on you both already, not to mention giving you a free place to live. We have to spend conservatively. We don't know what the future holds, and we don't have a steady source of income yet. We need a plump savings account to get us through whatever comes our way."

I scoffed. "Um, you don't get to tell me that I can or cannot get Botox. I'm a grown woman, and I *need* that Botox so I can *get* my next source of income... a rich husband! How am I going to snag a husband when I look like Walter Mattheau as my age catches up to me and my face sags down to my knees!"

Julian pulled a face. "Ugh. That was a horrible image I can't unsee."

"Your face isn't going to sag like that," Diane said. "You may get a few wrinkles as time goes on, but who cares? Aging can be a beautiful process."

Rolling my eyes, I snorted. "The only people who say that are the people who can't afford all the skincare I've been able to afford. I'm not wrinkling. I won't. I'll just go pick a new piece of mine and Julian can call our dealer and sell it."

"It sounds like we have a drug dealer." Julian chuckled.

Even though it was completely above board, it sure felt like we were dealing drugs. Julian would get ahold of the guy online, he'd come by and take some of my clothes, then after selling them online, he'd drop off a wad of cash to tide us over. Every time one of my beloved pieces of couture slipped through my fingers, I felt a piece of me leaving as well.

The anger over my situation bubbling just beneath the surface exploded as it poured out my mouth, and I yelled, "My damned ex-husband and the government may have taken my money, my homes, my clothes, and my dignity, but to hell if they're taking my face too! I've already forgone my weekly facials, dermaplaning, collagen therapy and all the other skin treatments I've been having done for years. But I am *not* giving up my Botox! I won't!"

"We can always try tape?" Julian reached up and touched his temples, pulling the skin tight. "Lots of women who can't afford Botox tape their face. I'm sure we've got some Scotch tape lying around here. Maybe we could try it?"

I tightened my fists and closed my eyes tight. "I'm not Scotch taping my face together. I. Need. BOTOX!" I screamed, and the power of my words sent Julian and Diane huddling together. Tears squeezed through my closed lids as another wave of loss washed over me. It seemed every time I started to find my stride in this horrible new world, like a wrecking ball to the gut, suddenly I would be reminded once more just how much I'd lost... how far I'd fallen. And the landing hurt like hell every single time.

"Okay, okay!" Diane soothed, then carefully reached over and touched my shoulder. "We'll find a way to work it in the budget if it means that much to you."

My teary eyes snapped open. "Really? I can get the Botox?"

Diane chuckled. "You can get the Botox. But that means we need to do something more for money if we're going to start splurging, because your couture is going to run out eventually, and then we'll be broke again."

"Like what?" Julian asked.

Diane let out a long exhale then answered, "We need to get jobs."

"What?" Julian and I shrieked in unison, then Julian kept on. "CeCe? Work? That's preposterous!"

Diane twisted her lips then shrugged. "This is our life now. We need to start working to pay the bills."

Horrified at her suggestion, I argued back. "I'm going to marry a rich man! *That's* my job!"

"And I'm going to help her. That's *my* job!"

"And how is that going for you? You got any prospects in sight?" she said, her voice tinged with incredulity.

I shrank a little. "Well, no. But that's just because we don't have enough money for big outings to the city so I can find one."

"Mmmhmm." She pinched her lips. "So, you need money to go and find a husband?"

"Yes, but that's why we are selling her clothes," Julian argued. "We've almost got enough now. We save the good, sexy outfits so she has something to wear and entice them, then we get a hotel room in Baton Rouge to stay in for a while, and we spend our days at the Baton Rouge Country Club. There will be plenty of old rich guys milling around there. We researched it at the library the last time we were there."

"See." I pointed at Julian. "We don't need jobs. We just need enough money to get me to the Baton Rouge Country Club, then enough time to snag me an old, decrepit rich husband."

"I see." Diane smiled. "And how are you planning on marrying this old, decrepit husband while you're still married to another? In case you've forgotten, we have no way to divorce them since they're gone with the wind. Or are you just planning on catching a sugar daddy to date and making him pay your bills?"

I soured my face. "Ew. I'm a proper lady not some bimbo. I need a legitimate marriage to a man to secure my fate. I mean, just to date a rich man means he could send me packing anytime he wanted, but with a marriage, and a prenup that ensures I don't walk away empty-handed, I can secure my future for good."

Julian nodded along. "Exactly. Only marriage will ensure our survival. We don't give out the milk so they get the cow for free." He stopped and tipped his head. "No, wait. We don't give out the cow..."

"Why buy the milk when you can get the cow for free?" Diane asked, smiling.

He pointed at her. "Yes! That. That's why we have to find one to marry, not just date."

"And the fact you're already married? Tell me again how you're getting around that not-so-miniscule obstacle?"

I wafted my hand in the air. "Simple. When I get a man to fall in love with me, we'll use his money to hire the best lawyers to get me out of my marriage, and then I'll be divorced so he can marry me instead." I smiled, proud of how much thought I'd put into this.

She twisted her lips. "Mmmhmm. I see. But what if it doesn't work out? What if there is no decrepit, rich husband waiting for you there?"

I opened my mouth to speak then closed it when I didn't have an answer.

"Why wouldn't there be a husband there for her?" Julian scrunched his brow.

"Um, because finding a husband isn't like going shoe shopping?" Diane chuckled. "Just because there are rich, old men milling around doesn't mean they will be a) single, b) looking to get married, or c) interested in CeCe. Meeting one is one thing, but it could take months and months, or years even, to get one to marry you!"

"Why wouldn't they want to marry me?" I scrunched my face.

She snorted. "Um, have you met you?"

With a gasp, I clutched my chest. "I'm fabulous!"

"You're a late-sixties, broke, spoiled, still married woman who will turn up as a possible criminal if they do one Google search about you. Oh yeah. Those men with twenty-something, easy, carefree bombshells clamoring after them are gonna be lining up for you."

The laughter that erupted out of her shook me right to my core. I had always considered myself a catch... a woman others would aspire to be and a woman that men would fall in love with instantly if I hadn't already been married. But hearing myself broken down into such simple, ugly terms seemed to shine a different light on me than I'd always imagined... and it was worse lighting than we'd encountered at Walmart.

"Plenty of men would love to marry CeCe!" Julian defended, and I thanked him with my eyes. "I mean, they really do have to be like really, really old so they are too old to get it up and don't have a need for the really young blondes, but we'll find one. I know it."

Those final sentences of his caused my heart to sink again. Was I really too old and used up to find a decent new husband? Was an old, diaper-wearing relic really the only thing awaiting me if I followed through on this plan?

"I'm just saying that you two had better have a backup plan if this is really all you've come up with. And I think you should also really reconsider putting all your eggs in one basket again... especially the very same basket that ended up with us in this very situation. Don't you want to learn to stand on your own two feet?"

"At this rate, they will be bare feet if I don't find a new husband!" I spat. "I am selling all my shoes just to survive!"

"So, then we stand on our own two bare feet," Diane said. "But we stand on our own. And if we get jobs, we won't have to sell your stuff anymore. You can keep it. Our jobs will pay the bills."

I waved her concerns away with a dismissive flick of my hand. "A job, darling? Please. I haven't lifted a finger in years. I have no marketable skills, unless you count shopping and throwing fabulous parties."

"And drinking," Julian added. "You're an excellent drinker."

"Well, maybe you should consider developing some skills. You're a smart woman, CeCe. You could excel in a real career if you put your mind to it."

"Oh, Diane, you always were the practical one. But can't you see? Marrying another wealthy man is the quickest way to regain my social standing. Plus, it's much more glamorous than punching a clock."

Diane leaned in closer, her tone filled with concern. "CeCe, you can't base your happiness on someone else's bank account. What if you fall in love with a man who doesn't have a fortune?"

"Well, that's simple," I said. "I *won't* fall in love with a man without a big bank account. So, problem solved there."

"And if you marry a man with a big bank account and he loses it, or steals it again, then what? You're right back where you started."

I narrowed my eyes. "Then I'll find another husband with money."

Diane buried her face in her hands, shaking her head. "CeCe, you're incorrigible. But if you're going to go through with this ridiculous plan, promise me one thing: you'll at least try to find a man who makes you happy, not just someone with a fat wallet."

I pouted, pretending to ponder her request for a moment. "Well, I suppose I could settle for a man who's moderately wealthy and exceptionally handsome."

"Alright, CeCe. But mark my words, one day you'll realize that there's more to life than just hunting for rich husbands. And in the meantime, I think getting jobs is the only thing to ensure we don't starve to death after we sell off the last of your couture."

"I'm not getting a job." I turned up my nose.

Diane crossed her arms. "Well then, since you don't need money and I do, I'm going to have to start charging you both for rent. And groceries. And gas for driving you around. How much do chauffeurs make these days?" She pressed a finger to her chin.

"You wouldn't!" My eyes flashed wide.

She grinned. "I would."

Julian leaned closer to me over her and whispered, "CeCe, we can't afford that. All our money needs to go to Operation Diaper Daddy. If we spend our money on day-to-day stuff, we won't be able to afford to go to the city for the few weeks this is gonna take."

I scowled, my mind racing with other ideas that didn't involve me getting a... I gulped... job.

I came up with none.

"What if I promise to give you a million dollars once I find a husband? Then will you skip this crazy idea of me having to get a job?"

Diane shook her head, a smug smile tipping her lips. "Nope. I'm not putting my stock in this crazy scheme of yours. I'm putting my stock in us being strong, independent people. We can do this. Hundreds of millions of people are doing it right now, and we're no different from them."

"But I *am* different!" I stomped my foot. "I'm CeCe VanTramp! I don't do jobs!"

"Then you're on your own." Diane sat back. "Good luck finding a husband."

"Ugh!" I erupted in frustration, flinging my hands into the air with theatrical exasperation. "Fine. I'll do it. I'll get a ridiculous job. But the very moment I snag a wealthy husband, consider this my resignation notice."

Diane gave me an amused smirk. "Works for me."

Julian extended a comforting hand across Diane, lightly touching my leg. "CeCe, I'm truly sorry about all this. The thought of you working is, well, quite unimaginable, but I believe in you. You'll do great, and everything will work out."

Diane raised an eyebrow, directing her gaze at Julian. "You're not off the hook either, my friend. You're getting a job too."

His jaw dropped in disbelief. "Wait, what? You mean me as well? No, no way!"

She chuckled heartily. "Of course, I mean you too! Did you honestly think CeCe and I would head off to work, while you'd lounge around watching soap operas all day?"

Julian seemed to contemplate the idea. "Well, I had this vague notion of becoming the stay-at-home husband, like a modern-day butler. Yes, the butler—that could be my job. I'll keep the house in order while you two strong, independent women venture off to work."

I wagged my finger pointedly in his face. "If I'm getting a job, you're getting a job."

"But, CeCe!" he protested, pouting. "I don't have any marketable skills either!"

Diane wore a smug grin. "See, I've been saying it for years—you've been nothing but a paid best friend to CeCe. You claim to have had a job, but I call it pure fiction."

Julian crossed his arms, a sullen expression on his face. "I did things."

Diane remained resolute. "Well, now you're going to do even more. In fact, how about we all take a little trip to Mawmaw May's right now and see if there are any job openings available? She told us she was hiring."

I sat up abruptly. "Hold on a second. You want me to work in a restaurant? As in, serving people? Are you out of your mind?"

"A job is a job." Diane pulled the Afghan off us as she rose from her seat.

I stood up, and Julian hopped up as well. "I thought you meant something like a job in a cosmetics store or a salon. You know, those kinds of jobs. High fashion jobs."

Diane tipped her head. "Have you seen any cosmetics stores or salons in Ruinville since we arrived?"

"Well, no," I admitted reluctantly.

Julian shook his head. "I guess not."

Diane lifted her hands with a shrug. "Then it's going to be hard finding a job in high fashion when there aren't any. The closest thing resembling fashion is Walmart, but hey, they probably offer benefits, so perhaps that's not such a bad option after all. Let's head there to fill out applications."

In unison, Julian and I gasped, pressing together as if our lives depended on it. "I absolutely refuse to work at Walmart!"

"Count me out as well! I stand with her!"

Diane strode toward the door, grabbing the keys from the wall. "Then it's settled—Mawmaw's it is. So, who's coming with me?"

Julian and I exchanged glances, and as I felt my last vestige of dignity slip away and crumple on the floor, I took a deep breath and followed Diane, resigned to the fact that I was about to embark on a journey I never imagined I'd be on.

I was getting a job.

Gulp.

CHAPTER TWELVE
Diane

Pulling teeth seemed a far easier task than getting CeCe and Julian out of the truck to come into Mawmaw's with me.

CeCe sat unmoving in her seat, refusing to look at me while I stood at the open passenger door. "I changed my mind. This is stupid. I'm not going in to ask for a job."

I leaned in the truck a little farther. "I don't like this anymore than you do, but I'm not being a baby about it. We need money. To get money, we need jobs. Mawmaw's is understaffed, and we know she's kind and would be great to work for. It's a no brainer. Now get your spoiled, ridiculous asses out of the truck."

Julian looked up at me with pleading eyes. "Please, Diane. Don't make us do this. Just give us a little more time. We'll find a rich husband and pay you handsomely in back-rent when we do. Please, please, please don't make us go in there and get a... job."

I hated to admit I took a little pleasure in the idea of seeing CeCe and Julian slaving away in a real job, but deep down my motivations weren't completely spiteful for all the years they treated me like garbage. We really did need incomes, and to hell if I was going to shoulder the burden alone while they lounged around my house, ate my food, and made me chauffeur them around while they enacted this crazy scheme of theirs. A scheme I doubted they'd actually pull off, meaning I'd be stuck with them far longer than any of us had anticipated.

They didn't want to work, and I got that, because though I'd never admit it to them, I didn't want to work either. After forty years of being a stay-at-home wife, I hated to admit how much I struggled with the idea of getting a job... especially in a restaurant I'd bussed tables at as a teen. It felt like a giant step back in life, and the thought of toiling away waiting on tables instead of having people wait on me made me cringe. Then I cringed again that I'd grown so entitled that deep down, I *did* feel like waiting tables was beneath me. It pained me to realize how much I had internalized a sense of entitlement, and how far I'd fallen from the young, idealistic young girl I barely recognized. But feeling beneath me or not, we needed a job, and I wasn't going to tackle this hardship alone.

"I won't!" CeCe squealed, and the way she threw the childish tantrum only reinstated my resolve to see her miserable serving the local crowds at Mawmaw's.

"Last chance. You come in and get a job or you two are out on your own. I'm going in. The choice is yours." I left the truck door open and spun on my heel, striding as confidently as I could up the steps to Mawmaw's porch. I certainly hoped I looked more confident than I felt, because deep down, I was absolutely terrified.

My last 'real' employment involved serving and bussing tables at Mawmaw's during visits to Aunt Addie, working at a campus bookstore during college, and a nursing internship the summer before I met Rick. Decades had passed since then, leaving me to wonder if my limited experience was enough to excel in the workforce now. Despite the years, I was determined to prove myself, especially if Mawmaw May gave me a chance—I owed her my best.

I paused at the door to the diner and took a deep breath. *You need a job, Diane. Mawmaw May is kind and will help you relearn some skills. You aren't going to be like CeCe and depend on anyone else ever again. You've got this.*

Lifting my chin high, I reached for the handle.

"Wait! We're coming! Don't cut us off!" Julian called, and I turned around to see him and CeCe hustling across the gravel parking lot toward me.

I stifled my smile.

"Fine. We'll do it." CeCe pushed a piece of her windblown hair from her face. "But I'm never going to forgive you for this."

"You won't have to forgive me." I pulled open the door. "You'll thank me for teaching you to take care of yourself."

She huffed her disagreement, but I didn't bother turning around to argue. Instead, I straightened my shoulders and walked in with confidence I hoped would get us some jobs.

"Diane!" Mawmaw May greeted me with a huge grin when she spotted us. "Welcome back! Grab any open table you want. I'm the only server on, so I'll get there as soon as I can."

I glanced around at the tables all filled with locals, many of which we met at our rummage sale, and found an open booth. I gave them all friendly little waves, and they did the same in return.

"You two go sit down," I said to CeCe and Julian. "I'll talk to Mawmaw May about getting us jobs."

They grumbled, then stalked across the dining room like scolded children sent to the corner for a time out.

"Actually, that's what I came to talk to you about," I said to her as she ducked behind the bar to make some drinks. "We all need jobs, and I know you're short staffed."

Her eyes lifted and widened with excitement. "You want to work here?"

I lifted my hands. "To be clear, I haven't worked since I was twenty, and those two over there truly have no real-world work experience. We will need a big grace period to learn our way around here, but if you'll take a chance on us, we'd love to help out."

"Hired!" she shouted so loudly that the diners all glanced over.

I heard CeCe and Julian wail in protest, but I didn't turn around to pay attention to their dismay.

"Really? You'll hire us?"

She shoved a scoop of ice in a glass then started filling it from the gun. "I am desperate. I can't keep going at this pace. You three just stop in tomorrow morning when I'm not slammed, and we'll figure out where we can put you. If we can get you trained enough, you'll be ready to start tomorrow night."

I grinned widely, excited to be one step closer to standing on my own two feet again. "Thank you, Mawmaw May! You won't regret it!" I glanced back at CeCe and Julian who both had their heads pressed down on the wooden table, and I chuckled. "Okay, maybe you will regret it, but I swear I'm gonna work so hard for you, and once those two accept the fact they are working class now, they will as well."

Her warmth flooded out of her as she reached forward and touched my cheek. "I'll be so happy to see you all the time, Cher. I'll see you in the morning."

"See you in the morning." I leaned into the weight of her touch.

A customer waved for her attention, so she winked and rushed away. I turned around and walked over to the two defeated lumps pouting at the table.

"We start tomorrow," I said, remaining standing. "We'll come in the morning to get trained, and then tomorrow night is our first shift."

CeCe didn't look up from where she had her head buried in her arms. "I hate you."

I smiled. "I hate you too, but that doesn't change the fact you're going to have a job tomorrow."

Julian looked up at me with puppy dog eyes. "Are you sure I can't be the butler? I'll keep the house so tidy and make sure everything is done. The chore wheel!" He sat up straighter, his eyes lighting up. "I'll take care of the whole chore wheel! Just don't make me do this!"

CeCe shot upright. "Is that an option? I'll do it! I'll be in charge of the chore wheel and Julian can do the job!"

His mouth dropped open. "Hey! That's my idea! You can't steal my idea!"

After a few moments of being entertained by the two of them bickering back and forth, I interjected before it turned into a hair-pulling match. "No one is a butler. Butlers are for rich people. We are not rich. We are poor. Dirt poor. That means everyone gets a job, and everyone works. Starting tomorrow. Now, poor Mawmaw May is so busy I don't want to make her any busier and stay for food, so let's go home, make a pizza then watch our movie and get a good night's rest so we're ready for work tomorrow."

CeCe wailed loud enough she caught the attention of the tables around us, and a few men at the bar. When they turned around to look at us, I swallowed my gasp, recognizing John as one of the flannel-covered backs.

He gave me a shy wave, and memories flooded back once again of the beautiful boy I'd met when I was fourteen at my first summer carnival in Ruinville. The memory was preserved like a cherished photograph in the album of my heart, somehow untouched by time.

The first time our eyes locked. A few nervous glances and the exchange of shy smiles.

How he found me at the ring toss, frustrated I couldn't win the teddy bear, and offering to win it for me.

The sparks that ignited between us when he took my hand in his.

The nervous excitement exploding inside me at the end of the night when I leaned up and kissed his cheek.

He was my first crush, and the next time I'd seen him, he'd asked me to go for ice cream. It was the start of my first love and a chapter of my life I still cherished to this day.

"Did I just hear you're gonna be working at Mawmaw's?" a deep voice asked.

I spun around to see Sherrif Boshaw standing behind me, his distrustful eyes narrowing as they met mine.

"Hello, Sherrif Boshaw. Good to see you again. Yes. We'll be starting work here tomorrow."

He stepped a little closer. "Mawmaw May is like family to us. If I find out you've got some kind of trouble brewing for her, just know I'm gonna be right here watching you like a hawk."

I closed my eyes for a beat and took a breath. "Sherrif Boshaw. I know we had our little run in when I was a teenager, and I know that if you look me up on the internet right now, you'll see lots of crazy stories, but I can assure you, I'm no criminal."

"Mmmhmm." He bit the toothpick sticking out the side of his mouth. "That's what all the criminals say."

I sighed with exhaustion. "I'm not a criminal. And I would never do anything to hurt Mawmaw May. She's like family to me too."

"We ain't seen you around here for years, then suddenly you're back with a laundry list of accusations against you? Seems shady to me."

"I have nowhere to go," I admitted. "When my husband broke the law, without me knowing I'll add, he took off with all our money. I lost everything. Aunt Addie's place, and Ruinville, are the only things I have left. I swear I'm not here to cause trouble. I just want a fresh start."

A voice from behind me startled me when it said, "You giving Diane trouble, Bobby?"

I turned back to see John standing behind me. The close proximity of his body to mine sent a familiar shiver traveling up my spine. It was the same one I used to get right before he'd kiss me.

"I'm just making sure she knows we're watching her," Sherrif Boshaw defended. "Don't need no funny business in Ruinville."

"If I'm not mistaken, people are innocent until proven guilty. That's the law, right?" John said. "And you're a man of the law, correct?"

Sherrif Boshaw quirked a shoulder. "Yeah, I 'spose."

"And unless I'm mistaken, the state of New York and the FBI all found Diane innocent of all wrongdoing. Correct?"

With a grumble, Sherrif Boshaw gave a little nod.

"Then isn't it our duty to also treat her as an innocent citizen, Sherrif Boshaw? Lots of people get accused of wrongdoing every year that turn out to be innocent. I believe Diane here is one of them."

"I'm just saying, I know she was trouble when she was young too, so I've got to do my job and keep an eye on her."

John laughed. "We were all stupid kids at once. I did a whole mess of stupid crap as a teenager that you've forgiven me for." He paused. "May have taken a decade or so, but you know I'm a trustworthy man now. Right?"

"Well, I suppose," Sherrif Boshaw said. "You turned out all right it seems."

"Exactly." John stepped to my side, and I couldn't contain the little smile playing on my lips as he defended me. "I did a whole bunch of shady stuff, and I turned out just great. How about we trust that Diane is a good person too and give her the benefit of the doubt. She's just trying to rebuild her life. Isn't that right, Diane?"

I nodded in agreement. "I'm not here to cause trouble. I swear."

Sherrif Boshaw let out a hefty breath then dipped his chin. "Fine. But if you mess up, I'll be the first one to take you down."

His mustache twitched with a little snarl, then he spun on his boot and strode back to his table.

"Don't mind him," John said. "He's just bored and itching to find something to validate his existence. He hasn't seen any real crime here in years. Other than teens getting in trouble, of course... something I know we're both familiar with."

His eyes sparkled as he paused, and I knew his mind was drifting back to that night the same way mine did. Memories of his kiss... his touch... of that special bond we'd shared, flooded back into me.

John cleared his throat. "Uh, yeah. So, he's just bored. Don't take it personal. He's always been a grump, and he's getting worse as he ages. And now he's been watching too many of those true crime shows, and he's looking for trouble where it doesn't exist. I know you well enough to know you didn't do what they said you did. It may have been a long time since I've seen you, but I know you, Diane. Always have. Always will."

At first, the words he spoke warmed me straight to my core, but then I realized it meant he knew about my situation. I bit my lip, lowering my voice. "Thanks, Johnny... I mean John. I appreciate you sticking up for me. And it sounds like you know about my... situation?"

I looked back up into those familiar eyes. He gave me a little nod.

"Yeah. I, uh… everyone was talking about it. I hate to admit I looked it up online, and from what it sounds like, you got a really raw deal. I'm so sorry that your husband did that to you. I can't imagine what you're going through."

His gaze dropped to the ring I still wore, and I shifted to hide my hand behind my back. I'd almost taken off the ring a hundred times since that night the FBI knocked on my door, but to me, marriage was supposed to be for life. When Rick had slipped the diamond on my finger that day, I never wanted to take it off again. But now, things were so confusing. He was just… gone. Did that mean I was single? Still married? Stuck in limbo forever? Part of my heart mourned the loss of my marriage… the familiarity. The known. We hadn't been passionate lovers for years, but he'd still been my partner… my friend. But for the one part of my heart that broke at how he'd hurt and abandoned me, the other part of my heart beat wildly at the thrill of the unknown… at the prospect of finding new love again.

I looked deeper into John's eyes.

Or re-finding love again, perhaps.

"Diane!" Julian called from the booth behind me. "Can we go now? If I'm going to be stuck slaving away here for the rest of my life, I'd like to go spend one last night at home before I become indentured here."

I chuckled. "Sorry. I'm making them get jobs here. We all are. They aren't impressed."

"You're really gonna be working here again?"

"Yep. Let's hope I can remember how to do this."

His soft smile lit up my insides. "You'll be great, Diane. You always were. And I guess since I eat dinner here almost every night, I'll be seeing you soon."

"Yeah." I smiled. "I'll, uh, I'll see you soon."

"Night, Diane," he said.

"Good night, John."

He gave me one last look then turned and headed back to his stool at the bar. I exhaled a breath and tried to calm the excitement bubbling inside me at the prospect of seeing him again.

You're still married, Diane. Just focus on the job.

"It smells like deep fried death in here," CeCe said as she stood from the table. "I'm with Julian. If I'm gonna be stuck inhaling this crap every night, I want out of here now. One last night before our lives are over."

"Okay, okay." I started toward the door. "Let's go home."

I glanced over my shoulder one last time, and I caught John's soft stare. With a little smile, I gave him a wave, then headed out for our last night as unemployed, destitute socialites.

CHAPTER THIRTEEN
CeCe

"The what goes in the what?" I asked Mawmaw May as I stared down at the glass I'd just filled with a combination of tomato juice, some strange brown stuff I couldn't pronounce, hot sauce and vodka.

She continued wearing her patient smile. The same one she'd maintained since the moment I'd started my very first shift working.

Ever.

I hadn't thought I could fall any lower than the day I was ousted from my own penthouse and left homeless on the street, but nothing compared to the sheer horror of starting my first job. And at a rundown bar in the bayou no less. My parents must be rolling in their grave seeing their only daughter, born and bred for greatness, preparing to serve cheap beer and fried food.

I shuddered.

"Like this, Cher. The pickle and the meat stick go in the drink like this. Just skewer them with an olive. Then voila. A Bloody Mary."

I frowned. "I know how to drink a Bloody Mary, I just never realized how much goes into making them. I thought you said everyone pretty much drinks beer and simple mixed drinks like those rum and cokes I was making. This one is complicated."

She touched my arm and smiled. "You'll get the hang of it. In a few weeks you'll be buzzing around behind this bar like a pro. Everyone starts somewhere."

With another one of her big, warm grins, she spun off and pushed the half doors open as she went into the kitchen. While the short, wooden doors swung back and forth behind her, I caught a glimpse of Julian in the kitchen at the dishwasher. I couldn't see his face, but I assumed it was streaked with tears as he scrubbed disgusting food off plates in his new position as a dishwasher and busser. My poor, sweet Julian. I pressed a hand to my chest as I watched him tentatively grab a dirty pot, his fingers barely gripping the rim as he hoisted it into the sink then dropped it into the suds.

The only one who seemed to be thriving in this new horrific role of employee was, of course, Diane. She practically flitted around between the tables, grinning so wide at the customers I thought her face would rip... the face I wanted to clobber that smile straight off. We'd trained for two hours earlier in the day, and she'd been a complete natural. I'd hoped once our actual shift started, the pressure of the hungry diners would cause her to crack and abandon this stupid decision forcing us all into jobs, but no. Of course not. She seemed to be absolutely loving it and managed to keep that irritating glow about her as she practically skipped toward me with a new order.

"Two rum and cokes please, barkeep." She grinned.

I scowled, my eyes impaling her with a glare before I spun and stomped to the glasses, grabbing one and shoving a scoop of ice into it.

Her cheery voice grated on me as she said, "This isn't so bad at all! I'm getting to know so much about the locals already. I've had four tables so far, and everyone is just so nice. And I'm making decent tips! Doesn't it feel good to be making our own way?"

I topped the drink off with the soda gun, marched over to her and slammed it on the bar. "No," I answered, then stomped away.

I heard her chuckle, and it sent a shiver down my spine. "Don't be such a grouch," she teased. "You'll get some customers soon, and when you earn your first dollar, you're gonna be so proud of yourself. I'm proud of you already."

I didn't turn around. Instead, I closed my eyes, as if by sheer willpower, I could make this all disappear. This bar, this town, this entire God forsaken state. None of it would exist, and instead of degrading myself as a bartender at a hole in the wall in the bayou, I would be back in my penthouse, surrounded by the opulence I once knew. A small smile tugged at the corners of my lips as I conjured the memories of standing in my closet surrounded by vibrant clothes and the rich scent of luxury. How soft they felt as I reached out and ran my fingers across them. For a fleeting moment, I fell back to heaven, until a man cleared his throat behind me.

An internal growl rumbled just beneath my surface as someone rudely yanked me out of my daydream and dumped me right back into my nightmare. "Evening, Pretty Girl," he said, his voice unmistakable.

Reluctantly, I turned to see Bayou Bill, his devilish grin sending a disconcerting flutter through my stomach. "Looking mighty fine back there," he complimented, tipping his camouflage hat, embroidered with "Bayou Bill's Boat Tours" and an alligator logo. "Gotta say, you sure do class up the joint. You're the prettiest bartender in the whole damn South."

I fought back the urge to smile, but my lips betrayed me, quirking up at the corners. The way his eyes appraised me with an intensity I hadn't felt in a long time sent a warm flush creeping up my cheeks. In New York, we were surrounded by twenty-year-old models who garnered all the attention. But here, in this bayou bar, Bill looked at me like I had just stepped off the Victoria's Secret runway, and, against my better judgment, I found myself enjoying the feeling.

Young again. Beautiful. Sexy, even. Words I hadn't felt in far too long.

"I'll just take a draft of Bud Light if ya don't mind," Bill requested, resting his elbows on the bar, his gaze never leaving me.

"Sure. Yeah. Coming right up," I stammered, flustered by the strange emotions he stirred within me. As I spun around to get his beer, I closed my eyes and chastised myself for allowing a bayou local to make me feel such things.

Stop it, CeCe. Just because you've fallen to such unfathomable depths doesn't mean men like Bayou Bill are appropriate to flirt with. He's disgusting. A camouflage-covered redneck is still a camouflage-covered redneck, even if he does have the prettiest damn eyes you've ever seen. And that smile... Wow. It sure can turn your whole world upside down.

I halted mid-thought and scolded myself again, this time more forcefully. *Seriously, CeCe! Stay on track! Do not flirt back with the creepy gator guy!*

As I glanced over my shoulder at Bill, my stomach did an exhilarating flip. Under my breath, I muttered a curse and hurried to secure an empty beer glass. Once it was filled to the brim, I returned to his seat and set it before him. His eyebrows arched toward his hairline as he peered down at the frothy concoction.

"What?" I asked, my brow furrowing in response to his amused expression.

Bill leaned in closer, his eyes dancing with mischief. "Nothing. It's just, uh... it's all foam."

I glanced at the glass filled with snowy bubbles and shrugged. "That's how it came out. Not my problem."

"You do know there's a way to make it not all foam, right?"

Memories of Mawmaw May explaining the art of pouring a draft of beer resurfaced, albeit faintly. I'd crammed my head with so much information earlier today that it felt like it had leaked right back out.

I shrugged. "That's how I pour them. Take it or leave it."

"Or I can show ya how it's done."

"I can manage this on my own, thank you very much."

Bill leaned in even closer, his sapphire eyes twinkling with mischief. "You sure about that? It looks like the beer says otherwise."

"It's fine. I wanted it to look like that," I fibbed, my resolve wavering under his charm.

He chuckled, stood up, and sauntered around the bar, slipping behind it.

"Hey! What are you doing? You can't be back here!" I protested.

Bill seemed impervious to my objections and just gestured for me to follow. When I noticed Mawmaw May overseeing the situation without rebuke, I reluctantly trailed behind Bill to the beer taps.

"I worked here a few summers, and I know my way around. Just watch and learn, Pretty Girl. When you pour a beer, you gotta tip the glass like this," Bill instructed.

He lifted an empty glass to the metal spout and tilted it just before pulling the tap handle. The golden liquid cascaded down the side of the glass, and I watched in awe as he expertly filled the beer, yielding only an inch of frothy head.

"See? Like that. Now, it's your turn," he said, stepping aside and handing me an empty glass.

Though I felt embarrassed to be seeking assistance from Bayou Bill, I couldn't resist the opportunity to master the technique. I pressed the glass against the metal spout and pulled the handle. As the beer flowed, the foam began to fill the glass.

"It's happening again!" I exclaimed. "It's broken!"

"Like this." Bill chuckled, reaching over and encircling my hand with his own. The instant our skin made contact, I felt sparks of electricity dance between us. His body brushed against mine as he sidled behind me, leaning in close to help angle the glass just right.

"See, like that," he whispered, his warm breath sending a shiver coursing through my body. "It's all about finesse, CeCe. You need to treat it gently. Handle it with care... like a woman."

I couldn't recall the last time a man had made me feel this way. Twenty years? Thirty? Maybe never?

I cursed myself for succumbing to the magnetic attraction and for the way I leaned back into his body as I closed my eyes and fantasized about a passionate moment with him right there on the bar, our clothes discarded in the heat of desire.

"There. A perfect beer," he announced, flipping off the tap handle. Gradually, his hand slid away from mine, and as our physical connection broke, the spell I'd been under shattered as well.

I spun around to face him, aghast by the daydreams I'd concocted and mortified that I'd engaged in such a public display with Bayou Bill.

I frantically scanned the oblivious customers, anxiety gnawing at me.

Did anyone see that?

"All you need to remember is to tip the glass. See? Works like a charm." His charming grin couldn't dispel my shock.

I glanced toward Julian, who stood holding a tray of clean glasses, his eyes wide and mirroring the dismay I felt within. We stood frozen, exchanging horrified glances, and I knew that he'd witnessed the few moments of embarrassing canoodling with Bill.

Bill finally made his exit, strolling past Julian with his perfectly poured beer. "Hey, Julian," he said in passing.

Julian remained silent, his gaze locked with mine. After Bill found his seat, I gathered the courage to move my feet and rush over to Julian, seizing his arm and almost causing him to drop his tray of glasses.

"You saw nothing," I whispered urgently into his ear.

"I don't know what I just saw, but it definitely wasn't nothing," he replied in a hushed tone. "You were practically getting dry humped by Bayou Bill, and... I swear you looked like you were enjoying it!"

I stepped back, hands on my hips. "He was not dry humping me, and I did not enjoy it. He was showing me how to pour a beer."

Julian's eyebrow rose in a challenge, lips pursed together. "Mmmhmm."

I scowled. "It's the truth. You saw nothing because nothing happened."

His lips twitched with a smirk. "Mmmhmm."

"Julian!"

He sighed and rolled his eyes. "Fine. Nothing happened. I did not just come out here to see you grinding your ass against the gator guy." He glanced over at Bill as he sipped his perfectly poured beer, then he tipped his head. "Although, I will say he certainly is a fine-looking gator guy. I mean, once you strip away the weird clothes and the funny accent. Maybe give him a haircut and a cleaner shave." He tipped his head the other way. "You know... if you aren't going to keep grinding on the gator guy, maybe I should give it a spin."

"Hey!" I slapped his shoulder, and he almost dropped his glasses. "Stay away from him."

He grinned widely. "You like the gator guy."

"Do not," I argued back, but I hated that my words lacked the certainty I wanted them to have.

"Mmmhmm," he said as he walked around me and smiled.

Julian, in his teasing state, failed to notice a box of plastic cups protruding from under the bar rail. He struck it with his toe, stumbled forward, and with a deafening scream followed by shattering glass, he tumbled to the ground behind the bar.

"Julian!" I raced to his side where he lay face down, grabbing his hand and calling out to him. "Are you hurt? Are you okay?"

Diane appeared behind me, her voice panicked. "What happened? Is he hurt?"

Julian remained unresponsive, and my heart pounded in my chest as I stared at my best friend, lying in a heap.

"What happened?" Mawmaw May asked as she joined us.

Bill peered over the bar. "He tripped over that box and fell. Is he alright?"

"Julian! Are you hurt?" I demanded, shaking him.

Finally, he rolled onto his back and looked up at me, his eyes shimmering with tears. "Am I hurt?" he asked, his gaze locked onto mine. "Am I hurt? Yes, I am hurt! I'm a dishwasher in a Podunk town in the freaking bayou! My pride is hurt! Everything hurts! This can't be my life!"

He wailed as he lay on the dirty bar floor, and I had to muster every ounce of my strength not to flop down beside him and join him in lamenting the cruel world.

"What the hell happened?" Gumbo Gus barked, emerging from the kitchen.

"A little accident," Mawmaw May answered. "I don't think he's hurt though. Is he?"

"He's okay," Diane answered.

Gumbo Gus grumbled disapprovingly, shaking his head. "This is a bad idea, Mawmaw. They shouldn't be working here."

Mawmaw May approached him, placing a reassuring hand on his shoulder. "They need our help. It's the charitable thing to do. Just give them a chance to learn, Gus. They'll be alright. You'll see."

Charity. I scoffed inwardly at the irony. I had spent my life donating millions to charitable causes, yet now I found myself on the receiving end of charity. The thought almost made me break into hysterical laughter. For a fleeting moment, I considered reaching out to those organizations and asking for a refund, but the reality hit me hard—there was no going back. This was my life now, our lives, and as much as I loathed every second of this existence, I had to help my friend push through it.

"Come on, Julian," I said, my voice determined as I reached down to grasp his hand. "Let's get you up."

"I'm just going to stay here. Forever," Julian mumbled, his defeat palpable on the rubber-matted floor.

"We have to keep going, Julian," I urged, my words a desperate plea. "Just a little longer, and then we'll find our next husband, okay?" I whispered, the promise hanging in the air between us. "Just keep going. We have to keep going. We'll be back in a penthouse in no time."

His glassy eyes met mine, seeking reassurance. "You promise?"

"I promise," I said, my voice unwavering. "I'm getting us out of this stupid town."

"Good. I hate Brokeville. We don't belong here." A glimmer of hope flickered in his eyes, and a faint smile tugged at his lips. With a firm grip, I helped him up, refusing to let despair claim us.

"Are you okay?" Diane asked, her concern evident as she lightly brushed Julian with her hands. "Any injuries?"

He shook his head. "No. I'm not hurt. Maybe a light bruise or two tomorrow, but that's it."

"Thank God," Diane exhaled, leaning forward to embrace him gently.

Julian stiffened initially but gradually softened into her comforting hug.

"I got a broom," Bill announced, entering the scene with a broom and dustpan in hand.

"Oh, you don't work here. I don't think that's your job," I protested, though he ignored my objection, advancing toward the scattered broken glass.

"Happy to help ya out, Pretty Girl. Anytime," he said, his grin infectious.

I couldn't suppress my smile, but the knowing looks exchanged between Julian and Diane brought me back to reality. "Okay, show's over, everyone back to work!" I declared, attempting to regain control of the situation.

They returned to their respective tasks, leaving me alone with Bill. He assisted me in cleaning up the mess, his effortless charm putting me at ease and irking me at the same time. After we finished, he returned to his seat at the bar.

"Thanks again for your help," I said, placing a fresh beer in front of him.

He glanced down at it, grinning appreciatively. "Not bad, Pretty Girl. Almost a perfect pour. You're really getting the hang of this."

Although I hated admitting the truth in his words because I, CeCe VanTramp, *shouldn't* be getting the hang of bartending, I couldn't deny the sense of accomplishment that washed over me. Yet, my triumph was short-lived as another challenge emerged in the form of a disheveled man with wild eyes and even wilder hair.

I gasped.

The scary man we'd passed on the road that day we came into town.

"I... dr.. be...col... one.. ank...you... me... Wa.. nic," he sputtered, his words unintelligible.

Terrified, I looked to Bill for help, my eyes pleading for rescue.

"CeCe, meet Whacky Wade. Whacky Wade, meet CeCe," Bill introduced, his ease in understanding the man's garbled speech astonishing. "He got hit by lightning 'bout twenty years ago, and his words have been all jumbled ever since. You'll get used to it."

I pointed at Whacky Wade. "You think I'll understand that?"

Bill chuckled. "He said he needs a cold pint of beer, and his name is Wade. It's nice to meet you."

My amazement turned into disbelief when Wade nodded in agreement.

"How is anything surprising me anymore?" I muttered to myself as I poured another beer for him. Wade expressed gratitude in more strange jargon, and I shot a look at Bill to help translate his chaotic words.

"He says thank you, Pretty Girl." Bill said, then leaned forward. "Well, I added the Pretty Girl."

When he winked, I cursed my face for flushing, and I glanced back to the kitchen to see Julian staring at me over the wooden doors, an accusatory smile lifting his lips.

Shaking off the accusation I saw in his eyes... the one I hated to admit was true... I grabbed a rag and started wiping the bar like Mawmaw May had instructed me. More people filed in, and soon Diane and Mawmaw May were both hustling up spitting out drink orders for me to make. When I got all twisted around over a big one, Bill pushed up out of his stool and strode behind the bar again.

"What are you doing back here?" I asked as I frantically searched for the bottle of Johnny Walker.

Bill pressed his hands to my hips and scooted me over, then reached down and stood back up holding up the bottle. "They keep that one back here."

"Thanks," I said, still trying to erase the tingles in my skin where his hands had just been.

"Tell ya what," he said as he grabbed a glass. "Let me put those years I spent tending bar here to good use, and I'll help teach ya the ropes tonight."

"You will? Really?" I said, my eyes lighting up at the offer.

"I won't look as good as you back here, of course, but I'll show ya what I know."

With his wink, my stomach did that somersault thing I'd thought had ceased back in my youth.

"Thanks, Bill." I moved aside to allow him space. Together, we tackled the large order of drinks, his expertise guiding my uncertain hands.

As the night wore on, Bill showed me how to close the bar, his patient guidance easing my nerves. When we finished, he tipped his hat and headed for the door. "You think ya got it down now, Pretty Girl?"

"No," I replied honestly. "But I'm closer. Thanks for your help tonight."

"Anytime, Pretty Girl," he said with a wink, his departing smile leaving me oddly breathless. I watched him leave and couldn't help but let my eyes indulge in the way his rear end filled out those jeans.

"Well, we did it!" Diane exclaimed, collapsing onto a barstool. "Our first shift is complete! That wasn't so bad, was it?"

"It was awful!" Julian's voice echoed from the kitchen, his tone laden with sarcasm.

I stared at the closed door, where Bill had just vanished, my smile growing despite Julian's comments. "It was awful," I agreed with Julian, not wanting to admit the truth to Diane.

Serving those repugnant customers had been a trial, but in that moment, I had never felt prouder. I had worked, taken a step toward self-sufficiency, and, against all odds, survived.

CHAPTER FOURTEEN
Diane

I meticulously transcribed the order onto my notepad, utilizing the shorthand that Gumbo Gus used, a skill I'd been gradually honing. Phrases like "chix" for chicken, "BCB" for bacon cheeseburger, and "FA" for fried alligator filled the page. It felt somewhat peculiar to jot down "SOS," a distress signal, but in Gus's world, it simply meant "sauce on the side." With focused, lip-chewing concentration, I meticulously wrote the order. A grin formed on my face when I examined the properly completed list.

"Ha! I'm really getting the hang of this!" I triumphantly declared to CeCe, passing her at the bar as I hung the order in the window.

CeCe, occupied with the struggle of opening a beer bottle, responded dryly, "Well, aren't you a special one?"

I signaled Gus with a cheerful bell ring, indicating the order was ready, and then I gave a smile to Julian. He returned it with a glower then resumed scrubbing the baked-on gumbo from the dirty pot.

Even though Julian and CeCe still weren't as thrilled about working and supporting themselves as I was, the past week we'd really started to find our stride. We'd even gone an entire evening last night without anyone breaking anything, and Julian had only burst into tears once instead of every few minutes like he had the first few shifts.

Progress.

"Hey, Diane," a deep voice said, and I turned to see John walking toward the bar.

Just the sight of him sent a shiver down my spine. I fumbled with the hem of my apron, suddenly conscious of every detail in my appearance. His mere presence made me feel like I was walking on a tightrope, trying to find the right balance between maintaining my composure and giving in to the butterflies that caused my stomach to churn. Nervous excitement coursed through me as I smiled at the man who made my knees tremble with his smile, just the way he used to when I was a smitten teenager. Although I had seen him at the bar nearly every night for the past week, his effect on me showed no signs of waning.

"Hey, John," I said back, keeping it short and simple like I did every night. We'd exchange a few pleasantries, he'd have his dinner, and when he left, we'd exchange a few more words.

"How's it going?" he said as he walked past me. "Busy tonight?"

"Not bad," I responded.

"Looks like you're all getting the hang of things here?"

He sat at the bar, and CeCe snorted. "We haven't killed anyone or burned the place down, so I guess that's something."

"That's something," he answered with a smile. "And I'm the fire chief, so if you do start a fire, I'm right here to put it out before you turn the place into nothing but ashes."

I pictured him in his sexy fireman uniform battling the flames, and my heart revved up again. My tables needed my attention, so pushing the tantalizing images from my head, I left him at the bar and hurried off to take orders and deliver more food. Even while I worked, my eyes always continued sliding over to John as he ate his usual dinner, and I felt jealous he was sitting at the bar with CeCe instead of at a table where I could spend more time with him. Although, I was also grateful that I didn't have to serve him because I worried I'd turn into a bumbling idiot every time he grinned at me.

When he finished his dinner at his usual time, he tossed back the rest of his beer then left cash on the counter. CeCe took the money off to the till, and he strode over toward me before he left.

"You outta here?" I asked.

He placed his hands in his pockets and rocked back on his heels. "Yup. Got an early start tomorrow. Need to get some shuteye."

"Yeah? Got a fire planned at sunrise or something?" I teased.

He chuckled. "No. The firehouse guys and I are working on our gumbo recipe for the big fundraiser getting thrown in the town center in a few days. You going?"

I scrunched my brow. "I hadn't heard about it."

"Yeah. Kinda last minute. One of my guys, Tyrell Landry, broke his leg yesterday, and he'll be out of work for at least a month or two. His wife is pregnant and on bed rest, so they won't have income at a time they really can't afford it, not to mention the extra expenses from his surgery. We're throwing together a fundraiser on Saturday to help him cover his bills while he's out of work. Nothing too fancy. Just a little community shindig."

I smiled. "I remember there used to be a ton of fundraisers in Ruinville."

"We still do 'em," he confirmed. "Taking care of our own is a part of why I chose to stay in Ruinville. Having a great community around you is a gift many people don't appreciate."

"Yeah. I get that more than you know," I said, realizing maybe I could have found more happiness here in this small town than I'd ever found in my life in New York.

But before I could ponder that question more, Mawmaw May rushed over, enthusiastically waving a piece of paper. "Don't forget your gift certificate!"

John accepted the gift certificate from her. "We really appreciate you chipping in."

She playfully swatted his shoulder. "Don't be silly. We adore the Landry family around here. Happy to contribute to their cause. The certificate is good for two full dinners and two drinks, so don't let them skimp out on you during the auction."

She emphasized her point by wagging her finger at him, and he nodded in agreement. "I won't, Mawmaw."

Mawmaw May turned her attention to me, her eyes lighting up. "And what about you, dear? Are you contributing anything?"

I hesitated, caught off guard. "I'm just hearing about this now, actually."

With a reminiscent gleam in her eye, she said, "Your Aunt Addie used to be at the forefront of every fundraiser in Ruinville. She was famous for those delicious cookies of hers.

Maybe you should bake some cookies for the fundraiser. I'm sure she'd love that."

Nervousness coursed through me as I tried to recall the basics of baking, and even though I wasn't sure I even remembered how to crack an egg, I nodded in agreement. "That's a fantastic idea. I'll make sure to do that."

"Wonderful!" Mawmaw clapped her hands in delight then sped off to another table.

As I tried to remember anything about baking, I must have worn the worry plain on my face.

John tilted his head thoughtfully. "You don't seem too sure about this."

I sucked in a deep breath through my teeth. "It's been quite a while since I've baked anything, but I'll give it my best shot."

John smirked, a hint of humor in his eyes. "Just make sure you have a fire extinguisher handy."

I chuckled. "I might just need it. Hopefully, I won't set Aunt Addie's house ablaze while trying to bake cookies."

"Well, if you do, just call 911 and I'll be there."

I smiled and laughed. "Keep your pager on. This could go south fast."

"Well, I think it's a lovely gesture," John said. "Mawmaw is right. Your Aunt Addie would be proud. I'm looking forward to seeing you at the town square on Saturday."

His eyes sparkled, creating a warm glow that resonated within me. "Yes, I'm looking forward to seeing you too."

As he headed toward the exit, he paused and turned back. "Hand me that order pad and your pen."

I wrinkled my nose in curiosity but complied, handing over the order pad and pen. John jotted something down on the order pad and then handed it back to me. I glanced down at the number on the paper.

"My number," he explained, a teasing glint in his eyes. "You know, in case you set the kitchen on fire and need a direct line if 911 is backed up."

I burst into laughter, tearing the number off and stashing it in my apron. "Thanks, John. Let's hope I don't have to use this."

He paused for a moment and added, "Don't hesitate to call. Anytime."

With a swift nod, he walked out the door, leaving me feeling like the whole world had suddenly turned upside down again. After taking a moment to regain my composure, I headed back to the kitchen to check if my order was ready.

"Diane and John sitting in a tree," CeCe began to sing playfully.

I narrowed my eyes and quickly retorted, "CeCe and Bayou Bill, sitting in a tree..."

Her eyes widened, and she abruptly fell silent. I couldn't help but flash a mischievous grin. Bayou Bill was a regular presence on the nights CeCe was working, and no matter how hard she tried to hide it, she looked like an elated schoolgirl when he flirted with her.

Probably the same way I looked when I saw John.

Neither of us wanted to invite more playful teasing, so we promptly returned to our duties, finishing our shifts without further mention of the two men who'd been frequenting the bar.

"See you all tomorrow night!" Mawmaw exclaimed, waving goodbye to the three of us.

I blew her a kiss and then led my exhausted coworkers out to 'Ol Blue.

"You driving us home tonight, CeCe?" I asked, hoping she would practice the driving skills I'd been forcing her to hone. First, we'd just gone around the yard for a while, but she'd made two successful drives down the road. Well, successful if you called her screaming every time she had to shift success, but we hadn't crashed, so I called it a win. I'd taught Julian as well, but he put up such a big fit about driving anymore that I stopped even asking.

She shook her head and whipped open the passenger door. "No. It's bad enough you're making me learn how to drive this hunk of junk. I draw the line at doing it in the dark and when I'm dizzy from exhaustion. You drive."

Not wanting to a get in an accident on the way home, I didn't argue. We climbed in, settling into our seats with sighs of relief.

"When are my feet going to stop hurting?" CeCe whined as she kicked off her Walmart-bought sneakers, a far cry from the heels that had nearly crippled her during our first shifts. "You said wearing these monstrosities would prevent my feet from swelling and aching."

"It'll still take time for your feet to adapt. We aren't accustomed to eight-hour shifts on our feet. Mine hurt too, but we're definitely better off in sneakers than Manolo's."

"Speak for yourselves," Julian chimed in, gesturing to his designer Prada loafers. "These are much better than the clodhoppers you two are wearing."

CeCe rubbed her socked foot. "So, your feet aren't hurting, then?"

Julian frowned. "No, they hurt like hell. They just look a lot better."

I chuckled as I fired up the old truck and began our drive home. When we arrived, we followed our usual routine, starting with checking for Peggy to ensure she didn't surprise us. We had stumbled upon her around the yard a few times, resulting in frantic screams and zig-zag dashes as we scrambled away from the bewildered creature. Thanks to our work at Mawmaw's, we could take home the near-expired meat, and we had a new nightly ritual of feeding Peggy that would hopefully stop her from venturing into the kitchen for a snack.

"Who has the leftovers box for Peggy?" I asked.

Julian responded, "It's me," and handed me the white Styrofoam box that Gus sent us home with.

I took the box outside and tossed the meat toward the water's edge. All three of us sprinted inside when we spotted Peggy emerging from the water, sliding her way toward her nightly treat.

"God, I hate that thing!" Julian yelled as he rushed to the front door.

"Open the door! Open it! Open it!" CeCe raced up the steps after Julian.

We all tumbled inside, gasping for breath as we caught our composure. One by one, we removed our shoes and purses and collapsed onto the couch.

"Ugh. I hate working almost as much as I hate that alligator," Julian huffed.

CeCe echoed the sentiment and propped her legs up on Julian's lap.

I shrugged. "I won't lie and claim I love it, but I am genuinely proud of us for what we've achieved. We're self-sufficient now, and that's something to be really proud of."

Both Julian and CeCe rolled their eyes, and Julian made a playful plea. "Just hurry up and find our sugar daddy, okay, CeCe?"

"I promise. Soon." She patted his leg. "I've almost saved enough tips to get us a weekend in the city, so we can start our search."

Julian squealed with excitement then leaned over to kiss her forehead.

I silently bore my irritation with their ridiculous plan of finding an old, wealthy man to depend on instead of learning to fend for themselves. Still, I had given up on arguing the point, as they were on their own journey, and I was on mine.

My new mission, I quickly remembered, involved learning how to bake cookies.

"Oh, crap. I need to find that recipe," I said, heaving my weary body off the couch.

CeCe tipped her head. "What recipe are you talking about?"

"My Aunt Addie was renowned for her chocolate chip oatmeal cookies, which she used to sell at every fundraiser. They've asked me to make some for the fundraiser this Saturday."

Julian chimed in, pouting, "When are we getting *our* fundraiser? We deserve one too."

I patted his head. "We're doing just fine. There are people who need it more than we do."

"Doubtful." He pushed my hand away.

With my new mission to step into Aunt Addie's shoes driving me on, I left my exhausted roommates and ventured to the kitchen, searching for the boxes of recipes I recalled from my teenage years. I brought them down and settled into a chair at the table, sifting through countless recipes, each one brimming with memories of cooking with Aunt Addie or savoring her delicious meals on the porch.

Apple pie. Chicken jambalaya. Chocolate bundt cake. Bananas Foster. Fried green tomatoes with crawfish.

My mouth watered as I recollected the tantalizing smells and flavors of Aunt Addie's incredible dishes. As the memories washed over me, so did the guilt I felt for losing touch with her. I pressed a hand to the recipe card with her elegant handwriting.

"I'm so sorry I wasn't there for you, Aunt Addie."

I knew she wouldn't have held it against me... she was too kind, but it didn't quell the burning need I had to make her proud. And that would start with taking up her mantle in contributing to the fundraisers just like she used to. When I saw the cookie recipe, tattered and torn, I grinned as I hoisted it triumphantly. These were her famous oatmeal chocolate chip cookies, and I would do whatever it took to bring her joy back to the community she loved so much.

Then I frowned when I stood up and looked around the kitchen completely clueless where to begin.

CHAPTER FIFTEEN
CeCe

Julian and I squealed in unison as I squeezed the truck into the tiny parking space at The Crawfish Corner Store, the local Ruinville grocery store. When we managed to get in without hitting anyone, I breathed a sigh of relief.

"I hate Diane for making me drive this piece of crap! It's bad enough she makes us ride in it, but now she's all, 'I'm not a chauffer. You two need to learn to drive yourselves around.'" I mimicked her voice with an exaggerated hand gesture and growled as I turned off the ignition.

It backfired, causing Julian and I to scream once again.

"I hate this thing! I hate this thing! I hate this thing!" Julian pounded his fists on the dashboard.

I tossed the keys at him. "Well, I did my part. Now you have to drive it home."

"Please don't make me." He pouted. "It's scary. I really don't like it."

I raised an eyebrow. "And I do? No, if I have to drive this blasted truck, you have to drive it as well. We both know equally little about it. It's your fault we're in this situation anyway. Why did you have to go and tell her we still have valid driver's licenses? We could have lied and said we weren't legally allowed to drive this pile of crap, but nooooo... you had to open your big mouth, and now look at us."

He sucked the air through his teeth. "Yeah. I probably never should have said that."

My eyebrows lifted higher as I pursed my lips. "Well, you did. And now we're stuck driving it. *Both* of us. Now, we had a deal: I drive here, and you drive back."

With a whimper, he reluctantly accepted the keys. "Fine. But if I die behind the wheel of this thing, I'm coming back to haunt you."

"Deal," I agreed with a stiff shake of his hand. "Because I'll probably be a ghost too, and then we can haunt people together."

His eyes lit up! "Oh! We're starting with that bitch Mindy Masterson who stole our seats at Fashion Week!" His eyes widened. "Oh! Oh! Then there was this guy, Tim Chase, in high school who made my life a living hell. Can we haunt him too?"

"Of course we can. We'll make a haunting hit list."

He clapped. "Yay! I mean, I don't want to die in this hunk of junk, but at least if we do, I have something to look forward to."

We shared a brief, playful smile and then hopped out of the truck, making our way into the grocery store to gather the supplies Diane needed for her attempt at cookie-baking.

I held up the piece of paper Diane had scribbled on. "Alright, we've got our list. Now we just need to find everything. Divide and conquer?"

Julian hesitated for a moment before nodding. "I'll take the top half."

I ripped the list jotted on the yellow note paper and handed Julian the top portion. We each headed off in opposite directions to hunt down the items we needed. Diane was determined to fill Aunt Addie's shoes by providing her famous oatmeal chocolate chip cookies for the fundraiser in two days, leaving us in charge of the baking supplies.

"Alright, let's see... oats. Where on Earth are the oats?" I muttered, feeling somewhat lost in the small grocery store.

"Need some help, Pretty Girl?" Bill's voice caught me by surprise, and I turned to find him grinning with his trademark knee-weakening smile.

"What are you doing here?" I planted my hands on my hips. "Are you stalking me?"

Bill chuckled and clucked the side of his cheek. "Nah, it seems we're just drawn together, you and me. The universe keeps pushing us into each other's paths. You ready to stop resisting?"

I scoffed. "Never."

His grin grew wider. "You will. What's got ya looking so lost?"

"Oats," I replied. "I need to find oats and all these other ridiculous items on this list so Diane can attempt her hand at making special chocolate chip oatmeal cookies."

Bill's eyes lit up with excitement. "She's making Aunt Addie's famous oatmeal chocolate chip cookies? Oh man! I thought we'd never get to enjoy those delicious treats again after we lost sweet Aunt Addie."

"Well, don't hold your breath," I cautioned. "She's not exactly a culinary wizard. These cookies might taste like dog food."

He twisted his lips. "Hmm. I guess I'll take a heed of caution with my first bite then. Do ya need help finding the ingredients?"

"Would you?" I asked, handing him the list. "I'd really appreciate that. I'll wait right here."

Bill's laughter vibrated through his shoulders. "Okay, princess. I'm not your errand boy, but I'll go with you to show you where everything is. I won't do your shopping for you, though."

I frowned. "Fine. Let's go."

"This way, Pretty Girl."

I hated that he called me that, but more than that, I hated how much I loved it. It made me feel young and beautiful again; something I hadn't felt in a very long time. I followed along behind him learning about how the grocery store was laid out, and when we grabbed the baking soda, the last item on the list, we turned the corner and smacked right into Julian. A sly grin crossed Julian's face when he saw us together.

"Well, well, well," Julian quipped. "Crocodile Dundee. What a surprise."

"Hey there, Julian," Bill responded with a smile.

"I just ran into him, and he's helping me find the items on the list," I explained.

Julian raised an eyebrow and smirked at me. "Is that all you're using him for?"

I glared at Julian. "Yes."

"Mmmhmm," Julian muttered, doing nothing to hide the disbelief in his tone.

"Just let me know if you found everything on your list," I said, ignoring his implications.

"I did." Julian pointed to his small red shopping cart. "The only one I'm not sure about is the vanilla. I got vanilla ice cream. Is that right?"

"That sounds correct to me," I said with a shrug.

Bill snorted. "For cookies, y'all are looking for vanilla extract, not vanilla ice cream."

"How the hell do you know that?" I propped a hand on my hip.

He mirrored my gesture. "Because I know my way around a kitchen, that's how. I've been single all my life. You either learn to cook or you starve. Julian, go put that ice cream back and CeCe and I will go get the correct vanilla. We'll meet you back at the register to check out. Come on, Pretty Girl."

He jutted his chin toward the center aisle, and I begrudgingly trailed along behind him. After he showed me what vanilla we were really after, I followed him back to the checkout line. We added up all our items, and I paid the lady with the cash I'd made in tips the night before. Bill grabbed the bag of chickens for alligator bait he was there to pick up and then followed me through the parking lot.

"Ready for our date?" Bill leaned casually against our truck, his arms crossed over his broad chest, camouflaged attire contrasting with the everyday surroundings.

I scoffed, a smirk tugging at my lips. "You've been asking every night, and my answer remains unchanged. Never."

Julian flashed a mischievous grin, but I brushed him off.

"I'll keep asking until you say yes, so you might as well say yes now. If you don't enjoy it, I promise not to bother you again, Pretty Girl."

I arched an eyebrow. "One date, and you'll leave me alone?"

Bill lifted two fingers into the air. "Scout's honor."

Perplexed, I scrunched my face. "I don't know what that means, but do you promise?"

He vowed, his hand over his heart, "I promise. Just give me one chance, and I swear that if you want me to leave you alone, I'll never bother you again."

I hated that the thought of him no longer coming around and flirting with me made my heart ache, but I couldn't imagine going on a date with someone like... well... *him*.

"I... I can't," I replied. But instead of desolation in his eyes, I only saw that relentless spark of determination.

Bill tipped his hat and began to walk away. Once again, I couldn't help but appreciate the view of his departure.

"Come on, CeCe, we need to get going. Oh. And guess what? You're driving." Julian hopped into the passenger seat.

I narrowed my eyes. "No, you're driving! That was the deal! I drove here, and you drive home!" I ran over to open the passenger door, but he promptly locked it.

"No!"

"Julian!" I yanked at the handle. "Open this door and let me in! I'm not driving!"

"No!" He crossed his arms, stubbornly avoiding eye contact. "I refuse to drive. You have to do it, or we'll sit here all day. I swear it!"

I narrowed my eyes at my stubborn friend then glanced over at Bill as he walked across the parking lot. Wanting nothing less than to drive 'Ol Blue again, an idea sprang into my mind, and I gave Julian a wily smile. "Fine. Sit there all day for all I care. You're on your own! I'm getting a ride with Bill!"

Julian's eyes flashed wide as he spun in his seat to look at me. "What? No! Wait!"

"Bill! Wait up!" I called as I rushed after him.

He paused and spun back around, the sexy smile lighting up his entire, rugged face.

"Can you give me a ride home?"

"Of course, Pretty Girl. Just as long as you don't mind that I first have to make one stop along the way."

I paused, wondering if I was asking for trouble getting tangled up with the likes of Bayou Bill, but with a sigh, I agreed. "Fine."

"CeCe!" Julian shrieked as he ran across the parking lot after me. "Don't leave me! Please don't leave me here!"

I turned and pointed a finger at him. "You are on your own. Drive the ingredients back to Diane yourself. I'm going with Bill."

His eyes swelled with worry. "But... but... I don't want to drive the horrible truck!"

"Well, neither do I, and now that you tried to force my hand, you're driving it alone. Serves you right. Maybe next time you'll stick to the deal."

His lower lip stuck out.

"Just remember, third gear sticks," I said, then I spun and left him standing in the parking lot feeling a small sense of victory in having mastered that little driving detail.

Bill led me over to a massive truck that matched his camouflage attire. Gazing up at it, I couldn't help but feel that 'Ol Blue looked like a mere toy in comparison.

"You can't be serious," I remarked with a hint of disbelief. "You drive this thing?"

He grinned that enigmatic smile of his and opened the passenger door, flipping down a small sidestep. He held out his hand and said, "After you."

Unsure if I had lost my mind completely to take a ride with Bayou Bill, I reached out and took his hand. Those sparks crackled across my skin once again, warming me up right down to the core of my being. With a gentle lift, he helped me into the truck then closed the door behind me. A moment later, he hopped up in the driver's seat, fired up the truck, and away we went. I glanced out the back window to see Julian standing defeated in the parking lot, and I gave him a little wave he didn't return.

***

After driving fifteen minutes out of town, Bill chatted away about alligators and pointed out intriguing points of interest along the way. However, he remained tight-lipped about one crucial detail—our destination. Each time I asked about our impending stop, a mysterious smile and three simple words were his only response: "You'll see soon."

Though it should have been exciting going on an adventure with a man I hated to admit I found quite intoxicating, anxiety mounted with each passing mile, and I felt a growing unease as we ventured further from civilization. My heart pounded in my chest when Bill turned the big truck onto a winding gravel road, leading us to the edge of the water. In that moment, it was just me and a man named Bayou Bill, deep within the remote swamplands, and a sense of isolation settled over me. I was alone in the wilderness with a veritable stranger.

What in the hell was I thinking? I don't even know this guy!

Beginning to feel like I was starring in my own personal horror movie where the audience was screaming at the stupid woman who'd jumped in a vehicle with a man she barely knew to get driven out to a remote location, I regretted the impulsive leap I'd taken into Bill's truck.

"Seriously. Where are we? What are we doing here?" I asked, my anxiety mounting.

He put the truck in park, looked over and answered with a smile. "You'll see soon."

With visions of horror movies and crime thrillers playing out in my head, I discreetly reached into my purse and located my small bottle of mace. I mentally berated myself for my recklessness, but I was determined to protect myself if necessary. Though my life was far from perfect at the moment, I clung to the hope that I'd rise again, refusing to meet my demise at the hands of a stranger in the middle of some murky swamp.

As Bill hopped out and started walking around the front of the truck, my anxiety transformed into fear. The thought of my face on a *20/20* special detailing the search for a missing city socialite raced through my imagination. I slid my finger along the safety switch of my pepper spray, preparing for a confrontation if he suddenly flipped the switch from the charming man who'd coaxed me into his truck into the ax murderer I built him to be in my mind.

An icy hand of fear gripped my heart as Bill pulled open my door. I whipped out my pepper spray prepared to unleash my city girl fury, holding it at his eye level as I demanded, "That's far enough! Where are we? What are you doing with me out here? I demand you take me back to civilization. Now!"

He looked at my pink pepper spray can and chuckled. "Really? You agreed to come with me on my errand, and now you're gonna mace me for it?"

My finger hovered over the trigger. "You won't tell me where we are or what we're doing here! If you think I'm just gonna let you murder me and bury me out in the woods so you can visit my dead body shrine, you've got another thing coming!"

I prepared to depress the spray, but his charming smile disarmed me.

"Really, CeCe? That's where your head has gone? That I brought you out here to murder you?" His laughter shook his shoulders, and the visions of him I'd crafted into a stone-cold serial killer started to look foolish.

I frowned as I began to calm down. "What! It's possible, isn't it? You could definitely be a murderer! Or a sex trafficker! Haven't you seen the news lately? Can you blame me?"

He laughed harder then pointed at me. "Hell, for all I know, *you* could be the serial killer. Maybe you're putting on a show, and you're gonna mace me then stab me to death while I'm incapacitated. Perhaps you're some notorious serial killer who goes around slicing up unsuspecting men."

My mouth dropped open, taken aback by his audacious theory. "Preposterous! That's a completely ridiculous theory!"

He shrugged, his smile remaining. "No more preposterous than me being a serial killer out to slaughter you."

His logic, while unconventional, strangely alleviated my fear, and my finger loosened its grip on the spray. Bill's gentle smile and reasoning shifted me back to some semblance of sanity.

His smile softened along with his voice. "I'm not trying to harm you. I swear. I just had to come out here with this chicken and feed it to my gators. One of my mamas just had babies, and I wanna make sure she gets some extra meals right now. It was supposed to be a surprise, which is why I didn't tell you what I had planned. I'm bringing you out here to take you on a little boat ride. It's a beautiful ride to get to her, and I thought you'd enjoy coming along with me."

His words, delivered with sincerity, transformed the fear that had gripped me into a sense of relief. My mind began to rationalize as Bill's hypnotic blue eyes soothed away my runaway anxiety.

"So, you're not taking me out here to kill me?" I asked, and the ridiculousness of my words finally started to sink in.

He shook his head. "No. Are you taking me out here to kill me?"

I chuckled and slid my finger off the pepper spray trigger. "No."

"Well, that's great news to me then. Does that mean we can get on with my little stop? If you're really still scared, I can drive you home and just come out and feed her early tomorrow."

Though I had no desire to embark on a boat journey through the bayou, the thought of a new mother and her offspring going hungry gnawed at my conscience. I tilted my head. "How far away is she?"

"Only about ten minutes," Bill answered. "It should take less than five to feed her and the young ones, and I can have ya back here in thirty."

I chewed at my lip, torn between options. I pointed my finger at him and shook it. "Fine. I'll go, but just in case you change your mind and decide you do want to kill me, don't think I'm going to let your charm and pretty eyes lure me into becoming a helpless victim. I'll fight you, Bill. And I took plenty of self-defense classes in the city. I can handle myself," I lied.

His smile grew. "The only thing I heard in that sentence is that you think I'm charming with pretty eyes."

A blush crept up my cheeks, and I fumbled for a response, but my thoughts fell short.

Bill extended his hand. "Come on, Pretty Girl. My boat's right over here."

Despite my mind screaming at me to choose the safer option and go home, my hand seemed to betray me as it reached out and took his. It felt like an invisible magnetic pull I didn't want to resist, and I let my disobedient body follow him to the dock.

"Here she is." Bill waved an arm toward the peculiar boat with a massive fan attached to the back.

"What on earth is that?" I recoiled at the sight.

"That's my boat," Bill replied, grinning. "I call her the Gator Glider."

My brow furrowed. "That's a boat? It doesn't look like a boat."

He shrugged and walked down the small dock closer to it. "It's not as fancy as the boats a highfalutin girl like you is probably used to, but she's a good one. Come on. Hop on."

Once again, my sensible instincts urged me to run for safety, but my stubborn feet refused to move. "Is it safe?"

"Very. This swamp boat is what I use to take people out on tours. Come on. It's fun. You'll see. Just give it a chance."

Bill offered his hand, and after glancing back at the truck and weighing my choices, I decided to embrace the adventure and joined him, stepping onto the boat. It moved beneath me, and he tightened his grip to keep me from wobbling right off.

Once we were safely on board, he grabbed some peculiar earmuff-like devices and tossed them to me. "Put these on."

"On my head? No way! They'll mess up my hair!" I protested.

His grin widened. "We're going to be flying through the swamps on an airboat. Your hair is going to get messy, but I'm putting my money on the fact you're still gonna look great. Just put on the ear protection."

Frowning, I placed them on my head. Bill gestured for me to sit on the bench seat in front of the captain's chair. Uncertain about what to expect, I jumped a little when the boat roared to life, and even with the ear protection, I was taken aback by the noise. I glanced over my shoulder at Bill, but the nerves inside me started to dissipate as I caught sight of his warm smile. Though I had always been high-strung, whenever I looked at Bill, it seemed that he had the power to alleviate all my insecurities.

"Hold on, Pretty Girl!" he yelled, the words barely discernible over the engine's roar.

I screamed when the boat took off at high speed. We glided effortlessly across the water, and as we navigated around bends, I clung to my seat and screamed louder. In the midst of my fear, I cursed my rash decision to go with him, silently pleading for the safety of dry land. However, as we curved through yet another turn, my scream transformed into laughter. My apprehension gave way to delight, and I found myself grinning so widely that I had to cover my mouth to prevent any unwelcome insects from flying in.

We zipped and weaved through the picturesque waters, and I felt an undeniable sense of freedom out there in the bayou with Bill. I extended my arms and closed my eyes, surrendering to the wind whipping through my hair. For the first time in a long while, I wasn't worrying about money or about my appearance or the crushing need to regain my social status. Fashion and jets and jewelry faded to black as I let myself go to enjoy this fleeting moment where I felt...

Free.

I looked over my shoulder and met Bill's gaze, and I felt a connection that transcended the ordinary.

I was free... with him.

He smiled at me and spun us around another corner that forced me to grip my seat as I squealed with delight. Then the boat gradually slowed, and with it, my heartbeat returned to a normal pace. Bill switched off the engine, and suddenly, silence enveloped us. I removed my ear protection and turned to see him grinning down at me.

"Well?" he asked, and I couldn't help but beam in response. "I knew you'd love it," he said before I could even find the words to reply.

"I loved it," I breathed out, my words filled with genuine enthusiasm. "That was more fun than I've had in... well, ever."

"Good. I had a feeling you'd have fun out here." He descended from his Captain's chair, reaching for the bag of chickens he'd brought along. "Come here. You're in for a treat."

With a mixture of trepidation and curiosity, I followed him to the edge of the boat.

"There!" Bill pointed, his hand gently guiding me as he turned me to face the rippling water.

My heart quickened as I saw the alligator head emerge above the surface, causing me to involuntarily squeal and instinctively lean against Bill. "It's coming this way! Eek!"

Bill's arm slid around the small of my back, providing a reassuring haven within his embrace. "That's Nancy. She won't hurt us. She's just joining us for dinner. And look."

I strained my eyes to observe more ripples on the water, gasping with delight as the little baby alligators popped up alongside their mother. "Oh! Babies!"

Bill's grin was evident in his voice. "See? What did I tell you? Pretty cool, right?"

Reluctantly, I acknowledged the cuteness of the tiny creatures, my heart strangely warming at the sight of the little alligator family. "I am not a fan of alligators, but that is pretty neat. A little family."

"Here ya go, girl. Enjoy!" Bill tossed the chicken into the water, and Nancy eagerly snatched it up.

Bill guided me back to the bench seat where he settled down beside me. We watched the small family enjoying their supper as we sat in comfortable silence broken only by the soothing sounds of the water and the bayou's wildlife.

"Are you glad you came?" Bill asked.

I didn't feel the need to hide my happiness with one of my usual snarky remarks to him. "I am. This is truly special."

"I'm glad you think so, too. I love being out here, far from everything. I take people on tours here every day, but I always return alone for a while to soak it all in quietly."

"I can see why. I never imagined I'd find something like this enjoyable."

"Something like going on a boat ride with a serial killer?" he teased.

I playfully nudged him in the ribs. "Oh, come on. It was a legitimate concern."

Bill wrapped his arm around my shoulder, and even though my mind scolded me for allowing the intimate embrace, my body just leaned in a little closer.

"Well, only one of us has been under criminal investigation by the FBI. I think I should be the one worried out here alone with you."

Though his comment was playful, I recoiled, my face hardening. "I am *not* a criminal!" I spat back, starting to pull away.

He tightened his grip around my shoulder, guiding me back to him "Hey, hey, I was just joking. I know you're not a criminal. Well, at least I'm pretty sure you're not," he teased.

"I'm *not!*" I retorted with emphasis. "I'm a victim. This was something that was done *to* me, not something I did."

His voice softened, and his usual playful tone faded away. "Do you want to talk about it? Tell me what happened?"

As I looked out at the serene waters surrounding us, I took a deep breath and embarked on my story from the beginning. It felt cathartic to tell the whole tale to a sympathetic ear, and Bill listened intently as I recounted my ordeal. When I reached the end of my woeful tale, he stared at me in disbelief.

"Wow. I'd heard bits and pieces of rumors, but none of them came close to describing the extent of what you've been through. You're incredibly strong to have survived all of that."

I met his gaze, my heart swelling at his words. "You think I'm strong? Because I don't. I feel weak every day. Pathetic, really. Like a loser who can't navigate the real world. Diane seems to be doing it effortlessly, and I'm... I'm floundering."

Bill gently tucked a strand of hair behind my ear. "You're not floundering; you're evolving. Growing, changing, and surviving. Even though you've been dealt a heavy blow, you're still standing. That speaks volumes. You're a beautiful, smart, confident, and capable woman. You're more impressive than any woman I've ever met."

The way he looked at me made me feel more beautiful than ever. Despite the absence of designer clothing, a perfect manicure, carefully styled hair, and meticulously applied makeup, he gazed at me with a level of appreciation reminiscent of how countless men in New York had looked at the models surrounding us. For the first time in years, I felt genuinely beautiful.

"It's all so unbelievable that this happened. I don't think I've fully processed it yet. Everything is gone—my money, my homes, my husband. He's probably lounging on a beach somewhere with a twenty-year-old blonde, sipping champagne and living the high life while I'm stranded in Ruinville."

Bill shook his head with a look of disgust. "The only truly unbelievable thing in this story is your idiotic husband abandoning you. If I were ever fortunate enough to call you my wife, I wouldn't care what challenges we faced. I'd never leave you. Ever. I'd drag you to the ends of the earth on the run rather than let you go, and I'd shield you from whatever hell came our way. Always."

A lump formed in my throat as I stared into his eyes, relishing the admiration in his gaze. The magnetic attraction between us seemed to pull me in until, without warning, I leaned forward and kissed him. The kiss took me by surprise, and after savoring the taste of his lips for a few seconds, I pulled back abruptly, wide-eyed and flustered.

"I, uh... I don't know why I did that," I stammered. "I shouldn't have. We shouldn't. This... I'm sorry. I shouldn't have done that."

His smile grew as he stared at me, then slowly, he slid a hand alongside my face and pulled me toward him. At first, there was a moment of hesitation, a flicker of uncertainty as if I were standing on the precipice of a life-changing decision. But when his warm breath mingled with mine as he whispered, "Woman, stop overthinking it and kiss me again," all doubts dissipated like mist in the morning sun. I let go of everything as I sank into his kiss, my world spinning out of control as our lips met in a passionate collision of emotions.

Never in my life had I experienced such passion, such deep, soul-bending emotion as I did bobbing on the water enveloped in Bill's strong embrace. Every decision I'd ever made had always been to impress others... to better my situation... to fulfill my obligation to my family to marry well, impress in society and live up to my family name. But here in the bayou in Bill's arms, I did something *I* wanted to do without a care in the world of repercussions.

I kissed the man who made my heart beat faster even if he was the last man on earth I dreamed I'd be kissing.

I didn't care. I kissed him deeper, relishing every moment of our crackling connection.

As our passionate kiss gradually waned, Bill's lips softened, and he planted several gentle, lingering kisses on my lips before finally leaning back and locking eyes with me.

"Wow," I whispered, my ability to articulate temporarily escaping me as my mind grappled with the intensity of the moment.

Bill concurred with a breathless chuckle. "Yeah, wow."

We shared a silent connection, basking in the aftermath of our electrifying kiss. Finally, I managed to regain my composure. "I... I should probably head back soon and make sure Julian made it back safely. I feel kind of bad leaving him stranded, although he definitely deserved it."

Bill chuckled. "You're probably right. He looked downright terrified when we drove off. Not sure if he was scared for you leaving with me or scared for himself."

"Probably both. In fact, we had better hurry back or knowing Julian, he'll call the police thinking you've kidnapped me."

"So, both of you have overactive imaginations when it comes to kidnappings?" He quirked a smile.

Laughing, I shrugged. "You live in the city long enough and you start to think everyone is out to get you. We aren't used to quiet small towns."

"Well, I'm glad you put aside your better judgement and came with me."

"Me too. This was... nice. Unexpected, but nice."

A smile passed between us, then Bill extended his hand, lifting it to his lips to plant a gentle kiss on the back of mine.

"Thank you for indulging me with this boat ride and for finally succumbing to that desire to kiss me, which I'm sure you've been valiantly fighting."

I laughed and playfully nudged him. "Don't let it go to your head. It was just a moment of weakness."

His eyes twinkled with mirth as he responded, "And do you think there might be more moments of weakness in the future?"

Bill's gaze bore into my soul, and I could feel the magnetic pull between us strengthen. "We'll see," I replied, trying to conceal my growing smile.

"We'll see," he echoed with a knowing grin. Leaning in, he placed another affectionate kiss on the back of my hand before leaving me breathless, perched on my seat alone, as he guided us back through the bayou.

CHAPTER SIXTEEN
CeCe

I stood on the porch, hand raised in a wave as I watched Bill drive away. I pressed my fingers to my lips, still slightly swollen from our kiss, and closed my eyes as I transported myself back to that incredible, unexpected moment.

I had kissed a man other than my husband.

I had kissed a man I never should have been kissing.

I had kissed a man I wanted to kiss over and over and again.

Before long, the front door swung open with a dramatic flourish, and Julian emerged, arms crossed in a mix of concern and irritation. "CeCe Louise VanTramp! It's about time! Even though I'm furious with you, I was getting worried and about to call the police! I can't believe you just jumped in a truck with a man you barely know! And then you didn't even make it home for two hours! You have some explaining to do young lady!"

I chuckled to myself having suspected correctly he'd be ready to call the police on me. Spinning around, I tried to suppress my smile, but failed.

Julian started to chastise me about leaving him behind in the parking lot, but then stopped mid-sentence and gasped. "Wait. What's going on with your face? Why does it—Oh my God! You got it on with the gator guy!"

My eyes popped open wide. "What! I did not get it on with the gator guy!"

Diane appeared in the doorway, wide eyes matching mine. "You got it on with the gator guy? Get out of here!"

I stomped my foot, hands clenched tight. "Stop it! I did not get it on with the gator guy! Bill, by the way. His name is Bill."

Julian quirked a knowing smile. "Mmmhmm. Say what you want, but I know that starry-eyed, post-coital glow. I can't say I've ever seen it on *you* before, but I've seen it in the mirror looking at myself many, many times. You got it on with the gator guy!"

Diane chimed in, eagerly pressing for details. "Tell us, CeCe! Did you really get it on with the gator guy?"

Exasperated, I gave in with a heavy sigh. "Okay, fine. We kissed. There, happy? But it ends at a kiss. We did not, nor will not, 'get it on.'"

Julian punched a triumphant fist in the air. "I knew it! I knew I recognized that glow! Oh my God! You made out with Crocodile Dundee! You dirty little tramp!"

He started tickling me, and though I tried to fight it, I couldn't help but burst into laughter, my smile reminiscent of my first kiss back in middle school. I'd told my best friend Emily about it underneath the covers with only a flashlight illuminating my grin.

"Stop! Stop it!" I batted him off but couldn't stop my childish smiling. "His name is Bill not Crocodile Dundee or 'the gator guy.' And we kissed. No big deal."

"Um, big deal. *Very* big deal! Okay, spill." Diane gestured to the porch swing.

With another sigh, I walked over and flopped down onto it, and the two of them squished up against me. We started a slow swing as I recanted the story, finishing with the kiss that had rocked my entire world.

Of course, I didn't tell them that.

"And then we kissed. That's all," I finished abruptly.

Diane huffed. "Uh, no. That's *not* all. Tell us about the kiss! What was it like? Was it good?"

Julian nodded along with her, expectant eyes searching mine.

It wasn't my usual self to open up about something so... emotional. In truth, I had kept emotions at arm's length for as long as I could remember. From the time I was sent to a boarding school in the seventh grade to acquire all the skills necessary to become a refined lady of high society, I hadn't formed any deep connections with others. Boarding school had a way of making girls view each other as competitors, and any display of emotion was considered a sign of vulnerability... something to be used against you like a pointed weapon. Like every other WASP, I'd mastered the art of concealing my weaknesses and repressing my feelings.

Since I'd last seen Emily when we were twelve, Julian was the closest thing to a confidant I had, but I'd never opened myself emotionally to him about things like love. I'd been married when we'd met, and though he regaled me with all his stories of passionate kisses, I'd never been in a position to share something so personal with him.

Yet here I was, seated on the porch with Diane and Julian, and feeling an overwhelming desire to express the exhilaration that was almost bursting from within. Still, I couldn't bring myself to do it. Even Julian, with his kind and adoring nature, had never witnessed me bearing my true emotions. He held me in high regard, and I had never dared to reveal my softer side. Rather than gushing about how incredible and life-altering that kiss had been, I chose to downplay it with a nonchalant shrug.

"Fine. It was fine. No big deal."

Diane leaned over and gave me a gentle shove. "It's a *very* big deal! You kissed a man! When was the last time you kissed anyone other than Arthur?"

My mind flitted back to high school. "I think it was James McDow under the bleachers at the homecoming game."

"So, high school? Wow. I can't even imagine kissing anyone else. It's been that long for me too," Diane said on a sigh. "Was it weird? Kissing someone other than your husband?"

I scoffed. "Just because I'm legally married, let's not refer to Arthur as my *husband* anymore. He lost that title when he abandoned me. He's my *ex*-husband."

She nodded. "Sorry. I just meant after all these years of kissing one man, was it weird kissing a new one? Did you like it?"

Julian giggled. "Of course, she liked it. She has the glow."

Heat flushed my cheeks as I tried to stifle my smile, but it burst free anyway.

"See!" He pointed at me, laughing. "She can't control herself! She's a giddy schoolgirl!"

I swatted away his finger, but he wasn't wrong. I *was* like a giddy schoolgirl, and I was doing a terrible job hiding it, so, for the first time since I'd bid goodbye to my best friend, Emily, I spilled out my emotions like verbal vomit.

"Okay! Okay! I liked it. No, I *loved* it! It was so romantic, passionate, and unexpected. His lips were so full and soft, and the way he touched my face." I sighed as I touched my cheek and leaned into my hand. "And his eyes. Have you seen his eyes? They are so beautiful, and the way he looked at me just made me feel... well, special. I felt like I was one of those models during Fashion Week that everyone ogles over. He looked at me like that. I can't even remember the last time anyone looked at me like that and it was just..." I trailed off when the lump in my throat choked off the rest of the words.

Diane pressed a hand to her chest, and I saw the admiration in her eyes. "That's so incredible, CeCe. Wow. I can't even imagine how that must feel."

I sniffled, sucking back the tears as I exhaled a shaky breath. "Yeah. It was pretty incredible. And I have no idea what I'm doing because I can't be going around kissing Bayou Bill again. He's not the kind of man I can ever be dating. It was just a little momentary slip. But wow. What a kiss."

Julian shrugged. "Why not? There's nothing wrong with slumming it for a little while. I used to do it all the time. In fact, the more scandalous they are, the hotter the sex. It just feels so... dirty." He shimmied his shoulders and waggled his eyebrows.

But I didn't feel dirty kissing Bill, though I knew I should. Ever since I was old enough to know what kissing was, I'd been pushed toward other notable families with their perfectly acceptable heirs. Those were the only boys I was allowed to think about kissing, but tonight, all I could think about was kissing my camouflage-covered gator guy again.

"There's nothing wrong with dating someone like Bill if he makes you smile like this," Diane argued. "Just because he's not a rich sugar daddy, doesn't mean he can't be a great guy. Women have other needs just as important as being cared for financially."

Before I could jump in, Julian scoffed. "Oh no. She's not going to *date* him because we are on a mission to find that said sugar daddy. But I'm saying she can get it on with the gator guy as much as she wants so long as she doesn't do something silly like fall for him." He snorted then froze and looked at me. "You won't, will you? Fall for him?"

I faked my shock. "Fall for Bill? Me? Never. No. He's simply not suitable. Like I said, it was just a silly kiss."

Diane rolled her eyes. "You two are such snobs. Suitable? Who even says that?"

I raised my eyebrows. "Only everyone, that's who. You weren't raised with money like I was. I was only allowed to date suitable boys who would make potentially suitable marriage partners. Arthur was practically chosen for me by my parents when I was twenty, and we were introduced solely to see if we made a *suitable* couple. Of course, we did, and it was expected then that we would marry. We both came from good families, and we got along great, so it made sense. We were, well, suitable."

She did nothing to hide the distaste on her face. "That sounds like a business deal, not a marriage. Did you even love him?"

"Of course, I loved him." I paused and tipped my head. "Well, in my own way, I suppose. I was never goo goo ga ga over him. Not *in* love with him, no. But I thought he was a good husband. Well, until he stole our money and abandoned me, that is." Anger slithered up my spine as I relived the betrayal.

"That's sad," Diane said softly. "I mean, I can't say I was goo goo ga ga over Rick anymore, but I definitely fell in love with him when I first met him. We drifted apart over the years, but I did truly love him for a long time."

"Like you loved your fireman?" Julian waggled his eyebrows and Diane's face burst into a deep crimson.

"Stop. That was a long time ago."

"Not so long ago considering you still look like a giddy schoolgirl every time he comes into Mawmaw's," Julian teased, then he turned and looked at me. "Hey! You look like CeCe looks right now after she got it on with the gator guy!"

"I didn't get it on with the gator guy! And I don't look like a giddy schoolgirl." I frowned.

He looked between us then burst into laughter. "You're both smitten kittens. Just admit it."

I was going to argue back, but Diane pressed a hand to her forehead and chuckled. "Fine. I'm a smitten kitten. Okay? Are you happy, Julian? Yes, I'm still crazy about him. It's been so many years, but I still swoon every single time I see him. But it's not like I can do anything about it. I'm still married to Rick."

She pointed at the ring on her finger, and I growled and took ahold of her hand. "We aren't married anymore, Diane. You need to drop that notion right now. We can't get divorced because we can't find the damn bastards, but that doesn't mean we're stuck in marital limbo for all of eternity. Just take that damn ring off and go get your fireman if that's what you want. Stop letting that dumbass *ex*-husband of yours keep ruining your life. I didn't let Arthur stop me from kissing Bill today, and I'm not the least bit sorry about it."

She looked a bit taken aback by the force of my words, but then she glanced down at her hand and slowly slid the ring off.

"You're right, CeCe. You're so right. Why am I even still wearing this stupid thing? It doesn't mean anything anymore. He broke our marriage vows when he abandoned me, and I'm done pretending I'm still his wife."

She lifted her hand and prepared to chuck the diamond ring into oblivion, but Julian shrieked and caught her hand before she let go.

"Wait! We can sell that!" he said, keeping her from launching a three-carat rock into the bayou.

She sucked the air through her teeth. "Oh yeah. You're right. This thing is worth money that we need. Yes. Do that. Take it to our guy."

"You sure?" Julian asked. "You want me to sell it?"

After looking at it one last time, she released her grip on the ring. "Do it. Sell it. My marriage is over and I'm done pretending it's not. That ring can help us a lot more off my hand than it can on my hand. Sell it."

"Good for you, Diane. Rick is an ass and I'm glad you're moving on. I'll take this to our sales guy." Julian carefully put it in his pocket.

"So, that's it, huh?" Diane said. "Just like that, we're considering ourselves divorced?"

"Just like that." I nodded. "We're divorced. And one day, when I find my next husband, we'll use his money to figure out how to make it all official and get divorced to those jerks for real."

Diane smiled, then looked back out toward the bayou. "This is so weird. I never planned on getting divorced. I was going to marry Rick, have lots of kids, change the world, and live a long, happy married life. And here I am with none of the above."

I almost didn't ask my next question, but finally said, "Why didn't you have kids? You seem like the type who would have wanted them."

She kept staring out at the bayou. "We tried. Many times. Even did some fertility treatments. It just never took for us, and then one day we just kinda stopped trying. I wanted them, though. Very badly."

"Me too," I admitted, and she looked at me quizzically.

"You did?"

I nodded. "Oh yes. I mean, first because it was expected of us in our family standing, but then when I got the idea in my head, I really wanted them. But I could never carry to term, and we lost several before I gave up trying as well."

Diane reached over and took my hand, holding it gently. "I had no idea, CeCe. I'm so sorry."

The unbearable pangs of those losses speared through me again, and I let out a sigh. "We never told anyone. It was too painful, so we just kind of went through it on our own."

"We didn't tell anyone either," Diane said.

It felt so odd that the two of us had been in each other's orbit almost daily back at the time, and though we'd fought the same battle, shared the same heartache, neither of us had known of the other's struggle. For a moment, I wondered how different that time would have been for me if I'd just shared my struggles with her... trusted in her like a friend instead of looking at her like the competition I'd always seen. We shared a mutual pain apart when we could have, perhaps, helped each other get through it.

Julian took my other hand. "I had no idea either. Why didn't you tell me?"

I looked at him and smiled. "It was before I met you. In fact, the day I took you in was the day I decided I was done trying. Instead of having a baby, it turns out I kind of adopted you and raised you up in society instead of a child."

He gasped and clutched his chest. "Really? You thought of me like an adopted child not just your employee?"

Diane snorted. "Employee? Seriously, Julian. You've never actually worked for her."

I ignored her accurate comment and shrugged. "Sort of. You were all lost and bewildered in the city, and I had so much to teach you. I suppose you filled that void for me."

He pressed a hand to his lips and whimpered. "Oh, CeCe. Or wait... should I call you Mom?"

"No!" I spit out sharply, then burst into laughter, softening the intense moment. "I'm not your mother. I'm your... CeCe. And you're my... Julian."

"Always." He leaned forward and hugged me. "I'll always be your Julian."

Diane slid her arm around my shoulder, and the three of us squished together in a hug. It felt strange sharing things with Diane and allowing myself to be vulnerable with someone I always considered top competition, but today, she felt almost like... a real friend.

Suddenly, a loud, piercing noise startled us, causing Julian to tumble off the porch swing with an audible thud.

"What's that sound?" he shouted so we could hear him over the incessant *beep, beep, beep.*

Diane's eyes widened in realization. "The cookies! I forgot I was baking cookies! It's the fire alarm!"

We leaped up and dashed inside, following the plumes of smoke billowing from the kitchen. Diane hurriedly opened the oven door, waving her hand in front of her face to clear the smoke as she grabbed a hot pad, removing what appeared to be the charred remains of what may have been cookies in another life.

"How do we stop that horrible beeping?" Julian yelled, spinning around in confusion.

Diane started spitting out directions. "CeCe, start opening windows! Julian, grab a towel and wave it at the fire alarm up there!"

I did as she asked, running around and yanking open all the windows I could, and when I finished the last one, I ran back into the kitchen to see Julian leaping up and down with a yellow and brown floral crocheted kitchen towel waving the last of the smoke away. Finally, the screeching stopped, and we all heaved out a collective sigh.

"Well, crap," Diane said as she stared down at the ashy remnants of her first attempt at baking. "I forgot to set a timer. I have to remember that for next time."

"Next time?" I planted my hands on my hips. "I don't think there should be a next time. This is the only place we have to live, and we don't want you burning it down."

"Well, maybe she's just looking for an excuse to call her fireman." Julian waggled his eyebrows.

Diane laughed off his comment. "Unfortunately, I was not. I really did just forget. But I'll get it right next time. I hope."

I shook my head. "I think we can just admit defeat here and stop pretending you're Betty Crocker. Just forget the cookies, Diane. It was your aunt's thing. It doesn't have to be yours."

She lifted her chin, straightening her shoulders. "Yes. It does. I let her down so much in life that the least I can do is pick up her torch and bake her damn cookies to raise money for causes she would have cared about. I'm going to learn how to make these damn things if it's the last thing I do."

Julian scowled. "And it just might be if we all burn up in your attempt at baking."

She laughed then dumped the burned cookies into the garbage. "I'm not an idiot. I can figure out how to bake cookies. I'll get going on another batch, and you two start pricing the stuff for the sale."

"Start whatting the what?" I said, confused.

Julian dropped his ugly floral towel on the counter and sighed. "Oh, yeah. We weren't here for this one, but it turns out that Aunt Addie's house was where everyone always dropped off their donations for any fundraiser sales. She did all the pricing and brought it down to the fundraiser to help raise money. So, now that she's not here, it seems this torturous task has fallen upon us."

"What? But... I don't understand."

Diane wiped out a bowl and set it on the counter. "What he means is that people kinda forgot Aunt Addie was gone and just started dropping stuff off today. First the Magnolia Maidens came, then the mayor, then more and more people just kept coming over dropping stuff off. I didn't want to say no, so I just stashed it all in the living room. We have to go through it and decide what each piece is worth then put them in boxes with other items of the same value. Apparently, it makes it easier for when they are setting up the tables to have it organized this way. We'll take it to the fundraiser when we go."

I backed up and poked my head out of the kitchen and looked in the living room, shocked I hadn't noticed the heaping pile of what appeared to be garbage when I'd run through before. But I suppose all the smoke and the screaming alarm had held my attention, but now it was focused right on the pile of horror.

"Didn't we just get a bunch of garbage *out* of this place, and now we took more garbage *in?*"

"Temporarily," Diane said as she cracked an egg into the bowl. "It all goes out the day of the sale. We just need to organize everything in groups and price it."

I stepped out of the kitchen and looked at all the old clothes then shook my head. "You want us to dig through old clothes? Like hobos?"

"That's what I said!" Julian agreed.

"No one says hobos anymore!" Diane called out. "Just start organizing!"

"Here. Put these on." Julian reached around me with a pair of bright yellow dishwashing gloves.

My face soured, but finally I slid them on and walked over to the pile, lifting up a floral shirt that likely sold through Walmart in the eighties.

"So, we have to price this?" I asked.

Diane popped her head out of the kitchen. "Yes. Just best guess. People can make offers if they don't like the price."

"Negative one thousand dollars," I said, then dropped the shirt on the floor.

"CeCe!" Diane scolded. "Be serious!"

"I am," I deadpanned. "We should pay them to take it."

Julian reappeared holding two wooden cooking spoons, and I furrowed my brow to look at him.

"There's only one pair of gloves." He snapped the spoons together like chopsticks. "I'll use these to put stuff in piles."

"Ah," I said, nodding my head. "Smart. Very smart."

Julian leaned down and picked up the shirt using his two wooden spoons, then carefully dropped it in a box.

"Five dollars," Diane said from where she watched us from the kitchen doorway.

"Fine," I sighed. "I still think negative one thousand, but I'll accept your suggestion it belongs in the five-dollar box."

As I started hunting for more things to drop in the five-dollar box, I heard Diane chuckle before she disappeared back into the kitchen in what I presumed was another attempt to burn us all up in a tragic fire. But twenty minutes later, she emerged from the kitchen, a huge smile on her face as she came toward us with a plate full of cookies that didn't look terrible. In fact, they looked and smelled quite edible.

"I did it!" She hoisted them up high. "I made my aunt's cookies! And you know what, they taste *good!*"

"You tried one?" I asked, arching an eyebrow.

"Yep." She nodded. "You need to take a break and taste one."

Julian and I shared a worried exchange, but when Diane came closer and showed us the cookies, I admitted how appetizing they looked.

"If I eat one, will you take over this ghastly job of pricing garbage?"

Diane chuckled and shook her head. "Nope. But you will be quite happy at how yummy they are."

"I'm starving." Julian eyeballed the cookies.

Diane selected a cookie, popped it into her mouth, and smiled as she chewed. "See, they're safe. I promise."

Julian set down his wooden spoons and carefully sampled a cookie, his face lighting up. "Wow! These are really good!"

"Right?" Diane beamed. "CeCe? Want one?"

Desiring any opportunity to escape the arduous pricing task, I removed the bright yellow gloves, placing them alongside Julian's spoons. I took a cookie and, after a quick sniff to ensure it didn't smell burnt or spoiled, I took a bite. The flavors exploded in my mouth, and I couldn't help but grin at Diane.

"You did it!" I exclaimed between bites. "You truly did it! Wow! I'm impressed!"

"I did it," Diane replied with a grin. "We did it. We're making it work. Look at how far we've come."

I glanced around the house, which, apart from the pile of items I considered garbage that I was practically standing on, was beginning to feel like home.

"Yeah," I agreed, smiling. "We're making it work."

Against all odds, it seemed the three of us really were starting to thrive in this strange new world of ours. Diane and I hadn't been there for each other in our past struggles, but it seemed this time, we were somehow there for each other now. Supporting each other. Helping each other. Encouraging each other. Maybe Bill was right. Maybe I wasn't floundering... maybe I was surviving. After everything we'd been through, we were still standing.

I glanced down at the pile of crap next to me.

We may be standing next to garbage, of course, but we were still standing.

CHAPTER SEVENTEEN
Diane

"This box is too heavy! You carry it. You're young and strong," CeCe pleaded with Julian.

He swiped a hand across the sweat dripping from his brow. "I may be strong, but it's nine thousand degrees right now in this heat wave, and I'm literally melting. I mean, I knew we were living in hell when we moved here, but I didn't expect it to actually reach the temperatures of hellfire itself."

CeCe narrowed her eyes and pointed up at her hair, no longer smooth and styled like it had always looked in New York. "At least the heat and humidity aren't making you resemble some sort of an electrified poodle. I'm starting to understand why every woman in this Godforsaken town insists on having such ridiculous, huge hair. It's not a choice but an acceptance. Without an army of stylists following me around with a smoothing iron and vat of hair product, nothing is going to combat this horrible humidity. Now I'm hot, I look like an idiot, and I can't lift that damn box of junk and carry it another inch. Please, Julian. You do it."

She stuck out her lip, then with a grumble, he grabbed the box from the tailgate of 'Ol Blue, grunting as he lifted it. "Ugh. Fine. Why in the hell did we put so much in the one-dollar box? It's freaking heavy!"

"Because Diane wouldn't let me make a negative one thousand box," she said back with a sneer at me. "One dollar was as low as we could go."

I hefted a smaller box, clearly marked with a ten-dollar tag in permanent marker. "It's all for charity. The higher the prices, the more we can raise for Tyrell. Let's drop the grumbling and get these boxes over to the donation area."

Together, we trudged through the bustling town square, already brimming with people setting up their various fundraising booths. They seemed to be handling the heat much better than us, but instead of grumbling about it every step like CeCe and Julian, I tried to bear it with some semblance of dignity—which was hard because they weren't kidding. It really did feel like hell itself had swallowed the town whole.

I greeted everyone with grins and small waves as we passed by, shocked by how many people I now recognized by name. I'd forgotten what life in a small town was like, and everybody knew everybody... including everyone's business. Since the entire town frequented Mawmaw's regularly, I now knew more information about the people of Ruinville than I'd even wanted.

I knew about Ardell's bunions. Charlie's broken lawnmower. Lionel's trick knee that predicted the weather. I also knew about the Porter sisters' fight about the new bonnets they'd bought that turned out to be matching, and I'd been part of helping break the standoff. The mayor's overindulgence in moonshine, and so much more. Life in Ruinville was like life in a fishbowl, and I wondered what they thought about me and my odd entourage. The whispers were starting to quiet when people would see us, and it was almost starting to feel like they were no longer looking at us like the outsiders we'd been when we'd come crawling into town.

I glanced over and saw Sherrif Boshaw and gave him a wave. He just glared back at me, pointing to his eyes and then me.

Well, *almost* everyone had stopped looking at us like interlopers.

We finally arrived at the central sales tent strategically placed near the gazebo. Sweat dripped down our foreheads as we panted.

"Oh, such a doll," Ruby said, and her little Magnolia Maiden clones nodded in agreement. "Thanks so much for organizing these. Your Aunt Addie always did such a nice job helping out. Makes it so much faster for us to set up if everything is already grouped by price. Just set each box on the corresponding table with the price sign, then we'll take care of getting everything on display."

"Happy to help," I replied with a smile, my thoughts drifting to Aunt Addie and whether she was somehow watching, smiling at me for taking up her mantle.

Julian plopped his box onto a white folding table with a one-dollar sign. I quickly found the table with a ten-dollar sign, and CeCe mumbled something about the absence of a negative-thousand-dollar table, which should be the largest one.

"That's the last of it." I took a deep breath after unloading my box.

"Excellent. Truly excellent." Ruby beamed, her bright red lips accentuating her toothy smile. "Would you like to help us sort through the items?"

Her gaze darted between us, and before I could respond, CeCe declared, "Cookies! Can't help. Got cookies to unload!"

Julian playfully pouted. "Oh darn, I was just about to offer to stay, but you're right, the cookies. We don't want them melting to goo in the truck."

With synchronized sad-face expressions, they spun then scurried back toward the truck parked at the opposite end of the town square.

"Thank you for doing this, Ruby. I hope you raise a lot of money from these items." I smiled at her before I followed my friends as they hurried away. I caught up to them just as they passed the kissing booth.

"What kind of degenerate do they have giving out kisses at this thing?" Julian jutted a thumb at it. "Probably a pig or something."

"Better than kissing some of the men I've seen around here," CeCe snarked.

"What if it's Crocodile Dundee?" He matched her smirk. "Bet you wouldn't mind kissing him again."

Her cheeks flamed red as she gave him a little glare but didn't spit back a pointed retort.

"It's not going to take all three of us to carry cookies," I said as I caught up. "You just didn't want to help out back there."

"Well, duh," Julian scoffed.

"You guys, we should all be pitching in as much as we can."

They stopped in their tracks and faced me, with CeCe striking a defiant pose. "Just because you're on some soul-searching journey to reconnect with your roots doesn't mean we are, too. We did the pricing. Our part is done. We're out."

"What she said," Julian chimed in.

Rolling my eyes, I sighed. "Fine. Stick nearby at least so I can find you when I'm ready to leave."

"When will that be? In five minutes?" CeCe asked.

"Um, no. We just got here, and I haven't been to one of these in years. I expect a few hours before I'm ready," I responded, ignoring their dropped jaws. "No one is forcing you to stay, but I'm not driving you both back home just to turn around and come back. If you two want to walk home or spend your money on a cab, you're welcome to. Otherwise, get comfy because we'll be here for a while."

CeCe looked around at all the booths and people milling about and asked, "Where can we go that won't attract weirdos trying to talk to us or put us to work?"

Julian perked up, raising his finger as if he'd had a eureka moment. "The bookstore. People in Destituteville probably don't read much. Let's hide out there for a while. No one will bother us at the bookstore, and I bet they have air conditioning."

CeCe grinned in agreement, and they both took off down the sidewalk.

"It's Ruinville!" I called after them. "Not Destituteville, Idiotville, Brokeville, Loserville, or any of the other incorrectvilles you keep calling it. Ruinville! Ruinville, Ruinville, Ruinville!"

They continued on, paying no heed to my correction, and that's when I heard a throat clearing behind me.

I turned around to see John standing there, wearing a curious smile. "It's called what now?"

I closed my eyes and dropped my head, a laugh escaping from my lips. "Sorry about that. Julian always insists on calling this town by the wrong name."

"Idiotville?" John raised an amused eyebrow.

I shrugged. "He's got his quirks."

John chuckled and looked around the bustling town square. "It's a great turnout. I'm sure we'll raise a lot of money for Tyrell today."

"Absolutely. We've got a great collection of clothes that I just dropped off for the sale. And I managed to make eight dozen cookies last night!"

His eyes widened with genuine surprise. "You made the cookies yourself?"

I beamed with pride. "I sure did. It took a few tries to get it right, but they turned out pretty darn great."

"And you didn't have to call 911 because you set the house on fire? Impressive."

I winced. "Well, almost. I did trigger the fire alarm and filled the house with smoke with the first batch, but we managed to handle it without calling the fire department."

He burst into laughter, his shoulders shaking as he shook his head. "Well, at least you contained the damage without burning down the house."

I joined in his laughter. "No, just that batch of cookies met its maker. But, I've learned how to bake cookies now, so I guess I'm making progress. I only set off the fire alarm one more time, sending CeCe and Julian tumbling out of bed screaming at one in the morning. They accused me of doing it on purpose."

"And did you?" He arched an eyebrow.

I shrugged. "Maybe it was an accident, maybe it wasn't. I'll never tell."

He laughed again, and I joined him. It felt good just being near him, like decades of my life would slough away with his close proximity, and suddenly I was a young girl again with a whole lifetime ahead of me. Every time I saw him, I wondered what my life would have looked like if I'd just come back here that summer instead of staying away. If I'd chosen him instead of Rick. A simple life in a small town instead of the grand one I'd decided I wanted instead. Where would my life have gone? As I looked deeper into those dusky blue eyes, I started to lose myself in his gaze until I shook my head to snap out of it.

"I, uh... I should probably go drop off the cookies at the bake sale," I said, breaking the brief spell.

"Do you need help carrying them?"

"Would you mind? My arms ache from stirring all the cookie batches and carrying clothes to the clothing drive. I'm not twenty-one anymore."

"Of course, it would be my pleasure," he said.

My heart skipped a beat as he looked at me with a soft smile. We walked together to 'Ol Blue, and he effortlessly picked up the boxes of cookies, making them seem weightless as he cradled them against his chest. We strolled across the town square in comfortable silence, sharing glances from time to time. Finally, we arrived at the bake sale.

After John had set the boxes of cookies down, he pulled out five dollars, handing it to Mayor Marjorie, who managed the booth, in exchange for the honor of purchasing the first cookie.

Nervous energy surged within me as he took a big bite, and I anxiously waited to see his reaction.

"Well?" I asked, my hands fidgeting as I stared up at him.

After he had finished chewing, he looked at the remainder of his cookie. "Well, I'll be damned. You've absolutely nailed her recipe."

"I did?"

"You did. Well done, Diane. Aunt Addie would be proud."

I squealed with excitement, clapping my hands and jumping up and down before I leaped up into his arms. The impromptu explosion of joy caused him to freeze for a moment, but then a second later, his arms wrapped around my waist, and he held me up in the air, my toes dangling above the ground just like they used to when I'd leap into his arms and give him a hug all those decades ago.

After realizing how inappropriate it was for me to be clinging to his neck, even though I wanted nothing more than to stay there for the rest of the day, I released my grip on him and slid back to the ground.

"Sorry. I didn't mean to do that. I just, uh... I just got so excited."

The warmth of his smile lit me up. "Don't be sorry. It was fine."

His gaze flicked down to my ring finger, and I swore I noticed a twinkle in his eye when he saw it absent my wedding ring. He looked back up at me, but just as he opened his mouth to say something, Chatty Cathy came running up, arms flailing above her head.

"John! Fire Chief John! We need help!"

He spun, ready to jump into action. "What's wrong?"

She landed in front of him, hands pressed on her knees as she struggled to catch her breath. "Timmy stuck his head through the fence around the pig petting zoo, and we can't get him out. His mom is worried the pigs are gonna eat off his face."

"What?" I spit out. "The pigs will what?"

She looked at me, eyes wide. "It's a thing! Really! Pigs will eat anything, including human heads. We saw it on TV once. Best way to dispose of a body. Just... hurry, please, John. Bring your fancy fireman cutter doodad or the jaws of life to get him out. We'll fend off the pigs if they get any funny ideas."

"I'm on my way," he said, then turned to look at me. "Guess I gotta go. Good to see you, Diane."

"You, too, John." I waved as he started away, then I called after. "And be careful of those killer pigs!"

He looked over his shoulder and laughed, giving me one last wave before he jogged away.

Still feeling embarrassed about my overexcited launch into his arms, I pressed a hand to my head and murmured under my breath, "Idiot."

After he disappeared from sight, my gaze scanned the bustling town square, trying to decide which game or booth to explore first. A nostalgic smile crept onto my lips. It had been forty years since I'd last attended a Ruinville fundraiser, and yet, the scene before me felt as familiar as if it had just been yesterday.

The setting was almost identical to the ones I'd known as a child. We used to come here every weekend, peddling cookies and delighting in the carnival of games, for there was always someone or something in need of a helping hand, and in Ruinville, a lively festival in the town square was the traditional way to make it happen.

Feeling a little out of place and lonely, I looked across the large grass square to the bookstore across the street. I strolled through the growing crowds and opened the door, the little bell above my head announcing my arrival.

"Welcome!" a friendly voice said, and I offered a polite wave to the little woman with huge glasses behind the desk.

As I meandered through the cozy aisles of the bookstore, I turned a corner and spotted CeCe and Julian wedged together on a bean bag chair in the corner. Their heads were close, and their hushed giggles filled the air as they immersed themselves in a book.

"What's got you two so engrossed?" I asked, prompting them both to look up, their expressions resembling teenagers caught in a mischievous act.

Julian shoved the book behind his back. "Nothing."

I walked toward them then opened my hand. "What is it? Show me."

With a groan, he handed me the book, and I almost dropped it when I saw it was *that* book. *Fifty Shades of Grey.*

"Eew! Isn't this like porn?" I quickly handed it back.

"We were reading the dirty scenes," CeCe whispered with a giggle.

"Well, playtime in the bookstore is over. You two are coming out to join me for the little fundraising festival."

They both pulled a face. "Go out there in the heat with all those people? Don't we see enough of them at MawMaw's? I hardly think we need to spend more time with them than we already do," Julian said, shaking his head.

"Agree." CeCe mimicked his head shake, and for a moment, it looked like they had a tube or something connecting their heads the way they shook in unison.

"Please?" I begged. "I just made a complete fool of myself in front of John, and I don't want to be out there wandering around alone."

"A fool of yourself?" Julian's eyes widened as he sat forward. "What did you do? Grab his butt? Stick your tongue in his mouth?"

"Get caught looking at his crotch?" CeCe jumped in.

I let out an exasperated breath. "No, no, and definitely no. I jumped into his arms and basically assaulted him with a hug."

Julian scrunched his face. "Why did you do that?"

"I was overexcited that he liked my cookies, and I just kinda lost it."

Julian snorted. "He liked your cookies."

CeCe caught the dirty joke and laughed.

"Would you two be serious for a second and just get out here and spend some time with me? I don't want to look like a lone loser. I need my friends."

The moment the word came out of my mouth, I froze, my eyes widening as I stared at them.

Friends.

Were they? Somehow in the time we'd been stuck together in this alternate universe, had they actually morphed from my archenemies into my... friends?

The word didn't get lost on them, and they both stared at me silently like I had three heads. Not wanting to make a big deal over the word still rattling around in my brain, I quickly kept talking.

"Please. Just come eat some food, buy a few things to support the fundraiser so we look good to the town, play a few games, then we can go home. Bill may be out there." I waggled my eyebrows at CeCe.

She tried to conceal her excitement but failed with the way her eyes sparkled.

"Are you buying?" Julian asked. "I don't want to waste any of my nearly non-existent dough on this crap."

I nodded. "My treat."

CeCe almost launched to her feet. "Free food! I'm in!"

Julian joined her, then I waved at the store clerk while they trailed behind me out of the store and into the festival now swinging into full gear.

"Whoa. There are a lot of people in Povertyville."

I started laughing. "*Ruin*ville, Julian. It's Ruinville."

He shrugged. "Same difference. If you name your town something that means *ruined*, I don't know what you expect."

"Follow me." I tugged his hand and dragged him to the center of the town square where a giant stone statue of a dog posed next to a huge, preserved tree stump.

"This is Rune." I pointed to the plaque beneath the dog's feet. "This is how the town got its name."

"But this is spelled R-U-N-E, not R-U-I-N like, well, we're ruined, because we are. Ruined in Ruinville."

"I'm going to tell you the story of how Ruinville came to be. My Aunt Addie used to love telling this tale." My heart warmed a little remembering sitting right here in front of this statue as a child as she regaled the tale of the founder of Ruinville.

Using her same flare for the dramatic, I started telling the story. "This town was founded by an explorer named Captain Samuel Beauregard, born to a noble French family in 1778. Drawn by the promise of both adventure and riches, Beauregard left his homeland and set sail for the American territories along with his dog named Rune."

I paused and pointed at the dog staring proudly out into the town.

"Upon arriving in New Orleans, he immediately assembled a small, determined crew of settlers and skilled guides, knowing that the swamps and bayous held the promise of fertile lands, exotic flora, and abundant wildlife. Leading his expedition up the winding Mississippi River, Beauregard navigated deep into the untamed wilderness of the Louisiana Purchase. As the party ventured deeper into the treacherous terrain, they faced countless challenges, from dangerous wildlife to hostile indigenous tribes and the ever-present threat of disease."

CeCe and Julian surprisingly seemed riveted by my story. As I continued on, I used my hands to emphasize the danger I now spoke of, including faking a sword fight that left Julian gasping as he clutched his chest.

"But Beauregard's charisma and fortitude inspired his companions to persevere. He learned the secrets of survival in the swamps, and fostered peaceful relationships with the Native American populations, gaining their trust and assistance in his quest. One fateful day, Rune took off after some local wildlife, and Captain Beauregard ran after him. He found Rune having treed an animal in the largest tree he'd ever seen in his life."

I paused to gesture to the stump. "This stump right here is the actual remains of that very tree which fell down in a storm a century ago. When Captain Beauregard got control of his dog, he looked around and realized he'd stumbled upon an untouched, breathtakingly beautiful location hidden deep within the bayou. He believed he had found the perfect spot to establish a settlement—a place where his dreams of a thriving community could come to life. With unwavering resolve, he oversaw the construction of the town, which he named "Runeville" in honor of dog that had brought him here."

"Then why is it Ruinville instead of R-U-N-E-ville?" Julian asked.

I chuckled, delighted to share the quirky twist of fate that befell the town's name. "Because, when he asked the sign maker to create the very first sign for his new town, the man didn't understand the difference between the words, and he misspelled it as R-U-I-N-ville. And not wanting to pay for a new sign, Captain Beauregard just kept it spelled the way, and that, my friends, is why we now live in a town called Ruinville."

They stared at me, blinking.

Julian tipped his head. "So, the sign maker was an idiot, and that's how this place came to be called Destituteville?"

I laughed and nodded. "Yes, Julian. That's how the place became known as Destituteville."

"Interesting!" he said then walked over and patted the giant dog on the nose. "Sorry your owner didn't correct that sign. I'd much rather be rotting away in Runeville instead of Ruinville."

"I'd rather be rotting away anywhere but here," CeCe said, looking around at the bustling festival with a distasteful frown.

"So, now that you know the story of the town, let's go enjoy it a little!" I grinned, hoping my enthusiasm would wear off on them, but they just stared at me, scowling. "I'm buying, so let's go."

Those words perked them up a little, and they trailed along behind me as we puttered around booth to booth trying all the foods and buying the little worthless nicknacks and items for far more than they were worth just so we could contribute to Tyrell's fundraiser. Zydeco music filled the air, creating an infectious rhythm that had me swaying with every step I took. I managed to convince them to play a few games like ring toss, balloon darts, and the bean bag toss. Nostalgia filled my heart to bursting as I remembered youthful summers spent running around the festivals with Johnny. When they lost at every game we tried our hands at, they grew increasingly irritable, much like disgruntled children longing to head back home.

As it seemed like a full-scale temper tantrum was brewing, I decided to give up my attempts to immerse them in Ruinville culture. "Alright, alright, we can go. But first, let's say hello to Mawmaw May to make sure she knows we supported the cause. I wouldn't want her to think you two neglected your civic duties."

Although they grumbled, they begrudgingly followed me over to where Mawmaw May was serving food at the crawfish boil.

"Hello, Chers!" she exclaimed with a wide grin as she spotted us. She scooped all three of us into a warm hug. "I'm thrilled you could make it to the festival. The turnout is fantastic, and the Landry family will be well taken care of, not having to work for the next few months."

"This is so fun to be back at one of these." I looked all around me. "It feels like time just completely stood still."

"Why change perfection?" She smiled at me. "We've been having these fundraising festivals for years. They draw a big crowd, make great money, and everyone has fun. And not to mention the great food. Hey! I heard you did a great job making Aunt Addie's cookies! Everyone's talking 'bout them!"

My cheeks swelled with my smile as my chest swelled with pride. "Really? People are talking about them?"

"Plum near sold out already I heard!"

"Wow! I'm so happy I learned how to make those. I wasn't sure if I could do it."

"Your Aunt Addie is up there just pleased as punch right now I bet." She reached forward and pinched my cheek. "Ya'll having some crawfish boil? 'Nother one is just coming up ready."

"Sure, why not," I said, and looked over at my two scowling friends. "I'm buying."

They lit up, and I handed Mawmaw some of the cash I'd made in tips the past few shifts I'd worked.

"Just have a seat and we'll be serving the next round shortly!"

"Wow. A crawfish boil, I haven't been to one of these since I was a kid." I walked over to the oversized picnic table covered in a plastic tablecloth and newspaper. We squished in between other hungry Southerners practically drooling as they waited for the food to be served. I didn't dare warn CeCe and Julian about *how* the food would be served, and just hoped like hell they would enjoy the experience as much as I used to.

I looked at their concerned faces as they stared at the locals surrounding us, then CeCe's eyes flickered with shock. I turned to see Bayou Bill walking straight toward us.

"Oh my God, he's coming over," Julian whispered as he practically shimmied in his seat. "Are you gonna kiss him again?"

"Shut up." She elbowed him hard enough in the ribs to make him expel a sharp breath.

"Hey, Pretty Girl," Bayou Bill said as he slid into the seat across from us. "You actually going to partake in one of my favorite festival traditions?"

She looked uncomfortable as she shrugged, her eyes looking everywhere but his. "I don't know. Diane just said we're having dinner here."

He grinned. "Oh, Pretty Girl. You're in for a real treat."

Mawmaw May called out "Incoming!" and we all sat back while they carried over huge pots filled with all the good stuff. My stomach growled with excitement as they dumped the huge pots on the table sending crawfish, potatoes, corn, and sausage scattering in every direction.

"What the hell? Where are the plates? They are dumping it right on the table!" CeCe recoiled, leaning as far back as she could from the food sliding to a stop in front of her.

"This is how they serve it!" I grinned back. "Just grab some crawfish and enjoy!"

"Eew! They have eyes! They're looking at me! They're looking at me!" Julian shielded his face and turned away. "Make it stop!"

Everyone around us dove right in, grabbing the lifeless little creatures and going to town the way only Southerners could eat at a crawfish boil.

"No!" CeCe practically screamed as she watched in horror while the man next to her ripped the head off one and started sucking the juice right out of it. The loud slurping sound even made me cringe. I hadn't quite remembered just how graphic these meals could be.

"Don't be shy, Pretty Girl. Grab a mud bug and rip it in half! Suck the juice from the head and rip the meat from its ass. Best damn thing that'll ever touch those pretty little lips." He paused then wiggled his eyebrows and whispered, "Well, other than my lips, of course."

"Make it stop!" Julian shrieked again as the woman sitting to his left dropped a carcass right beside him. "Its eyes! Its lifeless eyes are boring through me!"

The man beside CeCe slurped again, and this time it was too much. She started gagging, and the loud, guttural sounds triggered the same response in Julian, and he began gagging too. They both erupted into a chorus of disgust, and I sat between them silently praying they wouldn't vomit on the table.

"That's it! I'm out of here!" CeCe spat between wretches, then she nearly tumbled off backwards trying to dislodge herself from her seat squished at the picnic table. Julian clawed his way free and sprinted after her, and I looked up at Bayou Bill and cringed.

"I, uh, I completely forgot what these were really like and may have made a grave error in making CeCe and Julian sit down to a crawfish boil."

He chuckled and snapped a crawfish in half then popped the tail meat in his mouth. "She'll calm down. Bit high strung that one, but I'll go find her in a minute. Just want a few more bites before I go scoop her up from wherever she's hiding."

I chuckled at the image of Julian and CeCe clinging together in a bush somewhere gagging in unison, but I also felt terrible I'd misread the situation so much.

"I'll go find them." I pushed off the table, admittedly feeling relieved to get some space from the man hoovering down crawfish heads like an industrial vacuum at the car wash. It wasn't what I remembered, and I had to admit I wanted to get some space from the slurping and snapping too.

I walked quickly around the fundraiser, then found CeCe and Julian sitting on the tailgate of 'Ol Blue, arms crossed and frowns on full display.

"You're a monster," CeCe said as I approached.

I raised my hands in submission. "I don't remember it being that... graphic," I defended. "I just remember eating a bunch of crawfish off a table, and I thought it was cool."

"They were staring at me." Julian's frown deepened with disgust. "Literally staring at me while their entrails were falling out. You *are* a monster!"

"I'm sorry!" I slumped forward. "I don't remember it being so gross! I didn't like it either if it makes you feel any better."

"It doesn't," they answered in unison.

A siren screamed and drew the attention of everyone in the area. I spun around to see the firetruck pulling out of the station, and I caught a glimpse of John driving it away. Other firemen clutched the sides, their fire gear on full display. My heart sank that a call was pulling him away from the fundraiser, and I wouldn't get a chance to see him again tonight and try to spend a little more time with him *not* embarrassing myself.

"There goes your boyfriend," Julian said. "Maybe I should go catch up and tell him what a monster you are that you like partaking in horrifying carnage displays where people rip the head off creatures while they stare at you."

"Stop!" I said with a sigh. "I'm sorry. I didn't realize how traumatizing that was going to be. Can we just forget it and go home and make a frozen pizza?"

"Yes. I'm starving," CeCe said. "Which is surprising because that was so gross I thought I'd lose my appetite for life."

"Don't you want to go back and watch your boyfriend suck the brains out of some crawfish?" Julian said, then soured his face. "Ugh. And to think you kissed those lips."

"And she's gonna kiss 'em again," Bill said, startling us as he approached from the side of the truck.

"Bill!" CeCe jumped up to standing. "What are you doing here?"

"Coming to make sure you're okay," he said, ignoring Julian and I like no one in the world existed but her. "You looked a little green back there."

"That was horrifying." She turned her nose up. "Truly disgusting."

"Ah, it's not so different than eatin' lobster," he argued. "Just a lot smaller. You get used to it."

"Never." Her nose lifted higher. "I'll never eat those things."

"You said never about other things I happen to know you reneged on."

She spun to look at him, and though I know she tried her best to impale him with her signature glare, instead, her lips started curving into a smile.

"Take a drive with me? Got a really neat place to show you, perfect for staring at the stars." He extended his arm.

CeCe looked at us, then back to Bill and opened her mouth to say something I assumed was dipped with venom.

Before she could utter a word, he lifted a hand. "You can spend the next however long chastising me and pretending you don't want to join me, or we can just skip that part and you can tell me how much you hate me while we go for a drive. It's a pretty night and the stars are out in droves. Truly beautiful, and I think you'll really enjoy seeing them. And if that doesn't sell you, my truck has air conditioning, and if I recall, Aunt Addie's house and that old truck don't. Come on for a drive, we'll cool down and watch the stars at the prettiest spot you've ever seen. Just leave the mace in your purse. I'm not going to serial kill you as long as you promise not to serial kill me."

She tipped her head. "Air conditioning?"

He nodded. "Yep."

She pinched her lips, then after a long pause, she sighed, softening as she reached out and slid her hand through his arm. I nearly choked at how accurately he seemed to already understand her. Like some kind of a magical CeCe tamer, Bill had managed to gentle the mouthy beast with little effort.

"Seriously?" Julian said exasperated. "You're going on a drive with him and leaving me here traumatized and hungry? How long will you be gone? I want pizza?"

"Head on home and I'll get a ride back with Bill," she said, her eyes sparkling as they remained locked with his.

I couldn't help but smile seeing the way CeCe softened in his presence. Like a piece of sandpaper scrubbing against a rough piece of wood, he smoothed all her sharp edges. And she looked happier with her camouflage knight in shining armor than I'd ever seen her at any event in New York.

"I'll get her home safe," Bill said, then he turned back at us and winked. "Eventually. Don't wait up."

CeCe flushed red, then glanced back at us and grinned.

I gave her a little wave then slung an arm around Julian's shoulder. "It's you and me tonight, pal."

"Weird. We've never spent a night alone together."

"Movies and pizzas?"

His eyes lit up. "Yes, please!"

"Come on. I'll drive."

I glanced at CeCe and Bill one last time and smiled, then I looked in the direction I'd seen John speed off, and my smile faltered. I wished I was going for a drive with a handsome man tonight, too, but it seemed only CeCe was finding affection this evening.

I looked at Julian. At least he gave great foot rubs.

CHAPTER EIGHTEEN
CeCe

The gentle caress of the morning sun on my face and the alluring aroma of coffee slowly pulled me from slumber. As I awoke, I greeted the day with a contented stretch, but my elation quickly gave way to a startling revelation. A sense of warmth and the comforting weight of an arm draped over my shoulder were not my usual morning companions. I froze as I started to process my surroundings.

"Good morning, Pretty Girl," Bill's voice broke the silence.

I blinked my eyes wide, momentarily disoriented by the rustic wooden walls of the cozy cabin bedroom. A careful glance to my side and my eyes met the beautiful blue ones of my unexpected bedfellow, and the events of the previous night began to reassemble in my mind like a movie playing in fast forward, weaving together a tapestry of memories.

The beautiful walk by the water.

The breathtaking kiss beneath the stars.

The drive to his house where I could barely keep my hands off him.

The knee-shaking kiss at his front door where he pressed me up against it and sent my head spinning from the power of his passion.

And then...

I smiled wide as I remembered the night of incredible lovemaking unlike anything I'd ever experienced before. Never had I imagined how magical it could feel to connect with someone the way I connected with Bill. How he seemed to know everything I desired long before I imagined it, and he left me breathless and satiated, nooked up safely in his arms while I had drifted to sleep.

Happy.

Protected.

Satisfied.

"Damn, girl. Waking up next to you is better than a month full of Sundays."

He brushed a hand across my face, and I froze at his touch, wide eyes blinking back at him.

He smiled. "Now, before you start in on faking your horror about waking up with me, I'll just remind you that I was present last night, and I will testify that you had a damn good time and came to my bed of your own free will. But if you want to start sniping at me about how horrified you are, and that I'd better keep my trap shut and not breathe a word of this to another human or you'll gut me like a pig, I need a coffee first."

He wasn't wrong. There was a part of me that wanted to pretend this was a terrible mistake and I, CeCe VanTramp, would never choose to tangle with the likes of someone like Bayou Bill. That he'd better erase the memories of my naked body from his mind or I'd dig his brain out with a spoon, but...

I didn't want to fight it anymore. For weeks I'd tried to pretend my feelings for him were nothing more than enjoying being fawned upon by a handsome man. But after last night, I realized that things between us were so much more, and I was done waging war against it.

Instead of fighting it, I finally gave into the feelings for Bill that were stronger than I'd ever imagined I could feel for him.

For anyone.

"Good morning," I finally whispered as I wiggled deeper into his embrace, pressing my hand to his broad chest beside my head.

His grip on my shoulder tightened. "Wow. No witty comeback? No pointed words?"

I just shook my head softly. "No. I'm too tired for that."

I could sense his smile as he stroked a hand down my arm. "Well, good. Saves me the headache this morning. Did you sleep okay?"

Having no energy or desire to feign shock and bolt from his bed, I found myself embracing vulnerability and revealed my true feelings. "I think I had the best sleep I've ever had."

In response, he planted a soft, tender kiss on my forehead, and I let out a contented sigh.

"Automatic coffee maker kicked in. Would you like me to get you a cup?"

"I'd love that."

Looking up at him, I locked eyes with his striking blue gaze, and that familiar fluttering sensation in my stomach returned. His gentle fingers traced my chin, guiding my lips upward for a sweet, lingering kiss.

"I'll be right back," he whispered against my lips.

Even though I knew he would return shortly, I couldn't quite bring myself to roll away from the safe cocoon of his embrace. Being pressed against his warm skin offered a comfort that I didn't want to end, even for the promise of the coffee that my mouth practically watered to sip. Bill was an unexpected bright spot in the dark landscape that had become my hellish life. He was the only thing that seemed to bring a smile to my face when I thought about the endless hours slaving away at a bar, living in a hovel, and scraping by until I could find a new husband to lift me out of it.

As I gazed up at Bill, my heart ached at the thought of the inevitable goodbye when my true knight in shining, diamond-adorned armor finally appeared. I knew that my current rendezvous with Bill was merely a temporary escape from my harsh reality ... scratching an itch as Julian had put it.

So why did the thought of leaving his arms cause me such anguish?

Pushing the dilemma from my mind, I tried to put myself back in the moment and just relish the fact I'd enjoyed a spectacular, romantic evening for what felt like the very first time in my life.

"Don't you move, Pretty Girl," he said softly. "I want to see you still sprawled in my bed when I return."

"I won't," I said, then finally convinced my body to roll to the side and let him free to bring back my much-needed caffeine. When he stood, my mouth watered for a different reason than the promise of the coffee I could smell... the sight of that naked behind was even better than it had looked in jeans. I bit my lip while I soaked in the impressive physique of the man I'd not seen as clearly in the dark. Arthur had never been one for physical fitness, usually sporting a belly and flabby skin, so this treat to my eyes caused me to grin as I pulled the covers up to my chin and chewed on my swollen lip.

Bill glanced over his shoulder, and a playful smile tipped his lips. "I see you lookin'."

I giggled and pulled the covers over my head then peeked out again. He made no effort to cover himself and walked confidently across the room in nothing but his birthday suit. When he reached the bedroom door, he grabbed his camouflage terrycloth robe from the door hanger. Before he slipped it on, he paused to give me a little extra look and a wink, and I nearly melted into a puddle of goo as I swooned.

After he disappeared into the kitchen, I heard a phone ring, and a moment later, Bill appeared in the doorway holding up his cell phone, an amused look upon his face. "It's Julian. We're in trouble."

My eyes popped wide. "Oh shoot! I forgot to call home and tell them I was going to be staying over!"

He chuckled and walked over, handing me the phone. "I know. I just got an earful."

I cringed then held the phone up to my ear as Bill walked back out. "Hello?"

"CeCe Louise VanTramp!" Julian scolded. "We were worried sick about you! I just got home to find you missing, and Diane didn't hear a peep out of you last night. We had to call Mawmaw's to get Crocodile Dundee's phone number to find out if he'd murdered you sometime in the night! You have some explaining to do young lady!"

"I got in on with the gator guy," I said quickly in a hushed whisper. I figured the bombshell would stop him from chastising me anymore.

"I knew it!" he screamed, and I had to pull the phone away from my ear. "I knew you were gonna get it on with the gator guy!"

"She got it on with the gator guy?" I heard Diane say in the background. "Get out of here!"

"She did! She's a dirty hussy!" Julian teased, and I couldn't stop grinning as I replayed the passionate evening over and over in my mind.

"Wait a minute," I said, arching an eyebrow. "Did you say you just got home?"

There was a pause, then Julian blurted out. "I met someone. A reporter at the fundraiser. Just after you left, this super-hot guy came over to interview Diane about making her aunt's cookies. Some feel good family story or something. Whatever. We stuck around, he and I hit it off, one thing led to another, and guess what?"

"What?" I asked excitedly.

"I went to the city with him for a night out! The city, CeCe! With real people in real clothes that didn't come from Walmart! We went to a club. We danced all night. We had a little hanky panky, and I just got home an hour ago."

"Wow! You went to the city? With a boy? How fun!"

"It was so fun!"

"And I got stuck here all alone!" Diane called from the background.

"Sorry about that. I told you it wasn't planned. I just got to dancing and well, you know how that goes," Julian said to her, then returned his attention to me. "First off, we all need to get a cell phone with our next paycheck money because I had no way to call you last night, and you had no way to call me."

"And no one called me!" Diane scolded. "I was worried sick!"

"Okay, okay," I said. "We'll go get one of those pay as you go phones like Diane has now that we're not all glued together 24/7 like some dysfunctional walking, talking scrap book."

Bill appeared with a cup of coffee, and I lost my concentration as Julian started prattling on about his incredible night in the city. I discreetly mouthed a grateful "thank you" to Bill and then closed my eyes briefly as he paused to plant a tender kiss on my cheek.

"CeCe! Are you listening?" Julian demanded.

"What? Huh? Yes, of course."

"Ugh. You're not listening. Oh my God! Are you still getting in on with the gator guy?"

"No!" I said, then Bill slipped back under the covers clutching his cup of coffee and ideas started dancing in my mind again. "You know what. I'll be home in about an hour. I'll just talk to you then."

"Hurry up!" Julian demanded, but I hung up on him and snuggled back into the nook of Bill's open arm.

"I've got to take out a tour in about an hour and a half, so that works perfect. I'll just drop you off at home on my way to the boat."

I hated to think about getting out of bed and stepping back into reality, so I tried to ignore all the pressing things awaiting me outside our little bubble of happiness. Here, in this small cabin on the shore of the bayou, everything else would just have to wait.

When I looked deep into Bill's eyes and saw the raw desire dancing within them, we both set down our coffees on the end table, and I lost myself in him once more.

***

When Bill dropped me off at home, we stayed parked in front of the house kissing like high schoolers before he finally caught a glimpse of the clock and realized he was going to be late.

"Can I see you later, Pretty Girl?"

With no desire to play coy and pretend I didn't want to experience the magic with him again and again, I nodded quickly. "You have Diane's number. Just call me on that phone. I'll get my own soon."

"I'll stop in and see you at work tonight. What time do you start?"

I frowned thinking about the long shift awaiting me. "Ugh. Work. Yuck. Not until about four."

"I'll come in for dinner. How's that sound?"

Seeing him stroll into Mawmaw's was always the highlight of my nights, so I smiled and nodded. "Perfect. I'll see you tonight."

"Bye, Pretty Girl," he said, then kissed me senseless once again.

I hopped out of the truck and waved goodbye then scurried up the front steps. Julian whipped open the door, and he and Diane stood wearing matching grins the Cheshire cat would have envied.

Julian's eyes sparkled. "You got it on with the gator guy."

I grinned back, unable to suppress my happy smile, feeling like I might burst from all the excitement and joy buzzing around inside me.

"Well? How was it? What was it like? I can't even imagine being with anyone but my husband. Was it weird?" Diane rapid-fired questions.

"It was wonderful," I said on a sigh as I practically floated into the house. "You wouldn't know it by looking at him, but Bill is such a romantic. He made me feel like a young teenager again. It was just... it was perfect."

Diane closed the door behind me, smiling as she followed me into the living room where I flopped down on the couch. She and Julian each jumped into a seat beside me.

"So, it was good, huh? It wasn't weird at all after being with the same man for so many years?" Diane asked.

I shook my head. "You'd think it would be, but it just felt..." I paused, searching for the word. "Natural, I guess. Things with Bill just seemed natural. Comfortable. Kinda like we fit. Does that make sense?"

Diane sighed and her gaze drifted off out the window. "I had that once. I get it."

"With the fireman?" Julian asked, and she nodded. He shimmied his shoulders. "Ooooh, Diane! Now it's your turn! I kissed a boy. CeCe kissed a boy. When are you going to kiss a boy?"

Diane flushed red and shook her head. "I don't know. He hasn't even asked me out. I don't even know if I would go if he did. I'm still married."

I scowled. "Only by a technicality. They abandoned us, Diane. The vows are broke. We're as single as if they'd never existed."

"You don't feel guilty at all?" she asked.

"Not even the slightest. After all the hell he put me through, I earned myself a magical night like that one."

Julian's eyes lit up, and I knew he was dying to fill me in on his big night, so I asked.

"Oh, it was incredible, CeCe! The lights, the music, the clothes. I didn't realize how much I'd missed it all! His name is Abe, and he's a reporter from a TV station that did a little story on small town fundraisers, then they got wind that Diane is taking up her aunt's mantle making cookies, and they thought it was a great feel-good piece. So, after the interview, we started flirting, and before you know it, I'm riding back to the city with him. I swear I almost passed out when we pulled up at a club and I saw the lights flashing. Felt like home."

He sighed and leaned back against the couch.

"And the guy? Is he good?"

He shrugged. "He's fine. I mean, if it means I have someone to take me out in the city, I'll definitely see him again. I certainly wouldn't have dated him back in New York, but down here he's like Brad freaking Pitt."

"I'm happy you got a night out in the city. That sounds wonderful."

His eyes lit up. "He's got friends. Older friends. Like producers and things that could be a great in for you! I'm going to keep dating him and start scanning his friends until I find our next sugar daddy. How smart am I?"

Instead of my spirit lifting with the knowledge we were one step closer to leaving this madness, my stomach plummeted to the floor. It dawned on me, my face betraying my inner conflict, that meeting our new husband would mean saying goodbye to my tryst with Bill.

He scowled. "What's that look on your face? Why aren't you more excited? This is our ticket out of here, CeCe!"

I forced a wide grin. "No, I am excited. That's wonderful news, Julian. Nice work. I can't wait to see who you can find for me."

"He's gonna be great, CeCe. I'll find someone so rich and old that hopefully he won't be around for long, and after he kicks the bucket, we'll never want for a thing again."

"Or you could start supporting yourselves and make your own happiness," Diane said, but Julian just waved a hand up in her direction.

"You want to do your small-town cookie-baking stand-on-your-own-two-feet pauper thing, that's on you, but me and CeCe? We don't belong here. We belong in the city with limos and champagne and all the finest luxuries life has to offer. That's where our happiness lies. Isn't that right, CeCe?"

The happiest I'd ever remembered feeling in my life had actually been in Bill's arms just this morning, but I still craved the luxurious life that had been ripped away from me. I nodded in agreement with Julian, saying, "Yes. We don't belong here."

"Suit yourselves." Diane pressed her hands to her thighs and stood. "I'm going to make us all some breakfast. Eggs on toast okay?"

"Sounds perfect," I answered and settled back against the couch.

As Diane cooked, Julian went on and on about all the luxuries awaiting us in the city, but for some reason, the thought of stepping back into that world again twisted my stomach up in knots. The only thing that seemed to unwind them was thinking about another morning awaking in Bill's arms.

But I had a mission at hand, a promise I'd made Julian and myself, so I shook off the warm feelings Bill inspired in me and focused on Julian's plan to get us back to the penthouse where we truly belonged.

CHAPTER NINETEEN
Diane

I pulled up in front of the village hall and turned off the old truck. The loud *bang* announced my presence to everyone around the block, and instead of jumping like I still did, they just spun around and gave me grins and waves knowing exactly who'd just pulled up. I waved back at the familiar faces dotting the little bustling town square. The enticing scent of freshly baked cookies filled the cab of the truck, prompting me to retrieve the basket from the front seat before hopping out and scanning for the cookie fundraising table.

A few nights ago, Seamus O'Malley's dog got in a spat with an alligator, and after a race to the doggy ER an hour away, he'd come home with a dog stitched up like a quilt and a three-thousand-dollar vet bill. In typical Ruinville fashion, knowing Seamus didn't have three-thousand-dollars to spare, everyone pitched in for a last-minute bake sale to help raise some funds to pay for his pooch's emergency surgery. I'd whipped up a few batches of Aunt Addie's cookies to chip in the way I knew she would have if she were still here.

"I can smell them from here!" Mayor Margorie grinned when she saw me approaching with my basket. She rubbed her stomach and licked her lips when I got closer. "It ain't a fundraiser without Aunt Addie's famous cookies! Last week at the Tyrell's fundraiser, everyone was raving about them! I'm just tickled pink you learned how to make them. She would be too."

I smiled with that warmth that always flooded me when someone mentioned how proud my Aunt Addie would be. It still mingled with the guilt I felt that I hadn't made it back to Ruinville to make her proud when she was alive, but each day I sank deeper into her community and into her shoes, the pain of my past mistakes lessened. It was as though every cookie I donated chipped away at the penance I felt for abandoning her.

"Where should I put them?" I asked, looking around at the table overflowing with baked goods.

"Right in my belly," a deep voice behind me said, and I smiled, recognizing it instantly.

I turned around to find John behind me, his smile wide as he greeted me. I'd only seen him a few times at Mawmaw's since the fundraiser last week when I'd hugged him so awkwardly. I flushed red every time I saw him when those memories of how good it felt to be in his arms rushed back to me with each casual smile.

The heat rose up my cheeks again as I pulled the basket out of his reach while he pretended to greedily grab them. "These are for charity. You're gonna have to pay," I teased.

"Damn." He clucked his cheek. "I don't have my wallet on me. Mayor Marjorie, can you set six of those aside for me? I'll pay you later."

"Anything for you, John! Thanks again for coming by to check for the carbon monoxide last night. In fact, I'll pay for your cookies. You earned it."

"You don't have to do that. It was my pleasure," he answered.

With a tut-tut, Mayor Marjorie pulled out six cookies and wrapped them in a napkin before handing them to him. "Thank you for your service, Chief John."

"I'm not gonna say no to free cookies. Especially these." He grinned at her and then at me before taking the cookies.

Before she could answer, she looked down toward the table where Ruby was setting some cherry scones. "No, Ruby! That's the chocolate section! Those go over there!"

She hurried off in a huff leaving John and I standing alone together. He took a big bite of a cookie, closing his eyes and smiling as he chewed. "Worth every second of getting trapped for an hour after I finished checking her house last night. She had to show me her new porcelain figurine collection."

I cringed. "Yikes."

"Yeah. Yikes," he said between bites.

Mayor Marjorie and Ruby started arguing over the cookie spread layout, and John glanced over at the gazebo behind us. "We need to get out of here before they come running over to ask us for our opinion to break the stalemate. Come on. Let's go sit at the gazebo and catch up a bit."

As I glanced at Ruby and Mayor Marjorie still bickering away, I didn't hesitate to jump in behind John and hurry away from the squabble. We walked the short block to the center of the town square, settling into the familiar gazebo.

He chuckled. "Damn. I just had a flashback of the last time we were here together. Do you remember—"

I cut him off. "Do I remember us sitting here sharing an ice cream sundae when Tumbling Tom left his walker behind his truck and then proceeded to back out over it?" I pointed to the spot of the incident, and John burst into laughter.

"That guy had an 'incident' every damn day. Running stuff over, falling down, breaking everything within arm's length."

"That's why they nicknamed him Tumbling Tom." I laughed recalling how many times we'd seen the stubborn old man who refused to accept help or accept his old age. "He would *not* stop driving. Refused to slow down and stop acting like a kid when he was an eighty-year-old with a bad back, bad knees and arthritis. Oh man. We saw him wipe out more times than I could count! Whatever happened to him?"

"Made it to ninety-eight if you can believe it. We took his keys away in his early nineties after he drove straight through Dorothy's fence, but he just kept stealing them back. Finally had Gary, the mechanic, take the tires off his truck and put it on blocks. He was so pissed, but he finally gave in and stopped driving. Ah, good ol' Tumbling Tom."

"Man. I had completely forgot about him. Oh! What ever happened to that woman who had like ten cats, and she'd put them in that big wagon and drag them around the square every day?"

He chuckled. "She pushed those cats around every day until she died about five, six years ago."

As we sat there in the gazebo we'd spent hours upon hours in as teens, we recanted all the tales from our youth and laughed about the memories we'd made. Almost an hour passed, and I barely noticed the heat as we sat talking and laughing about days gone by, the familiarity between us growing with each laugh and gentle touch.

The sun glinted off John's watch as he glanced down at it.

"Got somewhere to be?" I asked.

He shook his head. "Nah. Was gonna meet the guys for a beer at Mawmaw's, but they'll live without me."

"It feels good to have the night off. Normally I'd be there serving you food and CeCe would be cracking open that beer."

"You're off tonight?" he asked, glancing up at me.

"Yep. Whole day off. Feels like a miracle."

Swiping a hand across the back of his neck, he hesitated before speaking. "Do you, uh... would you like to meet me for dinner tonight? I'm off too."

My heart raced with anticipation. A date? Was he asking me on a date? Unsure if that was his true intent but excited about the prospect of an evening with him, I smiled. "Uh... yeah. I would. That sounds great."

"Yeah?" He returned my smile, and the way his eyes lit up told me the answer to the unspoken question.

I may have been out of the game for a long time, but there was no doubting that familiar look in his eyes. It was definitely a date.

"Yeah." I grinned wider.

"Why don't I pick you up at say... six o'clock?"

My little girlish heart thumped away in my chest. "I'd love that."

"Great. I'll head home to change and finish some stuff around the house, then I'll see you in a few hours."

"Sounds good."

We stood, and there was an awkward moment where we nearly hugged, but then we just smiled and walked the opposite way. It was all I could do to restrain myself from running all the way back to my truck, exploding with excitement to tell CeCe and Julian that I had a...

Gulp.

Date.

***

I practically squealed to a stop in the driveway, jumping out before the familiar *bang* had even finished. With excitement like I hadn't felt in years pushing me on, I tore up the walkway and took the stairs two at a time, bursting through the screen door, panting.

"I have a date! I have a date!" I screamed as I tore into the house. "Where are you guys? I have a date!"

CeCe and Julian popped out of the kitchen, eyes wide as they tumbled out the door together.

"What? Who? Where?" Julian demanded as he grabbed my wrist. "Tell!"

"Who? Who?" CeCe said.

"With John! We ran into each other at the bake sale, and he asked me to dinner. Oh my God. I'm having dinner with John!"

Julian started jumping and clapping, and I couldn't help but join him. Soon CeCe started hopping as well, and the three of us bounced around in a little circle.

"You're have date with a fireman! So sexy!" Julian squealed.

"You have a date! A date!" CeCe's voice lifted with an unusual enthusiasm.

As the word *date* kept tumbling around, suddenly my excitement began to morph into terror, and I slowed down my jumping. "I have a date."

"A date!" They continued hopping in front of me.

"I have a date," I whispered in disbelief. "Wait. I have a date. A date? What the hell am I doing? I'm a married woman! I can't go on a date!"

They stopped jumping, and both tipped their heads.

"Wait. I thought we were excited," Julian said. "Are we not excited?"

"I was. I *was* excited, but now that reality is sinking in, I can't go on a date! What the hell am I thinking? I'm married!" I looked at my finger where the missing ring had left a permanent indent, it's absence still startling when I'd look down. "I'm still married, right?"

CeCe huffed. "I said it before, and I'll say it again. They left us. Abandoned us. Took off to God knows where. We aren't married anymore, Diane. Just because we can't find them to divorce their lying asses doesn't mean we're trapped to live like nuns for eternity. You're single. I'm single. Julian is, well, always single. Stop worrying about your damn marriage vows—the ones *he* broke—and get out there and have yourself a good time tonight! Did that man have *one* thought about you when he was committing felonies, stealing millions of dollars, and absconding with it like a selfish asshole?"

"Is it weird for you dating Bill?"

She scoffed. "I'm not *dating* Bill! I would never!"

Furrowing my brow, I leveled her with a stare. "You've slept over there almost every night this week."

Julian chuckled. "She's getting a different kind of 'D' from Bill than dating."

CeCe smacked his arm. "Julian! Disgusting!" Then she shrugged. "But not incorrect. What I have with Bill is just pure pleasure. Scratching an itch. I'm not *dating* him. I'm…"

"Getting the different 'D'." Julian grinned.

She hit him again.

"Well, it's true," he said, rubbing his shoulder. "CeCe and I have a plan and it's dating millionaires, not swamp things. There's a big difference between hooking up and dating. CeCe would never *date* someone like Bill. It's no different than that guy I was hooking up with at the gym last year. A hottie, but I wouldn't have been caught dead with him out in public, but I certainly enjoyed every minute of him behind closed doors. Right, CeCe?"

She paused, swallowing hard before lifting her chin. "No. It's just for fun. I'm not dating him."

"So, you feel nothing for him?" I asked.

She paused again, and though she answered with certainty, I heard the falter in her voice. "No. Nothing."

"Are you feeling *serious* about the fireman?" Julian asked.

"I… I don't know," I answered honestly. "I mean, my feelings for him were so deep and pure, but it's been over forty years! And yeah, he makes my stomach flip every time I see him, and all I want to do is kiss those lips once more, but,

I mean, what the hell am I doing? I can't do this. I'm calling to cancel."

CeCe reached forward and grabbed my arm. "You're not canceling. You owe yourself a date with this man. I mean, God help you if you fall for some broke Bayou fireman, but you're hell bent on living this life in this Godforsaken town instead of getting out like us, so why the hell wouldn't you at least give it a try?"

"I... I guess I'm scared," I admitted. "I haven't been on a date since I was in college. I wouldn't even know what to say or do! Then I'll be feeling like I'm cheating on my husband to boot, *and* I'm terrified I'm going to fall for him! Or I fall for him and he doesn't feel the same way about me!" My eyes bulged with another realization. "What if he's actually pissed I never came back all those years ago and this is some ploy to make me fall for him and then break my heart!"

"That's something CeCe would do." Julian chuckled. "But I don't see your fireman as being the cold, vindictive type."

I thought about the kind man I'd known so well in my youth and how he still seemed to be the same warm, honorable man today. "No. I guess you're right, that doesn't sound like him. I guess I'm just scared. I don't even know what to wear."

CeCe's eyes lit up. "Now that is something I can *definitely* help with. Come on. Let's get you dressed and ready for your date because you're going."

"I'm going? I'm really doing this?"

"Hell yeah, you are." Julian nodded in solidarity. "Now come on. Let's go turn you into Cinderella."

Even though terror and excitement filled me with equal measure, I pushed away the terror and decided to focus on the excitement.

I was going on a date with John... the boy who'd stolen my heart all those years ago and never gave it back.

CHAPTER TWENTY
Diane

"There. Perfect." CeCe smacked her lips, encouraging me to do the same with the lipstick she'd just applied. It had been ages since I'd last played dress-up with friends, and now here was CeCe VanTramp, of all people, acting like my high school best friend calming my nerves for my first dance.

"I look okay? You're sure?" I asked.

She and Julian stepped back, matching appreciative smiles accompanying their nodding heads.

Julian snapped his fingers with a flourish. "He's not gonna know what hit him."

I stood, admiring the reflection in the mirror. For a moment, I saw the young girl who'd stared in this exact same mirror before she'd run out the door and into his arms. Now I was a grown woman who's face and body had aged and changed, and I hoped he'd still find me as beautiful as he once had. Nerves crackled inside me as I truly acknowledged I was not only going on my first date since my husband had left me, but I was going out with my first love... the man who hadn't vacated my heart even with the decades we'd spent apart.

A knock on the door caused us to squeal, and I shushed them as I was sure Julian's high-pitched shrieks could be heard by everyone in Ruinville.

A dizzying blend of excitement, fear, and guilt whirled around inside me like a tornado. "Oh my God. Oh my God,"

I repeated over and over. "Is this happening? What am I doing? I can't go on a date! I'm... I'm married!"

They stopped their jumping and stood immobile, serious expressions transforming their faces.

"This is happening," CeCe said. "And you're not going to ruin this night worrying about your crappy ex-husband. And he's just that... an ex. You're a single woman going on a date with a single man. A man you used to love. So, get out there and have some fun. You deserve it."

Julian gave one sharp nod in agreement.

As I stood looking at them, my two archenemies now firmly planted in my corner, a smile lifted my lips. As shocking as the loss of my pampered life was, nothing was as astonishing as the friendship I'd found in the two people I least expected. I reached forward and pulled them in for a tight hug.

"Thank you," I whispered, then let them go.

They gave me a little smile and a wave, then I hurried down the stairs, opening the door to see John standing nervously on my porch.

"Hi," he said softly, his eyes panning up the skirt suit they'd helped me pick out. "Wow. You look beautiful."

A warm heat flooded my cheeks as I glanced down at my feet, then I looked up into his warm, familiar eyes, and suddenly all my anxiety about wanting to go on this date fluttered away. He opened his arm, I slid my hand through his elbow, and he escorted me to his truck.

We chattered on the ride to the one upscale restaurant in Ruinville, and my girlish jitters got the best of me on more than one awkward occasion as we settled into our date.

But by the time appetizers arrived, I started to feel more at ease with him, and he seemed to relax a little more around me. For almost two hours, we ate and talked, our familiar banter growing more natural with each minute ticking by. When we left the restaurant, it seemed as if time had spun backward while we'd dined, and instead of two grown adults strolling out into the streets, it was two teenagers, giggling and laughing without a care in the world.

"I totally beat you in that bike race." I pointed a finger in his face.

He shrugged. "Only because I let you win."

My jaw dropped, and I spun and poked him the chest. "Liar! I had you in spades!"

He grinned wider. "Because I let you have me in spades."

I poked him again. "That's it. I want a rematch!"

He slid a hand over mine to stop me from poking him, but the moment our skin touched it seemed like every nerve in my body crackled to life the way it did only with him. I'd loved Rick, of course, but I'd never felt the passion for him that I'd felt for John. I'd always chalked it up to a childhood love versus an adult one, but as I stood on the street with every nerve in my body lighting up from the simple touch, I finally knew that it wasn't just a girlish crush that had made me feel so differently about John; it was genuine love, and once again, I found myself basking in its illuminating glow.

He kept his hand on mine, and his playful smile softened as he looked down into my eyes. A familiar spark ignited in his gaze, and I recognized it well from the way he'd always looked before he'd kissed me. The same desire coursed through me as I glanced at his lips, my fears and insecurities fluttering away on the warm breeze.

We stood on that street, eyes locked, as an unfightable gravity pulled our lips closer and closer. I had no other thought in the world other than how badly I wanted to be back in those arms. I rose on my toes, his lips closing in on mine as I let the spark of our unbreakable connection reignite once more.

His warm breath ghosted my lips, but just before he delivered the exquisite promise flickering in his eyes, a loud squealing of tires caused us to jump. We spun to see a car swerve around a cat darting across the road, and it ended with a *crash* when it rammed into a parked car. I gasped, my hands flying to cover my mouth as other screams from onlookers permeated the night air.

John didn't say a word as he dashed off toward the accident, his large strides swallowing up the ground as he jumped into action. I took off after him and slid to a stop when we reached the woman, now climbing out of her car.

"Whoa, whoa," John said grabbing her shoulders and gently guiding her to the ground. "You shouldn't move. You could have a neck injury."

The woman I didn't recognize didn't fight him, instead sinking to the ground as he supported her neck. "What... what happened?"

He gave a quick glance over her body looking for injuries. "You were in an accident. Do you know where you are?"

"I... what happened?" she asked again.

Confusion and terror filled her wide eyes, so I knelt beside her and slid her hand gently into mine. Blood poured from a wound in her head, so I slipped off the light jacket of my skirt suit and pressed it to the wound. "You were in an accident. It looks like you hit your head. Just stay still until help arrives."

"It's Fire Chief John," he said into his cell phone. "I've got a single vehicle accident on the corner of Main and Third. Single passenger. Head injuries. Requesting paramedics."

She started to struggle but I squeezed her hand and lightly pressed down to steady her. "Don't move. You could have more injuries than you know. Just stay still. You're safe. We've got you."

I smiled my softest smile to soothe her, and she settled back again.

"I'm Diane. What's your name? I don't recognize you from around town."

"I'm Lucy," she answered. "I'm in town visiting my Aunt Marjorie."

Visiting her aunt... just like I used to do.

"Mayor Marjorie?" I asked, keeping her talking and calm.

"Yes. That's my aunt."

I grinned. "She sure is a firecracker, isn't she? You a firecracker too?"

"Guilty." Lucy smiled back then winced, reaching up toward her head. "Ouch. My head hurts."

John finished his call then hung up and leaned over my shoulder. "The air bag probably gave you a little concussion, and you've got a cut on your head likely from a piece of glass. Your windshield shattered."

"I'm starting to remember now," she said with a wince. "A cat. A cat ran out, and I didn't want to hit it."

"Good. You remember the accident. Means your noggin isn't too scrambled," John said. "Couple of stitches and some rest, and you'll be good as new."

"Just stay still until help arrives though," I said when I felt her stirring again. "Just to be safe."

Red and blue lights lit up the darkness as the squad car came flying down the street then skid to a stop. Deputy Boshaw jumped out and hurried over to us. John stood and gave him a rundown on the accident as well as Lucy's condition. I remained with her, keeping pressure on the head wound while talking to her to keep her calm. A few minutes later, the ambulance joined the growing crowd of onlookers, and the paramedics relieved me from my position.

After they did a quick assessment and secured her neck with a stabilizer, Lucy was hoisted onto a stretcher and wheeled into the ambulance to head to the hospital for a check. I used the sanitizer they gave me to clean the blood off my skin, then walked to the back of the ambulance and gave a wave. "Good luck, Lucy."

"Thank you so much for staying with me, Diane," she said before they shut the ambulance doors.

As they drove off, John stepped up behind me, and just feeling his presence so close made me close my eyes and exhale a happy breath.

"You were really something tonight. You know that?"

I turned around to face him, and those familiar stomach flutters returned the moment I looked into his eyes. "Me? Oh, that was nothing. I just helped stopped the bleeding and kept her calm."

He blew out a sharp breath. "That's not nothing. Most people would have panicked, but you never lost your cool once. You just jumped right in and helped that woman without a thought. Even ruined your nice clothes."

He pointed to the bloodstained jacket, but I just shrugged. "It's only clothes. I didn't want her to keep bleeding."

He stepped a little closer. "It wasn't nothing. I can tell you from years of experience, not a lot of people stay so calm in emergency situations. You were pretty great, Diane."

I smiled, a little swell of pride lifting my shoulders straighter. "Yeah?"

"Yes," he responded confidently. "You have a knack for this kind of thing. You want a job as a volunteer firefighter?"

I let out an awkward laugh. "I don't think you want an old lady on your fire department."

"You're no old lady," he said, stepping a little closer. "Old ladies don't look like you."

My heart revved with desire again, and I wondered how long it had been since I'd felt this way about a man.

Since him, no doubt.

"Well, I feel old. I'm a far cry from the young girl you once knew."

"I still see her. As far as I'm concerned, you haven't changed a bit."

I warmed at his words. "Neither have you."

"You really were amazing back there." He reached forward and slid my hand into his.

I squeezed it back, my skin igniting with the simple touch. "You know, I did kind of enjoy helping someone like that again. When I was in college, I took that summer internship at the hospital, and I had plans of going to nursing school. I was going to go join Green Peace or something and travel the world helping people in need."

"I remember. You were so excited about that internship. It's why you didn't come back that summer."

That guilt pinged inside my stomach. "Yes. It was the first summer I didn't return here. It was too good of an opportunity to pass up and then—"

I stopped before I finished saying I'd met Rick that summer and that was the reason I'd never returned again. Though the pull of John had always tugged at me, I'd passed it off as a childhood crush and instead listened to my father about what a wonderful man I'd found in Rick. How lucky I was to have met someone who could take care of me financially in a way that our family had never known. Someone to support my dreams and be my partner. And he'd been right. Rick was wonderful back then, but it had never quelled the feelings that remained for John. And I'd had to push them deep down inside me, hoping they'd eventually fade away.

As I looked up at him all these decades later, it became clearer than ever... they hadn't.

"Being a nurse and traveling the world helping people is a far cry from the New York socialite that you just told me about over dinner. How did you end up on such a different path?"

That same guilt I felt thinking about Aunt Addie flooded me again. Not only had I abandoned her when I'd met Rick, but I'd abandoned my dreams of helping others too. "I guess I just slowly forgot who I was one small decision at a time. Rick's career took center stage, and I didn't really realize until just now how far I'd followed him away from the things that were most important to me. Like helping people, for one."

"Well, you would have made an amazing nurse. I can attest to that," he said.

Deputy Boshaw interrupted our moment by clearing his throat. I turned around to see him standing, his thumbs tucked into his holster as he rocked back on his boots. His eyes lifted from the ground and leveled with mine. "Just wanted to say thanks for jumpin' in and helping. Paramedics said you did a great job."

My eyebrows inched up. "Wow. You're not going to ask me if I pickpocketed her while she was down on the ground? You know, being the thief I am and all?"

His eyes dropped. "Just wanted to say thanks. To both of you. Glad you were so close, fire chief."

"We're glad we were nearby too. And you're right. Diane did an amazing job." He squeezed my hand.

Deputy Boshaw didn't say more, but a look of understanding passed between us as he tipped his hat at me then walked away.

"Wow. Is he really going to stop looking at me like America's Most Wanted now? I swear that man thinks I'm the devil herself."

John chuckled and slung an arm around my shoulder. "He's just looking for trouble because he remembers what hellions we were."

I leaned my head into his chest, sighing as I felt the familiar safety in the casual embrace. "We were trouble, weren't we?"

He grinned down and started walking us toward his truck. "We were trouble all right. Too bad you've got blood on your nice clothes, and I think after all the excitement, maybe I should bring you home. Looks like we aren't finding any new trouble tonight."

My heart sank thinking about parting with him as he slid his arm off my shoulder then opened the truck door, but he was right. I couldn't very well continue our date walking around town looking like an extra in a horror movie. He shut the door, then climbed inside, driving us back to my house.

When we arrived, he opened my door, taking my hand and escorting me out like the gentleman he'd always been. As we started walking up toward the house, he glanced over at the old rickety tire swing hanging from the tree.

"I can't believe that thing is still there," he said, gently guiding us toward it. "Do you remember how high I used to get you going on that thing?"

I laughed, nodding as those memories flooded back into me. He'd smile up at me as I'd swing up so high it felt like I'd keep going forever, squealing when I'd reach the highest point, then sailing back down, and he'd do it again and again, until finally he'd stop me and pull me into his arms for one of those knee-quaking kisses.

With a gentle tug of my hand, he led me toward it, memories fueling me when we reached the swing. I paused in front of it. "I loved when you'd push me on this."

"Then take a seat."

My eyebrows flew to my hairline. "Seriously? What if it breaks? It's old!"

"Then I'll catch you."

The soft flirtation in his eyes lit up the little torch I'd carried for him all these years like a fiery inferno. I giggled like a young girl and looked up to catch his grin.

I glanced up to make sure the rope still looked secure, then I sat down on the old tire. As I grinned up at the man before me in the button-down shirt, I saw the boy in the blue jeans and white t-shirt who had kissed me senseless right here in this spot.

With a gentle push, he sent me away. My whole body warmed with memories as I sailed softly through the air. Each time I drifted away, all I wanted was the tire to bring me right back to him again. Over and over again, I swung to him and from him, our matching smiles growing bigger as I swung higher and higher. As I reached the pinnacle of height, I felt the old rope jerk, and my eyes flashed wide as it started giving way.

"John!" I screamed, as I flew back down toward him.

He launched forward, scooping me around the waist while I sailed by, yanking me from the tire just as the rope snapped and the tire bounced on the ground.

"Are you okay?" He pulled me tight to his chest.

My toes slowly touched the ground, but he kept his strong arm around my waist, keeping me pressed tight against him.

"I... I'm fine. You caught me."

"I'll always catch you, Diane. No matter how far you go, or how long you stay gone, I'll always be here to catch you. Always."

He brushed his fingers across my face, and my eyes welled up with tears as I leaned into his warm, familiar embrace. It was as if no time had passed at all. The scent of his skin, the feel of his strong arms around me—it was all so achingly familiar yet tinged with the bittersweet weight of time lost.

"I should have come back. I'm so sorry I never came back," I whispered, my voice trembling with emotion. "I just... I got lost in life. I had such big plans, and I tried so hard to forget you and this town so I could follow them. And I somehow forgot myself... my dreams. My desires. I'm so sorry I never came back."

"But you did come back," he said softly. "It just took a little longer than I expected. But I waited for you because I always knew you'd return to me. Someday."

"You waited for me? All this time?"

He shrugged. "I dated, of course, but it never stuck. Every time things started to get serious, I just couldn't make the final leap, and I'd end things. Deep down, I always knew it was because they weren't, well, you."

A lump formed in my throat. "But... you should be so angry. You should hate me. *I* hate me for what I did!"

"I could never hate you," he said softly, another stroke of his fingers brushing the hair from my face. I closed my eyes and leaned into his touch.

"I'm just so sorry, John. You deserved better. Aunt Addie deserved better."

He pulled back just enough to look me in the eye. "Life doesn't always go the way we planned, Diane," he said, his voice steady, sure. "People change. We grow. That's just how it works. Holding on to what could've been won't do anything but keep you stuck. We make mistakes, we learn, and we keep moving. That's the only way forward. You're not the same person you were back then, and neither am I. But that's not a loss. We're here, right now, and that's what matters. This moment, us together, is a new beginning. Diane, I never forgot you. Not for a single day. I always knew you'd return to me. You're here now, where you belong, and I don't plan on ever letting you go again."

As I looked into his eyes, I saw the young man I had fallen in love with all those years ago. Despite the decades that had passed, our connection had endured, and we had found each other again in the twilight of our lives. In that moment, I realized that true love, the kind that defied time and distance, was something rare and precious. And I knew that I had found it once more, with him, beneath the Louisiana stars.

With a firm pull, John yanked my lips to his. I melted into his embrace as he bent me back with the force of his passion. I flung my arms around his neck, gripping him tight to keep from tumbling to the ground as my legs gave way beneath me. There, suspended in his arms, he kissed me so deeply it erased every moment we'd spent apart. Like a clock spinning in reverse, with every brush of his lips against mine, the years that had separated us faded away until once again, I was a young girl swept away with the kind of love that never left you. The kind of love that chiseled its way into your heart, embedding itself there to live forever... the way John had lived in my heart even with the decades separating us.

Flickers of exquisite pain danced on my lips from the force of our reunion, but I didn't dare ease up. Instead, I kissed him harder as if I could erase every minute we'd spent apart. Emotions long thought dead swirled inside me, crackling to life like tiny embers that had sat smoldering for decades, just awaiting him to breathe life back into them. They ignited inside of me, warming me in the deepest part of my soul, and he breathed new life into me with every touch of his lips to mine.

When his kiss finally softened, I clung to him, breathless and satiated as he held me in his arms, his eyes searching mine.

"I missed you, Diane. God, did I miss you," he whispered against my lips.

"I missed you, too," I breathed back, then kissed him again.

As I sank back into the depth of my love for this man, a noise from the nearby porch startled us both. We broke apart our kiss, spinning our heads to see CeCe and Julian scurrying back toward the front door, tripping over the small table as they tried to make a getaway.

"Ow! Crap!" Julian jumped on one leg, rubbing his knee as he hobbled after CeCe.

"Quick! They'll see us!" CeCe whispered loud enough half of Ruinville could have heard her.

"We see you," I called to them on a chuckle, and they both stumbled to a stop, turning around to face us with sheepish grins.

"Sorry." Julian grimaced. "We saw you pull in and came out to see you, and uh, sorry. We didn't mean to disturb you. We were trying to get back in unnoticed."

"If that was you two trying to be stealth, please don't ever consider careers in espionage," I responded.

They glanced at each other and then smiled back at me. "Sorry. We'll go inside. Just ignore us. Keep on..." CeCe waved a hand at us and smirked. "You know."

They scurried back inside, swatting at each other before the door slammed shut behind them.

With the moment ruined, I let out a sigh and turned back to John. "Well, I guess that's my cue to call it an evening."

"And what an evening it was." He leaned down and gave me a gentle kiss. "I had an incredible time with you tonight, Diane. Maybe we could do it again?"

"Yes, please," I answered too enthusiastically.

He grinned. "Good. I'll give you a call."

"I'll be waiting."

He leaned down and brushed a soft kiss against my cheek, and I sighed like a smitten schoolgirl.

"Goodnight, Diane," he said, then turned and headed back to his truck.

With an immoveable grin plastered to my face, I watched him walk away, giving him a little wave as he pulled out. The moment the truck headed out of the driveway, CeCe and Julian spilled back out the door, their enthusiastic squeals permeating the quiet night air.

"You kissed him! Oh my God! You kissed him! We saw you!" Julian started hopping up and down at the top of the steps, the glass of wine in his hand nearly spilling.

"We saw it! You kissed him!" CeCe joined in the jumping, careful not to spill the glass clutched in each hand.

For a moment, I wanted to play it cool, but the memory of our explosive reunion washed away any chance I had of curbing my enthusiasm.

"I kissed him!" I screamed, then ran up the steps, jumping up and down with them as they joined me in my celebration.

"Tell. Us. Everything!" Julian yanked me by the hand to the porch swing then CeCe handed me the extra glass of wine they'd poured me.

The three of us settled down together, and like a giddy schoolgirl who'd just kissed her first crush, I started at the beginning and told my captivated audience every last detail.

But they weren't just a captivated audience, they were my... friends.

I shared my wonderful evening with my friends.

CHAPTER TWENTY-ONE
CeCe

"Ugh. The stupid beer is out again," I grumbled when the tapper sputtered foam. "Julian! Can you go change it?" I called back to him where he scrubbed dishes in the kitchen behind me.

"Um, hello! I'm slammed back here!" he called through the food window. "You have got to learn to do it your damn self!"

Frowning, I looked around wondering where the hell Bill was. He came and sat at the bar to keep me company every night I worked, and he always jumped in to do the yucky chores like dumping the trash or changing the keg if needed. But with no Bill in sight, and Julian and Diane both buzzing around during the dinner rush, the difficult job fell to me.

"Fine!" I spat toward him then stomped back to the cooler where the barrels of beer were kept. It shouldn't have been a difficult task, and Bill had showed me how to do it several times, but I hated wrestling with the lines and trying to wiggle free the tap that always seemed to stick. After lifting the barrels to figure out which one was low, I located the offender and pulled the handle to remove the tap. It remained stuck, so I grunted and groaned, pulling and pushing until I finally freed it.

"Ha!" I shouted to myself triumphantly. "Take that!"

When the barrel of beer didn't respond, I turned to find the new, full barrel. It was a short distance away, which required me to drag it a few feet across the floor to where my lines would reach. Panting and swearing up a storm, I finally got it into place, then remembering how Bill had showed me, I shoved the tap down into the top.

Having forgotten one important step—probably *the* most important step—a geyser of beer exploded up into my face, and I shrieked as I choked in the stinky, foamy liquid.

"No!" I screamed as I yanked back the tap and stopped the offensive spray.

Blinking fast as I struggled to contain my angry tears, I wiped the beer from my face then reached up and touched my soaked hair.

"Ahhhhhhhhh!" I screamed, clenching my fists tight as I let my rage over this ridiculous job, this ridiculous life, explode out of me.

"Are you okay?" Bill said as he burst into the cooler like a knight in camouflage armor. "What's wrong? I just got to the bar and heard you screaming like a banshee. Came runnin' thinking someone was skinning you alive."

I spun to face him knowing full well my makeup must be running down my face and my hairstyle likely ruined, but I didn't care to hide my hideous visage from him. "It blasted me in the face! I hate this! I hate this keg!" I kicked it. "This job! This restaurant! This town! This life! I hate it!"

As I stomped my feet in the puddle of beer pooled beneath me, he rubbed a hand across his mouth, stifling his smile. "You pushed down the handle before it was seated, didn't you? Got a little beer face wash?"

"It's not funny!" I stomped harder, clenching my fists.

I looked up to see his soft smile he couldn't, or wouldn't, hide, but as the tears exploded from my eyes, he quickly hurried to me.

"Aw, come on now. There, there, Pretty Girl. You're okay." He wrapped his arms around me, ignoring the fact that my wet clothes were certainly soaking his. "You're okay. It's just a little beer."

"My hair and my makeup are *ruined!*"

He leaned back, taking my face in his hands and smiling down at me. "You're still as pretty as a peach on a summer day."

"No, I'm not. I'm a mess." I stuck out my lower lip.

He smiled and leaned forward and kissed it, and as angry as I was about my situation, I couldn't help but soften to his touch. Diane always joked he was a snake charmer, and as much as I hated her referring to me as the snake, she wasn't wrong. Bill always seemed to know just how to soothe me no matter what this crappy life I lived threw at me.

The moniker also fit quite well when I'd called him several days ago screaming to come over and remove a snake that had slithered into our living room. He'd laughed after he'd caught the hideous reptile, holding it up to give it a kiss before sending it back out into the wilds where it belonged. As horrified as I'd been that a snake had infiltrated our already heinous hovel, I was equally thrilled that he'd come to my rescue in an instant. He'd even agreed to carry me from the couch where I'd stood to the upstairs bedroom so I wouldn't have to touch the ground it had slithered across.

Now here he was again rushing to my rescue, and I leaned into his embrace as I pulled myself back together.

"Why don't you go to the ladies' room and rinse yourself off. I'll get this keg changed and watch the bar until you get back. Sound good, Pretty Girl?"

I nodded, my shoulders slumped as I exhaled my breath.

He placed a little kiss on my forehead, then I stepped around him and headed to clean myself up. As I washed the beer off my face and wrung it out of my hair, I fixed my smudged makeup enough to be presentable again... at least presentable enough for the rabble that called Ruinville home. With one last glance in the mirror, I headed back out of the bar. The busy, chattering dinner crowd overflowed Mawmaw's, and every barstool had filled up in my absence. Bill looked at home tapping beers and pouring drinks, and he gave me a little smile as I slid back behind the bar to take over again.

"Thank you." I took the bar rag from him. "I appreciate the help."

"Anytime, Pretty Girl. I'll pour myself a beer and sit down there to keep you company. Just holler if ya get too busy and need a hand." With a wink, he walked off and filled himself a pint of beer then sat down.

It always surprised me how he'd spend his whole evening off sitting at the bar just watching me work, always jumping in to help out even though he didn't get paid. No one in my old world would have lifted a finger to help anyone without something in return. But in Ruinville, everyone helped everyone, and Bill was always hellbent on helping me. He'd been my unwavering support when it seemed I had no strength to stand on my own as I tried, and failed, to adjust to my diminished social standing.

And I was grateful for him every night. And I often showed him in ways that wouldn't be appropriate at work.

I smiled to myself, glancing up at the handsome man whose bed had practically become my own in the three weeks past. Never had I known such passion... such tenderness... as I had at the hands of the toughest looking man I'd ever seen.

Our little fling was a welcome reprieve from the daily grind of working for just enough pennies to feed myself and stay alive. Every paycheck went to everyday living expenses with no leftovers for the luxuries I still craved. In order to pay for things like Botox, nice clothing, facials or the regular salon appointments I still desired that would bring me back to some minuscule semblance of my old lifestyle, I would have to work two jobs... or three. The only way to make extra money for those luxuries, or in my opinion, necessities, was to continue selling off my slowly dwindling wardrobe, but one day that would all be gone too. Just like everything else I'd valued in my former life. The life that had been so cruelly ripped away from me..

A life I missed so much, the pain from my loss of luxury seemed to deepen every day, like some kind of disease slowly eating apart my insides, feasting on my self-worth like a parasite insatiable for its next meal. Unlike Diane who seemed to become more comfortable in this minimalistic existence with each passing day, I felt more trapped... more desperate... to escape the hellish landscape of this sweltering, bug-infested craphole I'd landed in.

I looked up and saw Bill watching me with that unwavering look of affection in his eyes, and as it always did, for a moment, it soothed the pains in my body and soul from a life toiling away behind a bar in the bayou. With just one glance he could ease the longing for the world I still mourned and make me think that perhaps happiness could be found without my riches. Perhaps Diane was right, and happiness didn't have to come from a fat bank account, but from a connection with this man that turned my world upside down every time I looked at him.

A customer shouting his order at me broke my happy moment staring at Bill and yanked me back into the reality of my life as a bartender in the bayou. With a grumble, I plastered on my fake smile and turned to greet him.

My shift felt longer than normal with the nonstop rush of Ruinville locals pouring in eager to watch the game on the big screen TV. The only bright spot in my overwhelming evening was the sheer volume of drinks the men downed during game night meant my tip jar filled faster than usual. Now that I'd splurged and bought myself a cell phone, I needed to bring in more money so I could afford to pay the fee every month.

As the crowds in the restaurant for dinner finally dwindled down while we neared the kitchen closing, I counted the minutes until the game ended and I could do last call. I glanced over at Bill, my body already tingling from the promises those eyes kept making about what awaited me after my shift.

"This isn't what I ordered," the man I'd never served before said from the end of the bar.

I looked over and scrunched my brow. "You ordered the chicken strips. Those are the chicken strips."

He raised his eyebrows giving me a look of indignation. "No. I ordered *catfish* strips. These are chicken strips. If I wanted chicken strips, I'd have ordered chicken strips."

I recoiled at the sharpness of his tone. I thought back to his order, certain of his words in ordering the chicken strips. "You ordered the chicken strips. I remember. If you want catfish strips, I can put in an order for them."

He sighed, rolling his eyes as he mumbled. "How hard is it to get a damn order right the first time."

Anger vibrated beneath my skin, causing me to shudder as I fought against my urge to unleash my fury on the man who *dared* to accuse me of being wrong when I knew damn well I was right. But instead of allowing myself the simple pleasure, I swallowed down my venomous response and forced on a strained smile. "Did you want me to put in the other order?"

"I'm on my way to New Orleans and just stopped for a quick bite. I'm in a hurry and don't want to wait for another order. Just take them off the bill and I'll eat these."

My spine stiffened. "If you're going to eat them, I'm not taking them off the bill. You ordered chicken strips, and that's what you got. You can't come in here, order food, pretend it isn't what you ordered, and then expect to eat for free. Either eat them and pay for them or get the hell out."

He narrowed his eyes. "You can't talk to me like that. I'm the customer! I'm not paying for what I didn't order! I want to speak to your manager, or are they as incompetent as you?"

You can't talk to me like that.

If only he knew who he was talking to. No one was allowed to speak to *me* like that! In my former life, such insolence would have been unthinkable. It only amplified my overwhelming feelings of how far I'd fallen and how much I didn't belong in this world. I didn't belong here behind this bar serving fried food to a man I once wouldn't have even had the displeasure of speaking with. He was beneath me, and yet here he was treating me like some hired help only put on this earth to do his bidding.

"Get. Out." I snarled, clenching my fists as I fought every urge in my body to punch him in his oversized nose. "What?" he sat back.

"Get! Out!" I erupted, unleashing months of suppressed frustration enduring a job I hated, serving people who once would have served me. "You ordered chicken strips! I gave you chicken strips! I'm not giving you *free* chicken strips! So GET OUT!"

With a muttered curse, he shoved the basket toward me, the contents spilling onto the floor. "Screw you, crazy lady! I'm never coming back here again."

I stared down at the mess of fries and breaded chicken at my feet, then looked up, narrowing my eyes as the venom pulsed through my body. I let my rage pour out of my mouth. "GET OUT!"

"Hey! You heard her! Get out!" Bill jumped to standing, his chest swelling as he pointed at the door. "Or I'll make you get out."

The shocked man rushed out the door, and I dropped down to my knees. It wasn't because I needed to be there to clean up the mess, but because every last shred of dignity had left my body and the painful loss stole the last of my energy to remain standing.

I'd just gone to battle with someone over chicken strips.

Me. CeCe VanTramp fighting a man over disgusting fried poultry.

I'd fallen so far I may as well collapse on the floor and stay there where I belonged.

"Are you okay? I'll go get the broom," Bill said, peering over the bar.

"I've got it," I answered back fighting the tears threatening to spill over.

"That guy was an ass. If you want, I'll go out there and kick the crap out of him. My pleasure, Pretty Lady."

Pretty Lady. How I almost burst out laughing now hearing the enduring term I loved so much. But I wasn't anymore. I'd never felt less attractive, less powerful, less... *me* than I did in that moment kneeling down on a dirty bar floor scooping fried food back into a plastic basket.

"I've got it. I just need a minute to compose myself," I said over the lump forming in my throat.

Bill knew me well enough not to push, so he slid back into his stool, and I stayed down on that floor long enough that I was sure my sore, overworked legs could lift me back to standing. And when I rose up from the floor, I rose with a deepened determination to get out of the life and back to the one I belonged in. A life in the city. A life of luxury. A life where no one would ever dare disrespect me and treat me like I was beneath them again.

I was CeCe VanTramp, and I would rise back to heights so high the man at the bar tonight would have to break his own neck just to see me.

I finished cleaning the mess and collected myself then went back to finishing up the closing chores of my shift. The bell over the door jingled, and the newsman Julian had been casually dating, Abe, walked in, a big smile on his face, and an older gentleman in a suit trailing behind him.

Decent cut suit. Maybe Armani. Designer haircut. No scruffy beard. No flannel.

Not a local. The older man was too swanky for Ruinville.

I tipped my head appraising the man walking tall behind Abe. He carried himself like the men I'd known most of my life. Confident. Powerful. Important. I could practically smell the money oozing off him. No, not a local indeed.

Recognizing him as a man of stature and wealth, I quickly smoothed my hair as best I could and checked my mascara hadn't smeared in the reflection of the mirror behind the bar with the flashing *Bud Light* sign above it.

Though I looked much better than I had hours earlier when I was soaked in beer, I could barely recognize the woman I once was in the reflection staring back at me. My upscale hairstyle was long gone. The fillers, expensive treatments and creams that had kept my skin glowing like a baby's butt had all worn off, and I looked tired and haggard. My makeup, once done daily by professionals, no longer made my eyes pop the way only my long-time makeup artist, Jackie, could do. How Bill stared at me like the most beautiful woman in the world I would never understand. If only he'd seen me back in my day as a renowned socialite in

New York. Though I wanted to bolt out from behind the bar and hide from the rich-looking man, with nowhere to go, I took a deep breath and turned around to greet Abe and his friend.

"Hi, CeCe," Abe said with a smile.

"Hello, Abe," I answered, matching his grin, having become familiar with him in the past few weeks he'd been coming around some evenings to pick up Julian for nights in the city.

He swiped a hand through his auburn hair and scanned the barstools looking for a seat. "Busy night."

"Yes, it's been a nightmare of an evening. If you couldn't tell from how I look a mess. You picking up Julian after work?"

"Yep. There's a band playing tonight at the club. We're going dancing."

"Ah, to be young again. I can't even imagine going out for a night dancing after being on my feet working all night. Everything hurts." The throbbing in my feet and the ache in my aging joints seemed to thump harder now that I acknowledged them.

Abe gestured to the gentleman standing behind him. "CeCe, this is my friend and the owner of our station, Chauncey Fontaine."

My little heart fluttered at the job title. *Owner of the station.*

I was right. This man did have money. No doubt he wasn't swimming in the kind of money I'd been accustomed to, but if he had enough money to buy a news station, he certainly had to have enough cash to help pull me out of this rubble.

I will rise again.

With my refound gusto for elevating myself out of this life and back to where I belonged, I flipped on my charm as I reached slowly across the bar, batting my eyelashes at him while he took my hand.

"Nice to meet you, Chauncey," I said, giving him my most alluring smile.

"The pleasure is all mine." He kissed the back of my hand, and I feigned a sweet blush at it. "Abe here has been telling me all about your story, and when he said he was coming here tonight after the show wrapped, I had to come down and meet you myself. I'd be lying if I said I hadn't gone and looked you up online."

Oh, thank God. He knows what I really look like.

Relief he'd seen me in my glory days and hoping the image of that version of me was burned into his head instead of the disheveled woman before him, I kept up my flirtiest smile. "You looked me up? Hopefully you only found good things."

"You lived quite a life, Mrs. VanTramp. Wow. What a tale you must have to tell. I sure would love to hear it, and maybe we could make some kind of a story out of it? I bet people would love to see an interview with you telling your captivating tale. When Julian told me about your situation, I thought to myself, 'This is a story everyone is gonna wanna hear. I gotta meet these three.' So, here I am, and I'd love to spend some time with you talking about your life. See what we can come up with."

Horror over the thought of appearing on television to tell my story of what a broke loser I'd become, but not wanting to waste this chance to spend a little time sizing up Chauncey's wallet, I just smiled coyly.

"Well, I don't know about telling the world about my story just yet, but I'd sure be happy to share it with you."

He grinned wider, and his grey mustache lifted with the movement. He wasn't handsome by any stretch of the imagination, but I noted he at least had all his teeth, since wearing dentures was the one thing I'd told Julian was a hard no for my next husband.

"Well, I'd love to take you up on that. Here's my card." He slid the shiny black card across the bar. "Call me, and I'd love to take you out to dinner. I know a place with the best lobster in Louisiana."

Lobster.

My mouth practically watered imagining a taste of the delight I'd taken for granted far too many times before. "I'd love that," I responded, taking the card and flipping it between my fingers, giving him my sexiest smile.

"Looks like the bar is full," Abe said. "Let's grab that table over there. I'll pop in the kitchen to say hi to Julian, then we can have a quick dinner before we head out. Maybe we can come back and visit with CeCe when some spots open up."

Chauncey nodded his agreement. "I guess we'll be over here for a while, but I look forward to seeing you again."

"I'll be waiting," I answered with a sexy drawl in my voice.

He tipped his head then followed Abe to an open table in the dining area. Diane hurried over to say hello and drop off their menus. I smiled and started a stroll back across the bar with a little extra skip in my step, happy my luck may be taking a turn that could lift me back up out of my life's destruction. When I looked up and caught Bill's penetrating gaze, it wasn't the usual adoration in his eyes staring back at me... this time it was a potent mixture of sadness and pain.

"What the hell was that?" he asked. "Did you just agree to go out with that guy?"

I glanced over at Chauncey, who symbolized a chance to claw my way back to the life of comfort and prestige I'd once held. Yet, guilt tightened around my heart as I glanced back at Bill. He had provided an unexpected happiness in a life I otherwise loathed. A different kind than I'd ever experienced before... that couldn't be bought with money or power. When I was in his arms, I forgot about all the things I'd lost... the affluence, the houses, the jets, the lifestyle. When I was in his arms, I was... happy.

But the minute I left them and stepped back into the reality of my situation, the unquenchable yearning to elevate myself once again always crushed me, erasing the happiness I found with only him.

As I looked into Bill's heartbroken eyes, my heart grew heavy with a tumult of emotions.

"Bill, it's just dinner. That's all."

"Seriously, CeCe? I'm sitting right here, and you agree to go out with that guy? Why? Because he's got a fancy suit and money?"

Silently pleading for him to comprehend the weight of my struggles, I reached out to touch his hand, something I never did in public since I was too embarrassed for anyone to know I was shacking up with Bayou Bill. Sure, there were rumors we were canoodling, but with our discretion, nothing anyone could confirm. But even though it was my first public gesture, he yanked it away.

"Bill, I thought you understood. You and I... we're just having fun. That's all. I have always planned to get out of Ruinville as fast as I could. I don't belong here. You have to know that."

He snorted softly, sitting back with the shake of his head. "You know, call me an idiot, but I thought you and I were doing more than just knockin' boots. I know you keep saying this isn't going anywhere serious and you don't want anyone to know you're running around with the likes of me, and I was fine with keeping it secret. I guess I stupidly thought that eventually you'd figure out that there's nothing wrong with being with a regular guy, and that you don't need a ton of money to be happy. But I guess I was wrong. I should have taken you at face value. You're just out for yourself and to hell with who you hurt in the process."

"That's not true," I tried to argue back, but in reality, he wasn't entirely wrong.

Or wrong at all, I supposed. I'd always looked out for myself as number one, but I had to. In my world, it was every man for themselves.

I reached for him again, but he just shook his head. "Clearly, I'm not what you want, CeCe. I get it. You want caviar and I'm nothing but crayfish. But I ain't no boytoy for you to play with until you find some douchebag of your 'social standing.'" He used his fingers like quotation marks while he looked over at Chauncey. "So, if you want to go out with him, then fine. Do what you need to do, but just so you know, that means you and me? We're done."

A strange sensation of guilt and devastation welled up inside of me as I looked into his eyes. It was all I could do not to say, "Screw it," and jump over the bar and cover him with kisses like I wanted. If my life could be spent just in his arms and his bed, I wouldn't need another dollar. But I glanced down at my hands, the ones that hadn't seen a manicure in months, and noted the worn calluses from opening beer bottles. Life in Ruinville—life without money—meant an existence of slaving behind a bar and scraping by for every cent just to do it all over again the next day.

And the next.

And the next.

A life of monotony, struggling each day just to survive to the next. A man like Chauncey was the only way to escape the suffocating grip of poverty that threatened to crush the life right out of me.

"I can't do this forever," I said to him, showing him my worn hands. "I'm not made for this kind of work, Bill. I'm just not. I do like being with you, more than you know, but I just can't live like this anymore. It's not who I am. I'm sorry, Bill, but... yes. I'm going to go out with Chauncey."

The pain in his eyes nearly crumpled me to the ground, but I gripped the edge of the bar and held on tight as I dug deeper into my resolve to remain on the course Julian and I had set. The course that would take us back to the penthouse where we belonged.

"So that's it? You're picking money over me? Over happiness?"

"Happiness?" I spit out. "You call *this* happiness?" I waved a hand at my surroundings. "I'm covered in beer, my hands are calloused, my feet are swollen, my knees and back ache in ways I never knew possible. I'm living in a dilapidated house I don't even *own* only because of Diane's generosity! I'm homeless! Broke! Broke-*en!* I have nothing, Bill! You have to understand that this is no life for me! I belong in couture in a penthouse, sipping champagne and planning my next vacation. I am not, and will never be, cut out for this life. I can't live like this!" With an exasperated breath, I slammed my fist down on the bar. "I need *out!*"

Though I felt better for a moment from the powerful release of my outburst, it only lasted a moment before the pain in Bill's eyes ripped straight through my soul.

"If that's how you feel, then consider me out too. Good luck with the rich guy." Without another word, Bill pushed back off his seat, spun on his boots and walked toward the door. My heart sunk with each step he took away from me, but instead of rushing after him, I clutched Chauncey's card tight in my hand like it was a beacon to remind myself of my promise... a promise to reclaim the life I deserved. A life of wealth. Prestige. Comfort.

When the door slammed shut behind him, I swallowed over the lump in my throat, the battle inside me waging war between the allure of regaining my wealth or the feelings for Bill that I realized ran deeper than any I'd ever felt before.

"What the hell was that?" Diane slipped up alongside the bar, jutting her head toward the door Bill had just disappeared through. "He never leaves before your shift is over, and he seemed upset. Is everything okay?"

I took a deep breath, steadying myself as I tried to recover from the surprising loss I felt from Bill's absence. "He's upset I accepted a date with Abe's boss, Chauncey."

Her eyes flashed wide. "You what?"

"I had to. He owns a news station, Diane. He has money. He's taking me one step closer to getting out of this hellhole. Not my white whale, but if I date him for a few months, he's sure to run in some circles with the big fish. I'll use him to get to them and voila. Within six months, I'll be stepping back into the penthouse. Don't worry, I won't leave you behind. You've taken care of me, and I'll make sure to take care of you. Maybe whoever I land will have a friend I can set you up with."

She just blinked at me for a long moment, her mouth falling agape. "Are you serious? You just took a date with some guy just because he's rich, and you did it right in front of Bill? What the hell kind of person does that?"

I rolled my eyes, not wanting to withstand anymore of her condescending words. "Me. I'm the kind of person that does that. I told you the plan. I've always had this plan. You may be content to sit here in squalor, but I'm CeCe VanTramp, and I will not let this be my life."

"This doesn't have to be your life, CeCe, but running to some guy to pay your bills isn't the answer either. This, working here, is just a steppingstone until we figure out what we're going to do with our lives... how we're going to support ourselves and find happiness, *real* happiness, on our own terms. I don't plan on working here forever either, but I plan on finding a career that I love and that supports me. You can do that too. You don't need a man to support you, CeCe. You can't give up now just because things are a little hard at the moment."

"A little hard? A *little* hard?" I laughed. "Things are more than a little hard, Diane! We're broke! Totally and completely broke! And I'm a sixty-seven-year old bartender! Do you have any idea how much pain running around all night puts my body in? I'm exhausted, and I'm done! I want out of this disastrous life you seem to love so much!"

"It won't be like this forever. I promise. We can find our happiness here, CeCe. Together. But not if you give up and take the first easy out you see."

I rolled my eyes. "You fell head over heels for your ex-boyfriend and now you want to live here in Ruinville and find your happily ever after. Well, good for you. But my happily ever after isn't at this bar, or in this town, or with these people. It's back in the city where I belong. So that's where I'm going, and Chauncey is the first step to getting back there."

"So, you broke Bill's heart so you can just run back to money with your tail between your legs, never learning to stand on your own two feet?"

I glared back at her. "I wasn't raised like you, Diane. I have never lived a day without money. Your roots may be here in the dirt of Ruinville, and la di da if you've decided to go back to them and shack up with your old flame, but my roots are firmly planted in a penthouse. That's where I'm from, and that's where I'm returning to. I never told Bill we were anything but lovers, and if he was mistaken, then that's on him. I'm doing exactly what I need to do to take care of myself and Julian, and that means going on a date with Chauncey. Judge me all you want, but those are the facts."

Even though I spoke with authority, I couldn't help but cringe at the harshness of my words.

A soft laugh escaped Diane's lips. "Wow. I shouldn't be surprised, but somehow, I am. I really thought you were changing—growing. But now I see you haven't evolved even a little bit. You're still the same shallow, spoiled, selfish woman I knew back in New York."

I stiffened at the severity, and accuracy, of her words. "I don't belong here. Neither does Julian. I promised him I'd get us out of here, and I'm making good on my word. I'm sorry if you don't like that."

Julian came out of the kitchen, smiling. "I heard my name. What are we talking about?"

Before I could answer, Diane popped a hip and planted her hand on it. "Oh, you know, just that CeCe blew off Bill to go on a date with your friend's money."

"Oh!" Julian grinned. "He asked you out? Already? Damn, CeCe! That was quick work! I didn't even know he was coming with Abe tonight or I would have prepared you and picked out a better outfit. But, you did it anyway even dressed in that! Oh my God, it's happening. Operation Diaper Daddy is under way!"

Diane narrowed her eyes. "Is there anything about this man other than his money that has attracted you to him?"

I didn't answer because she'd know I was lying when I said there was.

"I'm just curious how what your doing is any different than the young, beautiful models you used to condemn and call gold diggers when they ran around after old, affluent men only because of their money? You tore them apart both behind their backs and to their faces. Hell, you called *me* a gold digger to anyone who would listen when I started dating Rick." She gave me a hard stare. "Yeah. I know about that. So, you've spent your life ridiculing and condemning women who are doing *exactly* what you're doing now. I guess if it weren't for you hurting Bill, who didn't deserve that, I would actually think this was kind of funny. CeCe VanTramp becomes the thing she used to loathe. In fact, I believe you used to refer to them as nothing more than high paid prostitutes."

My jaw nearly hit the floor. "What! That is ridiculous! Going out with Chauncey does not make me a prostitute!"

"Marrying a man who happens to have money doesn't make you a prostitute. Marrying a man *for* his money is no different than accepting it for strutting down the city streets in thigh-high boots and a mini skirt. At least that's what you used to say all the time, so I'm just asking you, how is this any different?"

Julian jumped to my defense. "CeCe is *not* a prostitute! She's just only choosing men with the means to take care of us the way we deserve! There's a big difference!"

Diane grinned a sinister smile. "You know, I always said Julian was just your paid best friend, only in it for the money. But for the last few months, the way he stuck by you, I really thought I'd been wrong, and he truly was your friend. But now I realize I was wrong about both of you. You haven't changed your selfish ways, CeCe, and Julian only stuck around because you're his meal ticket, and he knew you'd claw your way back to the penthouse you both love so much. If you told him right now you were staying here in Ruinville, he'd leave you in a heartbeat."

"That's not true!" Julian defended. "I love CeCe!"

"It is true. It's absolutely true. You were both just using me, and each other, to get what you want. Well, congratulations. I hope you two are happy together in the shallow, miserable lives that await you."

Tears threatened to spill as I felt the blow of her words. "I'm not trying to use you, Diane. We appreciate you taking us in. You didn't have to do that, and I am grateful. But can't you even try to understand how exhausted I am? How hard it is to pull my aching body out of bed every day to do this over and over again?"

"Of course I understand!" she shouted, and it forced Julian and I back a step. "I understand all too well because *I* am also exhausted! *My* bones and muscles ache in ways that I never knew was possible. Just because I don't bitch and moan about it constantly, and I'm trying to put a positive outlook on this situation we both found ourselves in, you don't think I'm hurting too? Frustrated? Angry! Well, I am! I lost everything too! I may not have grown up with money, but for the past forty years, I lived like a pampered queen, and I hate how much I miss the luxuries of our old life, and how dependent I became on them. Do you want me to admit that every day is a struggle for me too? Well, fine. I admit it. There are days when I'm so exhausted after work I consider selling Aunt Addie's house, taking the money and running so I have some actual funds to support me. Did you know that?"

I remained silent, shocked at her admission. She's done such a good job hiding her struggles I didn't even consider how hard this was for her too.

"Life is hard right now, CeCe. For all of us. But it is *going* to get better. It has to. I have to believe that, and I'm not going to give in and give up, and I hope you won't either. We need to stick together and find our way forward together. And we don't need to sell our souls to do it."

I wanted to tell her that I was in and that now that I knew she understood how I felt that we could get through this together, but deep down, the pull to my old life was too strong. "I didn't know you were struggling so much, Diane. You hide it very well. But I just hope that it will help you understand why I have to go through with this. You may be strong enough to fight through on your own, start a career from scratch in your sixties and work your ass off to get to where you want to be, but I'm not. I just want my life back, and I think Chauncey is the best step forward to do it. I'm sorry."

"'On your own.'" She chuckled softly, repeating my words to me. "I guess that is where I've been so wrong. I didn't think we were on our own. I thought we were in this together, but I see now that's not how you feel at all. So, you're right. I'm on my own to figure out my path forward, and you're on your own to figure out yours. I wish you luck, but I'm not interested in being friends with someone who would hurt someone like Bill just to further her own agenda without so much as a thought. I think what you just did to him is terrible, and I hope someday you realize that." She let out a defeated sigh. "Abe was my last table, so I'm done for the evening, and you know what? You two can close up. I'm going home."

"But how will I get home?" I said as she set her apron down on the bar.

She shrugged. "It seems we're all on our own now, so you guys can figure it out."

Julian and I watched in shock as she stormed out the front door, slamming it behind her.

"Wow. Diane is rude tonight," Julian said. "But don't let her get to you. She's just jealous we're this much closer to getting out of this town."

Though I wanted to believe him, I knew deep down Diane's words weren't coming from a place of jealousy. Diane meant every word she said, and as much as I tried to rationalize the truth right out of every mean sentence she'd uttered, it became harder and harder to accept anything other than one simple fact.

She was right.

I had hurt Bill. I was selling myself for money. I was weak and couldn't stand on my own two feet like her. The truth of her words felt like a wrecking ball to my self-worth, and as I stood alone behind the bar staring at the empty stool Bill had recently filled, guilt gnawed away at my insides until I was certain they'd turned to mush.

CHAPTER TWENTY-TWO
Diane

CeCe glided down the staircase in her exquisite gown, exuding an aura fit for a red-carpet premiere. Julian followed, his face radiant and proud, the expression he always displayed whenever accompanying her to prestigious events.

I turned up my nose and ignored them the same way I had for the past week, too hurt and disappointed to acknowledge the two people I'd mistakenly thought were friends. How naive I was to believe in anything beyond their apparent exploitation of our friendship. It had taken every ounce of grace inside me not to throw them both out that night since they made it so clear we were on our own, but I'd heard Aunt Addie's voice in my head encouraging me to show mercy. Instead, I just ignored them while waiting for their scheme to unfold, inevitably resulting in their departure to the city, orchestrated by CeCe's manipulative charms where she'd finish by sinking her fangs into some unsuspecting rich man. A man like Chauncey who she'd convinced to pay for her to stay in a hotel in the city the whole weekend while they had their first date.

The impending storm became a pawn in her hands, prolonging what should have been a mere evening into an entire weekend's luxury. I'd heard her on the phone with him, telling him how much she wanted to see him, but she was worried about traveling in stormy conditions. Like a piece of soft clay, she molded him with expert skill until she had secured a town car, an opulent room at the most expensive hotel, and a spending account to shop and dine on his dime.

Ugh. To sell oneself to the highest bidder. Disgusting.

Not to mention, both her and Julian being gone meant we would be short-staffed at Mawmaw's, and I was going to get my ass kicked running extra hard while they sipped champagne and got massages.

With hurt and anger threatening to burst out of me, I turned my back to them and closed my eyes as I centered myself.

"We'll be back Sunday night," CeCe said with that heir of importance she used to have... the one that had been absent these past few months as we'd grown closer.

Or, at least I'd *thought* we'd grown closer until I realized just how foolish I'd been to believe they'd changed.

I didn't respond, instead walking out of the living room and disappearing into the kitchen.

A car pulled up the drive, and I glanced out the window to see the shiny, black town car parked out front. CeCe and Julian strode up to it, each smiling at the driver as they slid into the back seat. My jaw tightened as I practically growled at the sight of them, feeling the same way I used to when I'd see her coming to and from events the same way.

"Ugh," I growled out, then spun away from the window.

When the car pulled out and I was alone in the house, I hated to admit how empty it felt without them. Over the past few months, we'd started to have so much fun together. Watching movies, baking cookies, and living together like... friends.

Now I felt lonely and alone, and I hated the loss I felt from the absence of two people it seemed I didn't really know at all.

Instead of wallowing in my loneliness, I spent the day cleaning the house and baking cookies. When it was time for work, I drove 'Ol Blue through the rainstorm to Mawmaw's alone, once again missing the conversation of the two people who chattered nonstop on our drives to work each day.

As I worked my shift, their absence was palpable, and it felt strange not seeing CeCe behind the bar, or hearing Julian screaming about some gross food caked onto a dish.

I... I missed them.

And I hated that I longed for the company of two people I'd never imagined I'd care for. Two people who clearly didn't care about me. Considering they'd been saying they were enacting this "Operation Diaper Daddy" for months, I didn't know why or how I'd thought that the three of us were going to build up our new lives together. I'd just grown so accustomed to them being a huge part of my daily life, even though in the beginning, I'd hated having them around, now I couldn't quite imagine my life here in Ruinville without them.

With the weather getting worse by the minute, we were slower than normal, and John was on duty so he didn't stop in to see me like he normally did, which only made the isolation feel heavier.

CeCe and Julian were gone.

John wasn't around.

The restaurant was empty with the exception of two customers.

Since I knew it would be slow due to the storm, I'd told Mawmaw to stay home. The only one around was Gumbo Gus in the kitchen, and he wasn't the chattiest guy to pal around with.

I felt so alone. Despite being always surrounded by the rush of the city, I'd grown accustomed to this feeling in New York. Even when Rick was around, he was always so enveloped in his latest business deal, I often felt alone even sitting by his side. It hadn't been until I'd moved back to Ruinville and taken up residence with CeCe and Julian that I'd realized just how lonely I'd felt most of my life. And now with them gone, that familiar loneliness felt crushing.

The restaurant phone rang, and I picked it up, excited to talk to someone. Anyone.

"Hey, just checking in on you," John said.

I smiled the girlish grin the simple sound of his voice always inspired in me. "Hi. How are you?"

"Been busy with trees coming down across the roads. These winds are getting crazy and only getting worse. Moving up to hurricane status. I wanted to call and tell you I think it's best Mawmaw's closes for the night, and you all head home safely."

"That bad?" I looked out the window at the rain hammering against it.

"Yeah. And if you want, I can come pick you up and drive you back. I don't want you to get stuck out in the storm."

Though the gesture was sweet, and I desperately wanted to see him, I knew just how hard he must be working. I didn't want to be selfish and pull him away from someone in need just so I could sneak in a few extra kisses.

We'd been on four more dates since our first one, and each date had been as magical as the first, ending with kisses on the doorstep that made me weak in the knees and long to drag him into the house to let loose the passion that still burned between us. But I also loved just kissing him the way I used to before sex ever entered the equation, and I felt young and free again making out with him on the front porch like a couple of lusty teenagers.

Pushing aside my selfish desires, I shook my head. "I know you're busy working right now. I'll close up and head home now. I'll be okay."

"You sure? I'm happy to do it."

"Thanks, John. I'll let you know if I need a ride."

"Drive safe, Diane. And call me when you're home. If I don't hear from you within an hour, I'm coming looking."

I smiled, my insides warming knowing there was still someone who cared about me... someone looking out for me even though at the moment, I felt so alone.

"I'll call you as soon as I'm home."

We bid goodbye, then I told the remaining stragglers the weather was getting worse, and everyone needed to head home for safety. I let Gumbo Gus know to clean up fast, then he and I closed up and rushed out to our vehicles, holding garbage bags over our heads to keep us dry from the relentless rain.

After a harrowing ride home in conditions that left me nearly blind, I made it safely back to the house. I raced up the steps, fighting the unrelenting wind and rain, bursting through the door into the pitch-black house and out of the storm. Feeling very insecure alone in the shrouding darkness, I fumbled and found the light switch. I clicked it up and down, but no lights came on.

"Crap. The power must be out," I breathed, pulling out my cell phone and using it to light a path to the kitchen. I scanned the floor extra hard to make sure Peggy hadn't wandered in again, and I didn't step on the unsuspecting alligator. Luckily, Julian had thrown her a bunch of leftovers last night so she shouldn't be hunting the house for food, and with the door fixed, she hadn't snuck in since that first day we'd stumbled onto her.

After ensuring Peggy wasn't lurking around in the dark, I fumbled around in the drawers. I found the matches and hurried around, lighting up candles in each room downstairs. When I finished, I stood alone in the living room, the howling wind and driving rain making my usually warm feeling home seem more like the set of a horror movie.

"You're okay. You're a strong, independent woman," I said aloud. "You don't need CeCe and Julian. You don't need a man. You're just fine."

Trying to ground myself in the new reality of an upcoming life without CeCe and Julian at my side, I fought the urge to call John and beg him to come be with me. I sat down on the couch, covering myself with Aunt Addie's Afghan blanket and pulling it up tight around me like a warm hug.

With no power to turn on the TV, and nothing to do but sit in solitude, I picked up the phone to call John and at least tell him I'd made it home safe. Just hearing his voice would help ease the loneliness if only for a little while. But before I could call, a huge gust of wind shook the house so hard that I screamed. A moment later, I screamed louder when a tree crashed through the living room window, shattering the glass and smashing through the furniture. I launched off the couch and out of the way, racing into the safety of the bathroom and slamming the door.

"Oh my God. Oh my God," I panted as I flipped open my phone.

I got to my short list of contacts, and surprisingly, my first instinct was to call CeCe. After spending months depending on each other, it seemed she'd become my first thought when I'd needed someone... needed a friend. But with her being away in the city, it only drove home the hard truth that moving forward, she wouldn't be the person I would call when I needed someone. She'd be long gone. Fighting the harsh truth I still struggled to accept, I immediately pushed John's number.

"You home safe?" he asked when he answered.

My voice shook with the tears I tried to hold back. "I'm home but the power is out, a tree flew through the window, and I'm all alone trying to remind myself that I'm a strong, independent woman and I can be here alone, but I can't John. I'm scared. It's dark. Please come over. Please. I don't want to be alone."

My voice cracked as I lost my battle against the tears. Emotions raced inside me. A mixture of fear, sadness over the loss of the friends I'd thought I had, and the realization that maybe I wasn't as strong as I'd thought I was, because at the first sign of trouble, I'd called a man to help me.

"I'm on my way! Find a safe spot and stay where you are!"

He hung up, and I curled into a little ball, wrapping my arms around my knees as I wedged myself against the bathtub. My terrified heart hammered against my ribcage while I waited for him, and finally, I heard his voice calling into the house.

"Diane! Diane! Where are you!"

"John!" I called back, jumping up from my safe space on the floor.

The bathroom door whipped open, and John appeared still wearing his firefighter's uniform. "Diane! Are you okay?"

The tears burst free as I stumbled into his arms, collapsing into his strong, protective embrace. "I'm so sorry I had to call you. CeCe and Julian are gone, and I was just so scared out here alone in the dark. And the storm is really terrifying. I'm such a wimp. I'm so sorry I pulled you away from real people in need."

"Hey, hey, hey," he said, softly cupping my face and lifting it up toward him. "You're not a wimp. This is a bad storm, and anyone would be scared being home alone out here. Not to mention the tree currently residing in your living room. You did the right thing calling me. I want to be here for you."

"What about your job? Don't you need to be out there?"

He shook his head, stroking a thumb across my cheek. "The guys have everything under control. My shift is over. I'm here with you tonight. I'm not going anywhere. I'll never let anything happen to you, Diane. Ever."

Relief washed over me as I threw my arms around his neck and pressed myself into the familiarity of his warm cocoon. He held me tight, soothing away the fear of the storm and the sadness of realizing just how alone I'd been. John had always been there for me without fail in my youth, and now as a man, he was there for me again. Even though I still wanted to learn to stand on my own two feet, I realized there was nothing wrong with finding a little support from someone I trusted. Someone I could depend on.

Someone I...

"John?" I said softly as I looked up into those blue eyes.

"Yeah?" he responded, swiping a tear from my cheek.

"I... I love you," I whispered out my truth.

Raw emotions reflected in his eyes as he stood immobile staring down at me before whispering back, "I've always loved you, Diane. I loved you then. I loved you every minute we were apart. I still love you now. And I'm gonna love you until the day I die."

A small cry escaped my lips just before he shut them with a powerful kiss. I sank into his body, my breath whooshing out as he scooped me up with a sweep of his arms. His lips devoured mine as he carried me to the bedroom, the storm howling outside fading from my mind as we lost ourselves in each other once again. With every brush of his fingers across my heated skin, memories of our first time flooded me as if it were happening all over again.

And in a way, it was.

We were different people now, but even with the decades of distance between us, we'd found our way back together... our love withstanding years of absence and lives lived worlds apart. But there in that storm, we reconnected again, and we connected over and over until the last of the storm had passed.

***

"What are you thinking about?" I asked John as I stroked his chest, running my fingers through the soft, grey hairs at the center of it.

"I'm thinking last night was amazing," he answered, pressing a kiss to the top of my head. "What are you thinking about?"

I smiled as memories of our passionate reunion flooded my mind. "I'm thinking last night was amazing as well." I paused, crinkling my face. "I'm also thinking that I'm sorry I didn't get a chance to shower after work with the power being out. I must smell like a giant French fry."

He chuckled. "I can tell you the last thing I was thinking about last night and this morning with you in my arms is that you smell like a French fry. If anyone should apologize for not showering after work, it's me. I bet I smell like a big bonfire."

I inhaled the masculine scent and sighed. "I actually like it. It's sexy knowing you were out fighting fires. And the smell kind of reminds me of what I smelled like in the summers when I'd come home from having a bonfire with you. It brings back memories."

"Well good. Because I hate to tell you that I'm gonna smell like fires a lot when I get home from work, and I don't know if I'm going to have the self-control to shower before I can get my hands on you."

I sighed at the thought of him coming home and sweeping me into his arms, giving me more of that burning passion I'd experienced with him last night.

"You'll get no arguments from me there."

"Well good. Then you stop thinking about how you smell like a French fry. If you do, I haven't noticed."

He snuggled me tighter, and I glanced out the window at the grey, morning skies with no indication of the terrible storm that had blown through. "I'm also thinking that there is a tree downstairs in my living room."

He chuckled. "Yeah. There is that. I've got a chainsaw in my truck. I can chop it up and get it out of the house. We'll have to figure out getting that window replaced and see if it did any damage to the frame."

I groaned. "Great. Just what I need. More expenses I can't afford."

He tightened his grip on me. "I can help you out. Happy to pay for repairs."

I shook my head. "No. I appreciate it, but I swore I wasn't going to depend on a man to pay my bills again. I'll figure something out."

"You sure are a stubborn one."

Chuckling, I shrugged. "Yeah, but I spent too many years losing myself to someone else and letting money change me. I'm not doing that again. CeCe may be perfectly happy prostituting herself for a penthouse, but not me. I'm going to build this life from scratch all on my own."

"And... am I in this life you're building?" he asked softly.

I shifted my body, pressing my hands to his chest as I looked up into that face I had loved my whole life. "You are the most important part of my new life. Of course, you're in it."

He smiled and tucked a piece of hair behind my ear. "Good. Because I'm not letting you go again. You're stuck with me now."

I sighed and pulled myself up, pressing a kiss on his lips. "I wouldn't want it any other way."

"And, uh... what does this life of ours look like? You said CeCe and Julian would be heading out soon, but what about you? What do you want in life?"

I leaned back and snuggled into the nook of his arms. "You know, it was funny. That night of our first date when we helped that woman, I remembered how much I'd wanted to be a nurse and help people. I actually went to the library this week and looked into nursing schools online. If I can get financial aid, which I think I can considering I'm as poor as a pauper, I'm going to go back. There's a school just thirty minutes from here."

"A nurse? Wow. That sounds amazing, Diane."

I smiled. "Yeah. It really does. Figure I can keep working at Mawmaw's for the next couple years while I go to school, and it's been ages since I've been in college, so hopefully things will transfer, but I'll be done in a few years tops. Then I can get back to doing what I always thought I'd do with my life. Helping people."

Though I'd drifted far from the goals I'd set out for myself when I was young, somehow life had found a way to push me back down the path to exactly where I belonged.

It had taken a huge wake-up call of losing everything to remember who I was and what was important to me, but now that I'd regained my footing, I would never stray from my path again. And knowing John was going to be there to walk it with me made my heart swell to near bursting.

"I love that plan. And the fact you're planning on staying in Ruinville only makes it that much better. Though, I'd follow you anywhere if you decide you need to leave again."

"I appreciate that more than you know, but my life is here now. In this house. In this community. With you. It took me a long time to realize it, but I belong here. I always have, and I always will. Ruinville is my home. You're my home."

His chest lifted, then fell with his long sigh. "I really do love you, Diane. There's never been anyone but you. You stole my heart when I was just fifteen, and you never gave it back."

"And I don't plan on it. Ever. You're mine, and I'm yours. Always."

He grabbed me and spun me around, and once again we lost ourselves in the burning passion of our rekindled love.

CHAPTER TWENTY-THREE
CeCe

The town car pulled up in front of our house, and I felt an unexpected sense of relief in returning home. Then I was more surprised at the realization that somewhere in these past months, I'd actually thought of this ramshackle house as *home*. But home is exactly what it felt like as I stepped out of the car and back into the yard we'd spent the summer fixing up. The beautiful flowers Julian had planted bloomed bright along the walkway, and I smiled as I looked up at the house.

"What the hell?" I gasped when I saw the picture window shattered and the remnants of our tree strewn across the front yard.

"What's going on?" Julian asked, then he gasped and covered his mouth. "What the hell happened?"

"Diane!" I shouted, then took off running up the walkway faster than I should have gone in my heels. I was out of shape from wearing them, as I'd realized after spending a weekend in stilettos, but I didn't slow down until I burst into the house. "Diane! Where are you? Diane!"

She stepped out of the kitchen, that cold, distant look still planted firmly in place. "I'm here."

I pressed a hand to my sequin-covered chest. "Oh, thank God! I saw the window and thought something terrible happened to you!"

"I'm fine. Tree flew through the window on Friday night. John got it all chopped up yesterday, and I've just been cleaning up the debris today."

We'd only been gone two nights, but with how different things felt in the house, it may as well have been a month. From Diane's cold welcome to the gaping hole in the living room, this place I'd called home no longer felt like the warm sanctuary it had become in some of the darkest days of my life.

"This is *crazy!*" Julian stood in the living room with his hands planted on his head. Then his eyes bulged. "Can the alligator climb through the window?" His eyes widened more. "Is Peggy in here? Did anyone look for Peggy?"

As he spun around the room staring around his feet, Diane just groaned. "No. Peggy isn't in here. She's fine. I checked on her after the storm and threw her some leftover chicken."

He pressed a hand to his chest. "Oh, thank God. I was worried we were going to have a repeat of our first day here."

Memories of our first day walking into this place flooded into me, and as horrified as I'd been that day, I now looked back fondly at those first moments we'd spent here... together.

I looked over at Diane, still tight-jawed and aloof. "I'm just so glad you're okay. That must have been terrifying. Were you home?"

"Yes. I was here alone. And yes, it was terrifying."

The guilt of knowing she'd been here all alone during such a scary event nearly swallowed me whole. "I... I'm so sorry we weren't here. I feel terrible."

She waved her hand dismissively. "It's fine. I may as well get used to it since you two must be getting ready to move out and back to the penthouse. Did you pick one out when you were there? Got your sugar daddy ready to sign it over?"

A rush of emotions swirled inside of me as I thought back on our weekend. I'd been so excited to return to the lap of luxury. So ready to walk amongst my own people. Wear my fancy clothes without sticking out like a sore thumb. Dine on the best food. Sleep in the most comfortable linens. Indulge myself in the luxuries of life I'd once taken for granted.

And it had been all that and more, yet the happiness I thought I'd find remained absent the entire time I'd been away. Chauncey was a perfect gentleman, and without a doubt I'd charmed him into giving me nearly anything I dreamed to ask for. He opened my doors, held my coat, and treated me like the lady I was meant to be. But every time he drew near, I recoiled, my body rejecting the man it should have run to. With each gentle touch on my back or brush of his hand against my arm, shivers of disgust ran through my skin.

He wasn't Bill.

Instead of my weekend away erasing the affection for Bill like I'd expected, it had only amplified my intense feelings for him. I'd missed him in a way that I never knew I could miss a man. I ached for him. Yearned for him. And even though Chauncey had been a gentleman and not tried to bed me, the mere thought of another man's hands on my body caused me to nearly lose my lobster. And yet, if I continued on this path Julian and I had set down, the time would come where I would have to give my body to the man paying my bills. I'd have to swallow my disgust while he took me to his bed, force myself to endure him so I could remain cared for at his side.

I would be, as Diane so accurately pointed out, nothing more than a prostitute.

Rather than confessing how awful the weekend had been and how much I missed her, home, and… Bill, I remained silent in response to her pointed comment.

"Do you know how much the repairs are going to be? I've been saving up some money. I'd be happy to help out."

The oven timer went off, and she turned and walked into the kitchen. I saw the spread of cookies covering the counter and knew it meant she was baking for a fundraiser yet again.

"Another fundraiser?" Julian asked. "My God, don't these needy people have anything else to do?"

Diane spun around, her eyes narrowed in that way they'd seemed frozen in since the night I told her I was going out with Chauncey. "Actually, to answer *both* your questions: No, I don't need your money to repair the window. And the reason I don't is because once Mawmaw May heard about what happened, she organized a fundraiser in town tomorrow evening. This time, the money is going to *us* to fix the front of the house because it could be weeks or months before insurance will kick in, and they don't want us living like this in the meantime. It will buy the lumber and the glass for the window, and several of the men in town will donate their time to put it all back in. For free." She planted her hands on her hips. "So, these *needy people* you can't wait to get away from are all pitching together to take care of us in *our* time of need."

Julian sucked his lip between his teeth, his gaze dropping to the ground.

My eyebrows lifted in astonishment. "Wow. I can't believe people would be so nice to us."

Diane pulled the cookie sheet out of the oven. "Well, I can. Because this is a good town with good people who take care of their own. And you may not want to be one of them, and you may look down your nose at them, but they are still here for us regardless. I'm donating cookies to the fundraiser because, unlike you, I want to do as much as I can to help them while they help each other and us. Now, if you don't mind, I have baking to do. I'm glad you had a great weekend with your new walking, talking bank account. Just make sure to give me a heads up when you two are moving out."

Julian and I exchanged an embarrassed glance, then as the lump swelled in my throat, I lowered my head and walked quietly up the stairs to my room. After changing out of my upscale outfit into something far more comfortable—the kind of comfortable clothes I'd become accustomed to these past months— I collapsed backward onto the bed.

Julian knocked and entered, then plopped down beside me. "Are you okay? You seemed weird all weekend."

"I'm fine," I replied, though the words held no conviction.

"Is this because Diane is so mad at us? Don't worry. It's Diane. She's too nice, and she'll forgive us eventually. She always does."

"It's not that. I'm fine."

He rolled over, propping his hands on his chin. "CeCe Louise VanTramp. You'd better tell me right now what is the matter."

I rolled over to face him. "Do you like Abe?"

He pulled a face. "No. I was over him like two weeks ago, but I knew he was the key to unlock the door for you to meet someone like Chauncey. I threw myself on the proverbial sword for you. And I'd do it again. I love you, CeCe, and I'll do anything for you... even keep dating a guy like Abe who actually *pees sitting down.*" He pulled a face again. "I mean, if he's too lazy to stand while he pees, you can only imagine how lazy he is in other areas."

I chuckled as he rolled his eyes.

"No, I'm not into Abe, but I'll keep taking one for the team until you find your Mr. Right."

I reached over and slid his hand into mine. "Thank you, Julian. I truly appreciate everything you do for me."

His soft smile lifted his lips. "I would do anything for you, CeCe."

"Then stop dating Abe and go find someone who makes you happy. I don't want you to have to endure spending time with someone you don't like just for me."

He furrowed his brow. "Does that mean you think you've got Chauncey secured enough I don't need to keep Abe around?"

I shook my head. "No. I mean, yes, Chauncey is definitely in the bag if we want him, but that's not what I mean. I just mean that I've known you for twenty years, and I don't think I've ever known you to have fallen in love... *real* love." I lifted a finger before he spoke. "And I mean with a human and not the newest Gucci fall line."

He giggled. "Okay, you got me."

"Just promise me the next man you date will be one you *want* to date, and not one you feel like you have to date for me, or to impress people, or for any other reason than he makes you happy."

He furrowed his brow again. "Where is this coming from, CeCe? What's going on?"

Knowing the complexity of my answer and not wanting to delve into it, I just reached over and patted his hand. "Just promise me. You say you'll do anything for me. Well, that's what I want."

After a long pause, he finally said, "Okay. I promise."

"Good. Now I'm tired and need a nap. A whole weekend in the city was far more exhausting than I remembered. Be a good boy and let me rest."

"Okay, CeCe. Just let me know if you need anything."

He leaned over and kissed my cheek, then left and closed the door behind him.

My phone rang, and I glanced over to see Chauncey's name filling up the screen. Just the thought of having to slap on a fake smile and play coy to secure the pompous, arrogant man's affection made my skin crawl like I was covered in ants. I rolled over and ignored it, closing my eyes as I tried to imagine my life tied to a man I wouldn't, and couldn't, ever love. The thought that was once the goal of getting the life I wanted now felt like a prison sentence.

At what point did having money become more of a punishment than a gift? Just how much was I willing to give up so I could wear Chanel instead of Walmart, or trade sex and my pride for slinging drinks? I knew I didn't want to spend my life slaving away behind a bar, but I also now realized I didn't want to be a slave to a rich man either.

The only thing I knew for certain was that I missed Bill so badly that I could barely breathe. I rolled over and pulled the blanket around my body, closing my eyes and pretending it was him wrapped around me instead.

CHAPTER TWENTY-FOUR
Diane

The string lights twinkled above our heads as John whisked me around the dance floor. My smile grew wider with each spin and twirl, and when the music stopped, I collapsed into his arms, laughing until he closed my mouth with a kiss.

"We should do more evening fundraisers!" I said, breathlessly. "This is so fun having a dance under the stars."

He slipped an arm around my waist and guided me off the dance floor. "It is fun, but all that dancing made me thirsty. You want a drink?"

"I'd love one. I'm going to go check on the fundraising tables and see if they need help. I'll meet you over by the games tables in a bit."

He kissed me again, and I swooned from the simple gesture. It felt so familiar, like we'd been dating forever and no time had passed between us. While I regretted our time apart, I also understood that living our lives separately allowed us to appreciate each other in ways that would never fade. My love for him was absolute, and by the way he looked at me before he leaned down and kissed me again, I knew the feeling was mutual.

"I'll find you in a bit," he said, then I crossed my arms and watched him walk away, admiring the jean-clad view.

With a happy sigh, I stopped myself from skipping as I made my way to the fundraising tent. The familiar faces of the townsfolk I'd come to know so well all greeted me as I passed them by. When I got to the fundraising tent, my brow furrowed at the sight of Julian and CeCe standing behind a table arguing over a green tote.

"No! They should go over here!" Julian tugged at the tub.

"Over here! With the jewelry!" CeCe gave it a yank.

"What are you two doing here?" I asked, surprised to see them show up to a Ruinville event without me dragging them by their ears.

They stopped their tug-o-war, and both spun to look at me, the angry looks on their faces dissipating as they both gave me soft smiles.

"We, uh... we made something for the fundraiser," CeCe said.

My eyebrows shot to my hairline. "You what?"

She set down the tote on the plastic table and lifted the lid. I peered inside to see an array of dozens of little colorful bracelets.

CeCe lowered her gaze to the tote. "I, uh... I don't bake or sew or knit or any of the other things you all do making stuff for fundraisers, but I wanted to help out. I found some of Aunt Addie's embroidery floss and beads in my closet awhile back, and I knew what they were because I used to make friendship bracelets with my girlfriends in middle school. So, I thought maybe I could make some to donate to the fundraiser."

Words escaped me as I peered down into the tote at the colorful little bracelets.

"I helped!" Julian beamed.

"It took me awhile to get the hang of it again, and I stayed up all night to do them, and Julian came in and helped me do more today while you were here setting up. But they didn't turn out very good. In fact, I don't even know why we're arguing about whether they should be with jewelry or crafts. They probably belong on the negative one thousand table." She looked at the tote then scoffed. "They're terrible. This is stupid. I don't know what I was thinking. No one is going to want to buy these." She started to close the lid, but I reached out and stopped her.

"No," I said quickly, placing a hand on her wrist. "CeCe, they are wonderful."

She looked up at me with a strange lack of confidence and a new look of sincerity I rarely saw in those normally calculating eyes. "They are? They aren't dumb?"

"No. They aren't dumb at all. I can't believe you guys did this."

My heart warmed at the vision of Julian and CeCe struggling to tie bracelets just so they could contribute something to our fundraiser. The anger towards them that had been seething through me for a week started to fade as I looked back into the tub of thoughtfully made bracelets.

"You're sure they aren't stupid?" she asked sheepishly.

I shook my head. "No. In fact, I like them so much, I want to wear one." I reached into the bucket and pulled one out, then I saw two more in the same color scheme. "In fact, I think we should all wear one. For advertising."

I pulled out the three bracelets, extending my hand and holding out the three bracelets like they were white flags I waved.

Julian and CeCe exchanged a smile, then each grabbed a bracelet. We tied them on, then Julian shoved his hand out. "Friendship bracelets unite!"

I laughed and stuck my hand forward to line up with his, and CeCe did the same. We clinked the bracelets together, and looked up at each other, grinning.

"This is really awesome, you guys. I know people are going to love these, and I bet they sell out and raise even more money to fix our house." I paused, and my heart sank a little over the word *our*. "Or, I guess I mean my house since you two won't be there much longer."

CeCe took a deep breath then stepped around the table to my side. "About that," she started, then slid an arm around my waist and guided me over to the gazebo. Julian followed along, and the three of us sat down side by side.

"What's going on? Are you... are you leaving already?"

I couldn't believe the sadness that flooded through me thinking about Julian and CeCe leaving my life for good. There was a time where all I wanted was to get rid of the two people I despised the most, but now the thought of a life without them filled my heart with an unbearable sadness.

"No. In fact, the opposite," she said softly.

My eyes popped open wide. "Wait. What?"

With a sigh, she gave me a gentle smile. "You're right, you know. This place and these people really have each other's backs. I'm sorry it took me so long to see it. I didn't realize how special this place was until I left it again. The city," she paused and closed her eyes, grimacing, "it was terrible. I hated it. The snobby people. The arrogance everywhere. Having to fake smile and fake laugh and fake...

well, everything. I can't stand Chauncey, or any man like him, and I don't want to live my life with a man I can't stand just because he has money. You were right, Diane. It's a terrible life I thought I wanted so much."

I just blinked back at her, too stunned to say anything.

"I don't want to go backward. I don't want to go safe. I want to learn to stand on my own two feet like you did and find a path in life that doesn't mean I have to sell my soul for the riches. I want to... I want to stay here with you."

"You do?" I managed out.

She looked at Julian and his shocked expression. "I do. That is if you'll still have me?"

I couldn't contain my smile as I nodded. "Yes. Of course, I will. I would love to have you stay, and together we'll figure out what's next for us."

Her smile lifted to match mine. "I would love that, Diane. Thank you. Thank you so much."

"Wait... what's happening?" Julian asked, lifting a finger as he scrunched his face in confusion.

CeCe turned to face him, her face folding into a soft frown. "I'm so sorry, Julian. I know I promised you that I'd get us back to the penthouse, but I just can't do it. I hated every minute of this weekend. I thought I wanted that life again so badly, but once I was in it, I felt like I couldn't breathe. Like I was suffocating. I know I don't want to bartend forever, so I'll need to come up with a new career, but it isn't going to be as the wife of a wrinkled, old rotting millionaire. I understand if you have to leave me here and go find someone else to help you get back to the life of luxury you love so much. I'll miss you terribly, but I'll help you in any way I can."

His eyes shone with tears. "I wanted that life back because I thought it was what you needed to be happy, and I would do *anything* to make you happy. I would never want you to sacrifice your happiness for me. CeCe, my life is with you. You're my best friend. My *family*. No amount of money or prestige could ever take me away. If Ruinville is your home, then it's my home too. To hell with couture and private jets... we can get by with Walmart and 'Ol Blue." He took her hand in his. "As long as it means I have you." Then he reached over and slid my hand into his free one. "And you."

I couldn't contain the tears as they spilled from my eyes, and I reached forward and swallowed them both in a hug, squeezing them so tight, I worried they couldn't breathe. "I can't believe you're choosing to stay with me. I was so sad thinking about a life without you both. I'm so sorry I've been so angry at you lately. I've been... mean. It wasn't that I was mad you were choosing an easy life, and honestly, I can understand the appeal. Starting over is hard. It was that choosing that life meant I'd be losing you both. I didn't handle it well, and I... I'm so sorry, and I'm just so glad you're staying. You've become so important to me, and I just... I'm just so damn happy. We're going to figure it all out, and we're going to figure it out together."

They squeezed me back, and I heard CeCe sniffling. The three of us remained locked in our hug, and finally CeCe sniffled once more and sat back.

"From riches to Ruinville, but at least we're together," she said.

We slowly released our grips on each other, and I wiped the tears from my eyes. "We're together, and that's what matters. And hey, you gotta admit, Ruinville isn't half bad once you're used to it."

She shook her head. "No, it's not. At first, I thought this place was hell, but the more time I spend here, the more I realize this is the happiest I've ever been. The people are, well, weird, but they've got each other's backs. And our backs too it seems. There's no better place for us to start over than right here in Ruinville."

"Everyone really is so nice," Julian agreed. "You don't find many places like this that would help people out in need so much."

"It is a special place. And one I'm so honored to live in," I said back. "I know it isn't the life we used to live, and it took a lot of getting used to, but it's my home now, and I don't ever want to leave it. Not for anything."

"I don't want to leave either," CeCe said then she lifted a finger. "But I really do mean it though. I'm not bartending forever. I'm going to need your help figuring out exactly what to do in this new life of ours."

Julian's eyes widened. "Same, girl. I will not be a dishwasher for the rest of my life. I mean, look at my hands! They're wrinkling! I'm a monster! I love you, CeCe, but there are limits to that love. We need to find me a new career stat if we're staying here."

I wiped the happy tears from my eyes and smiled at them. "We'll find you something you love just like I think I have."

The both looked at me, confused.

"I'm going to nursing school part-time while I waitress at Mawmaw's, and in a few years, I'll be a nurse like I had always planned before I met Rick!"

"What?" they responded with huge grins.

"A nurse? That's amazing, Diane!" CeCe said.

"You're such a good caretaker. You're going to be great at it!" Julian beamed.

"I'm so excited about it. It's going to be a lot of work balancing waitressing with going to school, but when it's all said and done, I'll have a career that I love, and I'll be helping people the way Aunt Addie always raised me to do. I was never supposed to be a socialite. I didn't marry Rick *for* his money, but it certainly changed the trajectory of my life. And not in a good way."

"I was always supposed to be a socialite," CeCe admitted. "That's what I was raised to do. Marry a good man with money, build the family fortune, elevate the family name. That was my whole existence. And I did care for Arthur at one time. I didn't *just* marry him for his money the way I was planning to do to get out of here, but I certainly didn't feel about him the way I feel about..."

She cut herself off before she finished, and her face fell with a heavy sadness.

"Like you feel for Bill?" I finished for her.

She nodded. "Yes, like I feel for Bill. Although after what I did to him, he's never going to forgive me."

I scoffed. "That man is crazy about you, CeCe. If I can forgive you for being so terrible to me all those years, he can forgive you for one night of weakness."

"You think?" she asked sheepishly. "But how? What would I even say after how awful I treated him?"

Julian lit up. "A grand gesture! You need a grand gesture to show him that you truly care about him now and he's not just some boy toy anymore."

"What kind of grand gesture?" she asked.

Julian frowned. "I can't think of anything at the moment, but I promise, if you want the Gator Guy, we are gonna get you the Gator Guy. I'll come up with something brilliant. I am the man with the plan. Oh! Now that Operation Diaper Daddy is over, how about we call this Operation Gator Guy Getter. Triple G."

She lit up in the way I only saw her do when she talked about Bill. "Okay. We'll come up with a plan. Operation Gator Guy Getter is underway."

They squealed and clasped hands, and I loved seeing the light in her eyes again that had seemed to go out the minute she'd said yes to Chauncey.

"So, we're doing this? We're all staying in Ruinville to start new lives together?"

They looked at each other and nodded. "If you'll have us, we're staying with you."

I grinned widely. "Then you're staying with me."

CeCe blew out a breath. "You truly are amazing, Diane. You took us in after we'd been so awful to you all those years. Your Aunt Addie really did help raise you better than all the nannies in the world ever raised me."

My heart warmed at the kind words and the image of Aunt Addie standing proudly beside me, smiling.

"You two were terrible to me." I chuckled. "Truly awful. But I wasn't an angel myself when I started fighting fire with fire and torturing you back. But that was in the past. This is a fresh start for us all."

Julian sucked the air through his teeth. "Yeah. Sorry we were such jerks before."

"I am sorry about the way we treated you," CeCe said. "I was just seething with jealousy all those years, and the only way I knew to handle that, was to try to take you down to my level."

My eyes flashed wide. "*You* were jealous of *me?* What are you talking about! You're CeCe VanTramp," I said her name properly instead of the way I'd always botched it on purpose.

She tossed her head back and chortled. "Oh yes. I was green with envy. When I married Arthur, I was the belle of the ball. Then Rick met you and suddenly you sucked all the air out of the room. You were younger, more beautiful, smarter, kinder... you were all the things I wasn't, and I could barely stand to be next to you. And then you started wearing better clothes, getting better jewelry, getting the admiration of everyone in our social circle. I always felt like I was ten steps behind you, and it drove me to madness."

My jaw dropped. "That is *crazy!* The only reason I ever started wearing fancy clothes and caring about stupid things like handbags and social standing was because you tormented me so badly about being frumpy that first year with Rick, I finally started trying to fit in and elevate myself to your level."

She chuckled. "I only teased you that first year because I was jealous. You were a natural beauty, and you didn't need all the glitz and glamour I needed to stand out. But then you started fitting the role of a socialite, and it drove me to even more madness."

I smirked. "Well, to be perfectly honest, once I realized how much I could make steam come out of your ears by outshining you and beating you to the latest fashions or outbidding you at auctions, I reveled in it."

Her eyes popped open. "I knew it! I knew you were doing that on purpose, but you always looked so sweet and innocent about it, I started to think I was going nuts! You scandalous thing you! And here I thought you were a kind-hearted do-gooder!"

I started laughing and shrugged. "I told you. Living that life turned me into a different person. One I'm not proud of. I'm sorry that I took such pleasure in driving you insane."

"Dear God, did you ever." Julian blew out a puff of air. "Do you remember that time she showed up in the same Armani gown at the auction right before you, and I had to shove you back in the limo and drive you home before anyone saw you wearing matching dresses? I thought you were going to light Manhattan on fire that night!"

I laughed, a devilish grin splitting my face. "I did that on purpose. I found out what you were wearing, bought it, and made sure to arrive before you, then stand in plain view of where your limo would arrive so you'd have no choice but to rush home."

CeCe gasped and slapped my shoulder, then we dissolved into hysterics.

"You villain!" she said, smacking me again.

I shrugged as my laughter petered off. "Tormenting my tormentor was the highlight of my shallow existence. So, I, too, am sorry for all the pain I caused you over the years. And I'm really sorry again for being so hard on you this past week. That wasn't fair. I was just scared of losing you, and I handled it badly. Can you forgive me?"

With a soft smile, she nodded. "Of course I can. And can you forgive me for all my past mistakes? I never should have treated you that way."

With warmth filling my heart, I nodded. "I forgive you, CeCe. We were different people then, and now that's all behind us, and the three of us are in this life together."

Julian stuck out his wrist, showing his bracelet. "Best friends forever."

We giggled at the childish expression, but it didn't stop us from sticking our wrists out to tap our bracelets together.

"So, what now?" I asked as I looked at the faces of my two dearest friends, the ones I felt so grateful were staying in my life. "I'm heading to nursing school as my next step, but now we need to figure out your next steps."

CeCe nodded then looked around the town center buzzing with people. "We will. But first, there is one thing I have to do. Now that we've made things right with us, there is one more person I need to make amends with."

"Bill?" I asked.

"Oh! It's time for a grand gesture!" Julian jumped to his feet.

CeCe and I rose to meet him, linking arms together.

"I'll do whatever it takes," she said. "Just help me find Bill and convince him that he's the one for me. Because he is. I don't know why, or how, but my God do I need that man in my life."

"He really does bring out the best in you," I said.

She nodded. "He does. He makes me so happy, and he accepts me for exactly who I am. I have to fix this mess I made with him. I really hurt him."

I squeezed her arm. "We'll fix it. Together."

"Operation Gator Guy Getter is underway!" Julian exclaimed, then took off, towing the two of us behind him.

CHAPTER TWENTY-FIVE
CeCe

The three of us walked around the fundraiser together, my eyes desperately scanning for Bill, and hoping he'd come. Knowing the fundraiser was for me, and knowing he'd avoided me the entire week since I'd broken his heart, I started to lose hope he'd show. But just when I was about to give up my search, Julian slammed on the brakes, causing Diane and I to crash into him.

"There he is! Gator Guy!"

When I saw him drinking a beer beside the ring toss, my breath trapped in my lungs. Even in an outfit I once would've deemed too embarrassing to be seen on any man of mine in public, I now saw Bill's rough and rugged style as undeniably handsome. I yearned to feel those strong arms wrap around me once again and taste the lips I had kissed a hundred times. How could I have been so blind not to see the incredible man who'd been standing right in front of me the whole time? The old rules of high society I had followed like absolute law seemed so silly now with him standing so close but still so far away. Bill was handsome. Sexy. And I should have been proud to be on his arm.

Instead, I'd tossed him aside like garbage.

When he looked my way and our eyes connected for the first time since that fateful evening I'd cast him aside, hurt and anger swirled inside those icy blue orbs the same way it had that night. I shrank beneath his devastated gaze, my own eyes sending out a silent plea for forgiveness. But he just took a big swig of his beer, tossed it in the recycling bin the same way I'd tossed him away, and walked off.

"He hates me," I whispered, struggling to fight the tears.

"He doesn't hate you," Diane soothed. "He's just angry. Hurt."

"He hates me, and I deserve it. I treated him like crap."

Julian rubbed my back. "I'm telling you. A grand gesture. That's the way they always do it in the movies."

"What the hell kind of a grand gesture should I do?"

He pursed his lips, tipping his head as he thought. Then with a shrug, he said, "I don't know yet, but I'm gonna figure it out. I've watched enough rom coms to be able to concoct the ultimate apology comeback tour."

With my shoulders slumped from the defeat of his outright rejection, I let Diane and Julian walk me back toward the gazebo where they were starting the Basket Bidding.

"What the hell is Basket Bidding anyway? I haven't seen one of these at these never-ending fundraisers before," I said as we found a spot inside the growing crowd gathering around the gazebo.

Diane pointed to Mayor Marjorie, holding a microphone where she stood in the center of the gazebo. "Basket Bidding is a really fun tradition they've had going on for... well, forever. They do it at evening fundraisers, like this one. People put together a basket filled with various foods, and then people bid on the basket, and the winner dines with the basket owner. It's just a fun way to raise some money and have a meal with a friend."

"Oh, that's kinda fun!" Julian said. "Too bad there aren't any cute guys for me in Ruinville, or maybe I'd bid on someone's basket." He waggled his eyebrows, then his face fell. "Wait. That's a problem. If we're really staying here, how in the hell am I supposed to find someone to date? The only gay man in town is... me. This feels very reminiscent of growing up the only gay in small town suburbia. There's a reason I never went back there after I left. I didn't fit in there, and I'm not sure that I will ever fit in here."

It occurred to me how much he was sacrificing to stay in my life. Not only was he willing to give up our life of luxury, but he was right. Finding love in a small, Southern town wouldn't be easy for Julian.

"Are you sure you want to stay? I swear I won't hold it against you if you have to go," I said, reaching out and touching his hand. "I would miss you more than words could ever say, but I would support your decision."

He shook his head hard. "No. You're right, CeCe. This town, this place, it may not be what I wanted, but I think it's what we need. Both of us. I said it before, and I'll say it again, my place is with you. We're going to find our way in this new life of ours, and we're going to do it together."

Those damn tears started welling up in my eyes as I looked at the face of my most loyal friend... or as he'd correctly stated earlier... my family.

"I love you, Julian. And I promise we are going to find you someone amazing. And if we can't find him in Ruinville, once we get enough money to buy a real car and not that dump truck we drive around in, we can go to the city on the weekends and start the hunt for the perfect man who deserves someone as wonderful as you."

He grinned and slipped an arm around my waist. "Awe. Thanks, CeCe. You're always looking out for me. We'll just have to make a really, *really* big radius on my dating apps so I can try to find someone for myself." His eyes widened. "Like *really* big because I seriously think I'm the only gay man in the entire county." Then he paused and pressed a finger to his chin. "Well, maybe the only *out* gay man in the entire county. Perhaps there are some hidden gems still locked up in the closet that I can help free." He waggled his eyebrows, and we laughed.

"Well, if it makes you feel better, if Bill never forgives me, we'll both be stuck being single in Ruinville. We can just grow old together."

Diane gave me a little pat on the arm. "He'll forgive you. I've seen how he looks at you. Just find a way to apologize... as many times as you need to. He'll come around."

"I hope so," I said, my heart constricting with the thought of having lost him forever.

The microphone squealed as Mayor Marjorie turned it on. Everyone gathering around covered their ears. Us included.

"Oops! Sorry!" she apologized, then stepped further from the small speaker. "Okay. That's better. Welcome everyone to the highlight of our evening... The Basket Bidding! As you all know, I'll be presenting the baskets and their talented creators, and you all call out your bids until we have a winner! And don't be stingy. Our friends need our help repairing their house after that terrible storm, and we're not going home until we've raised enough money to fix it!"

She pointed our way, and the whole town turned to look at us, each clapping and offering encouragement and kind words. I'd been to dozens of fundraisers in my day, hundreds even, and until I arrived in Ruinville, I'd never felt the sense of camaraderie and the real giving spirit. The fundraisers I'd been to had been to show off your money and parade around making sure everyone knew you were a good person. But in Ruinville, they were here for each other.

And tonight, they were here for us.

My soul warmed a little more as I stood in their presence, surrounded by the familiar, though still admittedly strange, people that now considered me one of their own.

The three of us waved our hands, mouthing thank you to everyone around us. Finally, Mayor Marjorie kicked off the auction with Arlene. She stood proudly on the gazebo holding her wicker basket while Mayor Marjorie rattled off from a list all the contents inside. Homemade pie, gumbo, turkey sandwiches, and her famous jam. Hands flew in the air as people spit out their bids, finishing with Gumbo Gus winning the tasty sounding dinner.

Arlene came down from the gazebo, slid her hand through his arm and they strolled off to find a spot to enjoy it. Next up, Mawmaw May stood up tall with her oversized basket, and a bidding war went rampant with everyone vying for the delicious goods her talented hands had created. With sixty dollars as the winning bid, she squealed with delight over the amount she'd raised, then hurried down the steps to meet Sherrif Boshaw.

One after another, the proud owners of the baskets stood in the gazebo while everyone fought over who would be lucky enough to claim their prize. It seemed half of the town had slaved away in the kitchen just to put something together to help us raise money.

"This is really fun!" Julian whispered. "And they are raising us some serious dough! I can't believe they are doing this for us."

"I can." Diane smiled. "We're part of a community now. All of us."

As I smiled at her, still shocked by what a sharp turn I'd taken in life that had landed me permanently at the side of a woman I once loathed in a town I once thought of as my own personal hell, my attention snapped back to the gazebo when I heard Mayor Marjorie announce the next basket had been made by Bayou Bill.

"What?" I gasped. "He made a basket for our fundraiser?"

"Oh my God! There he is!" Julian whispered, pinching my arm with how tight he squeezed.

"CeCe! He knew this fundraiser was for us, and he's still contributing. That must mean something! If he truly hated you, he would never be up there trying to help you out!" Diane practically squealed.

When I saw him step up on that gazebo holding a beat-up blue cooler, my heart rattled against my ribcage. My God how I missed that man. I missed how he made me laugh. How he protected me and made me feel safe. How he accepted me even at my worst. How he'd cradle me in his arms at night and hold me as I fell asleep. Kiss me so deeply I may as well have been at the bottom of the ocean.

I missed him. I missed everything about him. And I couldn't stand being away from him for even one more minute.

"In this basket," Mayor Marjorie said then paused, "er, cooler, we have a six-pack of Bud Light, two ham sandwiches, two bags of potato chips, and a candy bar. Do I hear ten dollars?"

The crowd chuckled at the simplistic offering, but when I saw Darla, the town floozy I knew held a torch for him, batting her eyelashes and lifting her hand, I knew she wasn't in it for the ham sandwich.

"Ten dollars," Darla said with a seductive smile.

Julian gasped. "CeCe! She's after your man! That hussy!"

Rage and jealousy collided inside me as I watched her twirling her hair while she grinned up at him. I'd been in my fair share of battles at auctions before, but tonight, I knew this was a prize I wasn't willing to lose.

I narrowed my eyes. No one was winning Bill's basket but me.

"Twenty dollars!" I shouted, lifting my hand in the air.

Diane spun to face me. "CeCe! What are you doing? They're raising money for *us*! We're not supposed to be bidding!"

Bill's eyes searched the crowd and landed on mine, and I swore I saw the corner of his lip smirk.

"Grand gesture," I said confidently, holding his gaze as I smiled.

"Oh! The grand gesture! Good one! Yay!" Julian clapped.

"Thirty dollars!" Darla shouted back.

"Fifty!" I countered.

She narrowed her eyes and leveled me with a glare. "Seventy-five dollars!"

"One hundred and fifty dollars!" I called out.

The crowd gasped, and this time Bill's smirk lifted in a full half-smile.

"CeCe! We don't have that kind of money!" Diane whispered.

"Chauncey gave me five hundred dollars to buy something I loved. I didn't see a damn thing in the city that enticed me, so I just shoved it in my purse. I've got five hundred dollars, and I'll spend every damn penny to buy the one thing in this world I truly love."

"Wow! One hundred and fifty dollars!" Mayor Marjorie laughed into the microphone. "Can anyone beat one hundred and fifty dollars?"

The crowd went silent, and Darla stomped off, defeated. I grinned my triumphant smile I'd used often thwarting an enemy in a bidding war.

"Going once. Going twice. SOLD to CeCe VanTramp!"

Bill and I locked eyes as I moved through the crowd toward him. He came down the stairs slowly, his alligator boots clicking on the wood with each step. When I finally reached him, he paused on the last one.

I stopped at the base of the stairs, my heart pounding with nervous excitement as I stood in front of him.

"Well, well. Her highness isn't afraid to be seen in public with a lowly man like me?" Bill quirked an eyebrow, his gaze teasing yet searching.

"Bill, I'm an idiot. I want you and everyone in Ruinville to know it." I waved a hand at the people listening intently, and for the first time in my life, I didn't give a damn. "When I told you I needed to get out of here and find someone better, I was just exhausted and scared. This life here isn't what I thought I wanted, but it turns out, it's exactly what I need. *You're* what I need." I reached out and pressed a hand to his faded shirt. "I'm sorry that I tried to keep our relationship under wraps like I was ashamed of you. It's you who should have been ashamed of me and my behavior. I'm sorry that I was too weak to stand on my own two feet. Most of all, I'm sorry that I hurt you."

His eyes softened, a flicker of hope reigniting within them. My heart swelled to see the remnants of the way he once looked at me.

"Bill, I thought I wanted a life of riches and status. But all I want is you. Screw the caviar. Give me the crayfish."

His face split into a grin, and a tear slid down my cheek just before he dropped his cooler, snaked a hand around my waist and bent me backward into a kiss that left me limp in his embrace.

The crowd cheered as we clung to each other, and I heard Julian's high-pitched screams above them all. Bill kissed me until I ran out of breath, but I didn't care. He was the only oxygen I needed.

With the crowd still whooping and cheering, he set me back up on my feet and slung an arm around my neck, leaning down and whispering in my ear, "Damn, Pretty Girl. You sure know how to say you're sorry."

"It's the first, and probably the last time I've ever done it. Don't get used to it."

He laughed and kissed my cheek. "Don't worry, baby. I know who you are, and you know what? I love you anyway."

My whole body blushed at his words, and I turned around and tossed my arms around his neck, pulling him down for one last kiss that left the townsfolk screaming even louder. "I love you too," I whispered against his lips.

With pride swelling inside me, I grabbed his hand and led him out of the gazebo. Julian and Diane jumped up and down clapping as we passed them by, and I gave them a little smile and whispered, "Thank you."

Julian blew me a kiss, and I returned it, then I gave Diane a little wink. Bill led me to the edge of the dance floor where several couples were spinning around.

"You sure about this? You really want to stay here in Ruinville with me? You're not gonna miss your fancy schmancy boyfriend?" He gave me a teasing smile.

"I've never been more sure of anything in my life. I went back to my old world for a weekend, and that's all it took for me to realize I didn't belong there anymore. I've changed... grown, as you said, and I don't want to go back to the person I was before. All I could think about every minute of every day was you. I want you, Bill. I'm always going to want you."

He grinned wide, then extended his hand. "Well, in that case, care to dance?"

I arched an eyebrow. "You dance?"

"What? You think just because I don't wear no flouncy tuxedos means I don't know my way around the dance floor?"

I grabbed his hand and smiled. "Well, by all means then. Show me."

He yanked me into his arms, and I laughed as he twirled me around. Instead of worrying about how I looked to the people spectating, or if my hair was getting blown out of place, I let myself go in his arms. We clung to each other as we moved as one, and when the song slowed down to a slow dance, I rested my head on his chest and settled into his arms.

For the first time in my life, I felt at home. Truly at home.

"Mind if we join you?" Diane asked.

I peeked up to see her and John walking hand-in-hand onto the dance floor. They looked absolutely perfect together, and I loved seeing the way she lit up when she looked at him. I imagined it was exactly the same when I looked at Bill.

"We'd love for you to join us," I said, and Bill and I spun a bit to give them more room.

Diane settled into John's arms, and the four of us rocked away to the slow song until I heard Julian clear his throat from the edge of the dance floor. I looked up to see him standing, arms crossed as he stared at me.

"Hi. It's me. The fifth wheel. I'm feeling left out."

I chuckled and looked up at Bill. "Do you mind?"

He laughed and opened his arm, flagging Julian to come and join us. With a little squeal, Julian hurried across the dance floor and wrapped his arms around us both. The three of us kept dancing as Diane and John laughed.

"Sorry, but I'm not going to be a wallflower just because you two broads hooked up. Until you help me find my own happily ever after, you're all stuck with me."

"I don't mind sharing my Pretty Girl," Bill said, then turned us around. "But you're not coming in the bedroom."

Julian pulled a face. "Ew. No. I just don't want to be sitting home alone every night while you guys are all off being romantic."

"Then consider yourself our third wheel as long as you need to be." Bill smiled at him and spun us both again.

I laughed as I tightened my grip around Julian's waist. "We'll find your person, Julian, but even after we do, you're still gonna be stuck with me. Always. You're my family."

He swooned as he pressed his cheek to mine, and I gave it a little kiss. When the song ended, Julian exited the dance floor, and Bill took me for one last spin. I let the last of my fears go as I lost myself in his embrace, and I smiled as I imagined the new life I couldn't wait to begin.

A life with a man I loved and the two best friends a girl could ever dream of.

CHAPTER TWENTY-SIX
Diane

I walked through the living room, admiring the new window that John, Bill, and a few other guys had installed two weeks ago. A month had passed since that tree had come crashing into the living room, and now with the final paint and finishing touches, you couldn't even tell anything had happened. I looked outside to see Julian tending the garden, and with how content he looked out there, you'd never know the tantrums he'd thrown months ago when I'd asked him to help. Oh, how he'd screamed that he didn't want to touch the soil and get his hands dirty. Now he had grown to love gardening, and he'd even replanted a tree to replace the one we lost in the storm.

CeCe waltzed down the stairs and joined me, chuckling when she saw him. "Maybe being a gardener is Julian's calling. I mean, look at the masterful color designs he's created. He's got your garden looking as good as the flowers at any event I've ever attended in New York. He has impeccable taste and style, and he seems to really love it. Oh! Or an event planner! He would make an incredible event planner!"

I looked at her and my eyebrows rose. "You know. That's actually an awesome idea! There are so many weddings and events in Ruinville, I bet he could corner the market on event planning! I know I would certainly want him in charge of my wedding if I was getting married."

CeCe waggled her eyebrows and bumped me with her shoulder. "Oh... marriage? Are you and John thinking about taking the plunge?"

"What? No!" I laughed, then it petered off. "I mean, honestly, we've only been dating a month, but it feels like I've been with him forever. We haven't exactly talked about it, but I would marry him in a heartbeat." Then I frowned. "Although, that can't happen since you and I are both still legally married. I don't even know what to do about that."

She sucked the air through her teeth. "Yeah. My original plan was to find a rich guy then use his money to hire fancy lawyers to figure out how to dissolve our marriages, but we all know how that plan turned out. Crap. You're right. We're both stuck in our situation until we figure something out, and now we don't have a big bank account to remedy it."

I shook my head. "No, we don't, but you know what? We don't need it. We've been doing just fine on our own, and I know that together, you and I can figure this out. We'll go to the library and do some research. There must be some way to get divorced from husbands who disappeared, then if either one of us decides we're ready to remarry, we'll be divorced and ready to go."

She smiled the way she always did when she thought of Bill, and I gave her a bump with my shoulder back. "You're thinking about marrying Bill, aren't you?"

Her face bloomed with an array of reds, then she sheepishly said, "I'm not *not* thinking about it."

We shared an excited look, then giggled a bit.

CeCe let out a contented sigh. "Well, no matter what, step one is we get divorced. Let's make that top priority.

Then, when we're ready to remarry, we'll be all set for Julian to plan our weddings."

"We have to tell him we finally found his career path. This is it. This is what he needs to do."

"It really is. He's going to love this idea. Let's call him in and tell him."

CeCe and I walked to the door and opened it to call for Julian. He finished up spritzing the flowers, then hurried in to find out what had us so excited. After telling him our idea, he practically bubbled over with excitement, already spewing out ideas for the different types of receptions he could design.

We settled down on the couch together to talk more about our ideas for starting him a business, then after we finished gabbing about Julian's exciting new endeavor, I shared my own news with them.

"And, I also have exciting news to share," I said proudly.

"What is it?" Julian asked.

"I sent out my application for nursing school and... I got in!"

"You did?" CeCe gasped. "Diane! That's wonderful!"

They enclosed me in a hug, and I squeezed them back. "I'm so excited. It's going to be a lot of work when school starts, but I'm ready to take on the task and get back to the career I always wanted."

"You're going to be a wonderful nurse," Julian said. "And I'm going to be a wonderful wedding planner! Eek! It's all coming together!"

CeCe frowned. "I still don't know what I'm going to do for a career. I'm finally settling in to bartending, but seriously, everything hurts so bad at the end of my shifts I can barely walk. I'm too old for this."

"There isn't anything you can think of that would make you happy for a career?"

She shook her head. "Unless Bill can afford to make me a stay-at-home wife, or professional lady of leisure as I prefer to be called, then no. Honestly, I just want to be with him all the time, and nothing else I can think of seems to bring me any kind of joy."

"Nothing?" Julian asked. "There must be something you love to do besides..." he waggled his eyebrows, and she smacked him gently.

Wanting CeCe to find the same enthusiasm for something of her very own like I now had for nursing school, I urged her on. "Come on, CeCe. Think back. What was something you were passionate about before you met Arthur?"

She let out a breath and shrugged. "Nothing. I was groomed from birth to be a society wife. That was all the aspiration my parents ever set out for me."

"Think harder. What did you used to do for fun?" I asked.

She furrowed her brow, thinking hard, then finally she lit up. "Write. I used to love to write and tell stories. In middle school, I would come home from school every day and scribble away in my little notebook making up all sorts of fantastical stories."

I slapped her leg. "Well, there you go! Let's find some way to get you into a writing career!"

With a snort, she shook her head. "Yeah, right. I'm too old to try to start a writing career."

Julian scoffed. "Nonsense! You're never too old to start again! And now that you've lived such an exciting, full life, think of all the stuff you'll have to write about!" He paused, and his eyes got big. "Wait! Chauncey was hellbent on interviewing you to tell your story about what happened to us. Maybe instead of letting someone else tell it, *you* tell it! Write a book about your fall from grace and how you picked yourself back up again. People would *love* to read that!"

"You think?" she asked, her interest peaked.

I nodded enthusiastically. "Yes! Yes, that's it! Write our story, CeCe! Oh, please. You have to."

She chewed on her lower lip, then finally they spread into a grin. "Okay, what the hell? I'll try it!"

"Yay!" Julian clapped. "A nurse, an event planner and an author. *Now* we're talking!"

As excitement bubbled inside of me for the journey we were each about to embark on, a car pulling up the driveway caught our attention.

"Was Bill coming by?" I asked CeCe.

"No, he's got a fishing tour today. It's not John?"

"Nope. All day fire training with the guys."

A car door slammed, and the three of us got off the couch and walked to the front door. When we looked out through the screen to see the two men coming up the walkway, my knees nearly gave out on me.

"Oh my God," Julian gasped. "Is that Rick and Arthur?"

"It is," CeCe breathed barely above a whisper.

On many occasions since they'd abandoned us, when Julian, CeCe and I would get a little tipsy on wine, we'd discuss what we would say if we ever saw them again. We'd stand in the living room giving our righteous speeches and laugh about how we'd tell them exactly where to shove their apologies. But now, faced with the reality of our husbands approaching us, those practiced words evaporated like morning dew in the Louisiana heat.

We stood frozen in shock as our husbands came up the steps, their faces so familiar and yet they looked like strangers to me. Julian went first, and after I finally convinced my feet to move, I followed him out onto the front porch with CeCe stumbling along behind me.

"CeCe!" Arthur hurried up the steps toward her, his big smile stretching his plump cheeks.

"Arthur?" She stood, stunned.

He pulled her into a tight embrace, but she remained stiff, her arms plastered to her sides as he squeezed her.

"Diane." Rick grinned sheepishly running a hand through his thinning, grey hair as he stepped in front of me, then with jerky, awkward movements, he reached out to hug me.

"No," I said sharply, stepping out of his reach. My voice shook, but not from fear - from rage. "Do not *touch* me. What... what the hell are you doing here? Where have you been?"

The sight of him standing there in his expensive pants and finely pressed shirt, looking exactly the same as the day he'd disappeared, sent a fresh wave of anger through me. How dare he show up here, in the home where I'd rebuilt my life from the ashes he'd left behind, wearing that familiar apologetic smile that had smoothed over so many minor transgressions in our marriage. But this wasn't forgetting our anniversary or working late through dinner - he'd stolen millions of dollars and abandoned me without a word.

"Diane," he pleaded. "Please don't be angry."

Arthur let go of CeCe, seemingly oblivious to her frozen shock. "Can you believe it's us? Bet we surprised you, huh?"

Julian stepped protectively in front of us, crossing his arms tight. "What the hell are you two doing here just showing up like this? And answer, Diane! Where in the hell have you been? Do you know what kind of holy hell you put these two through? Well, do you? Speak!"

They recoiled from his sharp scolding, and Rick lifted his hands in submission. "We are so, *so* sorry for disappearing. We had to. Once we realized the feds were onto us, we had to take the money and run, and we couldn't say a word to either of you because we wanted to ensure your total and complete innocence."

I let out a sharp laugh that held no humor. "Our innocence? How thoughtful of you to protect us while you were stealing millions and running off into the sunset."

"It was our mess," Rick continued, "and we didn't want you ladies caught up in it. The best thing to do was disappear, leave you clueless to show your innocence, and now that enough time has passed and they aren't hunting us so hard, we came to get you so we can sneak out of the country together. We've got everything all set up to start a brand-new life. We'll be safe, and you'll never have to worry again."

I glanced over at CeCe, seeing the same mix of disbelief and indignation on her face that I felt bubbling inside me.

"Never have to worry again?" CeCe spit out, finally coming out of her trance. "Like we didn't have to worry when we were being interrogated by the FBI? Or when we were thrown out of our homes? Or when we had to learn to stand on our own two feet because our husbands abandoned us?"

"We couldn't risk contacting you," Arthur defended. "We did what we had to do to protect you."

"Protect us?" I stepped forward, jabbing a finger into Rick's chest. "Do you have any idea what it was like? Standing there while the FBI ransacked our home? Having all our so-called friends slam their doors in our faces? Having to start completely over with nothing?"

"Diane, please." Rick caught my hand, and I glanced down at it, so strange how unfamiliar the simple touch felt to me after decades of spending our lives together. "We feel awful about what happened. We made a mistake. A big one. But we're here now, and we feel terrible you've had to live like this. Just come with us so we can get out of the country quickly. We'll explain everything on the jet."

I pulled my hand free from Rick's grasp and stepped back, suddenly seeing with perfect clarity how different the man before me was from the one I'd married. How different he was not only from who he used to be, but how different he was from John. The kind, loyal, and honest man that I now loved.

Julian lifted a finger. "Wait a minute. We thought you already fled the country! Are you saying you've been here the whole time?"

Arthur nodded. "The minute we knew things were going south, we contacted a guy who handles things like new identities. He helped us get all set up and even helped us fake fleeing the country so the feds would be looking in the wrong direction. We've actually been hiding out in a small cabin in Utah he set us up in just waiting for things to simmer down. Now that the heat is off, we have a jet waiting, and we can all get out of here. Together."

Rick looked at me, and I swear my heart stopped beating for a few long moments.

Flee the country? Go on the run? What?

Julian clucked his cheek while shaking his head. "I don't know whether to be horrified or impressed at the depth of your devious plan."

Rick's gaze remained locked with mine. "We did what we did for your benefit. Believe us, it was horrible having to leave you like that without a word, but it was what was best for you. Please forgive us. We miss you terribly."

Arthur nodded his agreement.

John's face flashed through my mind and solidified the answer I already had to his question.

"Forgive you?" I finally managed. "*Forgive* you? You are out of your damn minds if you think you can just waltz back into our lives and beg for forgiveness, and we'll just skip off after you to live our lives with criminals on the run!"

CeCe's eyes narrowed as she stepped tighter to my side. "Yeah! Screw you, Arthur! You *ruined* us!"

He grimaced. "I know. I know. And we're so sorry about what happened. We made a mistake. A big one. But we're here now, and we feel awful you've had to live like this. But you don't have to anymore. Once we're settled, you'll never want for anything else for the rest of your life. Just come with us so we can get out of the country quickly. We'll explain everything on the jet."

Rick's eyes pleaded with me as he reached out his hand. It was all I could do not to slap it away... to slap *him*.

"Come on, CeCe," Arthur said. "Just wait until you see the mansion I've got us. It's right on the beach, and I didn't even let them decorate it because I know how much you love redecorating. It's just waiting for you to come in and work your magic."

"A mansion?" Julian asked, his voice intrigued.

Arthur grinned and nodded. "A mansion. Cars. Couture. It's all waiting for you again. Please, CeCe. Let me make it up to you. I know we screwed up, but I swear you'll never want for anything ever again."

Julian's expression perked with every uttering involving the luxury he'd loved so much. "Tell us more about this mansion," he asked, then he squeezed his eyes shut and shook his head. "No. Nevermind. Doesn't matter. What you did to them was *terrible!* Unforgivable! You can't just buy their forgiveness with fancy new houses and clothes!" He paused and whispered to CeCe. "He can't, can he?"

She stood immobile, and though the rage reverberating inside her was palpable, I'd also seen the way her eyes had lit up when he'd started rattling off more of the luxuries awaiting her. For a moment, I thought she was going to reach out and take his hand, stepping back into her old world. The place she'd thought she wanted to be at the exclusion of anything and anyone else. But instead, she straightened her shoulders and lifted her chin.

"No. Julian is right. None of that matters now. I won't come with you, Arthur. I don't want your stolen money or your shallow life anymore. My life is here now, with them." She reached out, grasping my hand, and Julian took her other one. "These two are my family now. Not you. You abandoned me, and as far as I'm concerned, our marriage vows broke the day you walked out, leaving me penniless and terrified in New York. We don't want your money, and I don't want a life with a man I could never trust again. The only thing I want from you is a divorce."

I squeezed her hand tighter, my heart swelling with pride that she'd chosen herself... chosen happiness instead of the ease of a life with money. A life with a man she no longer loved or trusted. She'd stared the temptations of an easy life right in the face and punched it in the nose.

"Diane?" Rick said softly, his eyes pleading with mine. "Please come with me."

For a moment, I saw him as he used to be - the man I'd fallen in love with, the one who'd held me through my father's death, who'd danced with me at charity galas and made me feel like I belonged in his world. But that man was gone, replaced by someone I barely recognized.

Jaw tensed and eyes narrowed, I shook my head. "Our marriage is over, Rick. What you both did is unforgivable, and even if we did muster up the grace to forgive you, we found a happiness here, together, that no money could ever buy. Please, just go back to your new lives, the ones you started without us, and stay there. We're not leaving Ruinville. Ever."

"But Diane," Rick stepped toward me, but I shook my head to stop him. He did, then heaved a heavy sigh. "I don't want to leave you like this. You did nothing to deserve this. Please, Diane. You were a wonderful wife, and I love you very much. We took a huge risk coming all the way down here to get you, but we did it because we knew we had to beg your forgiveness in person. Just come with us now because we have to leave quickly, but I know with time you'll forgive me. And I'll spend the rest of my life making it up to you."

"Make it up to me? You can't make it up to me! You destroyed our marriage... our lives... you *stole* millions from unsuspecting people!"

He shook his head gently, stepping toward me, but I stepped back. "We only stole from millionaires. It's not like we left anyone going hungry or swindled money from old ladies. It was nothing for them to lose that money."

"And that makes it okay?" I shouted, my anger seething.

"No. No, of course not. What we did was unimaginable, and I regret it all so much. We were just desperate, and then things spun out of control. But with the restitution from the sale of our assets, they are almost all paid back. It doesn't mean what we did was right, or that the feds will forgive us of jail time, but I swear we aren't terrible people. I'm still the man you love. I just need your forgiveness."

Though anger continued seething through me, I still saw the man I'd spent most of my life with. A man I'd once loved. Feeling Aunt Addie's warm presence inside me and knowing exactly what she'd do, I let out a long sigh, and with it, so much of the hurt and rage that had been eating me up from the inside out.

"Rick, I appreciate your apology and that you came back to get us. I even understand that you thought you were protecting us by abandoning us. I'm horrified that you stole tens of millions of dollars from people, but I get that you were scared and ran. It must have been terrifying for you."

He and Arthur both mirrored the same ashamed expression as Rick answered, "It was awful. We screwed up so badly, and having to run was the hardest thing I've ever done in my life. But we had no choice. It was that or a life in prison."

"I still can't believe you stooped so low as to steal from people," I went on. "And if you want even a chance at my forgiveness, if you won't turn yourself in and face the consequences of your actions, then you can at least promise me that you'll pay back every single penny you stole."

"I will. I swear it. As soon as we're safely out of the country, I will send money to recoup every one of their losses. I just don't want to go to jail, Diane. I won't make it in there. But I will pay back the money. You have my word."

I remained still, part of me wanting to demand he turn himself in and thinking of calling Sheriff Boshaw myself, but the other part of me couldn't stand the thought of a man I'd loved so much locked up behind bars enduring whatever hell may await him in prison. Feeling at least partially satisfied that he gave me his word to pay back his victims, I gave a sharp nod. "Good. That's a start at earning forgiveness from me and from the people you hurt. Gaining some redemption from this disgusting scheme you both pulled."

"I just hate that I hurt you with my terrible decisions. That you've had to live like this all because of my stupid mistakes." He gestured toward our modest home.

With a long sigh, I started to let my anger toward him dissipate. "Even though it was an awful time for us, and we really struggled to survive, we did it. We rebuilt ourselves without you. And as much as I understand you think you came here to save me, I don't need saving anymore. I've found a happiness and purpose in this life that I never imagined. So, I guess maybe I should be taking these last moments of time with you to say... thank you."

His eyes bulged. "Thank me?"

CeCe nodded in agreement. "Yes, thank you, Arthur. By doing what you did, you forced me to realize just how miserable I was in my old life. How hollow it, and I, was. Just a few months ago, I was dreaming of this day when you, or anyone really, would show up like a knight in shining, diamond-encrusted armor and whisk me out of my misery. But... I've changed now. I don't need a rescue anymore. I'm my own knight in shining armor." She looked at us and smiled. "*They* are my knights in shining amor. I'm happy here. Broke, but happy." She shrugged. "I'm with Diane. I'm staying put, and I'm never going to change my mind. So, if you two need to rush off to your jet before the feds find out you're here, then you can go knowing that we're okay now. We clawed our way out of the hell you put us in, and we found something wonderful. We found each other."

We squeezed hands and remained locked in our camaraderie as we held our ground.

"Are you sure?" Rick asked. "I don't want to leave you, Diane."

Those raw emotions I'd felt when I'd discovered him gone seemed to smooth away as I found the forgiveness I'd once never thought I'd muster. "You already left me, Rick. But I'm not angry anymore. I'm at peace with my new life and the end of our marriage. We're fine now. Really. You two can go off and start your new lives without us, because we're already living our new lives without you. Please. It's okay. You can go. And I forgive you."

Sadness flooded his eyes, so I broke my grip on CeCe's hand to reach out and touch his face, planting a soft kiss on his cheek. "Thank you for coming back for us. We appreciate it, but this is goodbye, Rick."

He wrapped his arms around me and squeezed. "I'll miss you, Diane."

I squeezed him back and answered, "I'll miss you too. Just take care of yourself, okay? No more stealing money."

He blew out a puff of air. "Lesson learned. We're on the straight and narrow now. We've got new identities, and we're never going to make those mistakes again."

"Good." I kissed his cheek once more. "You were a good person once, Rick. I wouldn't have loved you all those years if you weren't. You made a terrible mistake, and it destroyed our lives, but I've moved on, and I hope that you can too. I hope somehow you can look deep inside yourself and find the honest, trustworthy man I once loved, and never ever do this kind of thing again."

He nodded, and a tear slipped down his cheek as he stepped back.

"You're sure, CeCe?" Arthur asked. "Once we disappear again, we won't have any way to contact you. We have to stay completely off the radar."

"I'm sure," she said with a certainty that surprised me. "My life is here now. But thank you for coming back for me and for apologizing. It does mean a lot to me knowing you didn't abandon me completely, and that the man I spent all those years with must have cared for me after all."

"I did. I do," he said quickly. "And my God do I miss you. Every day."

"I've missed you, too, but it's time for us to bid each other goodbye. Our time together is over."

He sniffled, then pulled her in for a tight hug. "I'm sorry, CeCe. I never meant to hurt you. I just hope that you've found the happiness you deserve."

"I have," she said back with certainty. "I may be penniless and struggling to get by as a bartender, but I'll figure it out on my own. It's worth it to stand on my own two feet and create a life I'm proud of." She gave him a stern look. "But I'm also serious about that divorce. We can't afford lawyers to get unhitched from you two shady criminals since you are in hiding, so maybe we could depend on you one last time, and you could use some of that money you stole to make that happen for us. We'd really appreciate it."

Arthur chuckled softly. "We'll figure out how to make that happen if that's what you want."

"It's what we want," she answered, looking at me for confirmation, and I gave it with a nod.

"Then consider it done." He leaned forward and kissed her cheek. "But I'll miss you."

"I'll miss you too," she said, then stepped back.

"We have to get going," Rick cut in. "The jet is on the runway, and we need to go before anyone finds out we're here."

"Goodbye, Rick." My heart clenched with the words as I knew this would be the last time I'd ever see him. A chapter in my life closing for good.

"Goodbye, Diane."

CeCe and Arthur hugged one more time while Rick and I had one last embrace. Julian stepped up from behind us and slid an arm around each of our waists, and we stood together and watched them pull out of our lives for good.

"Well, that was unexpected," Julian broke the silence.

"Very unexpected," I agreed.

CeCe spoke just above a whisper. "That was so strange seeing them again."

"They felt like strangers, but at the same time, so familiar."

The car pulled out, and we gave one last little wave before they disappeared from sight, and we knew we'd never see them again.

"I'm proud of you, CeCe," I said as I turned to her. "It would have been so easy to say yes and go right back to the money you so desperately hunted for so long."

She smiled softly. "Honestly, I'm surprised it wasn't harder for me. Arthur was just offering me everything I ever wanted, but seeing him standing there just made me think about how I never loved him the way I love Bill. And I won't choose money over love ever again. Besides, I'm going to be a famous author and make my own money. I don't need theirs." She winked, and I burst out laughing.

"Oh!" Julian squealed. "If you become a famous author, do you think you could buy me a few odds and ends? Like a car? And maybe a new pair of Gucci shoes?" His eyes lit up more. "Oh! And remember that skincare lotion we used to love so much? Think we could get more of that?"

She laughed and slipped an arm around his neck. "My darling, I promise that if I can write a bestseller, I'll spoil you senseless again. You deserve it. You've stuck by me through the worst days of my life, and you've become my most treasured friend."

She kissed him on the cheek, and he practically melted with his sigh.

She looked over at me. "Well, one of my most treasured friends. It seems I got lucky enough to get two."

My heart warmed at her kind words, and I stepped over and wrapped my arms around them, pulling them together for a tight group hug.

"I love you, guys," I said.

"We love you, too," CeCe said.

Julian leaned back and lifted his wrist, showing off the matching bracelets we still wore.

"Best friends unite!" he said, and we laughed as we touched our bracelets together, then we folded into one more hug.

CHAPTER TWENTY-SEVEN
CeCe

Whacky Wade mumbled out a string of words that used to be unrecognizable to me as any human language. But just like Bill had told me when I'd first arrived in Ruinville, eventually I'd understand him.

"Another order of alligator bites, coming right up!" I said with confidence, knowing exactly what he'd ordered.

He grinned at me, and this time I didn't even cringe at the missing tooth greeting me from his smile.

"Busy night," I said to Gumbo Gus as I dropped the ticket at the window.

"I gotta say, CeCe, you've really got this whole ordering thing down. Took you long enough though," he teased.

Instead of giving him a healthy dose of snark, I just took the compliment and spun back to the bar brimming with people I'd gotten to know well over the year we'd been in Ruinville.

"You need some help, Pretty Girl? It's busy tonight," Bill said from his regular spot at the bar. Everyone in town knew if I was working, no one dare touch his stool because he came in to keep me company every night.

"I'm good, baby. But thanks for asking." I paused to lean across the bar and gave him a little kiss. A small happy moan slipped out my lips as it always did when they touched his.

"You just let me know if you need some backup. I'll be right here. And now that I got you to say yes to marrying me,

I'll be here every damn day for the rest of your pretty little life."

I glanced down at the small gold band on my ring finger, then winked and grinned, my feet practically fluttering me away as I spun off to take care of my next customer. The day I'd told Bill that Arthur had shown up to whisk me away, and I'd chosen to stay, he'd been so ecstatic to know I was really his that he'd jumped right up on the bar and proposed to me in front of the entire restaurant. He didn't even have a ring ready it had been so spontaneous, and I barely let him finish his heartfelt speech about his love for me before I was screaming, "Yes!" and launching into his arms.

The next day, he'd surprised me with a simple gold ring that had been his mother's wedding band to be a placeholder while he saved up enough to buy me a diamond, but I'd told him I wouldn't hear of it, and this ring meant more to me than the largest diamond in the world.

And I'd meant it.

I loved the cherished heirloom from a man I adored, and I had refused to take it off for even a moment since. Our wedding plans were on hold until Diane and I could get a divorce, and it had been months without a word from Arthur and Rick making good on their promise to handle it, but that didn't stop me from relishing every second of being a fiancée to the man I couldn't imagine life without.

"CeCe!" Julian squealed as he burst in through the front door. "I have news! I have news!"

He raced up to the bar, planting his hands on his hips, and staring down one of our regulars, Lionel, as he sipped on his beer.

Lionel looked up at him. "Hi, Julian."

Julian just tapped his toes, his eyebrows inching up. "How long are you going to be there? That's my usual seat."

"Oh. Did you want to sit here so you can hang out with CeCe?"

Julian grinned and nodded. "Yes, please!"

Lionel stood up and grabbed his beer, offering his seat to Julian. "There ya go."

"Oh! Well, thank you! Don't mind if I do."

Julian flopped into the seat, his eyes twinkling as he pressed his elbows to the bar and perched his chin in his hands. "Guess what."

"What?" I asked, excitedly.

"I have news."

"What kind of news?"

He leaned in, whispering quietly, "John asked me if I would be interested in switching places with him. He moves in with Diane, and I take over his apartment in town."

My mouth dropped open. "No way! He's going to ask her to move in together?"

"Shhhh!" Julian shushed me and looked over both shoulders. "It's a surprise! Don't spoil it!"

I glanced over to see Diane still oblivious as she took an order from a table.

"Get out!" I whispered, smiling. "That's fantastic! What did you say?"

Julian rolled his eyes. "Yes, of course! Duh! With my new business as an event planner already taking off, I have the funds for my own rent, and with my new budding relationship with Toby looking good, it's high time I follow in your footsteps and get my own place. I mean, I love living with Diane, but the walls are thin there. I don't want to be hearing them get up to their business, and I don't want them listening to mine. So, I'm taking John's apartment as soon as he asks her. Tonight!"

I clapped my hands. "This is so exciting! Oh, she's just gonna die!"

I looked at her again, smiling wide as I imagined the happy tears that would fall when John asked her to live with him. I knew it would have been a proposal instead, but unlike me, she'd been clear to him she didn't want to get engaged until her divorce was finalized. Silly detail to me, but it was important to her that they start their marriage with a clean slate.

"How is it?" Julian asked. "Living with a new guy."

My body warmed with the happiness that spread through me thinking about waking up with Bill every morning. I'd moved in with him shortly after we got engaged, and though I missed living with Diane and Julian, me being away had almost brought us closer. Instead of spending half the time together arguing over the chore wheel, now we spent our time together doing fun things like having dinner, shopping, and enjoying a day at one of the endless Ruinville fundraisers. Even though Julian had quit dishwashing when he'd landed his second event planning gig, Diane and I still worked together for the time being, and with Julian always coming to visit, we still saw plenty of each other.

"Well, this is exciting news. Did you tell Toby yet?"

He shook his head. "No. I'm going to surprise him and move in then invite him over for a romantic candlelight dinner. It's going to be perfect."

He smiled the way I smiled when I thought about Bill... a smile I'd never seen a man inspire in him before. Toby had moved to Ruinville just two months ago and taken a job as the new Deputy under Sherrif Boshaw, and Julian had practically come undone over the new handsome man in uniform. And what a happy delight that Toby was single and it turned out, batting for Julian's team. After several weeks of flirtation, Toby had asked him out, and the two had been practically inseparable since. My heart swelled to bursting seeing my sweet Julian so happy as he thrived in his new life.

"Eek! Here she comes! Don't say anything!" Julian shushed me.

"Hey, Julian!" Diane leaned down and kissed his cheek. "How was wedding planning today?"

"So good," he spit out. "I helped LulaMae pick out the most beautiful dress. They are getting married on her family's big farm just outside of town. We're doing a garden chic kind of design, and it's gonna be epic."

"I can only imagine how beautiful it will be knowing your talents."

He gave her a proud little smirk, then sighed. "Okay. I'd better run. I'm meeting Toby after his shift. I like to catch him before he changes because..." he paused and bit his fist. "You know how I feel about a man in uniform."

I chuckled and gave him a little swat to head out. He stood up, then paused and spun around. "Oh, I forgot to tell you, some mail of yours came to Diane's today. I grabbed it for you."

He pulled the folded envelopes out of his jacket pocket and handed them to me. I quickly flipped through them, then gasped when I saw *RegalLeaf Books* in the corner of one of the envelopes.

"What? What is it?" Julian asked, and I flipped the envelope around to show him.

"Remember I said I knew that woman in publishing from back in our New York days?"

He nodded. "Yeah. Gwen something or other."

"Well, after I got in touch with her and pitched her my book idea, she said to send her the first few chapters."

Julian sighed. "Which you wrote and they were *amazing*. I'm so glad you let me read them."

"Well, I sent them to her a few weeks ago via mail because, well, still no computer, and this is an envelope addressed from her. Oh my God. What do you think it says?"

Diane paused as she was passing by. "What's going on?"

Julian squealed. "CeCe has an envelope from that publisher she queried!"

Diane gasped and squeezed up against Julian. "Well, open it! What does it say?"

My fingers shook as I ripped open the envelope, and a potent blend of fear and excitement crashed inside my stomach as I pulled out the letter.

With a deep breath, I started reading.

Dear Mrs. VanTramp,

I received the first three chapters of your manuscript, and it is with great pleasure that I would like to offer you a publishing deal. Please call me at your earliest convenience so we can discuss the project further.

I didn't finish reading the rest of the letter because tears clouded my eyes as I cried out, "They want it! They want my book! I'm going to be an author!"

Diane and Julian screamed so loud everyone in the restaurant spun to see the commotion. But all they saw were my two best friends rushing around the bar to tackle me into the biggest hug I'd ever received.

"You did it! You really did it! I knew you could!" Diane kissed my cheek, gripping me tighter.

"We're gonna be famous!" Julian screamed, dancing in place while he hugged me. "You did it! This is amazing!"

"What's going on, Pretty Girl?" Bill asked as he walked behind the bar.

I let go of my two best friends and ran into his arms, sobbing into his shoulder as I told him, "I did it. They want my book. I'm going to be a published author!"

"Well, I'll be damned." He squeezed me so tight I could barely breathe. "I knew you could do it, baby. I'm so proud of you."

"I'm proud of me too," I admitted as I stepped back and wiped the tears from my face. "I can't believe this is happening. I did it. I'm going to be an author."

Diane and Julian came over and each slid an arm around me.

"I can believe it," Diane said. "I always knew you had so much more in you. And look at you now. You're making it all on your own. You don't need anyone to take care of you. You're a force to be reckoned with CeCe VanTramp."

"That's not true," I said, pulling them all in tight around me. "I'm not doing it on my own. I'm doing it with all of you. You're my people... my family, and I wouldn't be here without you. Thank you for believing in me."

With a huge *awe* they enveloped me in a hug, I stood behind the bar that had become a part of me, surrounded by the people I loved most in this life. In that moment, I discovered a level of happiness I never knew existed.

EPILOGUE
Diane

Six months later...

The hot sun beat down on CeCe, Julian and me while we sat on the porch swing sipping sweet tea.

"Damn. It's a melter today," Julian said as he waved a hand toward his face, fanning his glistening skin. "CeCe, when is your book getting published so you can make millions when you hit the bestseller list and splurge on a little air-conditioning unit at all three of our places. Or even one. Even if just *one* of our places had air-conditioning, that would be grand. I mean, my event planning business is really taking off so I could probably afford one in my apartment pretty soon, but I have to buy a car with my money first. I can't keep borrowing 'Ol Blue to get to my appointments. It's not exactly professional showing up and having it backfire sending everyone leaping for cover."

She smiled proudly. "It's with the editors now. Releases in six months."

"I'm just so proud of you, CeCe." I reached over and touched her thigh. "You wrote a book. A whole book. And it's good enough one of the biggest publishers in the country is putting it out! It's just amazing!"

Her shoulders lifted with her happy sigh. "You know, I just got a call from Gwen this morning, and you're not going to believe this."

Julian and I waited on bated breath.

"What? What is it?" He pushed at her when she didn't answer right away, just smiling a mischievous smile instead.

After another long moment while he waited for her answer, she finally said, "A film company got wind of it, and it sounds like our story is going to get made into a movie."

"Whaaaaaaaaat?" Julian screeched as his hands flew to his mouth.

"NO!" I shouted, covering my mouth as well.

CeCe just grinned and said, "Yep. We're gonna be a movie."

Julian and I leaped to our feet and started screaming as we held hands and jumped in circles. After a moment of pretending to be stoic, CeCe finally gave into her excitement and jumped up with us. Our happy squeals and shrieks could have been heard all the way in Hollywood where somewhere, some producer, was planning to put our amazing story onto the big screen.

"This. Is. Amazing!" Julian stopped jumping and pressed his hands to his head. "Oh my God. Wait! Who's gonna play me?"

CeCe just chuckled. "I don't know. We aren't anywhere near that far yet."

"Henry Cavill," he said quickly. "I think it should be Henry Cavill."

CeCe and I both pulled a face, panning him up and down with a querying gaze.

"Um, Julian?" I said. "You don't look *anything* like Henry Cavill."

He scoffed. "Well, that doesn't mean he can't play me. I mean it's more about the fact we share the same kind of cool, sexy demeanor than our actual looks." His eyes popped wide. "Oh! Brad Pitt. He's got that same kind of swagger as me too. I'd be happy with him as well. Wait. He's too old now. Damn it."

CeCe and I shared a look then burst into laughter.

"Don't worry, Julian." CeCe slipped an arm around his shoulder. "I'll make sure it's someone with about the same amount of sexy swagger as you. The casting will be perfect."

He grinned like a kid on Christmas morning. "Oh my God! I'm gonna be in a movie!"

They jumping started again, and we leaped and screamed until we finally ran out of breath. We collapsed back onto the porch swing in a sweaty, exhausted heap. Before we could discuss any more of the plans for CeCe's book and movie deal, a cloud of dust announced a car coming up the driveway.

"What time is it? I thought the guys weren't coming until six," Julian said.

The sunlight glinted off my watch when I glanced at it. "It's only five. John will be home from his shift around five-thirty, but Toby and Bill aren't coming for dinner until six. No one should be arriving yet."

When a dark SUV emerged around the corner, we all gave each other quizzical looks then stood up to get a better look.

A man in a jet-black suit and tie stepped out of the car, then he walked around to the passenger side and pulled a briefcase off the front seat.

"Can we help you?" I asked, concern tightening my face that somehow the FBI had gotten wind of the visit from our exes and soon we'd be in some interrogation room again getting harassed to give up their location.

Not that we knew it. Just like when they'd bolted off on us the first time, keeping us in the dark, they'd never mentioned where our new home would have been if we'd taken off with them like they'd wanted. Smart, I thought to myself as I prepared to see the man flash a badge and turn this wonderful day into another nightmare like we'd lived through the first time the feds had interrogated us for hours on end.

"CeCe VanTramp? Diane Whitlock?"

CeCe stepped to my side. "Yes. That's us. Who are you? What do you want?"

"I have a delivery for you," he said, stone-faced and expressionless... exactly like those damn Feds.

"What is it?" Julian asked, stepping protectively in front of us.

"For their hands only," he said, peeking out from behind his dark sunglasses, then pulling out two pictures. One of me and one of Diane before looking back at us seemingly to confirm we were who we said we were.

"Don't take it," Julian whispered. "What if it's a bomb!"

"Why would someone be bombing us?" I whispered back out of the corner of my mouth.

"We did make some enemies in New York," CeCe whispered.

I glanced at her, and she rolled her eyes.

"Fine. *I* made some enemies in New York. But I don't actually think any of those snobby socialites I offended would waste their time bombing me. I think we should take it."

The man stood in front of us, the briefcase extended in his hands, his face still frozen like some machine had sucked all the emotions straight out of his body.

Tentatively, I reached out and took the briefcase. Without another word, he spun on his heel and strode back to his SUV. We watched as he hoisted a large, black hard case suitcase out of the back, and then after setting it down, he pulled out another. After popping out the handles, he grabbed each one and wheeled them toward us.

"Oh my God. What is in those suitcases? Are those bodies?" Julian covered the small squeal coming out of his mouth.

The man didn't say a word, instead placing a suitcase in front of both of us, spinning on his heel and returning to his SUV before pulling away and disappearing as we stood there, confused.

"Well, what is it?" Julian asked, peeking over my shoulder.

"I don't know. Let's go find out."

"Toby is a cop, and he would say we shouldn't touch the suitcases without gloves. If there are bodies in there, we don't need our fingerprints all over them."

"They aren't bodies," I said confidently, then lost it when I glanced back at the strange, large suitcases. "Well, let's leave them and see what's in this briefcase first."

The three of us walked up to the house then sat on the steps. I carefully opened the briefcase, and with Julian's idea that it was a bomb firmly planted in my mind, I held my breath when the latch went *click* as it opened. Instead of an explosion, I found two manilla envelopes with the names *CeCe* and *Diane* written on each one.

"What is this?" I asked, pulling out the envelope with my name on it.

"Open it! What does it say?" Julian started, then he gasped. "Wait! What if it's anthrax! People put it on letters they mail and then..." He stopped and slid a finger across his neck.

"Julian! You need to stop watching so much true crime." CeCe rolled her eyes.

He frowned. "What? It's Toby's favorite. He's a cop, so it's kind of like job research when we watch."

"I don't think it's anthrax," I said as I looked at my name. "This is Rick's handwriting."

"This is Arthur's handwriting," CeCe pointed at the other envelope.

We shared a look, then quickly tore open the envelopes. I found a letter inside of mine.

Diane,

I just wanted to say how sorry I am for what I did to you. You truly were the most wonderful wife a man could have asked for, and you didn't deserve to be married to a schmuck like me. I made a lot of mistakes in my life, but marrying you wasn't one of them, and I hope that despite everything, you still feel the same way about me and don't regret the years we spent together. I know it's too late to win you back, and though I'll always miss you and regret the things I did to lose your love, I'll always be grateful to know that you found happiness again. I wish you nothing but the very best in your new life, and I hope that this legal documentation of divorce proceedings will help you move forward with your new start. Signed divorce papers will follow soon as soon as we've made it through the required waiting period. I'll miss you, Diane Please know you'll always be in my heart, and I hope the gift can help you and CeCe start your new lives off with a little extra comfort.

Yours always,

Rick

A tear streaked down my cheek as I stared at the legal papers signifying the end of a long marriage to a man I once loved. It was bittersweet closing that chapter of my life, but those papers also meant I could start my new one with John with nothing tying me to my old life holding us back.

"Well? What do they say?" Julian bounced beside us.

I wiped the tears from my cheeks. "It was a goodbye letter from Rick. He was wishing me well, and he sent the legal notice he filed for divorce."

CeCe sniffled and wiped her tears as well. "Mine too. Is it wrong I'm a little sad?"

I reached over and touched her leg. "No. It's not wrong at all. I'm a little sad too. We're officially saying goodbye to a huge part of our lives. That's not nothing."

"No. It's not." She sighed. "But I'm also really excited because it sounds like the divorce is underway, and pretty soon it will be official. We'll be divorced. And then... then I can marry my Bill."

She smiled widely as she clutched the papers to her chest.

"Okay, so divorce papers in the briefcase, but what's in the scary suitcases?" Julian asked, pointing at them.

"Rick mentioned a gift to help us start our new lives," I answered.

"Well, someone open them then!" Julian clapped.

We all stood up and walked over the suitcases. They each had a tag on them, one with my name and one with hers. When I tried to lift mine, I grunted and dropped it back down. "Wow. That's heavy. That big guy made it look a lot lighter."

CeCe strained against hers, then gave up. "I think Julian's right. It's bodies. We should have worn gloves." She gasped. "What if it's *their* bodies! Rick and Arthur! Like they killed themselves and mailed themselves to us as an apology!"

"CeCe!" I swatted at her. "Stop! They didn't do that. It's not bodies. Let's just open them out here and find out what they are."

I struggled to lay my suitcase down, then when I did, I carefully tugged at the zipper to open it up. As it popped open, I gasped when I saw layer upon layer of stacked hundred-dollar bills.

"Oh my God!" I stepped back.

CeCe and Julian screamed beside me as she opened her suitcase, revealing the same thing.

"We're rich!" Julian leaped into the air. "We're getting air conditioning! Whoo hoo!"

I stammered as I stared at mine. "This is... this is millions of dollars," I breathed.

"Millions," CeCe said quietly in disbelief.

Julian just kept jumping and hooting, praising the air conditioning Gods.

I looked over at CeCe and shook my head. "We can't accept this. It's... it's stolen money."

Julian stopped leaping and rushed to my side. "Whoa, whoa, whoa. What do you mean we can't accept this? Of course, we can."

CeCe softly shook her head. "No. She's right. This is stolen money."

"What do we do? We can't send it back. We don't even know where they are. Do we turn it in?"

Her eyes bulged. "We are *not* turning this over to the Feds. They will never stop hounding us trying to find them. No. We can't turn it in. It will just open up a can of worms I want no business with. And if we're being honest, he stole *my* money too, so in reality, this technically is mine."

Julian clapped once and pointed at her. "Yes! Exactly! This is *your* money so no way are we sending it back! So... air conditioners it is!" Julian beamed, then he grinned as he looked at the alligator sunning herself by the water. "Did you hear that, Peggy? We're rich! We can buy you chicken for days!"

CeCe wasn't wrong. He'd stolen her entire family fortune, which in reality, was probably far larger than the millions in these bags. That tidbit of information did make me feel a little less guilty about our sudden windfall. And knowing that Rick and Arthur vowed to pay back every penny to their victims, there wasn't any reason to try to give them back this money ourselves.

"So... we keep it?" I asked, hesitantly.

CeCe looked at the money, and then me. "I don't see what else we're supposed to do with it. Even if we did give it back, the government will probably just use it for something shady anyway."

"What then? It's not like we can deposit it in the bank or even buy big things. I'm sure we're still on the watchlist of the FBI."

She shook her head. "No. Definitely can't let anyone know about this. It needs to be our secret. Just the three of us."

As I stared at the money with guilt swelling inside me, suddenly, my face lit up. "I know exactly what I'm going to do with my money."

"Get central air in this house and then put it in my apartment too?" Julian asked, batting his lashes with a sweet smile. "And a car? Can one of you please buy me a car so I can look more professional for my appointments?"

"My Aunt Addie spent her whole life trying to help people. She died with barely a penny to her name because she gave away everything she had to other people in need. I'm not going to spend this money on myself. I'm going to use it to give anonymous donations to other people in need. Like Annabelle. Her barn roof caved in after that big storm last month. We raised money from the fundraiser, but it's going to cost thousands more. What if a little money fairy simply dropped off an envelope with enough cash to cover the rest?"

CeCe's face lit up. "Oh! I love that! Or the money they've been saving for the library remodel all year long. What if that twenty-thousand-dollars they are still raising suddenly appeared?"

"Yes! Exactly!" I smiled wider.

"And you, know, I don't need this money for myself," CeCe said. "I want to earn my own money now with my book and my movie. Who needs their millions when I know I'll be earning my own soon?"

"Exactly," I said. "We take care of ourselves now, and with this money, we'll take care of everyone else."

As I stood there with ideas for how to use this money to spread joy to everyone around me, the guilt over it fluttered away. I could almost feel my Aunt Addie's arms wrap around me as she hugged me, knowing that even though she was gone, I was now here to take care of the people and the town she'd loved.

Julian lifted a finger. "I love this idea and all, and I'm fully behind it but..."

"We'll buy you air conditioning!" I said, exasperated. "I promise. We can take a little tiny bit and put air-conditioning in all three of our homes."

He beamed. "Well, if you insist."

I chuckled, then glanced at my watch. "Well, if we really are keeping this a secret from everyone but ourselves, then we need to get these suitcases inside and hidden before the guys get here."

They both nodded in agreement, then we zipped up the bags and the three of us hauled our new-found riches into the closet, tucking them beneath a pile of blankets.

"We're gonna need a vault or something to hide this money," Julian said as we closed the closet door.

"We'll figure out a safe way to stash it. But for tonight, it's safe in here." I pointed a finger at them both. "Just nobody light any candles or do anything stupid to burn down the house. I don't know if those cases are fireproof."

"Luckily you live with a fireman now," CeCe said. "Hopefully he made sure your fire extinguishers were up to date. You know, just in case."

With so many people who could be helped with that money, I tried not to worry about its fate until we could find somewhere to stash it safe from the prying eyes of the government or anyone else who could ever tie it back to us.

"Oh! John's home!" Julian said, pointing out the window.

We quickly straightened ourselves up and hurried away from the closet, and I went out and met him at the front door.

"Hey, baby," he said as he slipped an arm around my waist and gave me a kiss.

We'd been living together for almost four months, and I didn't think I'd ever get sick of welcoming him home.

I inhaled the slightly ashy smell that always permeated his clothes, and I kissed him once more. "Welcome home, honey."

"Bill and Toby are right behind me. Ran into them at the store while I was picking up the wine you asked for."

He showed me the bottle and I thanked him, then we headed inside. Toby and Bill arrived a few minutes later, and after the six of us caught up about our days, I went to work making dinner—a new weekly tradition we shared.

We laughed throughout the entire meal, sharing stories and jokes, the six of us getting on like long-lost friends. When dinner was finished and we'd had our after-dinner cocktails, CeCe and Julian got ready to head out. Though I didn't miss having them trash the house on a regular basis and refuse to clean up, I did miss curling up for a movie with them every night, and giggling over which actors we thought were cutest. But we'd all taken a step forward in our new lives, and that meant we had each grown into needing our own places.

"Okay, tomorrow night, what do you say the three of us have movie night at my place and we can," Julian leaned in and whispered, "figure out what to do with the you know what."

"Perfect," I said. "I'll bring the wine."

I gave them each a kiss on the cheek, but just before they left, CeCe spun around. "Wait! Our divorce papers. I feel like we should show the boys."

I glanced over at the briefcase we'd set on the coffee table and smiled. "I think you're absolutely right."

We called the boys into the living room with us, then explained that today a courier had dropped off our divorce papers. We left out the part about the bags full of millions. Bill and John couldn't stop grinning as we opened the case, pulling out the papers that would end our previous lives and help us move forward into our new ones with them.

"So, this is really happening?" Bill asked, his eyes lighting up as he looked at CeCe. "You're getting divorced."

She grinned. "Yep."

"And then you can marry me." He matched her grin and spun her around, putting her down and dipping her backward in a passionate kiss.

John looked at me. "Seriously? They did it?"

I nodded, smiling at him.

Though I still felt that twinge of sadness in ending a marriage, when I looked up at the love radiating for me in John's eyes, I knew I'd made the right decision. We all hugged each other goodnight, then John and I stood on the front porch, waving at the two couples as they pulled out.

"Well, that was fun." I leaned my head on his chest. "I'm so glad you guys all get along so well."

"Yeah. Toby and Bill are a riot. I'm glad we get along too."

"Well, now that I'm officially getting divorced, you're gonna be stuck with me, which means you're stuck with Julian and CeCe, and that means you're stuck with Bill and Toby. So, you're better be sure you like us all before..."

I trailed off just short of saying the words "we get married."

We'd talked about it, but I'd told him I didn't want to get engaged until my marriage to Rick was officially over. It felt somehow tainted to get engaged to one man while I had no idea how long I'd be married to another. But now that weight had lifted, and suddenly the thought of marriage went from a daydream to a potential reality.

John's eyes sparkled as he stared down at me, and I saw a new spark ignite inside of them.

"Come here," he said, reaching down and sliding my hand into his.

I didn't ask where we were going, instead following him down the steps and across the yard to the tire swing he'd fixed last month.

"Have a seat." He placed a hand on it to steady it.

Smiling like I used to when he'd push me on this swing, I settled down onto it. With a gentle push, he sent me away, and I smiled as I swung back to him again. The cool evening breeze ruffled my hair as I swung back and forth on the tire swing, memories of carefree days flooding my mind. The creaking of the swing mixed with our laughter felt like a symphony from the past, a nostalgic melody I thought I'd never hear again until I somehow ended up back in his life.

"Do you remember the first time I told you I loved you?" he asked, then pushed me gently away.

I nodded, a rush of emotions flooding my heart. "Yes, of course I remember. It was right here on this swing."

He smiled with a familiar sparkle in his eyes, a warmth that hadn't faded over the years.

I swung back to him, but instead of pushing me away, this time he grabbed hold of the tire, pulling me to a stop.

"When I told you that day that I'd love you forever, I meant every word. Not a day has gone by since that you haven't taken up every inch of my heart. Life took us on different paths, but fate brought you right back into my arms. And this time, I don't ever plan on letting you go again. I've waited my whole life to ask you one simple question."

As he kneeled down before me, I pressed a hand to my chest, feeling the weight of decades of separation lift as he pulled a velvet box from his pocket.

"I've been carrying this around for months just waiting for you to be free so you could finally be mine. And I can't wait another minute more to ask you. Diane? Will you make me the happiest man alive and marry me?"

My eyes welled up with tears, the enormity of the moment washing over me. This man, whom I'd loved and lost in the maze of time, was here, and somehow, against all odds, we'd found our way back to each other.

"Yes!" I exclaimed, tossing my arms around his neck and covering him with kisses.

We tumbled to the ground, and he wrapped his arms around me, holding me tight while he kissed away all the years we'd been apart. I could barely stop kissing him long enough for him to slip the ring on my finger, and as soon as it was lodged into the place it would never come off, I pressed my hands to his face and kissed him again.

After I finally managed to stop kissing him, we rolled over onto our backs, staring up at the stars just like we'd used to. Despite the passing years, the sky remained unchanged from our teenage days, twinkling overhead in this town that would forever be my home.

When I'd arrived in Ruinville, I'd been heartbroken to see how my Aunt Addie had been living. That guilt had nearly torn me apart. But the longer I spent here, the more I realized it wasn't Aunt Addie I should have been feeling sorry for... it was me. She was the one who was happiest all those years she and I were apart, and now that I was here in her home, I finally understood just how lucky she'd actually been.

She had her friends in a town that loved and cared for her the way she loved and cared for them. The same town I now cherished as my own, proud to pick up where she left off. And not only did I have a man I loved with my whole heart, a man I had always loved, but I had two of the best friends a girl could ever ask for.

We had lost everything but then gained so much more. And now our lives were starting again, and I couldn't wait to begin this new chapter as a wife, a friend, and a member of a community I would be part of until the day that I died.

***

Want to keep the laughter rolling? Then don't miss The Wilder Widows series!

Four widows. Four wishes. One wild adventure!

Get this twice AUDIE nominated and SOVAS winning series for Best Humor Book in digital, print or audio form!

Start with the first book: **www.books2read.com/ thewilderwidows**
Or get the full series! **www.books2read.com/ wilderwidowsseries**

THANK YOU FOR READING

I hope you enjoyed *Riches to Ruinville*! The greatest gift you can give an author is your review. If you enjoyed this book, I would be forever grateful if you'd take the time to leave a few words, or even a star rating. Find out more about my other books and upcoming releases at **www.katherinehastings.com**.

You can also get new book releases, sales, and free book specials delivered right to your inbox by signing up for my eNews!
Sign Up Here!

Get social with me and join me on:
Facebook @katherinehastingsauthor
Instagram @katherinehastingsauthor
Follow me on:
Bookbub
Goodreads

Made in the USA
Monee, IL
20 October 2025

32437877R00256